Praise for *Trial Run*

"This book is a true psychological thriller that cannot be put down . . . An awesome jaunt into a world that may just be closer to reality than we think."

—*Suspense Magazine*

"Thomas Locke masterfully keeps the suspense level taut throughout the book. It is a rare author who can create such dramatic tension in a storyline that contains areas of technical discussion, like quantum computing, while still maintaining a character-driven plot. A fast-paced, constantly unfolding mystery with well-developed characters, *Trial Run* promises to begin a strong new series that manages to transcend the bounds of science fiction writing."

—*Manhattan Book Review*

"High tech mixed with intelligence gathering, combined with a fast-paced story and evocative writing. *Trial Run* grabs readers from the first page. Locke weaves words to create masterfully evocative descriptions, scenes, and characters. The science is presented in a Crichton-esque manner, compelling readers to believe that not only can it be true for some future date, but it is probably being used in some secret laboratory right now. *Trial Run* will make a great last-of-summer read. Once you start, you won't want to put it down."

—**BuddyHollywood.com**

"*Trial Run* is wonderfully told: a swift, engaging story that shows a large understanding of the human condition, our essential frailty, our drivenness, our need for connection. As three stories collide, Locke brings into play some key questions that face each of us as human beings: Do we know what is really going on? If we don't, can it destroy us? This is artful writing, full of suspense."

—**Jay Parini**, *New York Times* bestselling author of *The Last Station*

"A truly remarkable work. The interweaving of three stories is faultless, the tension explosive. The story involving the intelligence community and military is extremely vivid and very well crafted. A wonderful read."

—**Keith Hazard**, deputy director, Central Intelligence Agency

FLASH POINT

Books by Thomas Locke

LEGENDS OF THE REALM

Emissary
Merchant of Alyss

FAULT LINES

Double Edge (ebook)
Trial Run
Flash Point

FAULT LINES · 2

FLASH POINT

THOMAS LOCKE

Revell

a division of Baker Publishing Group
Grand Rapids, Michigan

© 2016 by T. Davis Bunn

Published by Revell
a division of Baker Publishing Group
P.O. Box 6287, Grand Rapids, MI 49516-6287
www.revellbooks.com

Printed in the United States of America

Library of Congress Cataloging-in-Publication Data
Names: Locke, Thomas, 1952– author.
Title: Flash point / Thomas Locke.
Description: Grand Rapids, MI : Revell, [2016] | Series: Fault lines ; #2
Identifiers: LCCN 2016003303 | ISBN 9780800724368 (cloth) |
    ISBN 9780800724351 (paper)
Subjects: | GSAFD: Suspense fiction. | Christian fiction.
Classification: LCC PS3552.U4718 F55 2016 | DDC 813/.54—dc23
LC record available at http://lccn.loc.gov/2016003303

Scripture quotations are from the Holman Christian Standard Bible®, copyright © 1999, 2000, 2002, 2003, 2009 by Holman Bible Publishers. Used by permission. Holman Christian Standard Bible®, Holman CSB®, and HCSB® are federally registered trademarks of Holman Bible Publishers.

16 17 18 19 20 21 22   7 6 5 4 3 2 1

This book is dedicated to

Emanuele Basile

Who started me on this journey
with the simple question:

What if

From the days of John the Baptist until now, the kingdom of heaven has been suffering violence, and the violent have been seizing it by force.

Matthew 11:12

BOOK 1

1

You're going to get yourself fired."

"That is a distinct probability," Lena Fennan agreed.

"Forget probable." Robin Galwyn was another junior analyst at First American Bank, hired the week before Lena. Robin would have been Lena's best friend in the city, if either of them had the time or energy for friendship. She occupied the cubicle three down from Lena. The two cubicles separating them were empty, the result of recent layoffs.

Lena was tall and rangy and still held to an athlete's build, though she was ready to drop her gym membership since she seldom found time to work out. She wore a rumpled suit from Ralph Lauren that had seen better days. Her long dark hair desperately needed attention. Her features were stained by the months of too much stress and not enough sleep. She had named Wall Street as her goal while still an undergraduate at Georgetown. She had played varsity basketball and she had majored in economics and she had made friends and she'd had a life. But deep down where it mattered most, Lena had already taken aim. A master's in finance at Rutgers had followed, with two summer internships at hedge funds to beef up her CV. Now she was here, getting ready to walk away from everything she had worked so hard to achieve.

All because of a voice from beyond.

Robin went on, "Vacation time for junior analysts is a theoretical construct. It only exists in a parallel universe. We survive by working longer and harder than anyone else."

Lena offered Robin the note she had just written, which was the reason they were almost arguing. The typed single sheet announced that Lena was taking a long break. For the first time since setting foot on Wall Street, Lena would not be reachable. Robin's task was to wait until Lena had left the building, then slip inside Wesley's office and leave the note on his desk.

Lena asked, "Are you in or are you in?"

"Oh, give me that." She swept the note from Lena's grasp. "I hope he's worth it."

"It's not a guy."

"Forget tall and handsome. I'm thinking limo and a private jet."

"It's not like that at all." Lena slipped her laptop into her briefcase, alongside the file she had been preparing ever since the Weasel had shot her down. Just touching the file's cover was enough for her breath to lock in her throat. At midnight last night Lena had received a wire transfer confirmation for 3.1 million dollars.

She rose on unsteady legs, picked up the suit bag she had brought from home, and said, "I have to get out of here before Weasel gets back. Wish me luck."

"Waste of a good breath." Even so, Robin hugged her. Hard. "Let me know where you land."

Lena left the bank's headquarters, her suit bag slung from one shoulder, her briefcase on the other. She did not use a purse. While she was still an undergrad, a visiting woman executive had commented that purses were for ladies who lunch in Kansas City. Since her arrival on Wall Street, Lena had seen any number of women execs who used purses as a fashion accessory. But the remark had stuck. Lena made do with a billfold in her Versace briefcase's side pouch.

She turned onto William Street and started looking for a taxi when it happened. Again. Another unmistakable message. Like the other two that had already wreaked such havoc in her world.

Your ally is inside.

The message arrived with the force of a punch to her brain stem. It rocked her so hard she tripped on the sidewalk and almost went down. Just like the three previous events. Which was how Lena had regarded them ever since she realized they were neither imagined nor random nor one-off.

Events. With the power to change her life permanently. Whether the change was good or bad, she had no idea.

She said out loud, "I've had just about all I'm going to take."

One grey-haired exec glanced her way and smiled. Otherwise no one paid her any attention. Other pedestrians probably assumed she was talking on a hands-free. Either that or she was just another junior analyst going off the edge.

Lena stopped and considered her options. The heavy pedestrian traffic flowed around her.

Regardless of how borderline insane this might seem, the previous two messages had proven to be definite hits. The first had drawn her into analyzing what at first had appeared to be just another crazy series of possibilities. The second had told her where to obtain the required funds.

And then there was the most jarring aspect of these events. The factor that had her bugging out in the lonely, dark hours.

She knew the voice. She should. She had been hearing it all her life.

It was her own. Speaking to her from beyond.

Unless, of course, some benign force was duplicating her voice to convey these messages. Lena could not decide which option spooked her more.

Lena sighed, defeated by success. She turned toward the door. Only then did she realize where she was.

"Oh. No." Two words separated by a tight breath. Denoting extreme shock.

She stood in front of the entrance to the law firm that represented her own bank.

Lena had worked with several of the firm's more junior associates. If she walked in there and explained what she wanted, word would get back. It was inevitable. Her bank was this law firm's single largest client.

A voice from behind her asked, "Excuse me, are you going in?"

Lena willed herself forward. She knew resistance was futile. And she had to move. Her plane left in three hours.

The foyer was a high-ceilinged marble morgue to the aspirations of all mere mortals. Three armed security guards flanked the black stone reception desk.

Lena walked over and spoke the same words she had uttered any number of times before. "I'm here for the First American meeting."

"ID?"

She fumbled in her case. Handed it over. Hated how the guard could see her fingers tremble.

He keyed in her name, printed out a visitor's badge, handed it back with her ID. "You know the drill."

"Yes. Thanks." Lena walked to where another guard stood by the elevator entry. He took her badge and swiped the readout and coded in the floor. She entered the elevator, pushed through a pair of very hard breaths, and willed herself to steady.

It was only when she exited the elevator that Lena realized where she had landed.

The partners' floor.

She had been here twice before. One of a dozen flunkies brought in to beef up presentations they were making, expected to sit by the wall and keep their mouths shut.

The reception area was decorated with a Persian carpet the size of an inland sea. Two late Tudor tapestries adorned the walls. A receptionist who looked more expensive than the carpet asked, "Can I help you?"

Lena's mind froze solid. The law firm of Arnold and Shaw employed over two hundred attorneys in their Wall Street branch. Senior partners reportedly earned several million per annum. If some meeting with First American was taking place on this floor, it meant whoever was coming from the bank's side had the clout to fry her to cinders.

The receptionist's bark had a musical lilt. "Hello? Yes?"

"I—I'm here from First American."

"And you're early." The receptionist pointed to the sofa by the rear wall. "The conference room is still occupied. You can wait over there."

But as Lena retreated, the event's second clarion call arrived.

Here he comes. Tell him everything.

He was small and dark-haired and wore trousers to a pin-striped suit and a starched white shirt. Lena put his age at late fifties. The way he moved suggested the tensile strength of an aging gymnast.

The man noticed her intense gaze and asked, "Do I know you?"

The receptionist said, "She's some staffer here for the First American conference. And the room is still being used by Mr. Shaw."

"Actually . . ." The word came out sounding strangled. Lena cleared her throat and tried again. "I really need to speak with you."

The man showed mild surprise. "I'm not involved with the First American account."

"This has to do with something else." Lena felt the receptionist's curiosity like a branding iron. "Can we have a word in private?"

Lena did as the event demanded and gave him both barrels. When she was done, his first response was, "Please tell me you didn't deposit the investment funds in a First American account."

"Wells Fargo."

He nodded. It was one of the first motions he had made since sitting down. He was quite possibly the stillest person Lena had ever met. "So when does your flight leave for Denver?"

She checked her watch. "Two hours and thirty-six minutes."

He picked up the phone, punched a number, waited. "This is Don Metzer. Have a car and driver meet me out front. Where are we going? Good question." He lowered the receiver. "Please tell me your flight is leaving from LaGuardia."

"Yes." Lena mouthed his name. Don Metzer. She decided she liked it.

He hung up and rose from his chair. "I'll go with you. We've still got a lot of ground to cover."

Lena remained where she was. "You understand I can't pay you. I'm counting every nickel."

"Attorneys operate all the time on a contingency basis."

"And the bank doesn't know what I'm doing," Lena persisted.

"I told you. I don't work on that account."

"When First American finds out, there could be a serious blowback."

He offered a sparse smile. "Music to my ears. Let's go."

"Let me make sure I have this perfectly clear." Don Metzer's diminutive size was accented by his position on the Town Car's rear seat next to Lena. She had always been sensitive about her five-ten stature, but if the attorney found anything uncomfortable in looking up to his newest client, he gave no sign. "You are flying to Denver and driving to Pueblo, where you intend to acquire a bank."

She glanced through the glass divider at the driver. "Is it safe to talk?"

"All our cars are wired so that I have to press and hold down this button to speak with the people up front. Plus our drivers are thoroughly vetted. They have to be. We use these cars as extensions of our offices."

"Half a bank," she replied. "Fifty-one percent."

"The first of three interlocked acquisitions . . ."

"The bank will form the centerpiece of a new holding company," she confirmed.

"And the bank's current owners will sell a majority share because . . ."

"They're hanging on by their fingernails. Since the 2008 recession they've survived by selling off all their major assets. They're down to the one original bank building. Their balance sheet is a mess. They've been on the FDIC watch list for two years."

"So you are acquiring them . . ."

"For their bank charter. Which is the most crucial element of my plan. That's why I'm starting with them." She found his method of interrogation oddly comforting. He started the sentence, she filled in the blanks. As though they already shared thought processes. "Everything depends upon this first step."

"Say they don't sell. You move on to . . ."

"I don't have an alternative. There hasn't been time."

"You've been working on this for . . ."

"Two weeks."

"You are of course aware that the average time required for an acquisition in the financial industry is seven years."

"No. But it doesn't matter."

"And you are in such a hurry because . . ."

She found herself actually tempted to tell him the truth. That a voice from beyond had insisted that everything had to be completed this week. She had only pitched the idea to the investment group on Saturday, four days ago. The money from the group had arrived the previous evening. Today was Wednesday. She had two and a half days to make it work.

Lena replied, "I can't tell you."

He seemed satisfied with that response. The limo pulled up in front of the departures terminal. "Give me a dollar."

She reached for her purse. "Why?"

"It is the old-fashioned method of sealing legal representation." He accepted the bill and wrote her a receipt on the back of his business card. "Now everything we've discussed is covered by attorney-client privilege."

"What about your firm's association with First American?"

"Leave that with me." He waited as she slid from the limo, then said through the open door, "Call me the instant you can confirm the deal. I'll catch the next flight out."

Lena was still struggling to find the words to thank him as she entered the terminal. She clutched his business card like a talisman.

2

The officer who came for her was the one Reese Clawson thought of as Flat-Face. Female inmates tended to know their prison guards far better than male prisoners. This was part of staying safe. Abuse among female prison populations was fairly constant. Not that Reese had much to worry about on that score.

The guard was short and wide and had freckles that were stretched into a second coloring. Her face looked smashed by a frying pan, flat and utterly round, her nose a miniature indent. Most of the guards shared two things—odd physical appearances, and gazes as dull and flinty as old iron.

"Clawson, you've got a visitor. Bring your gear."

She still had an hour before the morning claxon. Which was an odd time for visitors. But Reese was not surprised. She took her time closing her book and rolling off the bunk. Inmates did everything on their three-by-six foam mattress. Hers smelled bad, but it was not the worst she had known in her fourteen months of incarceration.

For most inmates, visitors meant a sliver of activity in their dull grey existence. For Reese, it meant something else entirely. She pulled her sweatshirt over her prison blues, then filled the front pouch with her meager belongings. The book she left on the empty bunk. Her hand lingered on the blank notepad, then she decided to leave that as well. Why she had spent prison money on a journal was a mystery. She would never have dared write down the events that had brought her here. Even so, she had experienced bitter glee over the havoc her words might cause. But the thoughts remained locked inside, where they belonged. Because if she started writing what she knew, she would sign her own death warrant.

Her cellmate was a huge Native American, so big she jammed onto the wall and spilled over the lower bunk's rim. She asked sleepily, "Going somewhere?"

"Out of state, most likely."

"What, you read smoke in the sky?"

"Something like that."

The woman shut her eyes. "See you when you wake up, girl."

Reese followed the guard down the concrete alley and through the buzzed security doors, down another hall, past the main security point, ever closer to the forbidden outside. She was good at pretending she did not care about ever breaking out. But now and then she caught a whiff of the world beyond the wire. And her heart skipped a beat. Like now.

She had assumed they were leading her to the narrow concrete-lined quadrangle where vehicles parked for prisoner transfers. Instead, the guard led her into an area she did not know, another windowless hall, another series of metal doors. As far as Reese was concerned, any change in the routine was interesting.

The guard stopped by a door with a wire-mesh window and waved to the security officer in the bulletproof cage. The door buzzed. The guard opened it and said to the person waiting inside, "Rap on the glass when you're done."

"Thank you, Officer." The visitor did not look up from the file open on the metal desk. "Sit down, Clawson."

Reese did as she was told. Not because she was good at following instructions. Because she caught another faint whiff of a fragrance from far beyond this realm.

The woman on the other side of the desk turned a page in the file she read. She wore a pin-striped suit and a white silk blouse with a frilly bow at the collar. The woman was bulky and mannish with long dark hair clenched tight inside a gold clip. On her, the frilly collar looked childish and odd, like she had intentionally dressed to draw attention away from her expression, which was cold and hard and calculating. She turned another page in the file and continued reading.

Reese had no problem with waiting. She had been doing little else for fourteen long months.

Since her arrest, Reese had been moved four times. When they had first picked her up, she had been sent from Santa Barbara to Raiford Women's Prison in central Florida. Then Tennessee. The last two had both been in Virginia. Endless trips in the backseat of cars that had smelled worse than her mattress. It was enough to drive her insane. Which was perhaps what they had intended.

The woman reached into her jacket pocket and pulled out what at first glance was a digital recorder. Which was probably why prison security had let the woman bring it inside. But Reese knew better. She had used the exact same device. The woman flipped a switch and waited until the light glowed green. The device sent out a jamming signal intended to blanket all frequencies. Such meetings as this were supposedly protected by attorney-client privilege. But this same code of ethics stated no American citizen could be held without charge for over a year.

The woman had still not looked up. She turned another page. "Do you know where you are, Clawson?"

The obvious answer was, the Lawyer Room. It was the inmates' name for the security chamber, the only place in the entire prison not wired for sight and sound. At least, not on record.

Reese Clawson had not been here before. Which was hardly a

surprise. Since she had also never been charged. Or had any need to ask for a lawyer. Up to this point, she had been fairly certain that any such request would have made that day her last.

The woman turned another page. She seemed to find nothing wrong with Reese's silence. "You are at the verge of the only chance you will ever have."

Reese did not respond. There was nothing to say.

"My name does not matter, because I am not here. We are not meeting." She finally looked up and revealed a gaze as flat and hard as a prison guard's. "Clear?"

"Yes."

"I have one question for you. Answer correctly, and you will move on to a different status. What that is, and where you will be operating, does not matter. Yet."

The woman liked holding this life-or-death clout, Reese could tell. Her eyes were brown as muck, dark as the life Reese had come to call her own. Reese also detected a secret anger and realized the woman was here against her will. She found that extremely interesting.

The woman went on, "Answer incorrectly, and you will be swallowed by the federal system. Permanently. Tell me you understand."

"Perfectly." All four of the prisons where Reese had been held were run by state penal systems. In each case, cells were rented by the federal government to house prisoners convicted in federal court. Federal prisons were so overcrowded they could no longer ignore the public scrutiny and outrage. It was easier to house the federal prisoner overflow in rented cages than build new facilities. But this also made it possible for the government to falsify documents and claim a particular inmate had been tried, convicted, and sentenced. To a life without any shred of hope of parole. Which was no life at all.

The woman's actions were overly slow, and deliberate as an executioner. She tapped the pages back into order. Settled them into the file. Shut the cover. Placed the folder in her briefcase and snapped it shut. Rested her hands on the table. Gave Reese ten seconds of the eyes, cold as a cell door. "What would you do to earn another chance at freedom?"

Reese gave the answer as much force as she could. "Whatever it takes."

The woman cut off the jamming device. She rose to her feet and hefted her briefcase. She walked to the door and rapped on the security glass. "That is the correct answer."

A black Escalade was waiting for them outside the prison gates. Reese was directed into the rear seat. The woman slipped in beside the driver, a bulky guy dressed in a tailored suit of slate and silk. He asked, "Any trouble?"

"No. Drive."

Everything Reese saw or sensed carried an electric quality. Even the woman's hostile silence was pleasurable. The world spun and the road unfurled and every breath took Reese farther from the existence she had feared was all she would ever know.

The woman said her name was Vera. Reese assumed it was a lie, but just the same she wanted to thank her for the gift. To offer any name at all suggested a future and a purpose big enough to require further contact. The Escalade was not new and smelled vaguely of disinfectant. The leather seat was seamed with the sort of ingrained dirt that no amount of cleaning could pluck out.

Vera said, "There's a briefcase behind you in the rear hold."

Reese turned around and pulled the heavy Samsonite case onto the seat beside her. It contained four thick files. She estimated their combined weight at between twenty-five and thirty pounds. Their contents were divided into a logical sequence—finance, product and fabrication, legal and personnel, customers. She was deep into her initial read-through when, an hour later, the Escalade pulled into the parking lot of a cheap highway motel, one that probably catered to the prison visitors.

Vera kept her face aimed at the front windscreen as she said, "There's a key in the case. Your room is straight ahead of where we're parked. Go inside. Work. Don't leave the room. An envelope in the briefcase holds cash. Order takeout. Don't make any other calls. If you try to run, federal marshals will be given a shoot-to-kill order. You have seven days to memorize the contents of those files."

Reese felt her face constrict into an unfamiliar form, but at least she could still name it as a smile. Not because of the command or the warning. Because this woman thought she would need a week. "Will there be a test?"

"Absolutely." Vera did not bother turning around. "Fail, and Jack here will dispose of you."

3

ena's third stop was by far the hardest.

It was three o'clock on Thursday. The first two deals had already been worked through. The owners of both companies had agreed in principle. Don Metzer was already discussing contract details with the Pueblo bank president. The owner of the second business, a vendor of ATM machines, was at this moment driving from Colorado Springs to Pueblo to work through his own transaction. Lena's conversations with both company chiefs had been staggeringly easy. She had offered, and they had accepted with the quiet desperation of men drowning in choppy economic seas.

That was not what made her approach to this third company so hard.

The previous night, Lena had not slept. Finally at two in the morning she had risen from her motel bed and sat by the window and stared at the lights speeding along the Denver bypass. What made the night so long, and this final meeting so hard, was accepting that it was all real. Which was strange, given everything that she had accomplished to this point. But her sense of a new reality had less to do with the current deal than with what it all meant.

Lena was an analyst by nature. And she knew these potent communications from beyond were not just some benevolent voice offering her a chance to become rich. This was about something more. Something greater. And by taking this first series of steps, Lena knew she was signing on. To what, she had no idea.

As she entered the third of her acquisition targets, the looming mystery weighed as heavy as her lack of sleep.

The company owner was Juan Chavez, who ran it with his only son, Enrique. Lena's research had revealed they were being squeezed hard. Revenue and profit margins were stagnant. If this had been a publicly traded company, they would have sold out long ago.

Juan was seated behind a scarred and messy desk when Lena was ushered inside. His son leaned against the windowsill beside his father's chair. "Like I told you on the phone, the company is not for sale."

"Thank you for seeing me, Mr. Chavez. May I take a few moments and tell you what I have in mind?"

Juan Chavez was so well-padded his features were mere indents in a corpulent ball. By contrast, Enrique was sharp-featured, tall, and handsome. If a lady liked men with the Latin lover's indolent attitude, which Lena most definitely did not.

The father waved a fat-fingered hand at a metal chair. "Sure, okay. We got ten minutes."

"First of all, I don't want to buy you out. I want fifty-one percent. For which I'll pay you one million dollars. Cash."

The presence of that much money, even if they didn't want to sell, set the father to squirming. His chair complained with tight squeaks as he shifted. "My company is worth more."

"It could be. Depending on how the valuers consider your assets. But more than half your trucks are approaching the end of their natural lives. And six have over two hundred thousand miles on the clock." She held up her hand. "We don't need to discuss valuation because it doesn't matter. One million dollars is all I can offer because it's all I have."

"We could maybe talk to you about selling, say, twenty percent."

"Sorry. It has to be a majority share for my plan to work."

Enrique cut off his father's protest with, "So what's this plan?"

"I want to build the first financial institute designed specifically to service the Colorado marijuana retailers."

"For real?" The son flashed a remarkably attractive smile. "You want us to go into the dope business?"

"No, Mr. Chavez. I want us to enter the money business."

Lena had uncovered this opportunity while researching the most bizarre situation in recent commercial history. In a growing number of states, with a variety of restrictions, trade in marijuana had been declared legal. This was made possible through a change of state law. But all financial operations were governed by federal law. In principle, every financial transaction by every buyer and seller was still illegal.

Banks would not touch the money. Credit cards could not be used to make purchases. The same went for checks. Buying from licensed retailers remained a cash-only business.

This resulted in huge problems.

These newly licensed businesses were required to record their transactions, register with the IRS as commercial enterprises, and pay their state and federal taxes.

But they could not set up bank accounts. Or deposit their earnings. Even the use of secured safety-deposit boxes was forbidden by most banks. The financial institutions' legal departments suffered multiple heart seizures over the threat of federal litigation. The bank's charter could be declared forfeited. The lawyers who advised them could be brought up on charges and be stripped of their right to practice law. Same for their auditors. The bank and everyone involved in the process risked losing everything.

And so problems for the retailers grew steadily worse.

They were, quite literally, swimming in cash. In Colorado alone, the state's tax authorities estimated the retailers would, in their third year of legalized operation, generate over three billion dollars in turnover.

Small business owners were investing in massive safes and armed guards and bulletproof doors. But robberies remained common, often orchestrated by these very same guards. Too many people were lured by massive hoards of ready cash.

And then a new problem surfaced. A crisis of national proportions. One that changed the entire landscape.

The transport company owner's son had lost his flirtatious smirk before Lena completed her overview. Juan frowned in concentration, his chair squeaking as he nodded in time to Lena's points. Enrique left his perch by the window and drew up a chair beside his father. The two men now shared the same hard stare. They were cautious, but they were also intent. Lena liked their silence. She liked how Juan's first words were, "So how come we're the last group to be contacted?"

She liked even more how Enrique replied for her, "Because we're not desperate, right?"

"Exactly," Lena replied. "I agree, in some circumstances a million dollars could be viewed as a lowball offer."

"But that's all you got," Juan said.

"Every last dime."

"So you form this new company that owns parts of the three groups. Then what?"

"In the short term, we become the only financial group serving the retailers. We don't just go in and offer them bank accounts. We offer them everything." She ticked the items off her fingers. "We install ATM machines in each of our customers' outlets. Because these machines are owned and managed by a chartered bank, each ATM is legally considered a bank branch. This means the machines will accept deposits as well as dispense cash. The usage of credit cards also becomes possible."

Enrique nodded in time to her words. "Then our trucks show up at the close of every business day."

"And you sweep up the money under bonded guard and transport the cash to the Pueblo State Bank," Lena confirmed. "Where the money will be deposited in special short-term accounts."

The two men gave that a long minute, then Enrique said, "So explain why you won't accept a smaller cut of our company."

"Because it's not about me. It's about who would be willing to buy this new entity."

Their eyes opened wide. "You're selling us out?"

"The very instant the federal government changes the regulations on these financial transactions. Which will happen soon."

Juan demanded, "How come you're so sure about that?"

"Because," Lena replied. "They don't have any choice. The absence of a legal means of handling all this cash has opened this up to organized crime. A number of cities in Colorado and other states have seen a huge upsurge in gang violence. That was what alerted me. The government is being forced to issue a new ruling. And soon."

"So your idea is to get in early. Offer these desperate retailers a legal method of depositing their cash." Enrique nodded slowly. "This is smart."

Juan studied his son. "You like this?"

"You got to admit, Pop, it's a totally new take on a major issue."

Which was exactly what Lena had thought. Until the Weasel shot her down. And the events kept pushing her, first to the investors and now here. Through experiences that changed everything.

But all she said was, "When the attorney general's new ruling comes down, we will have a lock on the market. One of the large regional banks, or perhaps a venture capital group, will snap us up. But for this to happen, we have to show them a clean deal."

Juan said slowly, "So you need a majority share."

"Right. It's essential to them that they gain outright control over each piece of the puzzle."

Enrique said to his father, "So the part of the company we still hold would be worth some serious cash, Pop."

Juan asked, "How much are we talking?"

"The value of your remaining shares could easily be five million dollars. Maybe more. Much more."

Father and son exchanged another long look, then Juan asked, "What's the downside?"

"For you, minimal risk. I will put a rider in each contract that if the feds take any legal action against the new holding group, you have the right to buy back my shares for eighty cents on the dollar."

The silence was heavy, stifling. At least to Lena. Finally Enrique asked, "What do you think, Pop?"

"She's given it to us straight. I like that."

"Me too."

Juan asked her, "You dealing with Preston Downs over at Pueblo State Bank?"

"My attorney is with him now. And the president of the ATM group."

He reached for the phone. "Why don't you give us a minute, let us check things out."

"Of course." She rose from the chair.

Enrique walked with her through the outer office. "I guess it's the conference that's got you pushing so hard."

"Excuse me, what?"

"They got some special name for the group, Colorado Marijuana Retailer's Association or something. They're having their first meeting."

She could not help herself. She actually shivered. "When?"

"Starts tomorrow. The papers have made a big noise about it. You didn't know?"

"Not until now." She disliked how she couldn't keep the tremor from her voice. "Assuming you and your father agree to this proposed deal, could I ask your help with something?"

He shrugged. "Depends. What?"

"Come with me."

4

Brett Riffkind entered the hospice care facility and almost collided with a couple on their way out. They were so broken up they probably did not see him or hear his apology. Even after a year of working in such facilities, such encounters still left him shaken.

Like with many hospices, the director's office opened into the front foyer, so all activities and visitors could be monitored. He knocked on the open door. "I'm Brett—"

"I know who you are, Dr. Riffkind. And you are four hours late."

"I apologize, Dr. . . ."

"Mrs. Birch." She was narrow and fuming and accustomed to ruling her domain with unquestioned authority. "Your patient has been enduring extreme discomfort."

"First of all, she is not my patient. She can't be. Since I'm not a medical doctor."

"Then what on earth are you doing here?"

"I came at the request of your patient." As the hospice director knew all too well. And over her strident objections. Which was the real reason for her irritation. "Again, my apologies. My flight was canceled and I had to rebook."

"You told me all that over the phone. And it does not change a thing."

"Right. So if you'll excuse me . . ." Brett turned away.

"Just hold on there, mister!" When Brett kept walking, she came rushing around her desk. "I haven't said you could go anywhere."

Brett ignored the stares from everyone in the narrow waiting alcove and kept walking. "You're going to tell me the patient is too far gone to endure four hours off her meds. Which she has insisted on despite your objections. Just as she has demanded I be granted access. Ditto on the disapproval. But this procedure has nothing to do with your wishes. Your lawyer has already told you that." He knew the room number because the patient's sister had told him. "How am I doing so far?"

"What you're proposing is most certainly not a procedure."

"The patient disagrees." Brett knocked on the door. "As does her family. And those are the only voices that matter. Your lawyer has told you this too."

The hospice director was still standing there when the patient's sister opened the door, which meant the director heard the woman in the bed say, "That lady is such a pain. Bad joke."

Brett regretted the exchange even before the door was closed. And said as much. "I watched a patient die this morning. It always gets to me."

The patient's sister asked, "You stay around for the end?"

"If they ask me to."

"Even when you don't like it?"

"Some of my subjects are not fortunate enough to have a sister there for them."

The patient watched the exchange with eyes that glittered with intelligence and defiance. Brett liked her already. Which only made his job harder. His hands trembled slightly as he opened his laptop and began the process of coding in. He put the tremors down to a long day.

It was the sister who stated the obvious. "Maybe we need to make peace with Mrs. Birch."

The patient spoke in the tight gasps of a woman intent on holding back the pain. "Not worth it."

"I can't be here all the time. What happens when I leave?"

"I don't like her. Nobody does."

Brett unwound the lead and plugged it into the special headphones. "How's the pain?"

"Not so bad. When I'm still. Breathing hurts. Maybe I should stop. Joke."

Over the eleven months he'd been working this gig, Brett had developed certain traits. They formed his own personal firewall. One of them was that he always referred to these people as his subjects. Or the patients. He willed himself to forget the names of all the family members. He never returned the embraces that often came after the procedure. But occasionally there were patients like this, who shamed him with their strength.

"I didn't introduce myself properly. I'm Brett Riffkind."

"Em."

The sister said, "And I'm Sandra."

"It's nice to meet you both. Your sister is right, Em. And there's one other issue to consider. Mrs. Birch will make it especially hard if anyone else here wants my services."

Sandra gave Em a chance to respond, then asked, "You always do this for free?"

"Expenses only. And that's another thing. Because the director is opposed to what's happening here, I can't stay in the overnight medical quarters or take my meals here."

Em said, "We can afford it."

"He's not talking about us, Sis."

"Oh. Right." A few panting breaths. "I really don't like her."

"It's your call," Brett said.

"Oh, go ahead."

Brett walked back down the hall. As soon as he rounded the corner and entered the reception area, Mrs. Birch burned him with her gaze. He knocked on the open door anyway. "Em and her sister would like you to join us."

The invitation was clearly the last thing Mrs. Birch had expected. "I'm not sure that's a good idea."

Brett turned back. "It's the only way you'll ever understand."

"This procedure was developed by Dr. Gabriella Speciale, an Italian scientist who spent years recording the brain-wave patterns of people meditating and at prayer. She isolated the primary shifts in mental states and identified the dominant brain-wave cycles." Brett directed his words to the patient. But Em and her sister already knew all this. The information was on hundreds of websites and blogs. Thousands. All over the globe. No one could have anticipated the outpouring that had resulted from his eleven months on the road. Especially not Brett. "Earlier studies had already determined that if you place a pure tonal sound in one ear and a slightly different tone in the other, the subject does not hear two different sounds. Instead, the brain forms a vibratory pattern. The rapidity of this vibration is determined by the difference between the two tones."

From her chair by the window, the hospice director radiated disapproval. Brett had no idea whether her tension would interrupt the patient's ability to ascend. But the way Em watched him with an almost ferocious intensity, he doubted it.

"The sequence starts with a pattern that invites the body into a state of complete relaxation. You remain completely in control of the entire process throughout. If you feel the least bit uncomfortable, you may simply return to full physical consciousness."

Em listened to him through the headphones. Brett used the type that completely enveloped the ear. Their bulkiness only highlighted the patient's wasted state. She asked, "You're sure I will ascend?"

"In our normal clinical trials, the standard rate of ascent on the first go is about thirty percent. Another thirty percent report a period of intense relaxation and nothing else."

"And the rest?"

"They bug out and run screaming from the room."

Em smiled for the first time. Her entire face flashed with the humor she had managed to hold on to, despite everything. The sight twisted Brett's heart.

Em said, "I'd like that. To go running. Anywhere."

Sandra asked, "What about with these procedures?"

Brett motioned to the Bible on the bedstead. "For subjects with strong faith who are not heavily medicated, the ascent rate is almost one hundred percent."

"I wouldn't call my faith strong," Em said. "More like a last gasp. Bad joke."

Her sister sat where she could share smiles with Em. "You're terrible."

"I know." Em's sharp gaze found the director. "I need to do this."

Mrs. Birch sighed but did not speak. She seemed fascinated despite her own best efforts to the contrary.

Sandra asked, "Have you ever lost someone when they've been, you know . . ."

"Ascending. No. Not yet, anyway."

Em flashed him another smile. "There's always a first time, right?"

Brett knew it was going to be very hard to say good-bye to this one. "I hope not. Ready?"

Em shut her eyes. "Let's do it."

5

Lena maxed out her credit cards by acquiring the smallest booth available and the last spot on the conference agenda. It meant they would be speaking first, which she assumed had been avoided by others here to address the group. She had no experience with peddlers of this stuff, legal or otherwise. But she doubted many of them would be fresh-eyed and alert at nine o'clock on a Saturday morning.

She said as much to Don Metzer as they surveyed the exhibition hall. The attorney had arrived at seven thirty that morning with their three new partners. They had taped a handwritten placard at the back of their empty booth and begged three folding chairs and a rickety table from a passing janitor. Now they stood at the railing of the rear balcony, which also served as the foyer to the main conference hall. Below them stretched aisle after aisle of the most bizarre convention on earth.

Don surveyed the scene with a faint smile and said, "Actually, speaking so early could be to our benefit. Our audience might be smaller, but we've got a better chance of catching them while they're still . . ."

She found his smile contagious. "Unstoned."

From her other side, Enrique chuckled. "Man, this is seriously twisted."

More than six hundred vendors were giving their booths a last-minute buff-up. Over the hall's sound system, Blondie sang a lament to life's wasted hours. Directly below Lena stretched an aisle of hand-blown bongs and tie-dyed shirts. The row to her left was reserved for confectionaries, where every counter was piled with chocolates and buns and brownies. Then came two aisles of machinery—self-watering pots, vacuum-sealing machines, carbon dioxide extraction systems, flicker grow lights. Farther back was row after row after row of the product itself. The fragrance wafting up to the balcony was pungent.

The ATM leasing company's president was a square-jawed aging jock named Gary Langdon. He ran the family business in a solid if unimaginative style. Enrique asked him, "You okay with all this, man?"

"Money is money," Gary replied. "The state my balance sheet is in right now, I'd lease bananas to the Denver Zoo's monkey house if it got me through next quarter."

A voice from behind them asked, "One of you dudes named Fennan?"

Lena swung around. "That would be me."

The red-bearded Viking cast a merry gaze over the banker's and lawyer's ties. The guy wore a vintage Grateful Dead T-shirt and a tag that declared him to be a staffer. "We need you on the podium."

"Give us three minutes." When he moved off, she turned to the third of her new partners, the oddest duck of them all. Preston Downs the Fourth, president of the Pueblo State Bank, was dressed in a three-pieced black suit, a needle-thin black tie, and a white shirt so starched the collar shone blue in the fluorescents. He was aged in his early sixties and looked ten years older, with a shiny bald head and cheeks so lean they formed caverns. Preston Downs the Fourth looked like a mortician sizing up his own casket.

Lena asked him, "How would you feel about being our spokesperson?"

"Are you certain that's wise?" His voice matched his physique, a low and somber drone.

"You best listen to the man," Enrique agreed. "These cats see him walk to the mike, they'll probably figure they're headed to the OD Corral."

To her surprise, Don Metzer said, "No, no, this is good. We're not after fitting in. We are offering a banking service. Stable, safe, secure."

When no one else objected, Lena said, "Okay. We're on."

"My name is Preston Downs. My family was one of Pueblo's original settlers. We ran a dry-goods business through the gunslinging era. We fed the cattle drovers and we buried the ones who didn't make it out. Our fortunes rose and fell with the town that we'd helped build up from nothing. And right now, the fortunes of my family and my town are both pretty close to rock bottom."

Lena surveyed the audience. They formed a remarkable collection of sizes and shapes and facial hair and tattoos and piercings. Her group possessed the only two ties. Lena figured she was the lone woman wearing makeup.

Preston Downs continued, "My great-great-grandfather established the Pueblo State Bank in the first month of the last century. Before then, our farmers and ranchers and merchants had to truck their money to Denver, or bury it in their backyards. Opening a bank didn't make much sense at the time—the town wasn't big enough to afford one. But we did it because our friends and neighbors needed what a bank could offer. Safety."

The man spoke with the slow cadence of a plainsman. He stood impossibly erect for a man of his years, and he addressed this audience with the same gravity as he would an audience of financiers. His manner and his speech came from a bygone era. Within three minutes of his starting, the conference hall was not just quiet. These people were engaged.

"I opposed the legalization business. But the people of Colorado have spoken. And I respect the democratic process. Even when I disagree with the result. That's what makes our country—"

He stopped because he had to. The conference hall had risen to its feet. They whistled and they applauded.

Don reached over and squeezed Lena's hand.

When the hall went quiet, Preston continued, "What is a crime now is how our government fails to guarantee the safety of our citizens doing what the state has declared a lawful enterprise. This situation is outrageous—" He had to stop a second time. And for him, that was enough. When the hall quieted once more, he said, "I've spoken my piece. I'm turning it over to the woman responsible for us being here."

Lena approached the mike, introduced herself, took the biggest breath of her entire life, and launched straight in.

She walked the retailers through her plan. Step one: new armored ATMs were to be installed in each retailer that signed on. The ATMs were granted "bank status" because the machine's supplier was now part of a bank's holding company. This meant the machines could be equipped to accept deposits as well as handle credit card withdrawals.

Step two: twice-daily pickups would be scheduled using the Chavezes' series of armored vans, a company that had been handling secure transport for over forty years.

Step three: accounts were opened by the Pueblo State Bank, which listed them as "special deposits."

What Lena left out of her presentation was the most worrying aspect of her plan. Don and the bank president both knew it for certain, but had granted her breathing space by finding no need to mention the obvious.

It all came down to a race against the clock.

Throughout these high-pressure days, three questions had raked talons across her brain. Was she correct in assuming this grey area was just that, and not genuinely illegal? Was the attorney general actually working on a ruling? If it was delayed for any reason, which would come first—the new ruling or a felony warrant?

Directed straight at her. Lena Fennan. President and CEO of the new holding company.

·ılı·

Lena completed her overview in eight minutes. She then turned to where the others stood and introduced them as her partners. She finished her remarks with, "We are still in the process of incorporating. We don't have contracts ready for any new clients to sign. We don't even have a cost structure. So right now, if you're interested, you have two choices. You can wait until all the legal hoops have been jumped through and we can write you up a contract on letterhead. Or you can accept us on our word. In that case, we'll do a handshake deal and our armored vans will be by to make their first pickup . . ." Lena turned to the Chavez father and son.

Juan called out, "We can start this afternoon."

Enrique added, "And go as long as it takes. Everybody will be seen to before we go to bed."

Lena turned back. "Your cash will be delivered to the Pueblo State Bank. Preston?"

He lifted his voice loud enough to carry over the silent crowd. "I and my staff will stay on duty all night if required."

Lena caught the bearded Viking's cutoff signal and said, "I guess that's it. If you're interested, you can find us at the emptiest booth on the exhibition floor."

They were mobbed.

6

Lena's and Don's only break from signing up new clients that entire Saturday was to hold an emergency conference call with the three partners at Don's firm who formed the management committee. The committee was required to green-light any new client. In Lena's case, this was especially important since the firm's largest single client was the bank. But Don played the senior attorneys like the pro he was. He named the firms Lena had acquired, then gave their revenue and the cost of the proposed acquisitions. His tone suggested it was barely worth the partners' attention, particularly on a Saturday afternoon. Which was echoed by the lawyers who utterly disliked how Don had disturbed their weekend.

Don hung up the phone and said, "Mission Control, we have liftoff."

The three company chiefs stayed on. Enrique spelled his father when the hour arrived to arrange pickups for their new clients. By the time the first trucks left, they had forty-two retailers ready to hand over cash. On a handshake.

Saturday evening, Lena went straight from the exhibition hall to the airport. Don was remaining in Colorado to nail down the

41

paperwork. As she sank into her seat on the flight, she wondered if perhaps she should have asked why he was willing to act against his firm's interests on this project. But there simply had not been time. And unless the attorney general's ruling came down in their favor, it really did not matter.

Don phoned her at work Sunday night, his voice reduced to a ragged lisp. "I've never seen anything like it. An hour after you left, we actually had one store owner break down and weep."

"How many clients have you signed?"

"The trucks have made sixty-three pickups."

"All on the basis of handshake deals."

"And Preston's comments from the podium. Having him serve as our spokesperson was a master stroke. Not to mention another seventeen firms that won't hand over their cash until they get the deal memo. Which I should have ready in a couple of hours."

"Thanks for backing me."

"That's my job." Don hesitated, then asked, "Something wrong?"

She stared around the junior analysts' bull pen. Robin had left just before Lena arrived. The seven other analysts were all heads down. At nine thirty on a Sunday evening. "I came back to the same old grind. I don't know. I guess I expected something different."

"It is. You just don't see it yet."

She turned away from the others and released the worry that had been plaguing her since the retailers swarmed their booth. "What happens when the feds hear about us?"

Don did not reply.

"This thing is so much bigger than I ever expected. We won't be able to keep the lid on for long. People are bound to talk, and sooner or later Washington will hear."

"I'm working on that."

"It better be good, whatever you come up with." She found it hard to swallow, much less form the words. "How long do we have?"

"Little late to be asking that." Don seemed unfazed by her worry.

"A few weeks would be my guess. Maybe a bit longer if I can work up a smoke screen."

Lena swiveled back to her workstation and stared at the reams of figures stretched over her three computer screens. Normally she could read them like a good book. "I'm just tired."

"Leave the worries to me. That's why I'm here." Don sounded impossibly cheerful. "Three things. One, we need to set up a daily conference time. Confirm the next one before signing off. What works for you tomorrow?"

She rubbed her face, tried to think. "Let's go for eleven."

"Done. Point two, you need to buy a pay-as-you-go phone. Only call me from that, and only to the number I'll give you when we next speak. Once the feds catch wind of what we're doing, we have to assume there will be listening ears."

Fear rose like a gorge once more. "And third?"

"Quit. Give notice. You're president of a company about to go ballistic."

Lena silently amended, *Unless the feds lock us all up.* All she said was, "I'll think about it."

⫿

Monday morning she arrived at eight forty, the latest she had come in since her first week on the job. The junior analyst bull pen was a hive of frenetic activity. Robin paused long enough to say, "Your job is to analyze risks. Not take them."

"That was the first decent rest I've had in a week." She slipped into her seat. "Amazing what nine hours' sleep will do."

Robin smirked. "So the vacation was that good, huh."

"It's not what you think."

Robin ducked like a turtle slipping into her shell and hissed, "Weasel at eleven o'clock and closing."

Wesley Cummins stopped where he could loom over Lena. The Weasel was very good at looming. "Fennan. My office. Now."

Wesley Cummins occupied the seventh-floor southeast corner office. Four windows. A tight glimpse of the Hudson River. Real sunlight. He was head of the bank's financial services division, the largest component of the mergers and acquisitions department. Some investment bankers considered M&A the unwanted stepchild of the Wall Street giants. Lena had never wanted to work anywhere else. But eleven months of sweating in Wesley's domain had almost cured her of what before had been her life's ambition. To be here. Standing in front of a man she had come to truly, genuinely, wholly loathe.

Wesley Cummins was a caricature of the self-obsessed Wall Street executive. Flash suspenders, flash suit, flash haircut, ridiculously overpriced tie. He was tall and would have been good-looking, had it not been for the simple fact that Wesley Cummins survived by being a professional thief. He stole his analysts' work, stripped away all mention of their names and the hours they had put in making him look good, and refused them permission to even touch the shadows of the banks' higher-ups. Which meant they had zero job security. They lived and breathed each day at the Weasel's whim. In the eleven months since her arrival, Lena had learned this was often the fate of junior analysts. Eighteen-hour days, no glory, quick departure. The story was so overtold the survivors treated it as one big yawn.

He bounced in his Italian executive chair of cherrywood and suede as he frowned over her handwritten note. "Did I green-light a vacation?"

Lena did not reply.

"No, I did not. But you went anyway. That's a firing offense if ever I saw one. Are you interested in staying on at First American, Fennan?"

Lena remained silent.

"You've got one chance of hanging on to the end of the week. I'm shooting you five new potential acquisition targets. I want them analyzed by start of business tomorrow."

"I need more time."

"You don't get to ask for more time, Fennan. That's what it means when you're—"

"I'll give you one new analysis each day. That's it."

"That's it? Did I really hear you say that?"

"And I want my name on the reports when you take them upstairs."

He stared at her like she had grown a new head.

"All reports I deliver from now on." She wanted to give it more steam. But it just wasn't in her. The full night's sleep still held her like a delicious elixir. "I want credit for the work and the hours—"

"Get out of here."

Lena walked back to her cubicle. Robin greeted her with, "You're fired?"

"Not today."

"Why not?"

"I have no idea. I did everything but beg him to give me the ax." She watched the files pop up on her incoming list. "I told him I wanted credit for my work."

Robin stared. "Not really."

"I know, can you believe it?" Lena tasted a smile. "Maybe next time I should tie him to the desk and get out the bullwhip. Maybe then he'd give me the new contract he's held back for the past ten weeks."

During their conference call on Tuesday, Don reported the team had signed up one hundred and seven clients. By close of business, the Pueblo State Bank was in possession of more cash than at any point since the recession hit.

When Lena rose before dawn on Wednesday, her first waking thought was the feds were bound to strike. They had grown too big too fast. The other Denver banks had to be complaining by now. The attorney general's office still had not issued a ruling. Which meant Lena's group was out there, exposed, swinging in the wind. She could almost hear the jail doors slamming shut.

An hour later, Lena sat in her cubicle, sipping a cup of green tea because her stomach was too knotted to accept anything bitter. "What am I doing here?"

"I've been wondering the same thing," Robin replied. "You're sure not working."

Lena pointed at her screens. "These numbers might as well be written in Egyptian."

"Last I checked, Arabic is the lingo in Egypt."

"There, you see? I knew that! What's happened to my brain?"

Robin started to quip, then looked farther down the corridor and said, "Weasel."

Wesley walked over and loomed by Lena's desk. "Got the report I ordered, Fennan?"

Lena picked up a file she had been working on before Don's call had come in the previous evening. Since then, she'd done little but worry. She offered the folder without looking up. It was the first time since her arrival in New York that she had offered subpar work.

Wesley accepted the file and said, "Need the others, Fennan. Chop-chop."

·||||·

Thursday morning, Lena was working with Robin through a mass of data sent in by a new prospective client. The client was a financial services company who was interested in being acquired. Actually, *interested* did not describe the company's attitude. They were beyond desperate. In reply to Lena's request for financial data, they had sent sixty-three boxes of files. Lena suspected the data dump was intended to mask a fatal flaw. Which only made her angry. And when Lena was angry, she attacked numbers like a ferret.

Lena did not even hear her phone's chime until Robin said, "Your purse is ringing."

"I don't have a purse."

"Purse, case, bag, whatever. Answer it."

46

Lena lifted out the phone she had purchased at Don's insistence. "Yes?"

"Where are you?"

"The bank."

"Go outside. Call me back."

"Actually, now isn't—" But Don was already gone.

Lena sat there staring at the phone, feeling the fear she had carried constantly ever since returning from Denver congeal. Don sounded worried. Frantic. Which could only mean one thing. She forced herself to rise from the chair.

"Was that your vacation man?" Robin's voice carried a knowing smirk. "He makes you buy a special phone? He's got to be married."

"He's not my guy." Lena's voice sounded metallic to her own ears.

"Hope he knows that."

It was raining when she arrived downstairs. Lena rushed down the street until she found a canopy not already occupied by smokers and hit speed dial.

Don answered instantly with, "We have an issue."

"How bad?"

"Too early to tell. The *Denver Post* contacted Preston at the bank's Pueblo headquarters. He turned the reporters over to me. I'm stalling, but it won't last long. The reporter knows too much for us to stay under the radar. We're front-page news."

Her gut felt filled with frigid concrete. "The reporter has been fed data by one of Preston's competitors."

"Preston thinks the same. Still nothing from Washington, right?"

"Not a peep. I'm checking every twenty minutes." She watched the rain form a liquid curtain off the canopy's edge. "What a mess."

"Don't panic just yet. I've been working my own sources." When she did not respond, he asked, "Are you paying attention?"

"With every fiber of my being," Lena replied.

"Okay, it looks like the AG is preparing to act. Generally major issues like this one are preceded by some quiet nudges, just letting the markets know well in advance. My gut tells me this is happening."

"Are you sure?"

Don remained patient. "Of course not. But it's more than a hunch. I've been at this game a long time, remember. Call it a seventy percent certainty."

She took a breath of the damp air, tasted diesel and the electric thrill of another chance. "Don, this is great."

He held to the same calm steadiness. "I'm glad you like it. Now listen. The reporter is bound to be calling. You need to stay cool and refuse to respond. Don't hang up, don't run. Just don't give them any more ammunition."

Lena knew she needed to return to the bank. The analysis she and Robin were working on was due that evening. She had no idea whether the deal actually carried such a short fuse or if it was just the Weasel's standard hassles. In either case, she couldn't leave Robin hanging. But she needed a moment. Lena turned up Wall Street and walked to Trinity Church. She entered the cool shadows and slipped into a pew. Her first week in New York, she had hunted down four such havens, places close enough for her to escape momentarily and just breathe.

She did not think things through. She simply sat and felt the electric tension vibrate through her body. She had no idea what to say to the press. She had never spoken to a reporter in her life. She couldn't say whether Don's idea would work. She needed to call her investors and give them an update. She needed another night's sleep. She needed a week away.

The rainstorm passed, and the church's western wall turned honey-colored in the sunlight. Lena emerged from the church, crossed the street, and rejoined the frenetic pace of Wall Street.

Fifty yards from the bank's entrance, her phone rang. Not the one she'd bought for Don. Her real phone. Her lifeline. This too was supposed to be an unlisted number, one she shared with family and a few close friends. But that meant nothing. She checked the readout and saw the number was blocked. She knew it had to be the reporter, and she still wasn't ready. She answered anyway. Waiting wouldn't help. "Yes?"

"Is this Lena Fennan?"

"Who is calling?"

"Ms. Fennan, this is Charley Farlow."

"Is this a joke?"

"No ma'am, it most certainly is not. I'm calling to talk a deal. And folks will tell you I don't joke about deal-making. I understand that's something we have in common. A lack of humor when it comes to numbers. I assume you know who I am."

"Of course I do." Charles Farlow had run his operation out of Atlanta for years, where he owned several cable networks. Back in the early nineties Farlow had invested in supposedly played-out Colorado mines, and then watched the price of gold go through the roof. Over the next dozen years, Farlow went from being seriously rich to being one of the nation's ten wealthiest men. "That is, if you're really who you say you are."

He chuckled. "I admit, going through a half-dozen layers would make this appear more legitimate. But I don't have the time. My jet's over at Teterboro revving its engines. I've got a meeting tonight back in Denver. If we're doing this deal, it's got to be now."

"You want . . ." Her brain was still too busy doing the hamster routine, spinning its mental wheel, to fully register. "You're here?"

"Tower suite, Waldorf Astoria. Why don't you head on over, see for yourself how real I am."

7

The same driver who had brought Reese from the prison to the motel returned with bags containing clothes. The room's directory had menus from a dozen different local restaurants. Reese took exquisite pleasure in ordering meals whenever it suited her, eating breakfast at midnight and dessert at nine in the morning. Each bite took her one step further from the rigid blandness of prison time.

Reese took repeated showers, reveling in the clean water and the privacy. She had almost forgotten how exquisite it felt to have a door lock on her side of the world. She positioned the table so she could stare out the front window, fascinated by the view. The parking lot fed onto a busy main road. Reese studied the people and the cars and the freedom they all took for granted. She did not mind being cooped up. She needed time to transit out of the prison mentality.

Whenever she grew restless, Reese pushed the beds together and used the free space for her workout routine. She punched the air and she ran in place and she held to the same tight internal zone that had gotten her through so much. Mostly, though, she read and she thought and she planned.

On the seventh morning after her release, Vera and Jack collected her in the same black Escalade. Neither of them spoke to Reese during the hour-long drive to a private airstrip. A needle-nosed Learjet 85 was parked at the end of the single runway. The midsized business jet had been introduced by Bombardier in 2007 and immediately gained its share of fans and critics among the ultrarich. The Lears were narrow and low-ceilinged compared to similar-priced Gulfstreams. But the Lears could land on a dime, and even this larger version required just three thousand feet for takeoff. But the real advantage to Lears were their engines. Lears popped to full speed in a heartbeat and had the force to smash their passengers deep into the plush leather seats. Fans of Lears referred to them as the Ferrari of the skies. A new Lear 85 had a range of three thousand nautical miles and cost seventeen million dollars. In a former life, Reese had counted such information as vital.

"Stay here," Vera ordered, and rose from the vehicle.

The driver watched the pilot emerge from the jet and salute Vera. "She wasn't kidding, you know. You get this wrong, I'm tasked with sending you away for good."

"The lady," Reese replied, "did not strike me as a kidder."

The driver studied her in the rearview mirror. "Me and the guys, we're taking bets on how long you last. I was feeling generous. I gave you another forty-eight hours."

When Vera signaled to her, Reese gripped the briefcase, opened her door, slid out, then said through the driver's open window, "I'd tell you to have a word with the others who bet against me in the past. But none of them are breathing."

Her clothes were one size too large, an off-the-shoulder sweatshirt and linen cargo pants with a cloth tie. Cork-soled sandals. Reese spent the flight leafing through the files she had memorized and staring at the clouds. The sun's position told her they were headed south. The flight lasted just under three hours. Vera worked her BlackBerry and did not speak. Twice Reese ate sandwiches from a tray in the plane's galley. The restless stirring in her gut was a silent alarm. She was missing something important. But she found an odd comfort in the fact that her sensors were still working at all.

Their descent took them through heavy clouds, then Reese caught glimpses of a rain-shrouded city with tall buildings by a large body of water. She assumed it was either Jacksonville or Savannah, but because she did not know their air speed she couldn't be certain.

They transferred from jet to limo. The city was indeed Jacksonville. Reese recognized the landmark Mathews Bridge as they crossed the St. Johns River. She had been there a few times, back in her former life, the one where she regarded the backseat of limos with the same bored tension as Vera apparently did now.

Reese completed her third read-through on the ride into town. They pulled into the Omni Hotel, then continued over to a small side entrance with its own green awning. When Reese saw the spa sign, she could not hold back the sigh.

Her evident pleasure only made Vera more sour. "There's a Neiman Marcus two blocks down on the left."

"I saw it."

"Go to the private shopper's department on the fourth floor. An account has been set up in your name. Get a business suit and whatever else you need." She checked her watch. "I'll be back for you in exactly five hours."

Reese's only response was another electric alarm in her gut. She rose from the limo and stood there under the dripping awning, staring at the empty space where the limo had been, running through Vera's final comments, knowing there was an underlying current. She was missing a vital clue. When it continued to elude her, she turned and entered the spa.

The receptionist was young, lovely, and clearly unsettled by something she saw or sensed about Reese. "We have you down for a facial, hair, nails, and a massage. Do you have any preferred order?"

"Sauna and rub, then the rest together," Reese answered, pleased that she managed the foreign words so easily. "And make sure the masseuse has fingers of iron."

Reese fell asleep almost as soon as the woman started working on her. Then something in her lizard brain shouted alarm, and she jerked so hard and came upright so fast the woman slammed into the side wall. The masseuse was big, well over two hundred and fifty pounds, and had skin the color of aged mahogany.

Reese said, "Sorry."

"Did I hit a nerve? Ma'am, I'm so sorry. They told me you asked for a deep-tissue massage."

Reese could lie, but she had to tell the woman something. She decided there was no reason to hide the truth. "I just got out."

The woman showed a knowing awareness. "You mean . . ."

"Federal pen. Fourteen months and three weeks. I've been out seven days."

The woman humphed a sound that was more sympathy than laugh. "You just lie back down, honey. Let Keisha work her magic." She stepped back to the table and said, "No wonder you're tight. I've felt steel bands that were less wound up."

The cosmetician was the last to finish and so the one to ask, "Will madam be wanting anything else?"

Reese had no choice then but to examine her reflection. The mirror covered the entire wall and had such brilliant lighting the somber truth glared at her.

Reese Clawson stared at a feral beast.

Her eyes had retreated into tight caves. But their positioning was slightly off because of the scarred indentation over her right eyebrow where Charlie Hazard had hammered her. Her jaw was somewhat askew from a second blow that had shattered bone. The prison doctor had been utterly unconcerned with preserving her beauty, and the result was a slightly off-kilter cast to her features and scars like angry valleys. The cosmetician had done her best, reducing the scars down to a pair of shadows. But they still served as arrows to the flawed bone structure.

Elements of her former beauty were still present, but only as hints to how far she had fallen and how hard her landing. No degree of professional shading could hide the cavernous depths to her cheeks. Prison life had turned her blonde hair both limp and semi-transparent, so the stylist had sheared it down to an almost military length. Her mouth had become permanently compressed, as though her full lips were a weakness she could no longer afford. Prison food and her workout regime had honed Reese down to all sinew and bone. Combined with her pasty complexion and rage-filled gaze, she looked like a throwback to some primitive race that devoured their enemies.

She smiled, and even before it was fully formed, Reese knew it was a mistake. The cosmetician was a young beauty and could not quite hide her wince of fear.

Reese said softly, "I believe we're all done here."

The private shopping department in Neiman Marcus was a carefully designed tactic to separate rich people from a great deal of their money. The central parlor was domed like a Grecian temple and lined with bar and buffet and eager staff, all of whom were slender and beautiful and perfectly groomed. What they thought of Reese arriving in sweatshirt and cargo pants was hidden behind polished smiles and words of welcome. She declined the champagne and accepted a plate of delicacies. She was not genuinely hungry, but Reese had lost her ability to turn down food. Young women brought in one outfit after another. Reese pretended to be interested. But in truth her focus remained internal.

There were mirrors everywhere. She could not escape personal examination, so she gave herself over to the inevitable. She did not feel the anger that was so embedded in her features. She searched hard and could only say she really didn't feel much of anything. Perhaps that was the purest essence of rage, she decided. To swallow it like a dark pill, have it become a component of her cellular form. It no longer needed to be felt. It simply was.

As she selected three complete outfits that she deemed worthy of corporate boardrooms, Reese gave over to digesting what she had learned. She mentally swam through the depths of figures and facts contained in the files. She made two decisions. She formulated a three-stage attack.

Then she focused upon the real mystery.

This entire episode, Reese decided, was designed with one thing in mind. Someone who could not contact her directly was determined to communicate with Reese. Now. Today. That was why she was here, being pampered and fitted. Whoever they were, they had designed this elaborate process to send her a message.

The further she proceeded along this line of thought, the more convinced Reese became that Vera was part of the message. An unwilling component, most certainly. But vital just the same.

The week in a motel, the limo, the Lear, the folders, the second limo, the spa, and now this. All of it intended to speak to her.

Now that she was seeing this in the right perspective, the message was clear enough.

All this boiled down to a four-word message that she finally understood.

Reese was not alone.

With the alterations to her new clothes completed, Reese packed everything else in her new Coach valise and left the store wearing a Lanvin suit that would have worked well at a fashionable funeral. She had no intention of attending anyone's wake, most especially her own. But the client's file had been perfectly clear on the people she needed to impress.

When she returned to the spa, the limo was waiting. Vera was nowhere to be found. Reese settled into the rear seat and gave herself over to the mystery's final component.

Who could possibly care enough about her to want her to succeed?

8

The Waldorf Astoria was an art deco throwback, a nod to the good taste and flair of a bygone era. Some New Yorkers turned up their noses at the lobby's inlaid mahogany walls and gilded columns and chandeliers and central clock shaped like an ornate pyramid. Twice Lena had come here for tea and a chance to pretend that she belonged among the moneyed crowd. This was the first time she'd arrived with any legitimate purpose.

She paused in the front foyer to suppress her shivers and phone Don. When he answered, Lena told him, "I think it's happening."

Beyond the main lobby was a second vestibule, guarded by a uniformed woman who politely asked her business. When Lena said she had been invited to meet with Charles Farlow, she was ushered into a discreetly hidden elevator that swept her up to the thirty-second floor.

Lena's footfalls formed a swishing hush along the carpeted hallway. She did not look at room numbers after spotting the security guard outside a suite's double doors. "I have an appointment with Mr. Farlow."

"Your name?"

"Lena Fennan."

He swiped the lock, knocked, opened, and announced, "She's here."

Charles Farlow was on the phone when his assistant led Lena into the main room. Farlow was as imposing as his photographs. He stood six feet six and moved with the lumbering grace of a grizzly. His voice rumbled smooth and low, thunder beyond the horizon. He paused long enough to wave a greeting and point Lena into a chair. Then he went back to pacing in front of the windows. A rampant beast of the financial jungle, claiming his domain.

He cut the connection and tossed the phone to his aide. "Handle that thing long enough for me to get to know the lady here." He walked over, swallowed her hand, and asked, "Do you pronounce it Lee-nah or Lay-nah or what?"

"I prefer Lee-nah, but you can call me whatever you like, Mr. Farlow."

"It's Charley, and that's a good answer in my book. You take coffee?"

"No thank you." She waited until he seated himself to ask, "Why am I here?"

"You've got something I want. What's it called?"

His aide offered, "Pueblo Holdings."

"Right. So I've got three questions for you. First, how did you know. Second, how did you come up with the plan. Third, how much will it cost me."

Lena was glad to hear her voice had somehow become unattached to her racing heart. "How did I know what?"

"That the AG is coming out with a rule change."

"I didn't—wait, he decided?"

Farlow's gaze carried an intensity that made his voice's easy rumble a fable. "You know, I actually believe you."

"I'm an analyst, sir. I analyzed." The tremors were too strong now to fully suppress. "The AG is really going to rule?"

"He already has. I paid a fortune to be the first with that news, and you beat me by a week. The announcement is going to happen this afternoon. Which means I want to wrap this up before my competitors come a-calling."

"Really, sir, Charles, I didn't know. I thought it had to happen. But I had no idea . . ." She felt a sweeping wave of dizzy relief so powerful she had to ask the aide, "Could I change my mind about that coffee?"

He asked her, "How do you take it?"

"Milk, no sugar."

She watched him pour from a silver thermos, took a sip, another, knowing Charles Farlow waited with growing impatience. But she needed the time. When she steadied, she set the cup on the side table and said, "My analysis suggested that the government had no choice. At the federal level, the threat of organized crime taking over the money side of legalized marijuana in an election year would be disastrous."

Farlow turned and told the aide, "Pour me one too. No, not those silly cups. Get me something my size." He accepted the go-mug and slurped noisily. "We'll come back to that. For now let's move on to door number two."

"How much time do you have?"

"Take as long as you want."

So she gave it to him step-by-step. Her preliminary analysis and being shot down by her boss and going to the Florida investment group and then traveling to Denver. She left nothing out, except of course the voice from beyond. The real reason why she was sitting here at all. Discussing a multimillion-dollar acquisition with the grizzly of American finance.

When his aide insisted they had to leave, Charles led Lena into the elevator and out to the waiting limo. All he said was, "Keep going."

Finishing her story lasted most of the way to Teterboro Airport. Throughout Farlow examined her with a gaze intended to pry open a titanium safe. When they pulled up next to the private aviation terminal, Farlow said, "So now we're down to my third question. I only deal in majority ownership. Tell me how, and tell me how much."

"You can have a hundred percent of the parent, which owns a majority share of all three subsidiaries." Her voice sounded ghostly, surreal in its calm. "I want thirty-one million dollars."

"Do you."

"That's the price."

"How many clients does your group have under contract?"

"I'd have to call and check for the latest update, but by last night we'd signed on two hundred and seven retailers. Which represents seventy-eight percent of the state's total trade."

"You have the power to make this agreement?"

"Full authority was given to me by the investors. I am the lone signatory on any transaction."

He pursed his lips, nodded once. "We've got a deal. With one contingency."

She had to fight down another wave of giddiness to ask, "And that is?"

"You come work for me."

The breath felt sucked from her body. "Excuse me?"

"I'm working to buy another two financial groups, both a lot bigger than yours. I want you to come run a portion of this new empire."

"Sir . . . I . . ."

He must have seen the decision even before Lena knew it herself. His eyes widened slightly. "You're actually going to turn me down?"

9

Brett climbed the stairs and set his suitcase down on the town-house's broad front stoop. He pressed the sorest point on his back and straightened with a soft groan. He had strained it the previous day, then made it worse by falling asleep on the plane. When he finally managed to stand upright, he pressed the bell. To his right, traffic rumbled and swished through the misting rain. He had only been to New York a few times, but he knew a five-story townhouse a hundred and fifty feet from Park Avenue and four blocks from Central Park would be worth a fortune.

The butler who opened the door was dressed in a black suit and bore the expression of a man trained to turn away mere mortals. "Yes?"

"I am Brett Riffkind. I believe I'm expected."

"Dr. Riffkind. Of course. Do come in." The butler stepped aside and observed as Brett painfully hefted his cases. "Shall I assist you with that?"

"I can manage, thanks." But each step only brought more discomfort.

"Do let me take it, sir."

Brett gratefully released the handles. "I just need the briefcase."

The butler set his suitcase on the marble tiles. "Your personal belongings will be quite safe here."

Brett followed him into a palatial foyer and stared up at the gilded ceiling—or tried to, because when he tilted his head his left side seized up again. "Oh man."

The butler observed him, patient as only a professional servant could be, then set his pace to match Brett's shuffle. The foyer opened into a grand gallery, eighty feet long and twenty wide, with four sets of sliding double doors, two to each side. The doors were carved and gilded to match the distant ceiling. "Wait here, please."

The butler knocked softly and slid open the right-hand door just enough to slip inside. An open door at the gallery's end led into a vast kitchen. Just inside the door was a mesh-backed office chair and small writing desk, probably used as a nurse's day station. Brett resisted the urge to walk over and sit down, as getting up was such a trial.

The doors slid back. "Mrs. Lockwood will see you now."

Brett shuffled into what once had been a grand parlor and was now redone as a hospital bedroom. The old woman in the bed looked waifish, but her voice carried remarkable strength. "I would say you look like death, young man. But that would be in the poorest possible taste."

"It appears that Dr. Riffkind has an issue with his back, ma'am."

"When Doris surfaces, see if she can offer him some relief."

"Very good, ma'am." The butler turned to Brett. "Dare you seat yourself, sir?"

"I better set us up first."

"How can I assist?"

Brett stood back and let the butler do the heavy lifting. The contents of his case were settled onto a hospital table fit with rollers and a foot brake. All the while the lady in the bed observed him with eyes bright and dark as a robin's. "When did you last eat?"

"I had peanuts on the plane."

"Frederick, fix our guest a tray."

"Certainly, ma'am." The butler rose from plugging in Brett's laptop and apparatus. "Scrambled eggs and toast and tea, sir?"

"That would be great, thanks."

"Shall I have Doris join you, ma'am?"

"She was up with me most of the night, let her rest. Besides, I doubt this young man has the strength in him to give anyone a hard time. When did you last sleep?"

"I napped on the plane."

She sniffed. "I mean a proper rest."

"Yesterday." Brett rubbed his face, then corrected, "Day before."

"Are you in the habit of destroying yourself like this?"

"My last appointment asked me to stay until the end. The doctors gave her only a few hours to live—she lasted seventy-two."

"You came straight from one deathbed to another?"

"I had already booked our appointment." Brett lifted the headset. "Shall we get started?"

"Put that thing away and sit down, young man. I am curious to know a bit more about you. That is, unless you're already scheduled to watch another poor soul breathe their last."

Brett made no effort to hide his relief. "Not for another week."

"Then make yourself as comfortable as you possibly can. When we're done, Doris will give you a good working over. She's trained as both a nurse practitioner and a chiropractor. Done me a world of good." She watched Brett brace himself on the chair arms and ease down. "What shall I call you?"

"Brett."

"And I am Agnes. Are you really a doctor?"

"Of neurosciences."

"A scientist who flits about the country, granting the near-dead a glimpse of what comes next. I find that interesting. Very few things interest me these days."

Brett remained silent. Either she asked or she didn't. He certainly wasn't going to help move this forward.

"Well, are you going to answer me?"

"I didn't hear a question."

She huffed. "What on earth has you carrying on like this?"

So there it was. Hearing the question once more should not have caused him such discomfort. Perhaps it was his back acting up. But Brett didn't think so. "I do this as penance."

"Penance."

"Yes."

"For what?"

"I was part of the original team that developed this project. I had a serious disagreement with the director. I offered the entire program to our competitor in exchange for a lab of my own and the freedom to do the work I wanted."

"You sold out your own team."

"I did. Yes."

She mulled that over, tasting several responses. "These direct responses are part of your penance?"

Brett swiped at the perspiration beading his forehead. "They are."

"The program director set this up?"

"No. I did."

"What on earth for?"

If it was difficult before, now it became excruciating. "After transferring the data, I began the original research into what has brought me here to you today."

"Studying death."

"Studying the moment of transition," Brett replied. "*Ascent* is the word for what you are about to experience. I ascended, and I became trapped."

"Trapped how?"

"Trapped," he repeated, hearing the sibilant roar fill his being once more. The rush of furious power, there to devour and destroy. "I was saved by one of our team. Since then, I have worked in this capacity."

"Gathering data. From people like me."

"I record what you experience, yes. And I pass it on to the team. What they do with it is up to them. But I don't use it myself."

"This is all quite remarkable." She studied him, her gaze the only component of her being that remained untouched by whatever illness held her to the bed. "You are hoping the team will let you back in?"

"No, they never asked me to leave."

"Then why . . . ?"

In all the times he had made this confession, he had never had a subject actually comprehend. This woman was, he realized, not just rich but remarkable. He felt himself drawn to her, which was dangerous. But he could not help liking some of his subjects. Even when it made their departure all the more difficult. Not simply because he became emotionally caught up in the end of another life. Because it brought back all the horrors he had known, the utter closeness of his own last breath.

Agnes said, "You can't ascend."

"Maybe someday."

"I can see that the loss has cost you dearly." Her gaze had the ability to probe far deeper than Brett would have preferred. "Are these ascents truly so wondrous?"

Brett booted up his laptop. "You're hopefully about to find out."

But the woman's eyelids had begun to droop. Her features ran like old wax, losing their strength with the rapidity only possible for the truly ill. She was asleep before Brett rose from his chair.

He left the items on the nightstand and shuffled away from the bed. When he reached the door he hesitated a long moment, then turned around. The woman slept peacefully. Brett wondered if he had completely lost his ability to remain detached. This would make three departures in a row where he had become emotionally involved. But there was no denying the fact that he already liked this woman far too much for his own good.

10

The Bridgeport Corporation's campus formed the nexus of Jacksonville's major industrial park. Bridgeport employed 130,000 people in six locations and was the third-largest employer in Florida after Disney and NASA. They supplied guidance and tracking equipment, hardware and software combined, for almost all US military jets and drones and guided missiles. Most military satellites were also powered by Bridgeport. The company's reach extended through all branches of the armed forces, and most of the intel agencies. They were the largest single supplier by annual billing to the National Security Agency. They were the electronic grease that kept America's spy and listening networks spinning.

Reese was kept waiting in the reception area for almost an hour. The sun had set and the majority of headquarters staff had left for the day. She did not mind at all. The lobby was as pleasant a place as any to reflect. There was no indication anywhere of what precisely Bridgeport did. The glass atrium was high-ceilinged and filled with blooming trees planted in great marble pits. A waterfall fell from one wall and maneuvered about the trees within a rock-lined stream. The musical noise formed a soft privacy curtain around all the groups that still waited to be called inside.

Finally Reese was ushered down a long corridor and shown into a conference room wrapped in a sunset beyond the glass wall. The two men rose and shook her hand and offered cards and gestured to the coffee service. Reese poured herself a cup because it gave her an opportunity to study the men. She didn't look at their cards. She didn't need their names. She called them Linebacker One and Two. They were retired military, down to the greying buzz cuts and bullish builds.

Reese said, "I need to know you're recording this conversation."

"We can't confirm or deny anything," Linebacker One replied. He had the flat drone of a man who had been stressed for so many days he had lost the ability to notice his own fatigue.

"Perfect," Reese replied. And it was. Because the man's response told her all she needed to know.

The men were formed by the same military mold, hard and well-fleshed with coppery gazes. They were here because some superior had directed them to show up and tell her no. Those were their orders. Selling them was not an option. Their job was to deny her entry.

Reese said, "I will only say this once. So pay attention."

The men shared a smirk and did not respond.

While still in the lobby, Reese had decided to toss out the instructions that shaped this test. Her orders from Vera were to obtain three contracts, each for one million dollars. Reese knew this pair's sole job was to bar the door. And they were very good at their job. For her to succeed, she had to use their broad shoulders as a stepping-stone.

"My name is Reese Clawson. I represent a new security and intel group. I am here to talk with you about Blake Donovan."

"Spell the name."

She did so.

Linebacker One pulled a BlackBerry from his jacket and typed. "We have nobody employed at Bridgeport by that name."

"Blake Donovan. Your directors have just offered him a contract to become the new chief of this division."

Linebacker One was apparently their chosen spokesman. "Even if this were true, which I'm not confirming or denying, we couldn't discuss this with—"

"He starts in two days. Which means you have to act fast." Reese set her case on the table and snapped the locks. "The man has a drug problem."

"Ms. . . ."

"Clawson."

"Our intel is the best in the business. It has to be. All senior employees are carefully vetted."

"Are they." She started laying out the documents, the ones she had been instructed to sell. "As you can see, the gentleman was given OxyContin following surgery for a torn ligament. Since then he has supplied himself with prescription painkillers through a PO box in Chevy Chase and a compliant pharmacist in Toronto."

Both men leaned their guts against the table to read. One said, "This postbox is not Donovan's."

"Of course he didn't open it under his own name." She turned over the next document. "Here is a photograph of our man opening the mailbox. Here is a copy of his signature on the box rental, a bank account, and a credit card. All in the false name. And here is a Maryland driver's license, the fake name, but our star's photo."

Two spoke for the first time. "This is bogus. It has to be."

Reese found pleasure in turning over the pages one by one. Linking her to a past she'd thought lost and gone forever. She had once been very good at this trade. The best. "And here are authentications. Five in all. Confirmation that the fake name's signature was written by the same man as the one who signed your contract as Blake Donovan. Followed by authentications that the photographs have not been Photoshopped. Surely you must recognize the name at the top of those pages. Since Bridgeport owns the company."

Linebacker One glared at her. "How did you come up with this garbage?"

She smiled, knowing it was a twisted expression, and finding pleasure in that. "Actually, what happens next is where things really get interesting." She passed over another photostat. "Recently Blake Donovan began having difficulty focusing. Who wouldn't, after four months of daily Oxy ingestion. So he used his trips to his former company's Mexican factory to make another set of clandestine purchases. By the way, certain amphetamines are available over the counter in Mexico. For ninety days and counting, the man has balanced his Oxy diet with uppers. Lovely place, Mexico."

One snapped, "Our drug tests would have uncovered this."

"Come on, you know how this goes. He uses the same tactic as professional athletes on the needle." She gave them a moment to object, then continued, "Which brings us to the last little item on my shopping list. Donovan's former employer caught wind of his new hobbies. But Donovan had uncovered a little secret of his own. Something about the extremely married CEO and a certain receptionist. So they worked out a deal. Donovan was given a glowing reference, and he agreed to leave quietly and swiftly."

One drummed his fingers on the table. "Evidence?"

"None I can share." Actually, she had none at all. Just the typewritten sheet she had memorized. Which was the clearest evidence Reese had for why she was seated here. Out of prison. Talking to them.

Two protested, "There's no way you can know this."

Actually, there was. And it was why she had been given this chance. Because she was the only person on earth with the know-how to carry this forward.

Reese replied, "Talk to their chief in-house attorney. He drew up the documents. But he also uncovered the drug use. He could lose his license to practice law for covering up a felony. He'll crack like a toasted walnut."

The pair exchanged a long look. Two conceded, "We'll check this out."

"Before you hurry off," Reese said, "there is the small matter of my bill."

One sneered, "This is a shakedown. We pay or you go public."

"Actually, this information comes to you free of charge. All I want is one small item. Do this and the secrets stay just between us."

"And that is?"

"An hour with your parent company's chief in-house counsel and finance director. Tomorrow morning. Nine o'clock."

"Neither of them are in town—"

"My offer," Reese replied, "is not open to negotiation."

11

ena Fennan had the reception area's sofa to herself. Her attorney, Don Metzer, sat in the padded chair to her right. As usual, Don showed the world an impenetrable calm. If he was even the tiniest bit worried about the firestorm they were about to endure, he gave no sign. He wore a pin-striped suit that was tailored for him on London's Savile Row. His shoes were made to order by Church on Jermyn Street. Lena knew this because Don had told her. Both the suit and the shoes were throwbacks to a different era, when Don Metzer had been a force to be reckoned with on Wall Street. But the power was gone, along with the perks, and now Don sat in a suit as old as his youngest kid, one tiny step away from insolvency.

Unless, of course, the chance really did exist that they would both survive the assault being prepared beyond those polished mahogany doors.

Don's calm presence kept Lena removed from the terror that should have been consuming her. She knew Don wanted to ask her about how she had happened to walk into his life nine days back. But he was a consummate professional. He was hired to be discreet. Even with his mystery client. Who plainly baffled him.

But he was here with her now. And he was willing to swallow his questions and his doubts. Even when his entire career was on the line. Because the opposing counsel prepping inside the double doors included the managing partner of Don's own firm. Or rather, former firm. Upon his return from Denver the previous evening, Don had quietly shifted from a position as salaried partner to something known as of-counsel. Don had told her that the firm's partners considered his move an act of insanity. But Don had done it anyway. Because of her and this project. He had taken the momentous step without even a murmur of complaint. Which was amazing enough for her to say softly, "I can't thank you enough for being here."

Don continued to stare at the window behind the secretary's desk. His voice was a soft drone, as bland as his expression. "What can you tell me about the people we'll be meeting with?"

She shifted in her seat and pretended to share his calm. She might not be properly terrified. But she had been unsettled and tense and worried for so long, she had almost forgotten what it felt like to be serene. Even so, at least she wasn't alone. "The bankers are Wesley Cummins and Roger Foretrain. The lawyers I don't know."

"Forget the lawyers. I know them. All too well. Tell me about the pair representing First American."

"Wesley Cummins is my boss. The week I started here, I renamed him the Weasel. He steals ideas, he claims all credit, and he fires analysts on a whim."

"First American sheds junior analysts faster than any other house on the Street," Don said. "What about the other banker?"

"Roger Foretrain is why I came to New York. He wrote the book on risk analysis. I read it in two days. The guy has the most amazing mind . . ." She noticed Don had turned from the window and was smiling at her. "What?"

"You say his name like you're in love."

She felt her face go red. "I've never even met him. Weasel forbids any of his team to set foot on the management floors. The first time I stepped inside the directors' elevator was today."

Don went on, "So you came to work with Foretrain, but then your direct boss ordered you not to speak with him."

"That is Weasel in a nutshell." But Lena was tired of thinking about the Weasel. The guy had dominated her life for the eleven longest and most bitterly disappointing months of her existence. Until nine days earlier. When the sky had opened up. And everything changed. But she couldn't think about that either. Not and endure what she knew was coming. She glanced at her watch. "They're half an hour late."

"Relax. We could be here all day."

"Roger Foretrain is never late. Not by a minute. It's one of his trademarks."

"I'm the fly in their coffee." Don stretched out his legs. He moved like a gymnast in a suit that was going shiny at the elbows. "No good lawyer likes to be blindsided. My managing partner is inside that conference room because your bank is the firm's largest client. Morley Shaw and his junior associate expected to bring you in there, isolate you on their turf, fry you to a crisp, and go treat their clients to a nice lunch. You were expected to count yourself lucky not to be brought up on felony charges. They never thought you'd show up with legal representation. Especially a guy with Street creds."

Lena was flooded with a sense of amazed gratitude. Something that had occurred repeatedly since drawing Don into her life. "What happened to you?"

Don nodded once, as though approving of her question. "How much did your research uncover?"

The truth was, very little. Lena planned to dig further. When she had time. Up to this moment, it had taken every ounce of her strength, every beat of the ticking clock, just to ride the whirlwind.

She replied, "Pretend I don't know anything at all."

"The short answer is, I bet on the wrong bank. I was partner in a boutique firm. We handled legal matters for a dozen smaller investment houses. Lawyers here tend to specialize, just like everybody else on the Street. My own team handled just two clients. Then our firm was bought out by Morley Shaw's group. My position was scaled back to what my employers at Arnold and Shaw call a salaried partner. Which means I no longer hold an equity share. Then the latest crisis hit, and one of my clients tanked. The other is struggling. Most of my junior associates were let go." His smile was as trim as the rest of him. "The bright future vanished. I stopped feeling loved. Or even wanted."

"Why didn't you go out and find more business? That's what partners do, right? They play rainmaker."

"I tried." This time the smile touched his eyes. "You and I have more in common than you know."

"They stole your client?"

"Not stole. Please. We're lawyers. They simply assigned my new client to a more senior partner, who gobbled it up and left me hanging."

"I'm so sorry."

"The Japanese have an expression for it. Salaried executives who are too senior to just fire are given a desk by the window. They clock in, they sit, they do nothing. Eight hours later, they go home. Most get the message and give up. But I couldn't. Not with a wife and a mortgage and two kids in private school."

"So why did your firm let you take me on?"

"Because you were seen as too small to matter. The three firms you were focused on were all Colorado based. Where neither my firm nor your bank have a footprint. The issue of co-clients is well established. All I had to show was that there were no adverse parties. Which there weren't. They let me keep your project because it wasn't juicy."

She felt burdened by everything Don wasn't saying. The risk he took, the trust he showed. "But to go of-counsel. That's just . . ."

"Inevitable," he finished. "They were looking for a way to kick me out and keep my one remaining client. I gave them what they wanted." Again the languid wave. Turning the page. "Can I ask you something?"

"Anything."

"You're half Chinese?"

"One quarter. My father's father. My mother says I swallowed up all the remaining Oriental genes. The only thing I got from her was my height. I'm over a head taller than Daddy. He's basically spent his entire life being either proud of me or exasperated by how I don't bend like Mom."

Don clearly liked that. "Your unbending nature has taken us for quite a ride."

The secretary's phone had been ringing constantly. When she answered now, though, she looked at Lena for the very first time. Lena's butterfly nerves had already started their frantic fluttering long before the secretary said, "Mr. Foretrain is ready for you."

As they rose from their seats, Don said for the third time that morning, "Once we get inside, don't say a single, solitary word."

"Understood."

"I mean it, Lena. Let me do the talking in there."

Lena knew Don had every right to be worried. She was in this situation because she had found it impossible to follow orders. "I won't open my mouth unless you give me the sign."

12

When Lena and Don entered the conference room, the two lawyers and Roger Foretrain were on their cell phones. They stood by the window, angled so they could pretend to ignore her and Don's entry. Beyond the glass, a late spring snowfall swirled. Lena's gut was filled with the same churning freeze.

She settled into the seat across from Roger Foretrain. The Weasel was seated to her left, with an empty chair between him and Roger. She wondered if Roger had ordered the Weasel to keep a distance. She hoped he had detected the vile heart that beat beneath Wesley's striped shirt. Or maybe he had pierced the man's hundred-dollar haircut and discovered his brain did not hold a single original thought. Lena hoped it was so. She had spent many midnight hours hoping that Roger did not actually like the Weasel.

Wesley Cummins paused from typing into his phone long enough to smirk at her and mouth the same words he had written at the bottom of her report two weeks earlier: *Crash and burn, baby*. Lena turned away. She was all done thinking about the Weasel.

Roger Foretrain cut the connection and tossed his phone on the table beside her incorporation papers. The female legal associate took that as her cue and stowed her own phone. The senior lawyer was slower. Morley Shaw used the space between the conference table and the window as his personal stage. His leonine features and sweeping silver mane and elegant suit all declared that here was a man accustomed to ruling over earth-shaping legal disputes, at twelve hundred dollars an hour.

Finally Morley Shaw cut his connection and settled into the seat beside Roger. He eyed Lena, sniffed, then turned to her lawyer and said, "Really, Don, I'm disappointed in you. Very disappointed indeed."

At first glance, Don Metzer was not up to a battle with Morley Shaw. He sat with his hands resting on the table. Motionless.

"This is your last chance," Morley said. "For the sake of your legal future, I urge you to move over to our side of the table."

"I'm here representing my client," Don replied.

"Who is about to be brought up on charges by your firm's client." Morley was as polite as he was dismissive. "Let's review how you come to be in this position at all. You falsely represented your client to the firm's management board."

"There was no misrepresentation," Don corrected. "The matter of her employment was included in the summary document. Which I have with me, if you'd care to review."

"But you failed to fully clarify the issue. Which a hearing of the bar's ethics committee will take very seriously."

"Ms. Fennan came to me with a simple M&A matter. I was engaged in the context of a corporate acquisition. This issue is ancillary to that engagement. The parties are all Colorado-based firms. Where neither our firm nor this bank have exposure. There was no conflict."

"No conflict then. But there most certainly is now. Believe me, Don. It has been my experience that the bar tends to come down very heavily on attorneys who go off the reservation. Which you as a partner have done."

"Former partner," he corrected mildly. "I went of-counsel twenty-four hours ago. Surely you remember that, Morley. At the time you said you thought it was a wise move."

The managing partner of Arnold and Shaw colored slightly. "You knew this was happening and were preparing for it. Which is how I will present your case, Don. And believe you me, I will personally take charge of this hearing." He pointed at the chair on his associate's other side. "Now remove yourself from this terrible situation and get over here while you still have a career to rescue!"

"Thanks, Morley," Don replied. "But I'm comfortable where I am."

Shaw lifted his arms in elegant disdain. "Really, Don, I feel obliged—"

Roger Foretrain's phone buzzed with an incoming message. He scanned the screen, clicked it off, and said, "Let's get on with it."

Morley Shaw disliked being cut off in mid-flow. He redirected his ire at Lena. "Ms. Fennan, your employers have opted to hold this meeting in lieu of having you arrested. Against my own advice, I must tell you."

Don interrupted, "Actually, there are no grounds for charges of any kind."

The managing partner's coloring rose several notches further. "It is precisely because of such weak and ill-advised counsel that we find ourselves here today."

The Weasel started swiveling his chair back and forth, the sort of tight little motions that an excited kid might make. He smiled as he watched her. This was what he lived for. Lena wanted to block him out, so she turned toward Don. Then she kept turning so she could examine the painting behind her. It was far more beautiful than the photographs she had studied.

When she turned back, she realized Roger Foretrain was observing her. He broke into Shaw's monologue with, "You know it?"

She had spent eleven months hoping for a chance to talk with this man. Even so, she glanced at Don. Her attorney kept his gaze on Morley Shaw but nodded. Lena turned back and said, "The painting is entitled *No Te Aha Oe Riri*, which translates as 'What has disturbed your peace?' It was painted in 1896, one of a series Gauguin completed after his return to Tahiti. He was sick, broke, and disheartened. His paintings from this era are darker and less idyllic than those from his earlier time in the islands. Many critics consider this to be one of the artist's finest works."

Maybe it was how the Weasel had finally lost his smirk. Or perhaps it was how every eye in the room was locked on her. Most likely, though, it was because Lena knew this would probably be her one and only chance to talk with the man who had drawn her to a life on Wall Street.

She went on, "You own nine of Gauguin's original oils and over two hundred of his sketches. You favor scenes where the painter portrays the Tahitian people, their thick lips and heavy hands and feet, all trademarks of Gauguin's unique perspective. You secretly keep a sailing yacht permanently moored in the Moorea harbor, and you sneak out there at least twice every year. This table, as well as your desk and the coffee set in your office, are all shaped from Tahitian mahogany. You flew over a senior draftsman to supervise their assembly."

The best way to describe Roger Foretrain was rumpled. He wore his tailored Turnbull & Asser shirt like a pajama top. His greying hair was a bird's nest, his glasses were as askew as his tie. "I don't remember seeing you. When were you in here before?"

"The first time I ever rode the executive elevator was coming up here for this meeting."

"You know an awful lot about a guy you've never met."

"That's my job, Mr. Foretrain. To gather up the hidden."

The senior lawyer cleared his throat. "Perhaps we should refocus on the matter at hand."

Without taking his eyes off her, Roger Foretrain unclipped the gold Rolex from his wrist and flipped it like worry beads. "Sure thing."

"Ms. Fennan, you are facing the threat of some very serious charges."

Don said, "I would ask that you address me as Ms. Fennan's attorney."

Morley clearly disliked that immensely. But he had little choice.

"Your client must relinquish all funds she has gained from this highly questionable enterprise."

"Let's back up," Don said. "We're here to understand what precisely are the bank's concerns."

"That should be simple enough, even for someone as far off the reservation as you, Don. Lena Fennan is one of the bank's employees. Her actions have violated the terms of her employment. Her contract contains a clause that specifically lays out her fiduciary duty to the bank."

Don said mildly, "My client conducted all these transactions on her own account."

"Did you even read her contract? Such transactions are a direct breach of their agreement!" Morley waved aside Don's unspoken rejoinder. "I'm the one asking questions now. Your client identified a potential investment, did she not."

"She did."

"Research that was conducted on the bank's time, using the bank's resources."

"That is correct."

Clearly Morley had not expected Don to agree so readily. "Frankly, Don, I am still having difficulty understanding what you're doing on that side of the table."

"As your client requested, let's set my personal motives aside for the moment."

"Ms. Fennan then took it upon herself to raise three million dollars in private equity funds. Did she not."

"Three point one million."

"She used these funds to acquire three firms."

"None were outright acquisitions," Don replied. "Ms. Fennan purchased a controlling interest. As I stated before, all three firms are Colorado based."

"Their location has nothing whatsoever to do with the fact that she acted in breach of her own contract!" Morley slipped on a pair of gold-rimmed reading glasses and extended a hand. His associate had the document ready. "By your client's own admission, she made a profit of thirty-one million dollars."

"Eighty percent of which went to her investors," Don replied. "My client's take before expenses was 6.82 million."

"The bank insists upon receiving all profits," Morley declared. "Your client's investors hold no legal right to one cent of this transaction."

Roger softly interrupted, "You made a thousand percent profit? In two weeks?"

Morley angrily hammered the air between them. "Let's stay on target here. The contract between your client and her investors is superseded by Ms. Fennan's duty to her employer." He used his forefinger to take aim across the table at Lena. "Young lady, all proceeds from that transaction must be immediately transferred to the bank, your employer. If your investors choose to take you to court, that is between you and them."

Don interjected, "Are you aware that my client put this proposal forward to the bank?"

Roger Foretrain leaned forward. "Say that again."

Morley shot his client a look. "Even if it's true, it changes nothing."

"Actually, it does." Don opened his briefcase and extracted a series of stapled pages. He passed out three copies. "Mr. Cummins, I assume you don't require a copy, since your comments are scrawled on virtually every page. I have highlighted several of them. Your handwriting is somewhat difficult to decipher. But I believe you will agree the comment across the top of page one reads, 'Adolescent rubbish.' On page two, Mr. Cummins asks, 'Have you been sampling these products?' On page three—"

Morley protested, "As I said, this has no bearing—"

"Then on page four Mr. Cummins suggests that my client's university degrees are falsified. And if you'll turn to the last page, you will see where Mr. Cummins writes, 'Denied with pleasure.' And down at the bottom he concludes, 'Crash and burn, baby. I would be doing the bank a favor to fire you.'"

The look Roger Foretrain cast his divisional manager stripped all the starch out of the Weasel's features.

Morley cleared his throat and said, "But Cummins did not follow through. Your client was not dismissed. Her actions are therefore still governed by her duty of loyalty."

Don stowed the document back in his case and resumed his almost subservient position, hands folded on the table. "Are you also aware that my client does not actually have a contract with the bank?"

This time both lawyers blanched. "That is utter rubbish."

Don paused then, and looked at the Weasel for the first time since entering the room. And smiled. "Twelve weeks ago, Mr. Cummins issued my client a new contract. Ms. Fennan considered the terms to be below her expectations. She refused to sign. As a result, Mr. Cummins froze her paychecks. She has not received any remuneration since. Not one penny."

The electric silence was finally broken by Roger asking, "How long did it take you to put together this analysis?"

Lena looked at the Weasel and allowed a trace of her fury to boil up. "Less than a week."

Don went on, "Given the fact that my client's direct superior stated categorically that the bank had no interest in her concept, and how she does not at present have any legally binding contract, a court of law would question any claim put forward by the bank."

"A court of law?" Morley's wrath lifted him partway from his seat. "A court of law? Do you have any idea what you are suggesting?"

Don seemed utterly uninterested in his managing partner's ire. "Actually, I do."

"The blowback could be catastrophic. To have you represent Ms. Fennan against our client could ruin us on the Street! Now either you relocate yourself to our side of the table where you belong, or I will personally bring you before the partners and demand that you be summarily dismissed!"

"No need," Don quietly replied. "I resign. Effective immediately."

Morley's inability to penetrate Don's calm only added to his apoplexy. "You cannot be serious!"

"I have never been more serious in my life. I quit. It's what you've wanted. Now you have it."

"You have ten seconds before I pull the lever. All your fiscal drawdowns will be rescinded. Your credit is erased. Forget pension, paycheck, equity! It's all gone. This very afternoon I will bring you up on charges before the bar! Are you listening to me? They'll carry you out with the garbage."

Don waited through a pair of Morley's raspy breaths, then replied, "Fine. I withdraw my representation from Ms. Fennan."

There should have been more satisfaction to the moment for Morley Shaw. But by this point he had been blindsided enough to suspect there was more. "Ms. Fennan is no longer your client?"

"That's what I said." Don returned the papers to his briefcase.

"In that case, Ms. Fennan, your employer—"

"Could I say one more thing before I leave? Not as her attorney. Just an interested third party."

"Absolutely not, this is no longer—"

Roger cut in with, "Go ahead."

"Lena Fennan has been offered a job by Charles Farlow."

Roger asked Lena, "Doing what?"

Don replied for her, "Charles Farlow has offered Ms. Fennan a vice presidency within his financial group and a chance to develop her own investment portfolio. I have been offered a position as her in-house counsel."

Morley sputtered, "The only way they could possibly have heard—"

Roger held up his hand. "Let him finish. You're not done, are you."

"I'm not, no." Don rose to his feet. "Lena will stay with your bank, but on certain conditions."

"She is in no position—" Morley was halted by a look from Roger that matched the intensity with which he had melted the Weasel.

Roger said, "Go on."

"You drop all consideration of claims against the profits Ms. Fennan made from this transaction. You instruct your legal team to withdraw any threat of action against both her and me. And you match Farlow's offer, the size of the portfolio, and the level of compensation."

"Anything else?"

"Just one thing. You fire the Weasel."

"Who?"

"Him. Wesley Cummins. He's gone." Don walked to the door, held it open, and lifted Lena with his gaze. "Just so you are aware, Farlow has offered Lena his full legal team to draw upon, should you decide to move forward with any complaint. Oh, and Morley, that offer of legal assistance covers anything you might wish to throw my way as well."

13

Lena sat in her former cubicle. She had not formally resigned. But whatever happened, her days here were over.

A sulphuric residue from the battle upstairs silenced the entire bull pen. Heads popped up, examined her, and disappeared again. Robin listened to Lena's account in utter stillness. Lena finished and just sat there. It felt good not to have to do anything, go anywhere, jump at the opening of elevators in fear that the Weasel was coming to wreak more havoc on her life. She tasted the odors of stale bodies in the overchilled air. It had probably always been there. Only now it was something she no longer belonged to.

When she'd first started working here, Robin's hair had been long and dark as a river. Lena knew one of her grandparents was from Ecuador. It was one of those things that had drawn them together, the various strands joined in the blender of modern American culture. Now Robin's hair was trimmed to frame her face, tapered feather-light about her neck.

Lena asked, "When did you cut your hair?"

"While you were away." Robin's voice drifted fog-like. "The long was such a hassle."

"It suits you."

"Thanks." Her eyes scanned the blank computer screen. "So your take from this is . . . like . . ."

"After Don's cut, five mil and change."

"You're rich. You got your ticket punched. Way to go." Only there was no elation to the words.

"It's not for spending. Well, it is. But . . ." It was Lena's turn to pause. The basis for all the events leading to this moment, the crux, remained unspoken. Trapped down deep. Where it was bound to fester. Sooner rather than later, she was going to have to tell someone. She was tempted to make that the closest thing she had to a true friend on Wall Street. Other than Don, of course. And Lena needed him too much to risk everything on a confession.

But before she could decide what to do, her phone rang. She inspected the readout, saw a Manhattan code, but did not recognize the number. "Lena Fennan."

"This is Roger Foretrain. Is it true what your attorney said? Charles Farlow's been sniffing around?"

"Farlow is most definitely not sniffing," Lena replied. "He acquired my company. He offered me a job."

"What did you tell him?"

"That I owed it to my present employers to give them an opportunity to respond. Which I did." Lena took great heart from the calm she heard in her voice. "Your twenty-four hours started at the close of our meeting."

A note of humor crept into Foretrain's voice, strong enough to defy the cell phones. "Can you stretch that to Monday?"

There was no reason such a request should cause her heart to hammer so. "I suppose . . . Yes. I can do that."

"I'm on my way to Boston, something that can't wait. Sunday evening my wife and I are attending a gala reception at the MOMA. Will you join us?"

"Will I . . . Yes. Of course. I'd be honored."

"The limo will pick you up at seven. Call my secretary and give her your address." He cut the connection.

Lena sat cradling the phone in both hands, trying to get her head around what just happened. She realized that Robin was watching her intently, the woman's slate-grey gaze back in full focus. "That was . . . Never mind."

Robin said, "So your time here in the Weasel's bull pen is . . ."

"Definitely over. Either they give me what I want, or I'm leaving for Denver. I might go anyway. But I need to know . . ." Lena stopped and took a very deep breath. So big it managed to release a hint of what was to come next. "I need to know if they value me."

"Whatever you decide, do something for me."

"If I can."

"Take me with you." Robin tried not to beg. But the appeal was magnetic in its strength. "Every new arrival on the executive level needs a willing slave."

Lena released the day's first smile. "Girl, why do you think I've been sitting here?"

14

B rett felt markedly better on Friday, partly due to expert treatment at the hands of Doris, the nurse practitioner, and partly because of a night spent in an actual residence. Agnes had woken from her brief rest while Brett was still eating his eggs and toast. In response to her questions, Brett had described the habits that had dominated his life for over a year. Frederick listened at the door and caught everything Brett told Agnes. Brett talked about eleven months spent traveling from hospice to care home, never taking more than his travel expenses, never spending more than a week in any location. One of the websites described him as the vagabond of death.

Agnes's only response to his confession was to suggest he use the downstairs apartment. Like many New York formal residences, the below-stairs space had been converted into a self-contained flat that was entered from the street. Frederick led him out the front doors, unlocked the metal gate, and descended a set of concrete stairs to a door set beneath its own narrow awning. The apartment was spacious, well lit from windows at the front and back, and beautifully appointed. It belonged, Frederick explained, to an only daughter who was never there. His tone remained bland, but his gaze hardened as he described a woman who could only remember to speak with her ailing mother when the butler placed the call.

When he was summoned late the next morning, Agnes watched him ease into the chair and observed, "You seem much better."

"I am, thank you."

"Doris is a gem. How was the apartment?"

"Fabulous. I can't thank—"

"Stay as long as you like."

Brett stopped in the process of keying on his equipment. "Don't tempt me."

"I'm serious. It's the least I can do. Frederick approves of you. His gentle hand rules this house. He agrees you need a respite from the road." She smiled at his astonishment. "Where is your appointment next week?"

"New Haven."

"You should stay here and commute up."

"I don't know what to say."

"Think about it. The offer stands." She shifted slightly and changed the subject. "Have you ever tried to ascend since your episode?"

"Three times."

"What happened?"

"Nothing. Not a single, solitary thing."

"And so you began your quest. The errant knight who takes on the hopeless struggle of others, fighting the dragon that can never be bested, only named." She sighed. "I am sorry for your misfortune, and I am grateful indeed for your famished spirit."

He forced his hands to lift the headset. "Shall I put these on you?"

"What are they for?"

"I will introduce a vibratory pattern through sound waves. This induces a state of physical rest combined with heightened mental focus. No one has ever reported feeling anything more than a slight buzzing sensation."

"Young man, the last thing I'm worried about is discomfort. All right, put it on."

Brett settled them over her ears. Her skin was clammy and felt cold to the touch. Which was often the case with people who were holding back on drugs for the ascent. "When was the last time you used pain medication?"

"Last night."

Doris, the main nurse, was seated by the draped windows on the bed's opposite side. "Actually, Mrs. Lockwood, it was early yesterday afternoon."

Agnes waved that aside. "The information we found online said it was best not to be drugged."

"Medication can impact the experience in some cases," Brett said. "Not all. Are you in pain?"

"I told you. Pain is not the issue. Proceed." Agnes watched him boot up his laptop. "I for one am terrified of dying. Approaching the final door has not changed that one iota. As far as I am concerned, young man, you are a godsend."

He did not know what to say to that. He never did. This was part of the problem, or rather, part of his act of penance. Doing this for no gain. Making this as selfless an act as he possibly could. Brett had spent his entire adult life focusing on what took him up the ladder's next rung. And why not, since he had always assumed that he deserved success. He was handsome, he was brilliant, he was gifted, he was . . .

He stared at the laptop screen as his fingers coded through the start-up process by rote. Even after eleven months on the road, after he'd witnessed the death moment so many times the faces swam together in his memories, all it took was one brief backward glimpse, one recollection of his former life, to hear the vortex's crypt-like roar. The sound of where blind ambition had taken him.

"Young man, are you all right?"

Brett forced himself to focus on the screen, the moment, the subject watching him from her sickbed. "I'm beginning the count now."

The nurse's chair squeaked as she leaned forward. Doris and Frederick had both asked to observe. Brett had no problem with visitors. Especially in a situation like this, where they cared so deeply for the woman. The problem was, there was nothing to observe. On the physical level, the only activity was Brett speaking softly into his microphone, addressing the inert form on the bed.

"You are entering a state of deep relaxation. Your pulse is now at half the rate of full wakefulness. Your breathing has slowed. You remain in complete control . . ."

The process had been developed by Gabriella Speciale, a psychologist and university professor from Milan. After years of research, she had made three remarkable determinations. First, people in prayerful and meditative states shared a series of identical brain-wave patterns. Second, these patterns could be replicated in others through introducing a graduated series of sound waves matching the brain's design. Third, through this process she could invite some participants to separate their conscious awareness from their physical bodies.

"You may now open your other eyes. You remain in complete control. You are free to observe whatever it is you need to see. The time is yours to learn. Ask whatever question you desire. You are completely safe. You may return to full consciousness at any point."

Brett gave her the standard three minutes, then began counting her back. The heart rate and breathing monitors on his laptop showed her smooth return to a wakeful state. As often happened, when Agnes opened her eyes she had to blink away tears.

Brett gave her a few moments to focus upon the physical, then asked, "How was it?"

"Quite remarkable, really." She had a lovely smile, one that defied her ailments. "I have a message for you."

Brett felt the hairs rise on the back of his neck. This was new. "Yes?"

"It comes from you. At least, that is who it appeared to be. Is that possible?"

His thoughts came in treacly slow motion. As did his words. "It is very rare. But it happens." And up to this moment, such contacts had only been between the future and current selves. Never a third party.

"He said to tell you your macabre lockstep has now come to an end." Her smile grew coquettish. "The gentleman speaks quite beautifully. Unlike your current terse manner. He asked if you might reside downstairs for a time. Of course I told him I had already made the invitation. He advises you to say yes."

Brett's lungs seemed incapable of drawing in enough air. He sat with mouth agape, gasping softly. Knowing he was free from the endless death watch brought no joy. He had no idea what to do next. He felt terrified.

Agnes turned her attention to the pair seated across the room. "It seems I am to stay around for a bit longer. I hope that's all right. Young man, would you be so kind as to remove these headphones? I feel like I'm talking inside a fishbowl."

15

The same limo and driver picked Reese up for her second trip to Bridgeport. Wordlessly the driver handed her a phone, and she spent an interesting few minutes enduring Vera's icy fury. But somehow the attorney's threats could not reach her. Perhaps it was the result of having spent a night wrapped in the luxury of a five-star hotel. But Reese didn't think so. A typical prison nightmare had woken her while it was still dark. She had gone through her workout routine, then sipped room-service coffee and watched dawn turn the river molten. Her sense of being in contact with secret allies had scripted both questions and partial answers over the sky.

Reese endured Vera's tirade, then replied that they could still shoot her tomorrow if she failed, which she wouldn't. Vera had gone silent for a full thirty seconds, then cut the connection. Her lack of response granted Reese a satisfaction she carried all the way back to the corporate headquarters.

This time Reese was only kept waiting about ninety seconds. She was ushered into the same conference room as the previous evening, but the two linebackers were nowhere to be found. Bridgeport's senior lawyer was a full head over six feet and could not have weighed a hundred pounds fully dressed. Their chief operating officer was a precise, buttoned-down accountant in a Brooks Brothers suit. He was aged in his late fifties and wore round black-rimmed spectacles that granted him an air of perpetual astonishment. Both men smoldered at being forced to show up. But somebody even higher up the food chain had been sufficiently impacted by Reese's news to demand they attend this meeting. This time no one offered her so much as a cup of coffee. She did not complain. She had endured far worse.

The COO clipped off the words. "We're here. We're listening."

She laid two stacks of papers facedown on the table between them. "I have two further items regarding the future viability of your company. Not this division. We are now talking about the entire Bridgeport Corporation. Which is why I asked to meet with people at your level."

They had clearly been prepped. Reese assumed they had listened to a tape of her previous meeting and checked out as much of her information as they could on short notice. They eyed the two stacks with genuine alarm.

The attorney demanded, "Who are you?"

"I represent a company you need to hire," Reese replied.

"We have in-house security and intel."

"I've already been sung that tune. And you're aware of what they missed."

"Only if what you say is true," the attorney countered. But his words lacked heat.

Reese remained silent. They were there. They were listening. It was enough.

The COO sighed his acceptance. "Two files."

"Correct. One you can have for free. The other will cost you nine million dollars. In return, you receive two years of this level of security protection."

She had been instructed to return with three contracts worth a million dollars each. Anything less would be construed as failure.

Termination would follow. Reese was working on the assumption that a single contract worth three times that total would suit her puppet masters just as well.

The attorney asked, "Which is which?"

She showed them open palms. "You decide."

"This is ridiculous," the attorney groused.

The finance director, however, leaned back in his seat. Studying her carefully now. "She is offering us solid intel. The first was seismic."

"If it proves correct."

"Our preliminary probes indicate she is spot-on." The chief operating officer was grey-haired and grey-eyed and grey-voiced. And highly intelligent. And far more open to her approach than the lawyer, who continued to smolder.

Reese wondered if perhaps their in-house security answered to the attorney. Which occasionally happened in larger corporations. The legal department kept their intel ops at arm's length. If that was the case here, the attorney would fear that his superiors saw him as responsible for having missed what she had discovered.

The lawyer said, "This entire episode is one giant charade."

The finance director shrugged and said to Reese, "Go ahead. Give us your spiel."

"Inside the documents on my left, we have a Bridgeport board member with a serious gambling addiction."

The attorney sniffed, "We hardly care about such personal peccadilloes."

"You should. His debts now stand at over eighteen million dollars. He has become involved with some very serious people who have bought all his outstanding debts. They are now in the process of selling his influence to the highest bidder. And will do him bodily harm if he does not obey."

They were so aghast it took a full ninety seconds for the finance director to ask, "The other?"

Reese patted the right-hand pages. "Door number two. Your very own in-house spy."

The attorney actually groaned. "Who is he selling to?"

"She," Reese corrected. "She has received three quarter-million-dollar payments from your top competitor on what is currently your largest project under bid."

The finance director turned greyer still.

"Gentlemen, the clock is ticking." She nudged both piles a fraction further across the table. "Choose."

·ı|ı·

It was late afternoon when Reese finally exited the building. A different limo idled at the curb. At her appearance, a young woman rose from behind the wheel and opened the rear door. Reese rolled down her window and asked, "Where are we going?"

"I've been informed that you're still booked into the Omni, ma'am."

The wind blew in a faint taste of the distant ocean, warm and caressing as only a Florida spring could be. She breathed the fragrant air, feeling as though this freedom was finally hers to claim. At least momentarily.

The phone rang ten minutes into their return journey. The driver answered, then reached back and said, "For you, ma'am."

Reese accepted the phone and said, "Clawson here."

Vera sounded bitterly disappointed. "You didn't follow orders."

"I obtained what you were after and more. Your so-called orders were not an option, and you knew it going in."

"You are hereby appointed head of the group. This is largely a figurehead position. Your number two will in many respects also be your superior."

"Who will that be?"

"You have the weekend off. He will pick you up at eight the next morning."

Reese knew Vera was expecting an argument. Demands over salaries, information, locations, etc. She had, after all, just won the first round. "Fine."

"You are here to serve one specific role. Do you understand what that is?"

That too had become clear over the passage of this day. "I'm your cutout."

Vera's displeasure seemed to increase at Reese's ability to pierce the veil. "Whatever happens, you and your associate take the fall. Your two names will be on all documents."

"I understand." And she did. If things went south, Reese and her mystery ally would be on the firing line.

"You are not to seek to identify your ultimate superiors. To do so would be reason for extermination."

Reese smiled at the highway leading downtown. The limo moved with the heavy smoothness of a beast built to withstand all such incoming threats. "I read you."

"You better. I am your only contact. I will require regular updates."

The connection was severed. Reese continued to smile as she handed the phone back to the driver. Having an opponent so clearly in her sights was one of life's little perks. Her superiors, whoever they were, would also be aware that Vera's reports would be tainted by her animosity. But results spoke for themselves. And Reese had always been good at delivering. Today just proved she had not lost her edge.

16

S unday evening, Lena stood outside her awful walk-up studio apartment on Trinity. She wore a little black Versace dress she had bought back in university for some event she could no longer recall. Everything from that time was tinged by a translucent fog, like her memories belonged to someone else's life. The skirt was a little too narrow, which meant it rode up and wrinkled with each of her long strides, but she had never met a man who complained. Her parents would have given her money for clothes. If they had ever seen where she lived, they would have demanded that she accept their help. But Lena had not come to New York to live off her family's largesse any more than she wanted to commute. She paid more than half her former salary to live within six blocks of Wall Street.

The entire southern tip of Manhattan was undergoing a massive change. Since 9/11 many banks and capital groups had moved out, never to return. The huge buildings going up these days were almost all luxury condominiums. Places like Lena's were being bought up, rezoned, and razed.

The limo moved down Trinity like a black killer whale. She did not wait for the driver to come around. But when she opened the door, she hesitated at the sight of another woman seated beside Roger.

"Climb in, dear," the stranger said. "I hardly ever bite."

"Lena, meet my wife. Marjorie, this is Lena Fennan."

"My husband is extremely impressed with you, my dear. Roger hardly ever speaks about someone as he has you."

"I suppose I should be grateful," Lena replied. Marjorie Foretrain had slid over far enough for Lena to sit by the side window. Lena wanted to be able to study them. So she settled on the little jump seat facing back across the footwell. "But I can't help regretting that it only happened when I was almost out the door."

"Hold that thought," Roger said, and pressed a button on his armrest. The divider behind Lena's head slid up. "You offered me this extra time."

"So long as you meet my conditions."

"Okay. First of all, your buddy Wesley isn't leaving."

"He is not my anything. And the issue is not negotiable."

"What if I gave you a third option?"

"I don't see how that is possible."

"But you'll hear me out."

"Okay. Yes."

"Good." Roger drummed the window with his fingernails, gathering his thoughts. "The Wesleys of Wall Street play a role that some would call important. Quite frankly, most analysts don't have what it takes to scale the financial heights. Wesley Cummins is there to weed out the underperformers."

Lena stared at the sweep of lights out the back window and fumed. Marjorie said, "Tell her the real reason."

Roger sighed. "Wesley's uncle sits on the bank's board."

"I didn't know that."

"No way you could. It's his maternal uncle. Different last name. And we intentionally keep such items buried. But it's true."

Marjorie was a trim lady as precisely turned out as a Fabergé egg. Her only jewelry was a large diamond pendant hanging around her neck. Her voice carried a distinctly New York sense of humor, biting and highly intelligent. "Word has spread all over the executive floors of your morning's theater. Wesley's uncle is suitably outraged. Which is not altogether a bad thing. The unappealing traits you discovered in the nephew are also present in the uncle. If you could find a way to pry him off the board—"

"Let's not go there," Roger said.

She smiled at her husband. "I was only saying what you've been thinking."

"Oh, so now you're a mind reader?"

"It's part of the job description. Didn't they teach you that at Columbia?"

Lena found the affection between them both genuine and appealing. She said, "If that's true, the uncle will do everything in his power to have me axed."

"Not," Roger replied, "if he doesn't know you're still with the bank."

"Sorry. I don't follow."

"We've taken a controlling interest in a boutique capital investment group. We intend to keep them at arm's length. They're lean and they move fast. And they've got a solid track record." Roger glanced at his wife as though seeking her approval. He must have found what he was looking for, because he went on, "I'll set you up as a separate entity within their group. You will handle your own fund."

She knew she had to be sharp. Focused. Intent upon wrangling everything she could from this ride. But what she really wanted to do was step outside the door and run shrieking down Broadway. "Where are they based?"

"Madison Avenue and 55th."

"So, still Manhattan." She willed herself to focus. "How large a fund will I manage?"

"How large do you want?"

"I have no idea."

"So what do you want?"

She said the only thing that came to her addled mind. "What I've wanted from the outset. To work with you. To learn from you. To . . ."

"Grow," Marjorie offered. "Reach your highest potential. Learn from the best."

Roger smiled at his wife. "I'll hold you to that."

"In financial matters," she added, smiling back. "I'll take care of the rest."

"No, no, you're right," Lena said. "That's exactly my desire here. I don't know whether the deal I've just put together is a fluke."

Roger nodded agreement. "All we can say at this point is, you went up to bat once and hit a triple."

"The young lady made a thousand percent profit in nine days?" Marjorie nudged her husband.

"It was a small bet."

"Not to her." She nudged Roger a second time.

"Okay, okay." Roger Foretrain acted like he was being forced to give bone marrow. "You knocked it out of the park."

Marjorie leaned back, satisfied.

When they entered the MOMA, Marjorie Foretrain served as the genteel bond between her husband and Lena. Roger played huffy because Lena had not leapt at his job offer. In contrast, Marjorie seemed pleased by her response. When Roger said he hoped Lena didn't feel obliged to bring her attorney into the process, especially after the bank had agreed to drop all complaints regarding the previous transaction, Marjorie said, "That's enough, Roger."

"I want to hear the lady say yes."

"The night isn't about what you want, is it, my dear. Tonight is Ms. Fennan's. She is the star being fought over. This is Lena's hour, to do with as she will." She smiled at someone Lena did not bother seeing, while her husband handed over their invitations. "Will you have champagne, Lena?"

"I'm already flying, thanks."

"Well, of course you are. Roger hates these events, he really does. He hasn't been good with crowds since he was a child, have you, darling."

"She really doesn't need to hear my private history."

"Private, that is the word to describe my husband. You really rocked him, knowing about his boat in Tahiti. He thought he had managed to hide that away from the entire world."

Roger snagged a pair of glasses, passed one to his wife, and said, "I'm going upstairs."

"There's only one reason why he's here at all." They joined the crowd pouring into the escalators. "Otherwise he would have stayed in the limo and sulked over not getting his way. Wouldn't you, dear."

"I don't sulk."

Marjorie rolled her eyes.

Lena said, "You're here for the Gauguin exhibition."

Roger looked directly at her for the first time since she said she needed to think over his offer. "You've seen it?"

"It's not open to the public yet."

Marjorie said, "Roger has been here six times. Or is it seven."

They passed through the portal decorated with a Gauguin motif and entered a different realm, one of vivid colors and primitive forms. The exhibition was full of chattering people who talked far too loudly and paid scant attention to the priceless artwork on display. Lena wanted to tell them to shut up. She saw Roger wince at a woman's particularly high-pitched laugh and knew he felt the same.

Marjorie halted before the first central dais and exclaimed, "What on earth is this?"

Lena heard no guile behind the question. But when Lena replied, Roger moved in close enough to catch her response over the din. She said, "Gauguin's first sojourn in Tahiti started in 1891 and lasted a little over two years. During his stay, he carved a series of small totems that he called ultra-savages. They weren't modeled after reality. They were his attempt to describe a world that had never been touched by European civilization."

Lena had seen photographs of several, but no picture could capture its latent force. *Savage* certainly described the item. Two figures, a man and woman, were fiercely intertwined around a section of tree trunk. They were big-lipped and strong-limbed. Lena studied them intently but could not decide whether they grappled out of love or anger or battle. She would never have thought such passion could be captured by a carving. The longer she studied it, the more she felt intertwined by the same conflicting emotions.

When she looked up, she discovered that Roger was studying her intently. She seemed to possess a new clarity of vision, as though her inspection of the artwork now carried over to this man. She saw how his world was dominated by swift analysis and instant decisions. Roger Foretrain was carved by the world she wanted to enter, and the one thing global finance could not afford these days was time.

She said, "Let's talk."

Roger followed her out of the display. She stepped past a sign saying the museum café was closed, into a hall shared only with a woman speaking intently into her cell phone.

Lena gave Roger the truth. "The reason I didn't respond is because I don't know what I want."

He glanced around as his wife approached and settled in beside him. "So tell me what you are certain of."

"I know I don't want to be paid for being a top gun when I haven't yet proven myself. And one success doesn't make a career."

His eyes tightened in what did not quite become a smile. "Agreed."

"I know I need guidance. I need access to people who are more experienced than me. I want that more than a bigger paycheck."

Marjorie said, "The two don't have to be exclusive, do they, dear."

"You're damaging my negotiating position," Roger replied.

"But the young lady is not negotiating. She is seeking to forge a bond. Isn't that right, dear."

Lena went on, "I don't want to be isolated in this other group. I want my fund, but I also want them to consider me part of the team."

"Very wise," Marjorie offered. "A balanced approach, minus the ego one often finds on the Street, and which I utterly detest."

"I'd like to have weekly appointments with you. Go over strategy. Analyze together. Have you feed me possible ideas. Walk with me through the next venture. And the one after that."

"I can do that."

Lena took what felt like the first free breath in months. "Then we have a deal."

17

Lena started to follow Roger and Marjorie back into the exhibit when it happened. This was the shortest event of all, a single word that carried the force of a royal command.

Wait.

Roger noticed her hesitation. "Aren't you coming?"

"You go ahead," Lena said. "I need . . ."

"A moment to gather yourself." Marjorie reached for her husband's hand. "Come along, dear."

"But we need to discuss terms—"

"You've succeeded at rocking her world. That's enough for now." Marjorie waited as the woman who had been arguing into her phone steamed past. Then she said to Lena, "Join us when you're ready."

Lena stepped back into the corridor leading to the café. She stopped in front of the glass wall overlooking the garden atrium. Rain spackled the glass, adding an illusive blur to her reflection. Lena knew she was staring at herself. But what she felt was that a second person had joined her. The sensation was so powerful Lena felt an undercurrent of fear.

The voice of all her events said, *I really was beautiful.*

Lena asked, *Are we talking? Finally?*

For a brief moment only.

Why now?

An excellent question. If I answer, will you do something for me?

Correction, Lena said. *Do something more.*

Lena knew with utter certainty this was far beyond some internal dialogue. Each word she received held the same explosive impact as before, a verbal assault that blasted her ever so gently. Now the absence of any response to her comment was a vacuum.

All right, Lena conceded. *I'll do it.*

There are two reasons for this dialogue, the voice said. *First, there is a final task.*

Final?

For me, not you. Which brings us to the second reason. I am dying. All the rules that kept us from this sort of discourse are fading with my time in this physical realm.

Lena spoke the word aloud. "No." When no response came, she asked, *How old am I?*

That would be telling. As I said, there are rules, even at this juncture. Now pay attention.

The images flashed upon the rain-streaked glass, seven in all, so powerful Lena spasmed tightly with each arrival. Then they were done, and the silence returned, and Lena could think of nothing to say except, *I'll do it.*

Of course you will. But that was not my request. Go to the third Impressionist gallery. Hurry. I don't have much time.

18

Brett loved being inside the MOMA. It was his first visit to a gallery of any kind in over a year. He yearned to visit the new Gauguin exhibit, but the crowds and the false gaiety repelled him. He moved through the Impressionist halls, one high-ceilinged chamber after another, drinking in the glorious colors like a parched and famished traveler. Which, of course, he was. One of the glories of art was its ability to transport him. This evening it granted him the opportunity to revisit the day's events and see them anew.

That morning he had entered the grand Park Avenue residence precisely at nine and been ushered into the sickroom, where Agnes was awake and eager to ascend for the second time. As he booted up his laptop, she asked, "Does everyone want to dive back in?"

Brett settled the headphones into place. "Very few. A handful in all the time I've been doing this."

"Why do you suppose that is?"

Brett had wondered the same thing. "The most common response of first timers is that they feel as though they've just experienced a small death."

"Fascinating," she murmured. "Though I would never describe any part of this process as small."

"I think their reluctance to repeat the experience is because they've ascended and discovered what they needed in order to find peace. The last thing they want is to bring death any closer." He touched the keypad and said, "I'm starting the count now."

Eleven minutes later, Agnes reopened her eyes and announced, "I've had another chat with your counterpart."

Brett could feel the gazes of her nurse and butler, but that was not what caused his voice to shiver. "Is there something I should know?"

"Several things, actually." She took pleasure in drawing out the moment, as though her message released her from the bed's captivity. "When was the last time you bought new clothes?"

"I . . . Last year sometime."

"That will not do. Not with this crowd. Frederick."

The butler rose from his chair. "Ma'am."

"Make an appointment for our young gentleman friend to be properly dressed and coiffed. That place on Park where my late husband shopped should do."

"Most certainly, ma'am."

She said to Brett, "There's a reception tonight. I had utterly forgotten about it. But it is happening, is it not, Frederick."

"One moment, madam." He slipped from the room and swiftly returned holding an engraved invitation. "The Gauguin opening."

"Of course. I remain an honorary member of the MOMA's advisory committee. One of the galleries bears my name. It was my husband's idea, giving my father's collection a proper home. Rather than letting my daughter sell them off to whoever has the biggest purse. Do you even like art, young man?"

"It's been a passion since childhood." Brett could see that the effort of speaking had spread a sheen of moisture over her brow. He knew the pain must be registering. Even so, he could not repress the clench of eagerness. "Did this counterpart tell you why I needed to go?"

"Most certainly." Agnes lifted a finger, all the signal her nurse required to jump into action. Agnes watched the broad woman prepare the syringe and continued, "He said you are to treat this as a life's turning."

·|||·

Back when Brett was on the UC Santa Barbara faculty, he had driven down to LA every few weeks, taken in a show or gallery opening, and gorged himself at one of the many art museums. He had never been bitten by the collector bug, which was good, because an assistant professor's salary did not grant him the ability to buy what he liked. He had not cared much for poster art or reproductions. Nor had he ever yearned for wealth, except at times like this. When he stood before a masterpiece and wondered what it would be like to have this on his wall, see it every day, and call such perfection his very own.

Being here in the MOMA, standing before paintings he knew so well he could claim them as friends, was a mixed bag. Part of him wished he had not come. Memories of other such visits carried the weight of everything he had lost. All the false assumptions, the blind ambition, the wrong moves, the terrible mistakes . . .

The vortex.

"Brett?"

He turned slowly, his heart already zinging. Before he had consciously fit a name to the voice, his entire being was flung about the room like a swallow dancing on unseen winds. "Hello, Josie."

"It is you." She was a vivacious bundle of intelligence and energy that defied her sixty-plus years. She peered at him with that myopic squint generations of students had mocked. "What are you doing here?"

"I should ask you the same thing."

"Here in the city because I run the neuroscience department at Columbia. Here at the exhibit because my husband teaches modern art at NYU and serves as a part-time curator." She clutched her purse with both hands. "Now you."

Brett wished he didn't have to answer. Especially to her. Dr. Josephine Banks had been his doctoral supervisor and Brett's biggest supporter. "I joined the research project."

"I know all that." Her grip tightened. It was not anger. Not really. Josie Banks simply carried passion into every aspect of her professional life. "You left me after I forbade you to take up that post."

"It wasn't really a post—"

"The project was run by that Italian, what was his name?"

"Her. Gabriella Speciale."

"Sure. And so it failed like I warned?"

"No. It has proven to be an enormous success."

She stepped closer. "So why the long face?"

He struggled momentarily and came up with, "They're not ready to publish. Not even close. We're talking years."

"You left them?"

"No. But I don't . . ."

She finished for him, "Have anything to show for your time."

Brett waited, his heart thudding, heavy with dread. Not over the question he expected her to ask next. Over his reply. No matter what the disembodied Brett might have said to Agnes about moving on, if his favorite teacher asked, Brett would tell her. Everything. He felt a genuine sense of brutal rightness standing here, preparing himself to reveal his dark side.

But Josie Banks surprised him by shrugging in disinterest. "New fields can take years to become established. Decades. But the Italian's concepts have proven to be authentic?"

"At every stage."

"Will you tell me about it?"

"Whatever you want to know."

"Later. Tomorrow, yes? Right now, tell me why you're in New York."

So he told her about Agnes, the year of monitoring the critically ill. At least he started to. She cut him off with, "This is utterly groundbreaking."

He nodded. "And it's just one facet of their project."

"All right. Yes. But the concept." Her eyes shifted rapidly back and forth, as though reading a journal article. Or preparing one. "There are two key elements, correct? The first is the temporal and spatial issue."

"Redefining boundaries," Brett confirmed. He had always liked this about her. How Josie Banks could take the vague whispers of a postgrad's idea and crystallize it into something real. "Physical confines can no longer be seen as boundaries for mental awareness."

"Physical confines." She released the purse so as to grip herself around her middle. "And then there is the other issue."

"Death," Brett said. "Its definition. The moment of the event. And the moment after."

She rocked back and forth, still scanning the unseen text. "I was wrong to urge you away from this."

"No." Brett sighed. "You weren't."

"You wasted nothing. It has cost you, I see that. But you have also—" She stopped, apparently caught by a sudden idea. "I need your help."

"Anything."

"One of my department heads has had a stroke. Her postgrad stand-in is insufferable. The students loathe him. There could well be a riot. Will you take over the class?"

Brett endured yet another swoop-and-dive. "I'd like nothing more."

"It's not a real post, of course. Just covering for the six weeks remaining of this semester. I believe the current week's lesson is on neurobiology's connection to quantum mechanics."

"I could teach that," Brett replied. "In my sleep."

"Of course you can." Josie slipped a card from her billfold and pressed it into his hand. Her smile carried a fullness that reached back through the years and the awful mistakes, and blessed him with that rarest of gifts, a second chance. "Your class starts tomorrow at two. I expect you in my office at one thirty. Be on time."

19

Lena watched from a distance as her legs carried her down the corridor and across the central foyer. She thought she heard someone call her name, but refused to be drawn from the intensity that left her hovering a fractional distance beyond herself. Out where a discussion across time was more real than the crowd and the gallery. And far more important.

Lena asked, *You are dying now?*

I share with you my last few breaths. Stop here. See the gentleman studying the Renoir? That is him.

Who?

Brett Riffkind. The love of my life. The breaker of hearts. The wounder of souls. Please. Let me touch his face one last time.

Brett stood before a Renoir lithograph entitled *Pinning the Hat*. It had been one of his mother's favorites. A framed copy had hung on her office wall throughout Brett's childhood. Standing here, he could smell the papers and ink and old perfume. His mother had been a noted mathematician and not especially good with her lone child. But they had shared art and museums. This particular piece had always intrigued Brett. Renoir was by most accounts a dour and somber man, yet he had managed to convey with piercing clarity the lighthearted gaiety of two young girls. This had been his first attempt to use lithography as a vehicle for genuine artistic expression. Brett could almost hear the girls' laughter, as though they mocked his inability to fathom the forces that rocked his world. To have his favorite professor arrive here and offer him a job, however temporary, was a vivid sign that his journeying had come to an end. The future opened in resplendent mystery. Brett was suitably terrified. And the two girls knew it.

For the second time that night, he heard a woman speak his name. "Brett?"

He turned and was immediately certain he had never seen her before. She was far too striking and intense to forget. She was perhaps even beautiful, but it was hard to tell, her face was so wracked by tragedy.

Brett assumed she was somehow linked to one of his former patients. Her bereavement was a bleak mantle that captured her face, her body, her walk. He asked, "Can I help you?"

The woman was almost as tall as he, rangy in the manner of a natural athlete. She shook her head, or at least he thought she did. Perhaps it was merely a larger tremor, one of many wracking her frame. She took another step, closing the distance to where he could see the unshed tears.

Brett knew he should say something. Everyone in the gallery was turned their way. Others had stepped into the three entries leading to adjoining chambers. All staring at this woman who breached the brittle gaiety with her tragic silence, who approached him with one outstretched hand. But Brett waited in stillness because he had no choice. He felt locked inside the moment, clenched by a straitjacket of confusion.

She settled her hand upon his cheek. Her touch was astonishingly gentle. He could feel the trembling, feel the way her fingers settled over the curves and indentations, holding him from chin to temple, almost . . .

As though she had done it a thousand times before.

Then her eyes spilled their burden of tears. The hand dropped to her side as though unseen puppet strings had been severed. Brett regretted its absence.

The woman whispered, "She's gone."

BOOK 2

20

All during Brett's conversation with the remarkable woman named Lena Fennan, the reception swirled about them like a half-forgotten tune. After she departed, Brett took a taxi back to the basement apartment off Park Lane. The instant he entered, he called Gabriella in Switzerland. There was no urgency to his news. But he had to speak with someone. Immediately.

When Brett finished relating the night's events, Gabriella gave it a long beat. Digesting what she had just heard. The line connecting Brett with Switzerland crackled once, echoing the energy coursing through him. Not exactly tension. Rather, a compound of astonishments that carried with them the force to propel him out of one existence and into another.

When Gabriella spoke, it was to address the third person on the phone with them. "What do you think, Charlie?"

"You go first," he replied.

Gabriella Speciale was a psychologist and a rare beauty. Her allure and Brett's own frustration had been the poisonous mix that had pushed him into the dark side. Brett had traded the team's secrets for his own lab, or he would have, except for how he had become trapped by the forces everyone now referred to as the vortex. The word was too small to contain all the terror and misery he had experienced, and which had almost consumed him. Would have, except for how Charlie had rescued him. Charlie Hazard, the supposed enemy who had won Gabriella's heart. His rescuer. His best friend.

Eleven weeks after Charlie had rescued him from the fate he deserved, Brett had felt well enough to depart. He had designed his act of penance during the long lonely hours, assaulted by what plagued him still. For much of that time, all Brett had to do was shut his eyes and the vortex's rushing fury was there. Waiting.

Gabriella had been utterly opposed to Brett's self-imposed exile. Her team was becoming increasingly fractured. She wanted Brett to remain. She wanted to help him heal. She wanted . . .

Charlie had silenced Gabriella's arguments with a few precise words. Brett was doing what he felt was best. He needed their support. Gabriella needed to let Brett go, so he could return.

"There are a number of issues here," Gabriella said. "But two are of immediate concern. Do you agree, Brett?"

He glanced at the digital clock set into the oven's stainless steel face. It read five minutes past midnight. Just after six in the morning Swiss time. "Yes."

"First is the manner of this connection. You met with a dying patient who ascended and was greeted by your temporal self."

Brett had not heard that term before. Temporal self. It indicated a significant shift. Previously Gabriella had been reluctant to even address the issue. Now she had named it. Clearly a lot had changed in the eleven months since their last conversation. Brett wanted to ask who else had crossed the river of time, but knew such questions would have to wait.

Gabriella went on, "Your temporal self says to this dying woman — what is her name?"

"Agnes Lockwood."

"She returns from her ascent and passes on the instruction that you are to halt your current duties and go to an exhibition. You do so, and meet a woman who has recently begun receiving guidance from her own temporal self. And this woman . . ."

"Lena Fennan," Brett supplied.

"Has never ascended."

"Never heard of it, or had any contact with us."

Charlie added, "Then there's how the temporal self dies in the middle of this connection."

"While saying farewell to Brett, her former love." Gabriella paused. "All these make for an astonishing set of coincidences."

"They're not coincidences," Charlie said.

"No. You are correct. That was not the proper term. I just . . ."

Charlie went on, "Then there's door number two."

"Ms. Fennan is instructed to attend a lecture you are to give tomorrow," Gabriella said. "Which you only learned about through a connection made at this same exhibition."

Charlie asked, "Was there any chance the lady could have overheard your conversation with the professor?"

Brett recalled the way Lena had approached him, the spectral walk across the gallery, the trembling outstretched hand, the unspilled tears. He shivered. "No."

Gabriella asked, "What is your lecture on?"

"Some aspect of neuroscience. I'll learn the exact topic tomorrow."

"You don't know what you're teaching." Gabriella pondered this. "Ask Ms. Fennan if she was made aware of your topic. Before you actually reveal anything. We are seeking confirmation of future knowledge—"

"He gets it," Charlie said.

"Yes. All right. Forgive me. I'm just . . ." She sighed. "It is so good to have you back, Brett. You are back, aren't you?"

Brett was grappling with that very same question, so Charlie answered for him. "He's back. Now tell him the rest."

"You remember Massimo?"

"Yes." The Italian student and three others had attached themselves to Gabriella in the team's earliest days. They showed a complete inability to follow the simplest instructions, which meant their ascents were of no experimental value whatsoever. Every now and then, however, they spoke of some occurrence that shifted the entire team's perspective. Otherwise they seemed scarcely connected to earth.

"Massimo's temporal self has said he and his friends need to take your place."

Brett shivered anew. "When was this?"

"Yesterday," Charlie replied. "They've been drifting around for the past twenty-four hours, bags packed, waiting for you to tell them where to come. Which is the main reason why Gabriella and I aren't too surprised about this call."

Gabriella sounded as though she had been infected by Brett's tremors. "Finish your work there and come home, Brett. We miss you."

Brett cut the connection and told himself there was no reason why that simple word should cause his eyes to burn. *Home.*

Lena returned from the MOMA to her ratty apartment and packed. There was very little beyond her work and her clothes, and she was done in less than an hour. She then located a suites hotel four blocks from her new office and booked a room for a week, starting the next day. The boutique investment firm of Baker Meredith was located in a high-rise at the corner of Madison and 55th Street, two blocks from the Trump Tower and four from the southeast corner of Central Park.

Lena made tea and drank it, staring out the window at the rain-swept street. The entire block was due for demolition. Somewhere to her right, Wall Street slumbered. She should probably have felt something over transitioning to her new existence. But just then there was no room.

After leaving Brett she had gone to the women's restroom and washed her face. She avoided looking at her reflection. She knew she was a wreck. When she found Roger and Marjorie, their expressions said they had seen at least a bit of her contact with Brett. There was nothing to be done about that. Lena had sought them out because the clock was ticking much faster than she would have liked. She said she needed to start in her new position the next morning, because there was a new project she wanted to investigate.

Roger had responded by quietly insisting she take the limo. Marjorie had hugged her, slipped a card into Lena's pocket, and said, "You definitely have what it takes." Which was almost enough to undo her yet again.

Lena turned from her studio apartment's lone window and stared at the three suitcases and the cardboard boxes waiting by the door. She needed to research the new project, but right then she needed a few hours' sleep. She climbed into her narrow bed. She kept on the lights, but the illumination was not strong enough to halt the memories and the questions that assaulted her.

She cried herself to sleep. Mourning the end to a love that had not yet begun, and the loss of a woman she had only tonight come to consider a friend.

21

Reese spent the weekend becoming introduced to idle hours. She read all the papers and news magazines the hotel's gift shop had to offer. She bought a swimsuit and sweats and shorts and sandals from the same shop. She could not go anywhere else because she had no money. She lunched poolside, she swam, she dozed. At sunset she left the hotel and crossed the bridge and walked the riverfront. There were moments of mild panic when she was seized by all the fears she had stifled while inside. She stood and gripped whatever railing was closest until the tremors passed.

She slept well, until a nightmare of being attacked by her cellmate jolted her an hour before dawn. Reese left the room and went downstairs, where a friendly night clerk offered her a pair of sneakers from the lost and found. She ran and she lifted and she fought down the terrors the only way she knew how.

The phone call came at ten minutes past seven Monday morning. The voice she'd been hoping to hear asked, "Are you awake?"

"Dressed, fed, ready to roll."

"I'm downstairs."

"I'll join you in five."

But when the elevator doors opened, Reese almost walked past the man she had once considered a close friend. Kevin Hanley had directed the second arm of an intelligence-gathering project where Reese had attained her career zenith, and where they both had experienced their ultimate downfall. Reese had spent many hours in lockup wondering if Kevin had survived the debacle. And now she knew the answer was both yes and no.

Kevin's transformation was as drastic as her own. But because she confronted them all at once, the result was shocking. Kevin had always worn a rather flaccid mask. This granted him the ability to hide in plain sight. Now he was simply grey. Hair, skin, eyes, expression. He had lost so much weight his skin sagged and bunched.

Kevin's response mirrored her own. His eyes widened and he mouthed a silent, "Wow."

She nodded. Perhaps someday other people's reactions would not bother her.

Kevin recovered and gestured toward the door. "Car's outside."

She followed him to the Tahoe parked by the valet's desk. Kevin exchanged a bill for the keys and slid in behind the wheel. "I'll drive. You need to read."

Reese set her valise and briefcase in the rear hold, hefted the folder waiting for her on the passenger seat, and slipped into the AC's cool wash. "Where are we going?"

"Motel by the Orlando airport. Three hours plus traffic."

She waited until they were on the interstate to ask, "What happened to you?"

"About what you'd expect. Highly public dismissal from my government job. Loss of all perks. Then my home. Bankruptcy." At least his voice was the same. Not even this litany disturbed his calm. "I drifted for a while. Took a couple of dead-end jobs. Scrounged off friends until they stopped answering my calls. Then these people got in touch."

"Do you know who they are?"

"My only contact is Vera. Same as you."

"Have you found out anything about her?"

He showed her a very flat gaze. "No."

Reese nodded her understanding. "Does our Vera have a last name?"

"Smith."

She hesitated, but knew she had to press. "Still, there has to be someone who wants us here. Someone with enough clout to let you prepare this elaborate welcome back."

"You got that, did you."

"Not only got it, but loved it. I owe you."

"You do, actually. Since I'm the one who pressed for you to get this job." He drove a few miles. "I didn't even know you were alive until I said you'd be ideal and Vera tried to have me fired for suggesting it. There were no records, no nothing. It was like the system just swallowed you."

She nodded. It was as good a description as any. "Like I said, I owe you."

Kevin gestured at the file. "You had best get started. There's a lot of ground to cover. Soon as we arrive, you're on."

Ninety minutes into the journey, Reese completed her first read-through of the file's contents. Kevin watched her shut the folder and spread her hands over the cover, then asked, "Any questions?"

"A few." There were not many surprises, though. Reese had assumed it would have to be something like this.

"Anything you want to ask now?"

She stared out the window at the passing foliage. Florida in late spring was astonishingly green. Around where they were now, just north of Daytona, they passed an invisible border and entered the temperate zone. Scrub pines gave way to palms and wild bougainvillea. The changes were subtle and missed by most visitors.

Reese asked, "Tell me what you think is happening."

Kevin nodded as though he had been waiting for this. "Soon after I reached the point of contemplating various ends to the misery, Vera called and offered me this assignment. The people hiding behind her waited long enough to be certain I would never feel any need to ask questions."

Reese ran a finger along the edge of the file. "That pretty much mirrors my assessment."

But Kevin wasn't done. "They wanted to make sure I would do anything they asked, no matter how appalling it might once have seemed. Without blinking."

She nodded a second time. There was no need to say anything other than, "Can you get me a gun?"

"I can get you any weapon you can think of, and some you can't imagine."

"A gun will do. And a silencer. And somebody to train me."

"Done."

He didn't ask. But she wanted him to understand. "I want to be ready in case somebody ever tries to put me back inside. And something else. The first chance I get, Charlie Hazard and his entire group are going down."

Kevin shot her a glance, deep and poignant. "Understood."

Reese settled back. There was a deep satisfaction in having them be in sync. She offered, "I was born south of here."

"I remember reading about that, you know, back in the day. Some Indian-sounding name, right?"

"Holopaw. On the road from Kissimmee to the coast."

"What was it like?"

"My granny used to say Holopaw was only good for raising stunted cattle and scrawny people."

"Sounds like an excellent place to leave behind."

"My daddy was not much of a father. Momma was sick most of the time. My granny was half Choctaw. She used to call me a changeling. Nobody knew where I came from. The rest of the family was dark enough to pass as Hispanics. Then up I pop, white-blonde hair and pale as a ghost."

The confession was unexpected and rare enough for Kevin to relax fully. Which was why she had spoken about her past at all. Reese seldom thought of her beginnings, much less discussed them. But Kevin was special. He had reached into the deep and offered her a lifeline. They were a team now. For better or worse. Joined by the last chance either of them were likely to have.

Kevin said, "And a beauty early on, I bet."

"So I was told. Especially by the men who started chasing me. But the difference between me and my family went a lot deeper than skin and hair. Nobody else in my clan wanted to be anywhere but right there in Holopaw. They raised goats for their milk and made cheese. A big outing was a day at the beach or hunting wildcats in the swamps farther east. Big ambitions meant saving to buy a new airboat."

He smiled for the first time since they'd met, and Reese knew she had done the right thing, raking over the coals of early memories. He said, "You just blew them away."

"I was the first of my family to finish high school, much less go to college. My granny said I was born to be mad, which was where I got my drive."

"Did you ever go back?"

"Once. My senior year. For my granny's funeral. What a mistake."

"Where did you attend university?"

"Princeton. Full ride."

"They recruit you there?"

Reese felt her body go still, congealed by the rush of memories. Everything she once had taken for granted. And lost. She forced out a strangled, "That's right."

Kevin lost his smile. "Sorry."

"No. It's okay. I just . . ."

"Don't want to go there." He nodded. "I read you five by five."

22

Monday morning, Lena stood on the curb fifty feet south of the bank's employee entrance. When Robin appeared, she called, "Over here."

Robin approached the car with wide-eyed wonder. "Your new job comes with a limo?"

"Apparently so. This morning I was working at my ratty desk in my ratty apartment." Lena waited while the driver popped the trunk, then helped Robin settle in her briefcase and box of personal belongings. "Roger's secretary called with the account and telephone numbers and said I'm supposed to use this company for my rides."

"Roger's secretary," Robin said. "Imagine that."

"The woman could not have sounded more bored," Lena said. "Is that everything?"

"You bet."

"Good. Because we're all done there."

Robin stared up at the Weasel's window. "Like that's a hardship."

"Did he say anything?"

"Not a peep. Just stood in his office doorway and glared."

They slipped into the limo's backseat. While the driver closed their door and seated himself behind the wheel, Robin took a photograph from her purse and propped it on the door. A girl of four or five beamed from the picture.

Lena asked, "Who's that?"

"My niece and godchild."

"Why haven't I seen her before?"

"I kept this photo in my drawer. Missie thinks I'm the greatest. She wants to follow in my footsteps. I couldn't bear to have her see how low I'd sunk." Robin touched the smiling face. "I wanted her to be with me this morning."

Lena smiled too. "I like that. A lot."

The driver asked, "Where to, Ms. Fennan?"

"Madison and 55th, please. But could you stop at the next Starbucks?"

"Sure thing, Ms. Fennan."

Robin watched the limo pull smoothly into traffic. "Everything's changed, hasn't it. For real."

The boutique investment firm of Baker Meredith was located in a black glass cube. It was one of many groups that had shifted away from Wall Street after 9/11 and never returned. The lobby security was professional and suitably sleek. The guard walked them to the elevator and said, "You'll need to have the receptionist call down with your details before we can fix you ladies up with permanent passes."

"Thank you."

As the elevator doors closed, Robin asked, "Where is your gear?"

"Everything I couldn't fit in my briefcase is packed in boxes. I moved this morning."

"Where, Central Park West?"

"Hardly. A suites motel four blocks from here."

When they exited the elevator, a young man in a rumpled suit and an expression to match stood waiting by the reception desk. He moved as soon as Lena entered the foyer. "Ms. Fennan?"

"That's me."

"Chester Briggs. I've been assigned to your team."

Lena instantly knew everything about the guy. Chester had been given duty as the firm's in-house spy. He expected to fail. As a result, he knew he'd probably be fired. Fear of dismissal was his constant reality. Just like it had been for them.

Lena did not bother with small talk as they signed in and collected their day passes. She introduced Robin and said simply, "She'll be working with us."

Chester grimly accepted the news and refused to meet Robin's gaze. He clearly assumed Robin's presence hastened his own demise. He led them back to a corner office and stood in the doorway, waiting to be dismissed. "The partners didn't say anything about you bringing your own personnel. I'll need to get another cubicle assigned."

"Wait on that, please." Lena took a slow look around. The executive desk was far from new, probably a castoff from some partner who had recently upgraded their office. Ditto on the chair and credenza. A beige leather sofa and three chairs were clustered in the far corner, surrounding a coffee table that appeared to be coquina with bronze legs.

Lena set her briefcase on the desk and stepped to the west-facing windows. Baker Meredith was on the forty-fourth floor. Looking right, she could see a green fringe of Central Park. Directly in front of her stretched the Theater District, then Hell's Kitchen, then the glistening waters of the Hudson River, and beyond that the Jersey sprawl.

Robin stepped up beside her and said, "The Weasel would positively croak with envy."

Lena nodded. The office was bigger than her former apartment. She turned back to where Chester stood in the doorway and asked, "Where is your cubicle?"

He pointed off behind him. "The bull pen's far side, over by the receptionist."

"Okay, your first job is to move close by. Try to get Robin into the cubicle next to yours. Do I have a conference room?"

He was trying to get his head around what she was saying and what she meant. "I don't . . ."

"That's job two. A spare office will do, but have them move out all the furniture, then find us a table and some swivel chairs. Stock the room with whiteboards. But if there's any delay, leave it. You two can work in here." Lena turned back to the desk and opened her briefcase. "Tomorrow morning we're meeting with Roger Foretrain. Dress accordingly."

Robin gaped. "For real?"

"Yes. Chester, do you know who Roger is?"

"The risk guy. Sure." He took a tentative step forward. "You're . . ."

"Pitching a new idea. We are. Together. That's how I work. The whole team stands on the podium with me. You don't get me coffee. You don't fetch my laundry. You don't pull long hours because that's what analysts are expected to do. If your work is done, go home. I'm interested in just one thing. Making the next deal." Lena realized Robin was laughing. "I said something funny?"

"Hilarious." She wiped her eyes.

"Chester, one more thing. You don't take assignments from anyone else."

He gestured back across the bull pen. "I'm working on a big deal—"

"Not anymore. Talk to the partners. Tell them if there's an issue, they should take it up with Roger. Now come over here." Lena set the pages she had printed that morning on her desk. All the info she had gleaned online. Everything she could find related to the most recent event. The thought that it was her last contact with the woman tightened her throat. "This is all I have. Your job is to flesh it out."

Robin leaned in close, already focused on the project. Chester, however, held back. "Uh, the partners were wondering if they could have a word."

"Not now, I've got an appointment." Lena checked her watch. "Walk with me, please. You too, Robin."

She did not speak as she crossed the bull pen. Baker Meredith occupied most of the floor, with partners and conference rooms ringing a massive central space. Lena knew the group had three senior partners and employed a hundred and nine people because she had checked. She felt eyes track her past the receptionist and into the foyer.

She said, "Let me guess. Foretrain told the partners to leave me totally alone. And they don't like it."

Chester was still working on a response when the doors pinged.

Lena stepped inside, motioned for them to join her, and went on, "They want to know how a total stranger has been handed her own portfolio. They want to shut me down. They're worried I'm Roger's in-house spy."

Chester licked his lips. "Something like that."

The doors opened onto the ground-floor reception area. Lena led them past security, out to where her limo waited. She said to Robin, "Take Chester for coffee. Tell him everything."

"Are you sure?"

"Yes." She turned to Chester. "I want you to talk with the partners, see if they'll attend tomorrow's meeting. Tell them we want them to come so they're aware from the outset of what we're doing. Roger is on our side, so we'll be better off having that first confrontation with him present."

Robin asked, "Where are you going?"

Lena drew out the card Brett had given her with the professor's name and the address at Columbia University. She handed the card to the limo driver and replied, "To class."

The world looked different from the back of a limo. When Lena had ridden in them before, it was because of someone else's clout. She had always been too nervous to do what she did now. Observe. Reflect.

Lena thought back over the events of the past eighteen hours. The limo seemed to insulate her from the emotional blasts as well as the city's din. Even so, Lena grieved in some mild sense for an old woman she wished she could have known better. Not someday in the future. Now. Despite all the upheaval in their final contact, Lena found herself comforted by how her future self had faced death not only with calm, but with the desire to relish a final taste of love.

Love.

The driver passed Columbia University's main admin building and turned off Broadway, then right, swimming against the tide of students. Columbia was a big-city university. The inner campus was veined with narrow lanes intended more for bikes and pedestrians. Surrounding this were newer structures that morphed into the Upper West Side. University security was very alert. Lena spotted three different cops giving her ride a careful inspection in the time it took them to go five blocks.

The driver halted in front of a new-old structure, redesigned and refashioned until it could no longer claim either a style or an epoch. When the driver started to rise from the car, Lena said, "Give me a minute."

He took in the flow of students and cycles, the narrow lane, the watchful cop. "I'm not supposed to stop here."

"Can you circle the block?"

"Sure thing."

As the driver pulled from the curb, Lena knew a fleeting desire to have him keep going. Back to her new suite of offices on Madison and 55th. She had all the mysteries one girl could handle. And the excitement. Because the preliminary research she'd done that morning indicated she had another project with a huge potential downside. One so large it could swallow her whole.

She had no desire to attend a class taught by Dr. Brett Riffkind, the man who had broken her future self's heart. Nor did she ever need to learn the details—did Brett Riffkind dump her, leave her for another, just die, whatever. The potential for wrong endings made the rear seat feel crowded.

It all came down to this. Sitting inside a limo. Doing what had been passed to her by a visitation from her future self. With her own dying breath. Lena dropped her gaze to the hand that had touched Brett's face. She could still feel his skin, see the confusion and pain in that shattered sapphire gaze.

Lena was a professional risk analyst. She was good at her job. She knew this next step was fraught with peril.

The internal argument was silenced by the limo halting a second time in front of the mismatched building. Lena sighed defeat. The simple fact was, she had told the woman she would do this. Attending Brett's class had formed one image from the final event. Another had been using him on this new project.

And Lena would honor her final pledge.

As the driver held open her door, Lena vowed that was as far as it was going.

She had said nothing to her future self about falling in love.

23

Kevin took the Beachline Highway west until he reached the Orlando airport exit. He then turned away from the terminals, hooking right onto a road that rimmed a man-made lake. Their destination was a Homewood Suites sheltered by palms and live oaks. A Marriott Courtyard rose to one side, a Ramada on the other. The winter season was over, the summer crush had not yet begun. The parking lots to either side of their hotel were empty. But the one Kevin entered was filled to overflowing.

Kevin parked under the foyer's overhang. A dozen or so visitors smoked and frowned as he and Reese rose from the car. There was nothing said. A single glance was enough for Reese to know these were not people who gave much attention to casual conversation. But their gazes were sharp to the point of famished, and they watched Reese's approach with a frantic edge.

She and Kevin passed through the jammed foyer and stopped by the hotel's shop for sandwiches and coffees, which they consumed standing at the counter that ran along the rear windows. People flowed about them, nervously waiting for the heads-up. Reese was grateful for the moment to adjust. She had never expected anything quite so intense.

She said, "You've taken this to a whole new level."

"We started small," Kevin said. "Internet advertisements handled by your favorite techie."

"You found Karla," Reese exclaimed.

"Actually, it was Vera and her mystery people. They are very good at locating the hidden."

Karla Brusius had been a principal ally in Reese's earlier project. Karla's presence meant Reese could rely completely on her technician. "This is great news."

He smiled and went on, "So the first two presentations we made, we had maybe a dozen people show up."

"When was this?"

"The first was four and a half months ago, the second six weeks later. We were just feeling our way. A little advertising in tech journals and regional university campuses. The people we were targeting, they are the ultimate cynics when it comes to standard PR. Plus we needed to see if the technology you read about in those files actually delivered."

"How many people made the cut?"

"Four the first time, three the second. Then Karla noticed that a couple of our new guys had started their own websites. Chronicling their experiences. They tried to keep it under the radar, you know, techie to techie. Then things online sort of exploded." He pulled several folded sheets of paper from his pocket. Flattened them on the counter between their meals. "This is from the most heavily trafficked site they put together."

The website's banner headline read "I Hate My Life." Reese didn't need to read further but did anyway. The home page accessed half a dozen different chat rooms, all holding to the same theme. Every person who came here had a valid reason to want out.

Out of their lives. Out of this existence. Out.

Reese said, "So you've identified a valid trend."

"I think so. Anyway, for our third session, we had twenty-eight at-tendees. The fourth, thirty-seven. This is our fifth time at bat." Kevin glanced behind him. "Karla said it had gone viral."

Reese bundled her sandwich wrapper and stuffed it into her empty cup. "So let's go see what the next level looks like."

Their meeting was set to begin at noon. Precisely three minutes before the hour, they entered the motel's largest conference hall and made their way to the front.

The windowless room was well lit and the chairs comfortable enough. Kevin and Reese seated themselves at the front of the room. Reese took her time and studied the crowd. They were a motley crew. A consider-able amount of piercings, body ink, and striking hair colors. Many in the audience wore T-shirts that read *www.Ihatemylife.com*.

"The shirts are a cute touch," Reese said. "Your idea?"

"I've never seen them before."

"Five assemblies. Exponential growth. And now your very own cheering squad." The crowd filled the room. Some looked like they had been there for hours. Several people in the front row ate impromptu meals. Reese asked the first of two questions she had been avoiding all morning. "How many trial subjects have you lost?"

"Seven in the first month. One in the second. Since then, none."

The trend was as interesting as the number. "How many function-ing operatives?"

"We call them voyagers. Karla came up with the title. There are eighteen remaining."

Reese patted the folder's cover. "So this new technology . . ."

"It plays a role in keeping our voyagers safe, sure. A big one."

"You think there's something else at work?"

Kevin hesitated, then said, "Let's leave that for later."

"All right."

"The answer is extremely . . ."

"Complicated."

He frowned at her choice of words, but said, "Why don't we focus on the new prospects."

So she asked, "Why the rush to build a larger team?"

"Vera's group is pressing hard for results." Kevin gestured to the podium. "Time to get started."

"You want me to handle this?"

"I prefer to vanish in plain sight. You've read the file. Given your past, I'd say you know more than anybody alive. Which is why you're here and not still rotting in some cell. Think of this as your on-the-job training. Because it's the last assembly I'll ever attend."

"My name is Reese Clawson. You all know what this is about, otherwise we wouldn't be here."

A massive guy was seated directly in front of her. He topped the scales at well over three hundred pounds. He spread his bulk over two chairs. His voice was as big as the rest of him, overbearing and obnoxious even when saying, "I've got some questions here."

"You've got one," Reese corrected. "You ask a second question, you're barred. You can never apply again." She gave that a beat, her gaze drifting over the crowd, then taking aim at him again. "So. You want to ask your one question now?"

The guy muttered, "I'll wait."

"One comment or question per participant," Reese told them. "Who goes first?"

A voice called, "What's the pay?"

"Raise your hand. Okay. What have you heard?"

"Nothing I can believe."

"Tell me anyway."

"Two hundred and fifty thou."

"Per annum. Everyone receives the same, including me," Reese confirmed. All this was included in the folder she had left on her chair. She waited through the rustle of comments, then went on, "First, though, you have to pass the tests. Those will take up the rest of today. If you pass, you're hired."

One of the wheelchair-bound women said, "It can't be that simple."

"Nothing about this is simple. But it is straightforward. Next?"

The big guy's chairs creaked as he lifted his hand. "What's the test?"

"What have you heard?"

"You pop us out of our bodies."

"Correct. We're dealing with controlled out-of-body experiences. Emphasis on the word *controlled*. You go where we say, you do what we ask, you come back. That's what we'll be testing today. Whether you can get out, and whether you can obey commands while you're . . ." She searched for the right word.

The massive guy in the front row finished the thought for her. "Free."

She hoped he caught her smile of approval. "Next? You there at the back."

"What's the success rate?"

"Small. Right at four percent of trial participants. Our preliminary surveys suggest that many people find the experience too close to dying. They want to do it. But they're afraid. Which is why we are here talking. It's come to our attention that being dissatisfied with your physical existence actually improves our chances of achieving positive results. We—"

Reese was suddenly flooded by a realization so intense she stopped in mid-breath. She gave the audience a long, slow look. The guy in the front row was actually not the largest person in the room. The chamber was packed, almost every seat taken, people standing by the side walls, with several wheelchairs along the back. Call it two hundred attendees. A smorgasbord of mismatched shapes and afflictions. But that was not what had halted Reese in mid-thought.

Not one of them cared how she looked.

Here before her were the outcasts. The jokes. The ones who'd never had a chance.

Until now.

Reese was filled with an empathy so intense her eyes misted.

Kevin half rose from his chair. "Reese? You okay?"

"Fine. I'm . . ." She studied the scowling giant seated in front of her. Just another no-hoper. Afraid even this chance would be denied him. Trying not to want it so much. "What's your name?"

"Carl."

"Don't worry about the odds, Carl. I'm sure you're going to do just fine."

24

Brett walked down the Columbia University hallway, knocked on Josephine Banks's open door, spotted the other woman seated in the professor's office, and hesitated.

Josephine waved him in. "You're right on time. Brett Riffkind, this is Rachael Standish, assistant academic dean. Brett, dump those journals on the table and pull up that other chair."

As Brett did so, the dean shifted her chair slightly, placing herself to the left of Josephine's cluttered desk. The transition said it all, as did her frown. Rachael Standish was angular, not gaunt, but rather big-boned and lean and opinionated and impatient.

If Josephine Banks was the least bit disturbed by Rachael's hostility, she did not show it. "Rachael wants to know if you measure up."

"Perfectly understandable." Brett had known dozens of academics like Rachael Standish. Hundreds. Most of them he liked. They lived for their work and their school and their students. They considered all outsiders as potential usurpers. Brett had no problem with needing to prove himself.

Rachael said, "The university has questions. And doubts."

Josephine said easily, "We also have a problem."

"One that should have been handled in-house," Rachael said.

"Actually, we can't." Josephine smiled at Brett. "Nice clothes. Is that part of your current research gig?"

"In a way." Brett wore the second of three outfits acquired the previous afternoon. He had purchased three because Agnes Lockwood's butler had phoned ahead and instructed the men's store. Brett's jacket was from Canali, a salt-and-pepper weave of silk and cashmere. Black woven silk Hermès tie. White-on-white shirt. Black gabardine Zegna slacks. Italian shoes he could have rolled up like socks. This one outfit had cost four thousand dollars.

Rachael Standish clearly was uncertain how to take Brett's appearance. She had expected to meet an out-of-work former academic who would carry a mantle of quiet desperation. Unemployed academics flooded this very tight market, frantically searching for something, even a temporary posting, that would grant them a hint of legitimacy.

"As I was saying," Josephine went on, "Brett was a gifted UCSB assistant professor who gave up a promising role in order to follow a highly controversial research track."

Rachael gave him another heel-to-hairline examination. "Controversial in what way?"

"Risky. Outside the boundaries of current parameters. I was opposed to it. Vehemently." Josephine smiled. "It appears I was wrong."

"And precisely what—" Rachael was halted by another knock on the door.

Lena Fennan stepped inside. Brett had been expecting her arrival. Even looking forward to it. And yet nothing could have prepared him for the impact.

The previous evening, Lena had looked shattered. Totally undone. She had stumbled through a fractured explanation with the quiet desperation of the recently bereaved. Brett had drawn her into a relatively quiet alcove and listened carefully to everything she was willing to tell him. About what Lena called events, and this final encounter with her temporal self.

What he had failed to fully realize was her beauty. Because last night it had been overlaid by a powerful sense of tragedy.

Not today.

Lena Fennan was not just lovely. She was fierce. She wore a travel-weary business suit of emerald green that caught golden flecks in her slightly slanted eyes. Beneath the jacket was a blouse of some shimmering material, probably silk. Her clothes were far from new, her shoes and briefcase were scuffed, and her dark hair spilled over her shoulder in careless disarray. But none of this mattered. An intelligent impatience sparked from her, so strong it reached across the office and smacked Brett in the gut. She was, in a word, stunning.

Brett said, "This is Lena Fennan. I invited her to attend my class."

The dean snapped, "It is not your class unless I say so."

"Until we say," Josephine corrected.

Rachael's irritation scattered over them all. "Inviting an outsider is out of the question, today of all days."

Had the dean not been so insistent, Josephine would probably have agreed. But the department chief's gaze hardened and her lips compressed, and she pointed out, "I invited you."

"That is hardly a point of comparison."

Josephine turned to Lena and asked, "What is your interest in Dr. Riffkind's class?"

Clearly Lena had not expected this level of hostility. She answered so slowly Brett had the impression she was making it up as she went. "I am thinking of hiring him as a consultant."

Brett did his best to hide the fact that he shared the women's surprise. Rachael demanded, "What exactly is it that you do?"

Again the slow formation, the building of her answer word by word. "I run an investment portfolio at Baker Meredith."

"I'm sorry, what—"

"We're a boutique investment group, six hundred million under management. We are examining a substantial investment in a firm tied to Dr. Riffkind's current work."

For the first time since Brett had entered the room, the dean sounded uncertain. "All consulting contracts with academic personnel must be approved by the university."

"That's what we're trying to determine, isn't it?" Josephine pointed out. "Whether Dr. Riffkind is to be employed."

"Temporarily," Rachael replied.

Josephine smiled and rose from her desk. "It's almost time for class."

"My name is Brett Riffkind. I was associate professor at UCSB in neurobiology. Two years and four months ago, I took a sabbatical to research one aspect of today's class. I don't know if the university still considers me on sabbatical. All I can say for certain is, I haven't been officially dismissed. The university thinks my work has potential, but they also see it as high risk. They decided to string me along, especially since I'm not drawing benefits or salary. So I remain caught in a sort of academic limbo."

Brett slipped out of his jacket and draped it over the back of a wooden chair beside the scarred podium. He took a good look around. Lena looked with him. The classroom was a wooden arena, rimmed by eleven curved rows that rose steeply from where he stood. The original wooden benches had thankfully been replaced by padded contour chairs. Each position held two plugs, for a computer and something else, probably a phone. A few of the hundred or so students had pens and pads at the ready. The majority were using laptops or tablets. All of them shared an expression of bored hostility.

"To give me a perspective of this class, how many of you are grad students in biology? Raise your hands, please. Six. Good. How many in psychology? Four. Neuroscience? Two. The rest of you are undergrad seniors, correct? How many are premed? Too many to count. Fine. Thank you."

Brett already knew this. Lena had walked to class behind the trio and had heard Josephine give him a swift overview, both of the class and of the issues they faced in the lesson plan. Lena liked how Brett used this opportunity to make the students respond. A small but significant icebreaker.

"Today's lesson is intended to introduce how quantum theory is tied to neuroscience. I understand your former professor and her assistant have both told you the whole concept is nonsense. I have a word for such people." Brett gave that a beat, then finished, "I call them dinosaurs. In ten years they will all be extinct."

He rested one arm upon the empty lectern as he turned around. Brett spoke with no notes. He examined the wall of blackboards. They were levered so he could raise or lower them as he pleased. The previous lecturers had failed to completely clear away their work.

Brett studied the cloudy confusion as he went on, "I understand the professor and her postgrad minion handed you a lot of theory and math to disprove the whole concept. In our first class I won't use either. I don't need to. Facts are facts. And that's all I'm going to discuss with you. Facts." He turned back to the class. "To begin with—" He was halted by an upraised hand. "Yes?"

A student asked, "Will we be tested on this?"

"Fair question. The answer is, today I'm the one being tested. That's why Dr. Banks and Dean Standish are seated up there on the top row. So let's leave that issue for the next class, if there is one. Okay? Good. Now for ground rule one. I am dealing with some very complex issues here. I want you to make note of your questions. Ask anything you want. I welcome them all. But only when I pause and invite your responses."

He examined the class for a long moment, then repeated the word, "Facts. The first fact is, the relationship between quantum mechanics and biology is no longer theory. It has been proven. Six times, to be precise. By carefully structured experiments that leave no room for doubt. Six experiments that have been noted by the world's most prestigious scientific journals. Facts, ladies and gentlemen. Today we begin dealing with the new reality."

Lena sat by herself so she could carefully examine both the man and this situation. She wanted to peel back the surface and determine why she was here. Or try to. So far all she could say for certain was Brett Riffkind belonged in front of a classroom. He dominated the lectern like a star. He managed to bend the room's high fluorescent lighting so that it aimed tightly and tracked his every movement.

"We are entering into a new and very strange world that is in the process of redefining our entire field," he said. "And it is not just biologists like your professor who feel threatened by this. Until about five years ago, quantum physics remained isolated in the lab. This was where physicists felt safe. They could control everything. They defined the box, the scientific parameters governing every experiment. But progress these days is all about tying quantum physics to the real world. The previous generation of quantum scientists is very uncomfortable with this step. Terrified, in fact. They dislike the uncontrolled messiness of the real world. Life, in effect, scares them."

Brett gave the class a long look. "And it should. Because for many of them, these new developments signal the end of their careers."

Brett gave that a moment, long enough to see that almost all of the students were now taking notes. He glanced at Josie Banks, seated up on the top rung, and liked how she flashed him an approving smile.

Brett continued, "Deep inside every cell of every living organism are waves of shimmering force that can be everywhere at the same time. Even our human senses, our mental faculties, are tuned in to the strange impact of quantum energies. To understand life in its fullness, we have to gain an understanding of quantum rules."

"Facts," he said again. He turned to the board and wrote for the first time. *Quantum Biology.* "The first successful experiment that tied quantum mechanics to the messy real world of neurobiology was a study of migration. How is it possible that a bird can migrate twice each year, depart from a specific tree, travel two thousand miles, and land by a specific lake that it last saw six months earlier? The answer, we now know, is a specific element of quantum mechanics."

Brett turned and wrote a second time. *Quantum Entanglement.* He faced the class once more and just stood there. He found a delicious pleasure in knowing they were his now. He recalled actors describing their first few moments upon the stage, when the audience remained a little hostile as they waited to be drawn in. Brett knew success in the class all came down to good theater. Either a professor had it or they didn't. Knowledge, timing, passion . . . It could all be summed up in one word. Engage.

"This first experiment involved a little fellow I like to call Robin Hood. Always before, the assumption was that birds navigated via the earth's magnetic field. But exactly how this was done remained a mystery. Five years ago, a Swedish scientist proved the bird's magnetic compass actually resides in the eyes. He did this by fitting English robins with little hoods that covered one eye or the other. The hood did away with the robin's ability to track. In future classes I'll give you the details and show you videos of the experiments. Today I want you to try to grasp the big picture."

Brett turned and wrote a third line on the central board. *Outlier.* "The importance of our little hooded robin cannot be overstated. This term, outlier, refers to data that is skewed so far away from the standard that it is discounted entirely. An outlier is the rogue element that demolishes a carefully controlled experiment. The one trial event that can't be fitted inside the scientist's safe little environment. Until this experiment, dinosaurs like your former professor classed all data pointing to the reality of quantum biology as outliers. Insignificant. Random quirks that could be erased and ignored. Because of our little robin, this is no longer possible.

"Inside the robin's eyeballs, magnetic energy creates a chemical reaction similar to what light photons do in ours. Experiments have proven this. The robin navigates along a direct and constant heading, even in the dark."

Brett circled the second line on the board. "All this comes about through quantum entanglement, a communication between particles that apparently happens faster than the speed of light. Einstein claimed this was impossible. He said quantum entanglement was ridiculous. Ladies and gentlemen, we now know that on this particular point, Einstein was wrong. We have proven that certain particles at the subatomic level are indeed paired, in the sense that they can communicate without any acknowledgment of either time or distance."

Brett did not state the next thought that came to him. Throughout that long year of playing the journeyman to death, Brett had become increasingly certain that here was the key. This was the link that served as the core of human consciousness, even when the standard physical boundaries were stretched. He glanced at Lena and found himself excited by the prospect of sharing his thoughts. The prospect that she might indeed play a part in his new beginning left him slightly breathless.

Brett forced himself to refocus on the class and continued, "Inside the robin's eyes, the earth's magnetic field creates electrons that are entangled. Each subatomic particle has two possible states. Until the particle is measured, it is in neither state but rather both states at the same time. But when the robin jerks its head, shifting from one position to the next, it determines the particle's measured state.

"Why Einstein discounted this, why he called it spooky, is because the state of this first measurement determines the state of all measurements to come. The vital factor as far as our little robin is concerned is this: the placement of these photons upon the earth's surface, and the distance the robin is from the equator, determine the measured state within the robin's eyes. Tiny variations in the earth's magnetic field are enough to change this measured state, thus altering the robin's compass readings. And this happens every time the bird jerks its head from side to side. This grants the robin its amazing ability to return to the exact same tree, two thousand miles and six months away."

Brett had not consciously timed his words, but in the pause that followed, he glanced at his watch and realized, "That's all the time we have today. We'll begin the next class with your questions."

Almost all the audience applauded.

25

Testing all the new applicants took Kevin until after midnight. Tuesday morning he arranged transport for the six new voyagers who had passed their trials. Then he and Reese left the motel and headed south on the airport highway, connecting eventually with State Road 192. Reese felt a sense of pleasure over coming back to her roots. This had once been known as the Kissimmee Highway and had been the main route from Holopaw to the coast. Her finest teenage memories all started with heading east as far as the road would take her, all the way through Melbourne and across the causeway bridge. There it changed names and became Fifth Avenue, before finally ending at a T-junction in front of the Indialantic boardwalk.

Today Kevin drove west, and the highway soon became four lanes chained on both sides by aging sprawl. The underbelly of Orlando and Disney was revealed, a tawdry parasite feeding off the theme parks, offering cut-rate alternatives to the expensive attractions farther north.

Kevin turned into the parking lot of a suites motel whose sign was repainted so the chain's name was erased. But the job was done poorly, and the sign's lighting flickered and sparked. The stretch of green separating the entrance from the highway held four banana plants so overgrown they blocked any view of the motel's entrance. At the sign's bottom was a hand-painted board that permanently declared "No Vacancy."

Kevin pulled into the shaded forecourt and cut the motor. "On the parking lot's other side is a low-rise with professional offices."

Reese turned and glanced through the rear window. The next building was in better shape, with three floors of mirrored glass. "I see it."

"We own that. A dentist and a chiropractor and a mortgage broker occupy the first floor. The mortgage guy is hanging on by his fingernails. Hasn't paid his rent since we've been here. We're not pressing."

"Good cover," Reese said, mostly to let him know she was following.

"The middle floor is our offices and official address. You want a secretary?"

"I don't even want an office."

"You've got one anyway. Next to mine. Fine view of the traffic and the power lines. Anyone stops by for an inspection, this is as far as they get. The top floor is assembly. Putting these neural nets together is a finicky job. Each one is made by hand, then it has to be individually tailored and calibrated. Vibratory calculations and positioning and stuff. We've got a good assembly team. Mostly Ecuadorians. The manager is from Ukraine. We pay double the going wages. They are loyal and they know to keep their mouths shut."

"What's the assembly rate?"

"Call it eighteen a month." Kevin hesitated, then added, "But we only get to keep enough to equip our new voyagers. The others are shipped out."

"Where do they go?"

"I have no idea."

"Who calibrates them?"

"For our team, a technician comes over with every new batch of trainees. Takes about four hours per novice. For the others, no idea. Not us."

"Where did the technology come from?"

Kevin reached for the door handle. "They didn't say."

"Wait a second." She saw how he didn't settle back. The tension was there in his face. Ready to argue with the unspoken. But Reese said it anyway. "Do we want to know who is pulling our strings?"

Kevin gave her a shooter's gaze and did not reply.

"Let's look past the risk," Reese said. "Just for a second."

"Can we? Ignore the risk, I mean. And survive."

"I didn't say ignore it. I said look past. Do we need to know?"

"You think we do."

She did not nod so much as rock side to side. "It could prove useful. Important, even."

"Insurance."

"Or knowing what to feed them, and when. And how much we can ask for in return."

Kevin did not so much relax as pull back a notch. Taking the pressure off his mental trigger. "That could be dangerous."

"Extremely," she agreed. But she knew he agreed with her. And knew also that Kevin was still sitting there discussing this because he had been thinking the same thing. "We'd need to hide the search by looking for something else. Hunt for something they want us to find. Because you and I both know they'll have spies planted inside our team."

"I have an idea who one of them is. Maybe two."

"Give me a chance to look for myself, then we'll compare notes."

Kevin opened his door and let the humid air wash over them both. "You have an idea?"

"More like a framework. So when the opportunity arises, then we can move."

"You'll tell me before you act?"

"I won't go unless you agree we should."

Kevin's gaze tightened once more, only this time it was with approval. "I was right to insist they bring you in."

Reese entered the motel just as the van carrying the novices pulled into the lot. The reception desk was staffed by a sallow-faced woman whose spiky hair bore a trio of colors that had never made it into the rainbow. Kevin handed Reese a plastic key and said, "You're in 211. I'll see to the newbies and meet you back here."

Reese ignored the eyes that tracked her as she crossed the foyer and took the stairs. She entered the room and found herself in a surprisingly luxurious apartment. The suites motel had been gutted, two studios reformed into large one-bedroom units, and kitted out with an eye for understated elegance. The shower was too nice to pass up, tiled in grey marble with a granite sink and stocked with towels and shampoo and lotions bearing the logo of some Park Avenue boutique. She dressed in sweats and checked her watch as she left the room. In and out in eight minutes. In prison, speed through semi-public spaces meant safety.

But when she returned downstairs, Kevin was already pacing an angry furrow by the front window. More people were drifting around the perimeters, no doubt drawn here by her arrival. But Kevin didn't have time for them either. He gripped Reese just above the right elbow and drew her outside. "I was planning to give you the ten-cent tour. Then you were going to address the troops. All this is important and it needs to be done."

"What's happened?"

"I got a call from Vera. We have a new assignment. They need something from us."

"From the two-step you're doing, I assume the timeline is tight."

"They need it now, Reese. Today. We've never been given anything like this."

She said it for him. "Vera wants me to fail."

"There's clearly some pushback over you making it this far," he said. "But Vera sounded genuinely stressed. You've met her. She doesn't have the capacity to pretend. She is being pressured. So hard, in fact, she sounded frightened."

"Then we've got to meet this head-on."

"What if we fail?"

She liked how he included himself in this. The normal Washington response to any new hazard was to walk away. Lower the threat level to number one. Instead, Kevin remained joined. Even when his concern was beaded across his forehead.

Reese switched positions with him. She took hold of his arm, leaned in close, and said, "First off, we're not failing. Second, this is exactly what we needed. This is our in."

All the hardships he had faced over the previous twelve months were there in his uncertain tone. "We're moving too fast."

"Correction. They're forcing us to move fast. Which means their system is fractured by pressure."

"Maybe," Kevin said.

But Reese was already moving. "Go see what Vera wants from us, then assemble the voyagers on duty. I need to have a look around."

Reese made a slow tour through most of the facility. She pretended to be fascinated by the café, the monitoring station, the three former conference rooms turned into departures lounges. There was no telling what the interior designer had thought of all this—the building's untouched exterior, the lovely apartments, the enlarged space to take meals, the new and beautifully appointed conference lobby, and three large rooms holding leather dentist chairs and an array of electronic equipment. A fourth was transformed into the monitoring chamber, sporting two walls of computer screens and five swivel chairs done in leather and chrome. The door to the monitoring chamber had a Keep Out sign. By the time Reese completed her circuit and returned to the lobby, she had a basic idea of what she needed to know.

Kevin hurried back through the sliding glass doors and held out a file. "This is all the data on our new target they've supplied us."

Reese made no move to take the file. "How many are in today's team?"

"Twelve. Two out sick."

"Three crews, right?"

"Two full strength, one that will be when you get the newbies up and running. I should have them kitted out in a few days."

"Make me twelve copies of that file." When Kevin frowned in response, she went on, "I want the voyagers to work with me."

He nodded slowly. Uncertain how he felt, but unwilling to object. "I'll be right back."

"Hang on a second. Where is the security station?"

"Manager's office. They're under orders to keep a low profile."

"Show me."

He was nervous and clearly feeling pressure that he wished she felt as well. Which she did. But Reese had learned not to reveal her emotions.

Kevin swung around the receptionist's desk and knocked on the blank door. There was a click, and they entered a warren that was meant to go unseen. A man and a woman were seated in the guard station, facing monitors and a long metal desk of equipment. A rank of guns was locked to the wall opposite them. A trio of whiteboards stood on swivel stands, filled now with photos and names of all the newcomers. Reese saw her photograph at the top of one board. She checked out the space beside her name, read her DOB, her education, her official positions with the fictitious companies that had formed her cover. Nothing about her work for the government or the more secret work that had come before, no comments about how she had spent the past fourteen months. She turned away.

Kevin told Reese the guards' names, which she instantly forgot, then he said, "This is Reese Clawson, my new number two. What she says carries the same weight as anything coming directly from me."

Reese felt her skin crawl as the guards observed her with the bland curiosity of professionals. They did not speak. One guard was male, the other female, both in their early thirties, heavyset and wearing jeans and pale blue T-shirts.

She followed Kevin through the next door and into the ready room. Another two guards were seated at the central table. The room smelled of microwaved lasagna. The guy was watching a basketball game on his tablet, the woman read a book. The pair slipped off headphones and listened as Kevin went through the same introductory process. When he was done, he told Reese, "Originally we had them stationed in the other building. But there were problems."

The guy said, "Nobody taught that crew to play nice."

"Mostly a lot of screaming and hissy fits," the woman said. "Some thefts. Two accusations of assaults."

"We determined one of the assaults was real and kicked them out," Kevin said.

"We had to get tough with a couple of the others," the woman said. She asked Kevin, "You told her about the four?"

"Not yet."

"There's this group," the guy said. "They like to pretend they run things. One female does not agree. She lives on the fringe."

Reese asked, "What's she called?"

"Ridley. Just the one name."

"She's a piece of work," the woman said.

"We do what we can," Kevin said. "Which included moving the security detail over here."

"And issuing us these." The guy pulled a baton from his belt, whipped it open, and hit a button. An electronic current shot across the forked tip. "We call them sparklers."

Reese thanked the guards and said to Kevin, "That's enough. Let's get to work."

She followed him back into the lobby and waited while he left through the sliding glass doors. Then she turned to the receptionist and asked, "Where's the gym?"

The woman inspected Reese while she chewed her gum. "Downstairs. But the pool's outside."

"Thank you."

"Hang on a second." The receptionist tilted her head, gauging whether she should say anything more. "Now's probably not a good time."

"You can reserve the gym?"

"Not exactly. But there's a person in there, and Ridley's not much on company. You know?"

Reese wanted to rush around the desk and hug the young woman. Instead, she nodded her thanks and headed for the stairs. Beyond the rear glass door she could see the oval pool and the two Jacuzzis and the tall enclosing fence. The area held a clutch of people awkwardly trying to have a good time. She took the stairs and walked the carpeted hall and stopped where she could look through the narrow window in the gym's door. The electronic lock had been disabled, and the light above it burned permanently green. Reese sighed softly. One glance was enough to know she had located what she had been desperately hoping to find. One crucial part of the puzzle she needed to put together in order to survive.

The gym held only one woman. She was in her late twenties and worked the heavy bag with fists and feet. At first Reese thought she wore a bodysuit. Then she realized the woman was heavily inked. Her legs and arms and neck. One continuous tattooed design, or so it appeared.

The woman must have known Reese was watching. A woman like this did not miss anything. Reese opened the door. Stepped inside. Let the door shut behind her. And waited.

The woman's strikes became harder, swifter, more vicious. She was not hitting the leather bag. She walloped Reese. Her every blow was a warning. *Back off.*

Reese waited her out. Finally the woman kicked the bag so hard the chain rattled. She halted the swings with her two fingerless gloves.

She did not look over. Reese remained silent as the woman's breathing eased somewhat, then said, "Can I ask your name?"

The woman let her sweat drip onto the mat at her feet. Weighing an answer. Finally she said, "Ridley."

"I'm Reese."

Ridley nodded to the floor.

Reese opened the door and stepped back into the hallway. Only when the door clicked and she was alone did she allow herself to smile.

Reese climbed the stairs and was halfway across the lobby when she spotted the man outside. She veered around the reception desk and walked through the sliding doors and entered the warm blanket of a Florida dusk. The overweight guy from her Orlando trials, Carl, leaned against the forecourt pillar. There were four metal benches arrayed around the perimeter, positioned for the smokers. The big man made no motion at her approach, gave no sign he noticed her at all. He sucked hard on a cigarette, the ash long and dangling. There were several stubs at his feet. He stared into the western sky streaked with clouds turned gold by the dimming light.

Reese stood there, taking her time. No need to rush, nothing to do that was more important than this. Finally she said, "Most people, they would look at you and think one of two things. Either they'd say, 'That guy is working toward an early grave, smoking and carrying all that extra weight.' But you've been hearing that all your adult life, and you don't let it even touch you anymore."

The guy's only response was to drop the butt onto the pavement, reach into his pocket, and pull out a pack of Marlboros and a plastic lighter. He fished out another cigarette, lit up, dragged deep, and went back to watching the sky.

"Others might think, 'Here's a guy looking for a little solitude,'" Reese went on. "'Just grooving on the sunset and his smokes. Cool dude just chilling on the beauty.' But we both know what you're really doing is marking time. We know you haven't even noticed the sunset any more than you do the movement of the hands on your watch. The sunset is nothing. The beauty is a joke. You're out here because you crave the night. You can move easy then. The dark is your friend. People don't notice you. You only live easy during the hours when others hide away in their safe little burrows. You're just like me."

He took in a quarter-inch of the cigarette with one drag, then said, "It's the same gig here, the same lies. Nothing's changed except for the money."

Reese started to touch his arm, then thought better of it. Guys like this really detested the touch of others. "What you just said, that's why I came out here."

His gaze flickered, a tight, splintered look her way. No more than a nanosecond. Like any direct look at reality was just too painful.

Reese put as much force into the softly spoken words as she knew how. "Don't give up on me yet."

She was almost at the door when he called her name. She turned around, and he asked, "What makes you think you can do anything about it?"

Reese wished it was easier for her to smile, or simpler for him to trust. "Go down to the gym and ask Ridley if she'll give me a chance. Either way, join me in the conference lobby. I'll show you what I have in mind."

26

Lena and Robin and Chester were joined late afternoon by Brett. Since leaving the class, Lena had spoken with Brett twice by phone, running through their research as it unfolded. At six thirty Lena had Chester order up dinner for everyone, asking only that the food come from somewhere nice. They ate a Greek-style meal of a dozen or so dishes, lamb and salads mostly, but with fries because Robin asked for them. Chester made them tea. They worked for another two hours, then Lena sent them home at nine. She ordered them to not work another minute. Do something nice, then get a good night's sleep, and be back at eight. Chester looked shocked at the idea of leaving the office with the task undone and coming in so late. But Lena was less concerned about having everything in place than she was having her team look rested and ready. Her final words were a reminder to dress accordingly.

Lena's room at the suites hotel was large for Manhattan, almost five hundred square feet, and shaped like an L. The kitchen ran along the same wall as the entrance and was flanked by a dining table that separated the living room with its giant flat-screen TV from the sleeping area. She was tired, but pleasantly so. She channel-surfed for a few minutes, then turned off the television and sat listening to the city's frenetic din. She thought about Brett, and how he had remained silent and watchful through most of the afternoon, speaking only when he was asked a direct question. His responses were thoughtful, measured. Lena hesitated a long moment, then reached for her phone and dialed the number he had given her.

When Brett answered, Lena said, "You're holding something back."

He replied, "I'm glad you called."

"There's something you're not telling us."

"That's right," he said. "There is."

"Something big."

"Very."

"Is it your research project?"

"Yes."

"Does your research impact our presentation tomorrow?"

Brett had adopted the same measured cadence he had used in the classroom. "The two issues, your project and my research, are joined at the hip. They could not be more involved. As for impacting the presentation tomorrow, I can't say."

Lena hesitated. There was a sense of facing an unseen boundary. Asking her next question crossed her into alien territory. Brett waited with her, seemingly content to give her all night. Lena tasted the air, then asked softly, "Will you tell me what your research is about?"

"Yes, Lena. I will tell you everything."

She disliked the tight tremors that coursed through her middle, and knew she could not handle anything more just then. "Tomorrow, then. After the presentation."

"Whenever you say," Brett replied. "Whatever you want to know."

Lena was still struggling with the sense of being drawn toward this man when they gathered the next morning. She had slept well, all things considered, and felt comfortable with the day ahead. But there was still a lot of ground to cover. By the time they left for Roger's office, Lena felt her team was as prepped as they possibly could be. She knew Robin and Chester were both worried about the project's huge downside risks and nervous over taking part in the presentation. But Lena's strongest impression, as the unseen wind drew her toward the next unfolding quest, was that she did not go into this alone.

They traveled to Wall Street in three limos. Lena shared one ride with Robin and Brett. Chester rode with the Baker Meredith partners. The third car held a clutch of nervous aides.

Lena found Brett's presence both comforting and unsettling. She was determined to maintain a firm boundary between her professional work and any romantic entanglement. Even so, the prospect of involving herself with a man who promised only heartbreak should have been a lot more repugnant than it felt.

The Baker Meredith partners were ushered into the conference room, while Lena's team was asked to wait. Lena took out her phone, called Don Metzer, and said, "You won't believe where I am."

The lawyer replied, "Hang on a second." Lena heard a door shut, then Don came back on with, "Tell me."

"Roger Foretrain's reception area. Seated in the same waiting room, on the same sofa, in the exact same position."

"Only the last time, you were waiting to get fired," Don said.

Lena made no attempt to hide her conversation from the team. "The only problem this time around is, you're not here with me."

"You're going to do fine," Don said. "Colorado still has me running flat out. I'm representing our partners in the sale of their respective forty-nine percents. Charles Farlow wants to own the whole shooting match."

"Ask him for a whole lot of money," Lena said.

"I'm going for a lot more than that. And I'm not asking, I'm demanding." Don spoke with the languid ease of a man who lived for battles like this. "Speaking of money, are you as prepped as on your last acquisition?"

"Not even close."

"How long have you had?"

Lena checked her watch. "Thirty-nine hours and counting."

Don laughed out loud.

"But I have a team. We know what we need to know. What we don't know, we can learn. What we're missing is our lawyer."

Don cleared his throat. "Lena, about that."

She knew what he was going to say. The absence of any messages from him since the acquisition had left her suspecting that Charles Farlow had recognized Don's skills and offered him a job. One he'd be foolish to turn down. But Lena did not want to hear that, especially not before she entered her first session with the Baker Meredith team.

Roger's secretary chose that moment to set down her phone, rise to her feet, and signal Lena and her team with a professional smile.

Lena said, "I have to go."

·|||·

Two steps inside the First American conference room, Brett was already extremely not impressed.

The conference room was far grander than anywhere he had ever worked. He assumed the Gauguin oils on the side wall were genuine. The view out the windows opposite was jaw-dropping. But none of this changed a thing. By the time he had settled into his fine leather chair, the surroundings had paled to insignificance.

Brett had endured too many meetings like this. Anyone involved in university-level research was forced to suffer through gatherings of opponents who pretended to listen. Today the people with money sat at the oval table's far end, clustered together like a battalion of enemy troops. They were already busy loading their guns. The atmosphere was charged with the compressed tension of unexploded ordnance. There were nine of them. The three senior executives from Baker Meredith were clustered together, with five aides seated directly behind them, pads and pens at the ready. Then came an empty seat, then Roger Foretrain. The man Lena spoke of with awe was seated apart from the others. He was the only one whose expression remained open, watchful. Even when he spoke, it was with a tone that suggested he hoped he was wrong to note, "No one expected you to ready a pitch your first week, Lena."

"This project is highly time sensitive," Lena replied.

One Baker Meredith partner was a male whose skin was an olive blend of various races, perhaps Indonesian or Filipino. The other male partner was an Anglo in his late thirties with weary eyes behind tortoise-rim glasses. The woman at their center was narrow and pinched and angry. She even managed to sniff in an aggressive fashion. "It is not a project until we say it is."

Lena did not give any indication that she had heard the woman at all. "Thank you for coming." She launched straight into a brief overview. Two minutes, start to finish. Then she nodded to Robin.

Brett thought Lena's two assistants both gave fair assessments. They were extremely sharp and good at their jobs. They had to be, to survive the notorious Wall Street culls.

But Brett knew there were two problems with everything they said. One, they were clearly both scared of the power represented at the table's far end. Two, they did not see what all the fuss was about. Robin covered the inventor, the apparatus, the record. Chester then dealt with the figures—the inventor's cost structure, the intended acquisition. They had even managed to obtain the buyer's in-house revenue projections.

Then they both hit the same brick wall.

About eighteen months earlier, the inventor had been approached by one of America's largest conglomerates, which offered him a huge pile of money for his device. The inventor had used the acquiring company's first inflow of funds to begin human trials. He had wisely started them in two different countries, Mexico and Italy. This was standard procedure for large pharmaceutical companies, which nowadays farmed out human trials to specialist firms. These firms used hospitals and subjects in lower-cost countries. They only returned to the United States for the final Stage Three trials, when the FDA was more closely involved, and they were counting down to payday.

But the inventor of this particular apparatus could not afford to use an outside company, even with the funds from his new backer. And the acquiring company did not offer to pay any more, because for them the inventor served the exact same purpose. He was their cutout. If something went wrong, the blame lay on him. Not them. The acquisition would not be finalized until the first human trials were completed. They were safe.

Which was good, because seven weeks into the first human trials, things went horribly wrong.

There were deaths. Five of them. Two in Italy, three in Mexico.

The families entered suit using US lawyers, which was completely within their rights, since the inventor and his entire production process were based in Savannah. Initially there were just two court cases, one representing the bereaved Mexican families and another for the Italians. Then the surviving subjects gathered together and entered their own suit, alleging potential long-term damages. One hundred and twenty plaintiffs in all.

The judges of all three suits found against the inventor. He declared bankruptcy. He was publicly disgraced. The backlash was enormous. The inventor was vilified, especially in the scientific press. Brett recalled reading something about it, but all this happened at the onset of his own downward spiral.

The company seeking to acquire the man's invention and all his patents quietly slipped away.

End of story.

Brett listened to the two overviews and knew what he needed to do. The two aides gave it their best. Their loyalty to Lena, and their trust in her ability to protect them, was touching. But they clearly did not see what the rush was about.

Brett saw the change happen at the room's other side because he was expecting it. He had seen it before. All too often. In his case, representatives of research-funding bodies had made their decision before he opened his mouth. They were officially required to enter into such funding pitches with an open mind. But the truth was, they sought a reason to shoot him down. Their secret objective was to detect some flaw in his proposal that would stand up to outside scrutiny. Once this was identified, they could relax. Their job was done.

Brett watched the bankers go through similar subtle shifts, how first the three partners seated at the table and then their aides all settled more comfortably into their seats. They could breathe easy now, enjoy the view, examine the artwork, drink their coffee, whatever. By the time Chester was midway through his analysis, Roger Foretrain was the only one still listening. Frowning, disappointed, but still alert. Looking for the reason that explained why Lena had felt a need to pitch this at all.

Brett pretended to follow Roger's gaze over to Lena. Like he needed reassurance that she was for real. He gave it a couple of beats, long enough to enjoy her beauty, not so long as to draw suspicion. Even with her gaze downcast and her natural exuberance dampened by the room's collective opposition, Lena Fennan was an astonishment. She radiated an intelligent intensity, an impatient grace. Her clothes were a bit rumpled and her hair somewhat confused, like she had not taken time for herself. Not just today. For months. Her rangy athleticism was overlaid by weeks of too little sleep. The banked-up fatigue bruised her features. Even so, Lena was . . .

Brett turned away when he finally settled upon one word that described her impact.

Lena Fennan arrested him.

The senior woman from Baker Meredith was in her late fifties and sounded like she had downed a gravel smoothie for breakfast. "I'm not clear on several points. First, why are we here? I mean, really. If one of my first-year interns had fielded this, I'd have him on the bus back to Des Moines."

Roger said, "We still haven't heard Lena's assessment."

"Come on, Roger. What could she possibly say that would make any difference? Five deaths!"

Roger leafed through his copy of their analysis and did not respond.

The woman, Baker or Meredith—Brett couldn't remember and didn't really care—took that as her cue. "Let's move on." She pointed her gold pen at Brett. "Who is this guy and what is he doing on our payroll?"

Brett took that as the signal he'd been hoping for. Lena started to respond. But she caught sight of the hand he lifted slightly off the table. Her dark eyes sparked when they met his. Fear, suppressed adrenaline, some confusion of her own. Brett forced himself to look away.

He said to the woman at the table's far end, "You're missing the point."

"Excuse me?"

"You're working under the mistaken assumption that Ms. Fennan has come here asking for money. Or your permission. You're wrong on both counts."

The woman squinted as the tension returned to the room's far end. Only Roger seemed pleased. He had come to be surprised. He turned back to the first page and read, "'Dr. Brett Riffkind, professor of neurobiology at UCSB, currently on a research secondment.' Doing what?"

"I'll come back to that," Brett replied. He kept his gaze on the woman, Baker or Meredith. "Right now we need to focus on the essential. Ms. Fennan does not need your money. Or your approval."

Robin and Chester struggled with the bland masks all Wall Street aides were expected to maintain. But clearly they were as baffled as the group clustered at the table's far end.

Lena's gaze was different. Blank. Dark. Oriental.

Beautiful.

Brett went on, "We all know you're not going to invest in anything Ms. Fennan pitches today. If she had shown up with an option to acquire Kuwait for a buck fifty, you'd still find a reason to shoot her down."

The woman gathered her items like a general removing her troops from the field of battle. "Really, Roger. This is hardly a reasonable use of our time or—"

"Give him a minute." Roger did not actually smile. But his features had settled into different, more comfortable lines. He asked Brett, "So tell us what we're doing here."

"Ms. Fennan is making this investment," Brett replied. "She has uncovered what everyone else missed. Again. She also has the funds. You know this for a fact, since she made her money from another investment that you thought was a loser."

"Not me personally," Roger corrected. "My question still stands."

"Ms. Fennan needs to know what percentage your firm requires to carry this on your books. Grant her the human resources and the legal basis for moving forward."

The woman protested, "We can't possibly be party to some hare-brained—"

"Forty percent," Roger said.

"Try again," Lena said, not looking up from her hands resting upon the table.

Brett actually felt a zing of energy shoot through him. He loved how they were in tandem here. Just loved it. "Give Ms. Fennan a reason to stay with your group instead of taking this to Colorado."

Roger was watching Lena now. "You tell me."

Lena met his gaze. "Twenty percent."

"Done." He asked her, "What do you need?"

Lena shot Brett another zinger of a glance, then turned back and replied, "A lawyer and a company jet."

27

The broad conference entrance hall had been remade into a very attractive lounge. A coffee area was stocked with energy drinks and pashmina blankets and pastries. Reese recalled how her previous teams came back shivering from a cold only they could feel, and drained by an experience that was visible only to them. Her current crew of voyagers was gathered around a pair of sofa sets and stressless chairs. As soon as she spotted the woman seated on the central sofa, Reese knew she was trouble. The woman was seated in the middle of the group, which meant everyone was forced to drag their gaze over her as they turned from one to the other. Reese saw how the female took genuine pleasure over their fear and their dislike.

Reese waited until Carl and Ridley had entered and settled into the far corner, over where the mock shoji screen masked the hall leading to the front foyer. Then she asked the woman, "What's your name?"

The woman was aged in her mid-twenties. Her blonde hair was shellacked into a tight helmet, her brown eyes flat, hard, and lifeless as glass. She said with a false cheeriness, "We're all about redefining ourselves here, you know? I'm thinking I'd like to change names. What about Heather?"

The words confirmed everything Reese had suspected. She had dealt with bullies like this woman in every prison where she'd landed. She said, "I want you to go collect your team."

Heather pretended at confusion. "But these are my team. Right, everybody?"

"You have five minutes," Reese said. "Otherwise I'm taking you off-line."

The cheery smile was slightly canted now, as if the muscles on her face's left side were unable to fashion the mask. "You are threatening me?"

"No threats," Reese said. She liked how the other voyagers were focused on her. She could almost feel their desperate hope that she might actually make a difference. She went on, "Twenty minutes from now, I start these voyagers on their new mission. If your crew isn't gathered so we can talk before that happens, you are gone. Finished."

The snakelike change was almost refreshing. "You can't do that."

"I can. I will."

"The rules—"

"I make the rules from now on. Five minutes."

Reese had spent a great deal of the past fourteen months reading. Most prison libraries were pitiful. The books were passed around until they fell apart, and even then they were wrapped in rubber bands and kept on the shelves. It was better to need both hands to turn a page than have nothing at all to read. Reese preferred nonfiction, but when the time lay heavy she read anything at all. She always looked first for books on psychology, especially those written about prison populations. She was interested in trying to understand what made herself tick.

Four people were seated with her now. They occupied one corner of the broad lounge that fronted the former conference rooms. Ridley and Carl had drifted back in and were perched in the corner. Watchful. Focused. Giving Reese a chance.

The four had almost nothing in common. A guy with dark hair slicked to his skull bore an astonishing array of metal piercings. The second woman was Indian or Pakistani. The other guy was Latino. He had eyes that burned with a very dark fire. He studied Reese with the intent pleasure of a hungry carnivore taking measure of his next meal. Then there was Heather.

The four shared just two traits. One was their age, mid- to late twenties. The other was their gazes. Flinty. Sharp. Fractured. Filled with a barely suppressed rage.

Reese had read how there was no clinical designation for the word *psychopath*. But the term had become widely used in criminal justice and prison settings. It was first introduced as an analytical criteria by Hervey Cleckley in the Diagnostic and Statistical Manual of Mental Disorders, a book that had fascinated Reese for weeks.

Criminal psychologists had developed what was referred to as a triarchic model for assessing psychopathic tendencies. Patients were graded on three factors. The first was *boldness*. A psychopath showed very low fear levels. They were extremely tolerant of stress. They actually enjoyed unfamiliar settings that carried a significant level of danger. This was matched by a very high degree of self-confidence. Psychopaths considered themselves the supreme ruler of all they surveyed.

The second factor was *disinhibition*. Psychopaths had virtually no impulse control. They showed no interest in planning and foresight. They had very poor behavioral restraints. What they wanted, they took. What they disliked, they destroyed.

The third measurement factor was *meanness*. Psychopaths lacked empathy. They developed close attachments only with those who could further their aims, feed their hungers. They exploited everyone else as sources of momentary pleasure. They were defiant of all authority. In extreme cases they found intense gratification in causing pain.

Reese had been fascinated by the work of one criminal psychologist in particular. This prison counselor described working with inmates who showed extremely high levels of factors one and three, and yet maintained a very tight control over their impulses. The social worker classed these as the most dangerous category of psychopath, because they could go virtually unnoticed in society at large. For all intents and purposes, they looked and acted entirely normal, until they struck. They used their environment like a carnivore in the jungle. They stalked, they attacked, they disappeared.

Reese had always considered herself one of these. She took no pride in the admission, felt no shame. She was what she was. Prison had not remade her. It had only distilled her down to her core essence. Which was why she felt so comfortable among this group. It was why their rage did not disturb her. They were all after the same thing.

Her job was to bring them around to her way of thinking.

Reese launched straight in with, "The key to surviving prison is joining a gang. I'm not talking about time some of you might have pulled in a county lockup. I'm talking about life in the boneyard. In general population, gangs are called either clicks or cars. The tag depends on the prison."

The guy with all the piercings asked, "You did time?"

"Your job is to stay quiet and listen," Reese said. She held to a casual tone. Her mask was firmly in place. Just like theirs. "Do that and you might survive."

The guy and Heather shared a smirk. But the Indian woman remained focused on Reese. As did the Latino.

"As I was saying, you find a car. You do what it takes to enter. My second lockup had just one car that accepted Anglos. They were led by a woman who enjoyed starting fights. In the boneyard, this type of woman was called an agitator. Her favorite tactic was to enter the yard, choose her target, and give them a chin check, a blow to the jaw. We called her Bug, which is the prison term for someone with serious mental problems. Bug liked to have new members of her car spend a week or so watching others get chin-checked, building up the scare factor. Anybody in the car who got hit was supposed to take it with a smile. When it came my turn, Bug waited a week, another, a third, and finally in the fourth week she came for me."

Reese went quiet. She was willing to wait all day. The rest of her team on the clock were chattering out beyond the shoji screen. Reese didn't care whether they heard or not.

Finally the Indian woman asked, "What did you do?"

"I jammed a pencil into her carotid artery and walked away. I don't know whether Bug survived or not. What I do know is, I did my time in solitary, then I took over that car and ran it until I got shipped out." Reese met the blank and angry gazes one by one. Then she said, "There's a new leader to your click. I don't chin-check. I'm not after aggro. I don't have time for it, and as soon as we reach an understanding, neither will you. Either you fall in line or you're out."

"You get rid of us, people die," the guy said.

"Maybe. For a week or two. Then my new car will have figured things out, and we'll be up and running. Only without you." She scanned the crew another time. "Now, I want to know two things. Straight up. First, how do you keep them safe. Second, how much are you scamming."

The crew faltered. The response was unified. They all showed the same instant of uncertainty. Reese had pulled away the veil and seen them. Done so calmly and without warning.

Even Heather showed a rare breakage to her cheery nonsense. "What are those two behind us doing here?"

"They're going to tell all the others about the dawn of a new day," Reese replied. "Here's what I think happened. You saw in each other a rare ability to transit without fear, even when some voyagers fell into those unexplained comas. Most of the others here just freaked. Only not you. And when that happened, you realized there was the chance to do something new. Something big. Join together and see how far you could take things. And it turned out to be pretty far indeed."

"Further than you could ever imagine," the Latino said.

"I don't need to imagine," Reese said. "Know why? Because you're going to tell me."

The guy hated it. His face worked with the bile of rising fury. But the Indian woman said, "We made friends."

The Latino ground his teeth, but something he saw in Reese's gaze kept him silent. Reese asked, "What kind of friends?"

"They welcomed us. They do what we ask."

The guy with all the piercings said, "They want something in return."

"Of course they do," the Indian woman said. "What in this life has ever been free?"

"But it isn't about this life," the Latino replied. "They haven't. They don't. Live."

Reese said, "So they're not real."

"Esteban didn't say that," Heather replied. "He said they haven't lived."

The Indian woman asked, "You know this how?"

"They told me," Heather replied.

"You asked them?"

"Of course I did. What, you're not curious?"

The guy with the piercings snarled, "Why are we telling her anything at all?"

"You heard the lady. She's hearing or she's kicking us out," Esteban replied. "I want to stay in."

Reese looked from one to the other. "So let me get this straight. You have allies who are . . ."

"Monsters. Something."

"And these allies, when you transit, they . . ."

"They anchor us," the pierced guy said, doing his best to melt her with his eyes. He hated being exposed. Just hated it.

Reese could no longer remain seated. She startled them when she bolted to her feet. But it did not matter. The potential was huge. The dangers even greater.

Finally she turned back and demanded, "So how much protection money are you scamming off the other voyagers?" When they responded by exchanging glances with each other, Reese pressed, "In or out. It starts now."

The Indian woman replied, "Two hundred a week."

"As of today, it's over." Reese halted their outburst by chopping the air. "You dance to my tune or you don't dance at all."

⫶⫶⫶

Reese was crossing the conference lobby when Ridley approached her. The woman was a couple of years younger than Reese, but her eyes were ancient. "In case you haven't heard, I don't play nice with others."

Reese liked having a reason to smile. "Thanks for waiting to spring that one until those four took off."

"I figured, you know, there was something going down."

"There is."

"Something the four in there didn't need to hear about."

"Right again."

Ridley wore her dark hair in tight curls, the only soft thing about her. Her tattoos formed a ring of fiery knives that encircled her neck. "So what's in it for me?"

"What do you want?"

Uncertainty flickered behind her eyes.

"Figure it out, then let's talk." She motioned to Carl, who hovered just out of range. "Join us."

Ridley asked, "You think the big guy here is going to make me behave?"

"This isn't about behaving. This is about taking it to the limits. I need a team of forward observers. Scouting out the terrain. Assessing risks. Checking out our options. Smart, savvy, alert, and born to think outside the box."

Ridley seemed to have all sorts of responses, tight and ready as her fists. But none of them fit. "For a bonus?"

"I told you, figure out your price and let's talk." She indicated Carl. "The best observers work in teams of two. One to spot and the other to watch both your backs."

Ridley had still not looked directly at Carl. "So what's with teaming me up with a trainee?"

"He hasn't been infected with whatever it is that has the others semi-terrified."

Ridley chewed on that. "I might be interested. What do you say, big guy?"

"His name is Carl." When Ridley did not speak, Reese gave her voice a hint of an edge. "Say it."

"What's the haps, Carl."

Reese went on, "I want you to work as Carl's personal trainer. Two loners working in tandem. Building trust out there where it counts. Introduce him to Indian country. See how far and how fast you can take him. When you're both satisfied, come back. Carl, the same offer stands. Whatever you want. The word I need to hear now is, are you in."

28

Brett had never been on a private jet before. The copilot served as steward and offered them a very polished welcome. He ushered them into their seats and offered drinks and pointed out the facilities. Then the jet took off and climbed with smooth ease to cruising altitude. The seats were pale doeskin. The tables were burl. The restroom was finished in onyx and burl and had a shower.

Lena spent the first half hour of the flight talking with Robin and Chester. They were gathered at the table closest to the pilot's cabin. Brett was not invited to join them, so he made himself a sandwich of thin-sliced filet mignon and creamy horseradish on bread that still smelled of the baker's oven. He ate standing up in the galley, wondering what it would be like to take such splendor for granted.

Finally Lena rose from her place and started back toward him. Brett was expecting rebuke, criticism, even perhaps rage. He had, after all, publicly usurped her position as leader of their team.

Instead, she gave him gratitude. "I owe you," Lena said. "Big-time."

"You don't. At all."

"There I was, trying to figure out all the wrong things. How to keep my job, whether I should move to Colorado. Or if I stayed, how I could build decent relationships with the Baker Meredith partners. Then up you pop and say exactly what needed saying."

Brett hid behind another bite of his sandwich.

"What I don't get," Lena went on, "is how you knew. Because you weren't talking to them at all. You spoke to me."

"You went at it as a professional analyst," Brett said. He used a starched linen napkin to wipe his mouth. "You wanted to present the bottom line, the risks and benefits, whatever you call it. But there's a problem. You and your team had already come to the same conclusion as everybody else."

Lena turned and looked back up the aisle to where Robin and Chester sat and stared glumly out the windows. "But it's not about that. Is it."

"You know it's not." Brett set the second half of his sandwich on the counter. "You're meant to make this deal. It's the last thing your temporal self said to you."

She spoke to the empty aisle. "Not the last thing."

Brett felt his face grow red. "Your temporal self said, 'Do this.' And how did you respond?"

Lena remained silent.

"You said yes. Not, you'd check it out. Not, if things looked good on paper." He gave her a chance to respond, then went on, "Lena, your job now is to find the reason to move forward."

Lena merely continued to inspect the central aisle and her two morose teammates. "I can't tell them how I know more, though."

"Probably not a good idea."

"So . . . do you know how to dance around the secret?"

"I think so."

"Because I need them to trust me."

"Yes. You do."

She glanced down at his sandwich. "That smells great."

"I can make more."

"Later. Right now I need you to address the troops."

Lena found the situation unsettling. Not in a bad way. Just disconcerting. She felt the same as she had that first night in Denver. People were relying on her. And she was relying on a voice from beyond.

Only this time there were differences. For one thing, Lena was seated next to a man who not only accepted her events as real but actually had a name for them. According to Brett, she had been contacted by her temporal self. Brett had not shared in such an experience. But he'd had events of his own. Many of them. And he had helped others have their own events. Lena knew she was going to give these ascents of his a try. It was only a matter of time. But right now she had to focus on getting through the next few hours.

Even so, she remained very unsettled. Not because of the project, not really, though there was a multitude of issues they had to work through. She had previously acquired a trio of companies. She was ready to face the challenge of doing it again. What she had trouble with was the man beside her. The threat he represented. Of growing old with a heart rendered useless by sorrow and empty longing.

"My field is neurobiology," Brett began. "These days, the discipline is dominated by numbers. These numbers come in three main flavors. First are the statistics, literally tons of data from experiments and measured results. Next is the interpretation of these results, which increasingly focuses on quantum mechanics, which is all about mathematics. And then there is funding. Defining your research in dollar terms and explaining how the outcome justifies the investment."

They were seated in four swivel chairs. Robin and Chester had half-finished mugs of coffee. The polished table separating them reflected the afternoon sun directly into Robin's eyes, so Lena slid down the two shades. She liked how Brett addressed them. He used the same manner as in the Columbia University classroom. His tone suggested that here was a man who knew his subject backward and forward. They could rely on his knowledge. They could trust him.

It didn't hurt that the man was easy on the eyes. Dangerously so.

"There is a warning we give to every new postgrad that goes like this," Brent went on. "Sometimes you have to ignore the numbers to see the obvious. It's a forest-and-trees situation. That's what we have here. We need to set your analysis aside."

"Everything we said was correct," Chester replied.

"Absolutely on the money," Brett said. "And it was crucial. Because we all needed to understand the obstacle. The reasons why nobody else ever moved on this deal."

"Five deaths," Robin said. "A bankrupt inventor. Public disgrace. Horrible publicity."

"All the reasons why everybody else has turned away," Brett agreed. "This project for all intents and purposes is not just dead. It's radio-active."

Lena watched Robin's and Chester's tension ease a notch. They accepted that Brett was not here to condemn their work.

The jet engines rumbled softly, the wind whispered. Finally Robin asked, "What did we miss?"

"I have no idea," Brett replied. "I can only make two observations. First, whatever it is, the missing key is so well hidden that no one else has managed to find it."

Chester asked, "And the second thing?"

Brett turned his chair slightly. Looked at Lena. And waited.

She spoke for the first time since sitting down. "This is an important project. And we're going to make it happen."

Chester sighed. "I totally don't get it."

Brett went on, "Forget the numbers. Throw out all the normal rules of risk analysis. From now on, we're taking a different track."

Robin's gaze reflected a growing awareness. "Because of Lena."

"Correct. We're going to trust that she has sensed another winner. She has managed to climb up and look over the barrier that has stopped everybody else in their tracks. Our job is to identify the hidden elements and then piece them together."

Chester said, "But how?"

Brett said, "Let's lay out what we know and look at it all fresh. Only this time we're already convinced. We don't need to sell this. We don't need to worry about our jobs or what anyone else thinks. Up ahead in Savannah, there's a deal waiting for us to put together. It's a good one. Our job is to find out why it's good."

"And who covered it up," Robin said.

"And what they didn't want us to discover," Lena said.

Chester looked from one to the other. "You guys are nuts." But he smiled as he spoke.

29

When Reese entered the monitoring station, Karla Brusius, her longtime aide and technical specialist, was seated before the long desk. Karla's hands rested easy on the controls, her oversized glasses slipping down her nose as she concentrated on the monitors. When she spotted Reese standing to her right, she said in greeting, "We are ready to go." Like it had been a couple of hours since their last mission. Instead of the longest and hardest fourteen months of Reese's life.

"It's good to see you," Reese said, slipping into the seat beside her.

"Kevin said he was going to try to bring you in," Karla said. "I'm glad he succeeded."

"Tell me what we've got to work with."

"The voyagers' readouts are individual now," Karla said, indicating the first row of screens on the wall directly in front of them.

"Because of the neural nets," Reese said, recalling Kevin's description.

"Correct. Each neural net has eleven microchips set at crucial points around the skull. These are calibrated so as to have maximum impact on the individual voyager's brain-wave patterns. The wave patterns identified as background noise—random thoughts and emotions—are all dampened. Those patterns identified as alpha, or related to heightened awareness and hyper-calm states, are magnified. The differences are too subtle to notice at first. Everything is computerized. There is a Cray operating behind this wall, handling the frequencies."

"I like this term *voyager*."

Karla nodded. "It seemed good to use a new term for this new method."

"How many voyagers can we work?"

"The most we have tried so far is sixteen. But I am sure we can do more."

"Can we handle more than one team at the same time?"

"Of course. Because the readouts are individually calibrated, we can split the teams however you like." Karla glanced over. "It's good Kevin brought you in. There have been . . . problems."

"That's why I'm here." Reese rose from the chair. "To make all the problems go away."

As Reese left the monitoring station, she tore the Keep Out sign off the door. The Velcro strips formed an empty black frame. She crossed the hall, signaling to the group still clustered by the coffee station. "Let's get started."

She waited until they had all entered, then dumped the sign in the wastebasket. "Anybody who wants to join us in the monitoring station during your free time, fine. My team is my team. Now take your positions."

Carl lifted his neural net. The cables dangled from his hand like rainbow worms. "I don't know . . ."

Reese lifted her chin and spoke to the ceiling. "Karla, you monitoring?"

A voice from the ceiling speakers said, "Of course."

"Come give us a hand." When Karla appeared, Reese went on, "Position Ridley and Carl together in the back right corner."

There were three rows of eight chairs each, twenty-four leather reclining dentist chairs. Each had an overhanging swivel arm attached to monitors and cable leads. Reese watched as the rest of her team slipped into their preferred spots, plugged in their neural nets, seated themselves, fitted the nets over their hair, and waited. Heather, the glassy-eyed blonde, took up a loner's position in the back left.

"Everyone has read the file on today's target, correct?" She got nods from most, though Heather turned to the side wall and sighed in mock boredom. "How have you handled probes like this in the past?"

There was a moment's silence, then one of the women said, "Two teams of four. First go, we scout the entire group. The monitor tells us to hunt for a weakness."

"That sounds solid," Reese said. There was no need to ask why Heather was not included.

She walked to the back row and waited until Karla had finished wiring in Carl's net. She did not try to hide her words. This was not about secrecy. Not yet. Clandestine actions would come later. She addressed both Carl and Ridley. "Remember what I said. You go out, you hang back, you watch. You don't take Carl any further than is comfortable for him."

When she received nods from them both, she walked back to the front and said, "Your first task is to go out safe and return the same way. Any danger, anything that unsettles, you turn back." She gave that a beat, then continued, "It may look like the same gig as yesterday. But that's just on the surface. Down deep where it counts, this is a whole new day."

Reese grabbed herself a cup of coffee as she crossed the lobby, then poured a second one for Karla. Her assistant had always taken hers with four brown sugars and a dollop of heavy cream. Reese had met inmates who replaced their drug of choice with such mixtures of fat and sweet. Reese had never thought about this before. She wondered if Karla was fighting her own secret cravings.

She passed by a trio of voyagers clustered by the monitoring station doorway. "From now on, this door is always open. You come, you go, it's your choice."

One said, "There isn't anywhere for us to sit."

"Good point. We'll change that later." Reese settled into the chair beside Karla and set her coffee on the station beside the open file. "We ready to go?"

"Green across the board." She sipped her coffee and smiled. "You remembered."

Reese took a long look around the boards and monitors and screens blanketing the front wall. Most was familiar, only far more detailed. "Tell me what's changed."

"The voyage is almost instantaneous, if they want to go at all." Karla used her cup to point out the heart rate monitors, which blipped along in red pulses. "They're all scared. Rates are higher, partly because of you and all the shifts you're making to their routine."

"And the other reason is . . ." Reese nodded when Karla's only response was to point at the monitor showing Heather's face. "Will the fear factor impact their ability to take off?"

"I told you. If they want to go, they go."

"So how do we manage the voyage?"

"We count them down. Otherwise Kevin told me to hold to the routine. Only accelerated. Five-four-three-two-one, go."

"You count them down." Reese mulled that over and decided she liked the change. It fit their purpose. Especially the pair she had just put together. "The two at the back are on their own separate channel, right?"

"The regular team is on com link one, your pair on two."

"What about Heather?"

A tremor rocked Karla's entire body, tight but visible. Coffee sloshed unnoticed over her hand. "She is linked in with team one. You didn't say you wanted her separated."

"Leave her exactly where she is."

"Heather scares me."

Reese sipped her coffee and nodded. "I understand."

"They all do. Her group, I mean."

"Probably a good thing." She had questions, but stowed them for later. "Okay. Let's do this."

30

Reese said into her mike, "Your target is a company called Kray Armor. You will begin your voyage. I will direct you with a question. The question is this: Where is their weakness? What lever can be used against the company? You will search only so far as you can and remain in total safety. You will be in complete control at all times. You have ten minutes."

Karla reached over, coded off Reese's mike, and whispered, "Kevin gives them twenty."

Reese thumbed the mike back on and repeated, "Ten minutes. We will do several quicker voyages today. The first is what we call a recce. You go, you check out the terrain, you return. Following this, we will assign specific targets." She pointed to Karla, who placed her hand on the main control. "I am starting the voyage now. Five, four, three, two, one. Go. You have ten minutes starting now."

Karla scanned the monitors, said, "All are in the green."

"I'm starting with team two." Reese tabbed the com link over and said to the pair at the back, "All right. Here we go. Carl, you are playing tagalong. Ridley, you monitor the others and you keep Carl safe.

Thumbs-up from you both to show you understand. Good." Reese sharpened her voice to the same military precision she used with team one. She gave them similar instructions, only the pair were held to an eight-minute voyage. Then she pointed to Karla and counted them up.

Then there was nothing to do but wait. Reese sipped her coffee, and in the act of setting it back on the counter, she realized what was happening behind her.

Over a dozen people were clustered by the monitoring station's rear wall. Most if not all of the off-duty teams, observing her with tense, fearful gazes.

Reese asked them, "What is going on here?"

No one spoke until Karla said, "Coming up on eight."

Reese swiveled back around, only to see the same mix of tension and dread on Karla's face. Her assistant said, "Twenty seconds."

Reese asked, "Can I speak with both teams together?"

"Com link three."

She keyed the mike and said, "I am beginning the count to end your voyage. I am counting now. One, two, three, four, five. You are back, you are safe. Welcome home."

All the monitors showed normal levels of conscious activity. The brain waves spiked, the heart and breathing lines accelerated within standard limits. There was nothing on any of the screens to indicate a reason for the tension that Reese could now almost taste.

Karla's swallow was audible. "All are back."

"Stay here. I'll check with them on results, then we'll go again."

There were so many people lining the back wall they pressed in on each other. As Reese approached the doorway, they shifted away from her and the exit, just like they had from Heather.

Reese left the monitoring station, crossed the lobby area, and entered the departures chamber. She liked the new term. Voyagers carried a sense of adventure. These were travelers who ventured into new terrain. They deserved a strong title, just like they deserved to be rewarded. They deserved . . .

Her forward momentum carried her two paces inside the chamber. But with that first look, her brain froze solid.

The voyagers remained in their seats. They stared back at the station by the left wall. All of them watched as Heather rose to her feet.

Only it was not Heather.

Reese could not say how she knew this. Even so, she was absolutely certain. At the level of bone and sinew, she knew. Some ancient awareness had been triggered, some genetic recognition she carried from the epoch of cave dwellings and medicine men and monsters cast in nighttime shadows. Heather was gone. In her place was something else.

The beast wearing Heather's skin arched her back, the muscles on her neck standing out like steel cords. She opened and closed her mouth several times, an almost reptilian move. Tasting the air. Savoring this glimpse into a world filled with prey.

And that was precisely how the beast eyed the others. The lips peeled back and the teeth clicked twice. Snap-snap, very quick, hungry and alert. The predator was in the open now. Sizing up which quarry to take down first.

Reese was not fully aware of moving. Only that her view of this beast shifted. Drew closer. She stationed herself between the beast and her team.

Her team.

The beast was clearly unused to human eyesight. The eyes did not track together. The voice was the most un-Heather component of her, a lyrical chant laced by an accent from some distant epoch. "Are you coming to join us too?"

"You are not welcome here."

The sense of facing a reptile grew stronger still, as the beast twisted its neck, the jaw fashioning a slow curve as the tongue darted out once, twice, a third time. The chant carried the rattle of leaves over an open grave. "But we would welcome you."

"Go and do not return."

A smile flickered in and out, fast as the darting tongue. "Shall I eat some of your precious others? Will you behave then?"

"Show up here again," Reese said, "and I will personally murder this woman and her entire team."

The neck arched again, the throat rasped, and only later did Reese realize that the beast had actually laughed. Then Heather gave a massive shudder, like she was being pulled apart at the seams.

And she was back. Just like that. The brittle smile, the dead eyes, the shellacked hair, all of it came together again and reformed into the woman.

Heather smiled at all of the petrified forms and said, "Isn't this fun?"

Reese took a moment to prepare her next move. Heather assumed the silence was due to fear and preened for the watchers. Reese stifled an urge to rip her apart. She took a steadying breath, then said calmly, "Everybody get ready for a second go. Same as the first, general observations only." She looked over at Ridley and Carl. "Everything okay?"

"He did good," Ridley replied.

"We'll debrief after round two. We voyage in ten minutes."

But as she left the departures lounge, a woman by the door said softly, "What you said to the monster, it won't make any difference."

Reese gestured for the woman to accompany her. When they were away from the others, Reese asked, "Does this happen every time? Not just with Heather, but the others, do they also . . ."

"I know what you mean." The woman was not just slight but frail, with birdlike limbs and a voice that probably had not once shouted in her entire life. "They're all the same."

Reese felt the cold rage surge through her once more. It was an aboriginal response, straight from gut to claws. "Look at me." When the woman lifted her gaze, Reese said, "Nothing is the same around here. They just don't know it yet."

31

Lena had asked Chester to arrange a meeting with the disgraced inventor before they left the First American building. As the jet touched down at the Savannah/Hilton Head airport, Lena asked Robin to call the former surgeon and reconfirm their appointment. They had an hour and a half before he could see them, so Lena guided them to an airport Starbucks and paid for four coffees. The golfers traveling to and from Hilton Head were affluent and ruddy-faced and loud enough to keep Lena's team from being overheard.

Brett sat with his back to the terminal and the crowds. "Let's review what we know and try to identify what we're missing. Dr. Bernard Bishop, aged sixty-six. Tulane undergrad, University of Miami medical school. Specialized in orthopedic surgery at Chicago. Married to the same woman for twenty-one years, then lost her to cancer eleven years ago. Two grown children, one living in Chicago, the other in upstate New York. Three grandchildren. Until this all blew up, Dr. Bishop was considered one of the nation's best spine doctors. His primary focus was the neck."

Robin added, "Specifically, the craniocervical junction, where the skull meets the spine. And the foramen magnum, where the brain and the spinal cord join."

Chester picked up with, "He was the on-call specialist for all the pro football teams in the southeast. Handled injuries to the cervical spine, vertebrae numbered C1 through C7. Did groundbreaking research and repair to the atlas, the first cervical bone. The atlas plays a crucial role in supporting the skull. It articulates with the occipital bone."

"Some say Bishop was the top neck guy in the world," Brett went on. "He was a senior surgeon here in Savannah and maintained a connection to the Mayo Clinic in Jacksonville. He kept residences in both cities, but his home has been here since he left Chicago. To be kept on by the Mayo for thirty-seven years tells us all we need to know about this guy's abilities as a surgeon."

Lena liked how he talked without referring to notes. Brett's hands rested lightly on the file's cover. He spoke conversationally, reviewing the work of allies. She asked, "Do you have an eidetic memory?"

He smiled and nodded, as though approving of her using the proper word, *eidetic*. "Not exactly. I read your combined reports three times. That's enough." He turned back to the duo and went on, "Like a lot of top guys, Bishop maintained a voracious hunger to grow and research and delve further. It's the trait of many highly intelligent and successful medical specialists. They spend their entire lives pushing against the boundaries of their chosen fields. In Bishop's case, he ventured into the area where brain surgery meets neuroscience."

"Brain waves," Robin said. "Neural mapping. Emotional trigger points. Where memories are held."

"Seven years of study," Chester said. "Numerous professional papers, plus more he coauthored on injuries to the brain stem."

Robin said, "I spoke with an editor at the journal where Bishop regularly published. She described Bishop's disgrace as a loss to the entire field."

"Neural mapping took off about eight years ago," Brett continued.

"Bishop started delving into this about a year later. The key was applying new methods of brain scanning."

Lena asked, "This is your field?"

"Not directly. But I have kept informed. Every neuroscientist does. They don't have any choice." Brett lifted one hand and gave a little wave. Putting that aside. "I'll give you the breakdown later. Right now, what's important is this. In the past seven years, more progress has been made on neural mapping than in all the rest of history combined. The breakthroughs in scanning technology have given us a Hubble telescope all our very own. Bishop was involved in this. He probably saw it as a natural fit, because the same improvements in scanning have helped spine surgeons immensely. Which brings us to the reason we're here."

"Three years ago, Bishop took it one step further," Robin said. "He became an inventor."

"First he retired from Mayo, freeing up three days each week," Chester corrected. "Then he started his very own garage company."

"Actually, he bought a defunct lab across the street from Savannah General," Robin said.

"And Bishop knew from that very first moment he was on to something big," Brett said.

Robin nodded in time to Brett's finger taps on the analysis cover. "He hired two research postgrads, an electronic engineer, two lab assistants, and a business manager. He invested virtually all his savings. He remortgaged his home. He promised his employees a cut of any profits. But he kept hold of all the company shares. He wouldn't take such a risk unless he was confident of a big payout."

"Sixteen months later, he comes out with the neural net," Chester said. "A cross between a helmet and a flexible webbing. With electrodes fitted in the same pattern as used to measure EKGs. But with a difference."

"He wasn't after measurement," Robin said. "Bishop intended to stimulate the brain."

"Specific areas of the brain," Chester said.

"Directing small electromagnetic impulses at problem areas," Robin said.

"And the neural net can be programmed to aim these impulses at different areas," Chester added. "Depending upon what health issue they are addressing."

"Because the net is imbedded with microchips that both monitor and stimulate," Robin said. "This was the breakthrough. This was what took Bishop's invention to a totally new level."

Brett leaned back and crossed his arms. He glanced over at Lena and smiled. The professor was clearly pleased with his students.

Robin and Chester both noticed the change. It freed them up, allowed them to accelerate. They were on a roll. More than that. They were taking aim.

"The initial results were totally off the charts," Robin said.

"Bishop's device showed amazing abilities to stimulate a whole host of neurochemicals," Chester said. "Serotonin, beta-endorphin, amino acids linked to logic and analytical thought processes and memories."

"Totally noninvasive. Seen as a low-risk treatment option. It could work on multiple symptoms at the same time."

"Insomnia, anxiety, mental disorders, motor-neuron ailments, epilepsy, even migraines."

"He ran initial tests with volunteers at Savannah General. This was what—two and a half years prior to his formal trials in Mexico and Italy? He worked exclusively with near-death patients who had given up all hope, with the permission of the hospital's directors and the patients and their families. He focused on illnesses where there was no known cure. He even had some preliminary indications that the device could stimulate the healing of injured nerves."

There was a silence. Lena could see the same thought reflected on both faces.

Finally Robin said, "Five deaths."

Chester said, "The hospital had no choice. Bishop was sacked."

"The FDA determined that such a noninvasive device was not strictly required to have been licensed. They did not pursue charges. The medical board followed the FDA's guidelines. Still, no hospital would ever give him another chance. He was bankrupt, disgraced, and reduced to working as a GP in an urgent-care clinic."

Chester frowned at his coffee. Sipped. Frowned some more. "I just don't get it."

Brett's smile grew broader.

Robin asked, "Don't get what?"

"This guy is the best. He doesn't make mistakes. That's what rules a surgeon's life, right? One false move, one slip of the knife, and his patient never stands up again or feeds themselves. He has to be right the first time, every time. Bishop has made a lifetime of right moves." Chester shook his head. "This doesn't add up."

Brett took a long breath. Stood up. Said to the table, "Exactly."

32

They walked around to the main passenger terminal and took a taxi because Lena did not want them arriving in a limo. She assumed they would need two vehicles, because there was no way for the four of them to be comfortable in one standard cab. But the first taxi in line was a battered minivan, and the wizened driver grinned at their approach and declared, "Y'all best know it's your lucky day, now."

"I sure hope you're right," Lena said.

"Yes, ma'am, I just saved you folks either some sweat or some cash, one or t'other. Ain't another cab in the rank that'll take four passengers without y'all showing up wrinkled and hot." He cackled as he gimped around to the back and opened the door and lifted in their carry-ons. Three of them carried overnight cases they had learned to keep by their desks. The driver grinned at Brett's hands, empty of all save the well-thumbed analysis. "Got caught out, did you?"

"More than you'll ever know," Brett agreed.

The driver laughed. "Hop on in."

The weather was Georgia springtime, humid and clear. Lena tasted a faint hint of salt through the driver's open window and knew a sudden longing for home. Orlando was as far from the ocean as one could get on the Florida peninsula, but on days when the wind blew strong off the Atlantic, the air tasted just like this, a citified mixture overlaid by the sea.

The driver left highway 16 at the 167A exit and entered old-town Savannah. Then he turned south, away from the tourist district, and drove down Montgomery. Ten blocks later he took a side street to Martin Luther King, then turned right again and continued south. The area was not bad, mostly mid-level commercial structures. But the side streets held the sort of shadows that would grow increasingly unwelcome the closer they moved to sunset. When Lena met the driver's gaze in the rearview mirror, he asked, "You sure you want to go there?"

"Yes."

"They's two clinics uptown, they got everything you need. They's set up to help the tourists."

"This one is fine."

He shrugged and did not speak again. Seven blocks later he turned into a low-rent commercial mall holding a payday loans, a dentist advertising in Spanish, a bagel shop, a bar, and a consignment store. The urgent-care clinic occupied most of the second floor.

The elevator was scarred with graffiti and stank. They took the stairs. The upstairs walkway was open to the late afternoon. A half-dozen men lined the balcony, watching the traffic and talking softly. They went silent as Lena's team passed and entered the clinic.

She gave her name to the attendant and joined the others at the back of the waiting area. Somewhere beyond the entrance to the examination rooms, a baby wailed. The patients and families were mostly dark, the features weathered by hard lives. Lena and her team could not have been more out of place with their business suits and their cases. They waited in silence for fifteen minutes, then a nurse opened the door and invited them back.

The examination chambers were curtained alcoves that faced a central hallway. Lena had seen similar systems in hospital emergency rooms. The nurse led them to a room at the end of the hall that was clearly shared by all the doctors. Four desks with computer terminals lined the walls. A young man with a clinician's white coat and tired eyes sat at the room's far end, eating from a plastic container of salad. He wore headphones and watched a reality show on his computer. He glanced over when they entered, then went back to his salad and the show. Clearly their business attire did not impress him.

Ten minutes passed. Lena stared at a calendar ad for a drug she'd never heard of and mentally prepped. Then the door opened, and a stocky man with a salt-and-pepper crew cut hurried in. He gave them a cursory inspection, then walked over and poked the other doctor in the shoulder. When the younger man slipped off his headphones, the newcomer said, "Give us a minute, will you?"

"No problem."

"Ask the others to stay out." He waited until the door closed, then said, "You have cards?"

Lena had one ready. Bernard Bishop was short and bullish and worn down. Bishop did not appear weary so much as defeated. As though he was propelled forward by a natural momentum, even when most of the man was long gone. His gaze was hollow, his voice toneless as he said, "What's First American doing buying the debts of a bankrupt doctor?"

"We're not here about your debts."

"Whatever you want, you've come to the wrong place. My attorneys have laid it all out. I've walked away from the chapter eleven—"

"Dr. Bishop, we need to talk with you about your invention."

He actually winced. Lena's words carried the power to fold him up, like a boxer protecting a broken rib. "Not again."

"Sir, can we please sit down?" When he looked ready to argue, she added, "You really want to hear what we have to say."

"I can give you ten minutes. I only get half an hour for dinner and I haven't eaten since this morning. Then I'm back on shift."

They pulled swivel chairs from various desks and seated themselves. Bernard Bishop remained isolated by choice, backed away from the four of them. Lena waited until she had as tight a lock on his attention as he could manage, then replied, "Sir, we are here to buy eighty percent of your company."

33

Bernard Bishop squinted at her, struggling to understand. Lena had the impression of watching a highly intelligent man trying to recall a language he had learned once but had now forgotten.

He said, "Come again?"

"Eighty percent of all remaining assets," Lena said.

He ran his left hand through the greying stubble. "Young lady . . ."

Brett said, "Her name is Lena Fennan."

The doctor had grey eyes rimmed by the dark caverns of countless broken nights. "You don't have a card?"

"My name is Brett Riffkind. Neuroscientist."

The gaze sharpened. "On faculty?"

"University of California. On secondment for the past three years."

"With the bank?" He did not actually sneer his opinion of that shift.

"Only for the past two days. I've been working with an international team on a new concept."

"Brett serves as our scientific consultant," Lena said.

The grey gaze remained locked on Brett. "What concept is this?"

"One that runs parallel to your own work, Dr. Bishop."

This time the wince was a mere flicker around the eyes. "You know there's nothing left."

Brett did not respond.

"It's gone. Seven and a half years of work. Not to mention my reputation and my rights to perform surgery. Gone." He turned back to Lena. He appeared angry now, resenting how she had brought the most unexpected news of all. A reason to hope. A false reason. It had to be. His gaze said it all. "There's nothing left. Not even for you vultures."

"All your assets," Lena repeated. "All your research. Everything."

He sat and smoldered.

"Name your price," Lena said.

"Get out," Bishop said. Too weary to even push hard.

In reply, Lena lifted her phone from her purse. "The bank's senior attorney is waiting for my call. The papers establishing our LLC have been prepared. Assuming one of these computers is yours, we will have the documents sent directly here. We will locate a notary and seal the deal. Tonight. But first we need to know your price. For your assets. Your research. And one hundred percent of your time." Lena gave the room a cursory glance. "Because you're leaving here and you're never coming back."

Bishop swallowed. "Time to do what?"

"That should be obvious," Lena replied. "Complete your work on the neural net. Bring it to market."

His mouth worked, but no sound emerged.

Lena took her cue from their conversation on the plane. She liked Brett's calm way of fashioning the impossible into reality. Time was pressing on them, so she had to be direct. She did not know why her temporal self had insisted on speed. At this point, she did not need to know more than that the deal had to be done.

Today.

When it was clear Bishop could not actually frame the protest, she said it for him. "We need to address the issue of the five deaths."

Bishop might have nodded. Or it could have been a shudder.

Lena forced herself to meet his gaze, though the pain in his eyes was hard to endure. "We are working on the . . ."

"Evidence," Brett supplied. "Incomplete, but strong."

She shot him a look of gratitude. She saw that Robin and Chester were both confused and unsettled by his choice of words. But that could not be helped. Lena went on, "Certain new evidence that has come to light. It has given us a strong indication that your device was not actually responsible for those deaths."

He touched the collar to his open shirt with fingers that trembled slightly. "How can this be?"

Lena shifted a fraction closer. "Sir, I cannot go into detail just now because we are under considerable pressure. But you need to understand. We need to complete this process immediately."

"But . . . why?"

Brett shifted forward. He moved a fraction to his left. Closing the distance between his chair and Lena's. It was just the two of them now. "Dr. Bishop, we need to assume that from this point on, we are going to be tracked and monitored."

A trace of fear flickered through Lena's gut, like lightning beyond the horizon. A faint rumble of thunder, easily missed. Unless she was listening for it.

Brett went on, "If we are correct, your opponents have murdered five innocent trial subjects. They want this idea of yours buried. They may still be watching you. We need to know how much you would require to sell—"

"Don't you understand? There isn't anything left!"

Lena waited him out, then persisted, "Sir, I need you to tell us how much you want in order to fully commit. How much for you to resume your work?"

Brett added, "How much will satisfy you, not today, but in five years' time? So that you will remain our ally and partner for the long haul."

When Bishop remained unable to respond, Lena offered the figure she had decided upon. "I would like to suggest that we settle on a million dollars. Half now. Tonight. Half in six months' time, once certain parameters are met regarding your progress."

The strain of hoping again left him hoarse. "This is real? You're not . . ."

"Real enough for Ms. Fennan to commit a million dollars of her own money," Brett replied. "Do you accept?"

He looked from one to the other, back and forth several times, the doctor dealing with the impossible. Life drawn from the ashes. Breath returning to the cadaver. Right before his eyes.

Bishop asked, "Who would do such a thing? Murder five innocents?"

Lena replied, "We're working on that."

After the legal documents were prepared by the bank's New York attorneys and sent down and printed, Lena split her team in two. She walked Bernard Bishop through the contracts, with Brett at her side to answer any specifically scientific questions and to ask a few of his own.

Robin and Chester prepped. They hunted down a midsized truck for sale and arranged to meet the seller the next day. Lena insisted on an outright purchase of the vehicle, rather than going for a rental, because she did not want a record of where they took Bishop and his work.

Robin then booked Lena and Brett on the evening flight back to New York. Chester located a branch of Bernard Bishop's bank that remained open late. He confirmed that the branch manager was also a notary public and would be on hand to witness documents they were bringing with them. They ordered two taxis, which were hard to find this far from Savannah's tourist districts and richer commercial areas. They booked three rooms in a lovely boutique hotel located on the city's most beautiful square. They wrote out a series of terse letters, whereby Bernard Bishop resigned from his duties at the clinic and ended his apartment lease. Bishop watched them with the unblinking intensity of a man unable to digest what he was experiencing, yet determined to remember every single tiny fragment.

The five of them took the taxis to the bank, where Lena introduced herself to the branch manager. The bank was modest and clean and intended to suit their mostly lower-middle-class customers. The manager was clearly not accustomed to dealing with a dark-suited New York executive who wrote out a half-million-dollar check on the countertop.

Brett stood back, as though isolating himself by intention. Lena had the distinct impression that he wanted to say something. She saw him study his watch, not just look at the time and glance away, but rather peer intently, measuring how much time they had before they left for the airport. She started to ask what it was, but decided this was not the place.

The waiting taxis drove them to a local self-storage. Lena used her phone during the drive to order a third cab to meet them. She shared her taxi with Robin and Bishop. The former surgeon directed them down a faceless line of metal-doored units. When he rose from the taxi, Bishop moved like an old man. He unlocked the door, then allowed Chester and Brett to lift the portal. He stood staring at the boxes, then said, "I haven't been here since I moved everything in."

The crates and cases formed a neat floor-to-ceiling U with a tight walking space down the center. Even in ruination and woe, the doctor had maintained his precision.

"Do you know where everything is?" she asked.

"I do. Yes."

"Point out the items that are irreplaceable. We'll take those with us. As many as we can."

Robin asked, "Is that really necessary?"

"I hope not," Lena replied. "Hurry."

Brett said, "We also need several fully functioning neural nets we can take with us back to New York."

"Each headset has to be calibrated to the individual user," Bishop replied. "I keep wondering if this was what caused the casualties, some mistake in my algorithms . . ."

"To repeat," Brett said, "neither your equipment nor the process killed those patients."

Bishop clearly wanted to believe, but couldn't. He indicated two boxes. "Six fully tested neural nets and a laptop with the software to calibrate. A notebook outlines the step-by-step calibration process. Perhaps I should mark it with a skull and crossbones."

They all pitched in, carrying cases and files and monitors and laptops and hard drives and neural nets from the unit to the taxis. They filled the three trunks and the rear seat of the third taxi. Finally Bishop said, "Those are the most critical components."

"Let's go," Lena said.

"Just a minute," Brett said. He stepped into the unit and motioned for the others to join him. When they were all inside, he told Chester, "Shut the door."

Lena asked, "What's going on?"

"This won't take long." When they were sealed in, the dusty air felt much tighter. The overhead fluorescents cast them in stark lines, creating dark crevices where they had pried away various boxes.

Brett looked at Bishop and said, "There's something you haven't been telling us."

Robin showed round eyes. "Now you're asking?"

"This isn't about danger," Brett replied. "Well, not directly. This is about data. The intel that isn't in your records. Is it, Dr. Bishop."

The man's gaze clarified for the first time since their arrival. He backed up until he touched the side crates.

Brett remained stationed by the opposite wall. There was nothing accusatory about his tone or his stance. Nothing to suggest why Bishop looked so terrified.

"Tell me about the subjects who were expunged," Brett said.

Bishop's mouth worked a few times before he managed, "How did you know?"

34

Reese walked down the conference area's long, broad corridor. She wore Ferragamo lace-ups, soft as sneakers. With each step, Reese punched the floor with her heel, thrusting her body from her foot all the way to her opposite shoulder. She knew it caused her hips to swing suggestively. She knew most of the guys were fascinated with her walk. She took it slow, a measured pace. Prison had taught her a whole cluster of new tricks. This was one nugget that had always served her well when working through a dangerous rage.

By the time she arrived at the reception desk, Reese was able to smile at the young man now on duty. He must have seen something in her gaze, because he started to rise and back away, but she said, "You're cool. I just need to have a word with security."

She stood where the camera could see her. When the guards made her wait, Reese resisted the urge to pound on the door. She knew it was the subtle message of security everywhere to the newbie. They weren't impressed, and they weren't going to jump to do her bidding.

When the buzzer finally sounded, Reese entered the security station and demanded, "Who's the senior duty officer?"

The guy who had showed her the baton raised a languid hand. "That would be me."

"Call Kevin. Ask him to clarify what he meant when he said my words and his carried the same weight."

The guy shifted uncomfortably in his seat. "Uh, that isn't necessary."

"What happens the next time I show up?"

He glanced at the woman seated next to him. "I buzz you in."

"Without delay."

"Right."

"Fun and games are . . ."

"Over."

"Just so we're clear."

The guy and the woman both nodded. In sync now. "Crystal."

"Good." Reese knew her smile carried a special menace. One powerful enough to make even a professional guard wince. "Sign me out a set of weapons."

⫚

Reese's return to the monitoring station played like a tune from the Pied Piper's flute. Even more team members shifted forward. Reese did not give any sign that she noticed them. She asked Karla, "Another coffee?"

"Please."

As Reese slipped back through the crowd, a waifish woman said, "We're supposed to shift teams after each voyage."

Reese waited until she had prepared two mugs to reply. "New game, new rules. We're still doing a preliminary recce. It will speed things up for the same crew to go again." Like nothing had happened. Like nothing was going to change. Just another day at the office.

She set the coffee on the panel in front of Karla and asked, "Everyone in place?"

"Except Heather. She says she needs to rest." Karla pointed to one of the wall monitors. "Esteban is her replacement."

Esteban observed the camera with a dark intensity, like he knew Reese was watching and he intended to crawl through the lens and devour her. Reese was not concerned that Heather had traded places with this guy. What was important was that one of the midnight crew was present. She asked, "Are we still using the same com links?"

Karla nodded. "One for the voyage team, two for your pair."

The communications lever was a narrow plastic tab set on a swivel. Etched into the surrounding metal was a ring of numbers: 1, 2, 3, 1&2, 1&3, and so forth. Reese keyed in the second link and said to Ridley and Carl, "It's the same as the last run. I'll count you down after the others. Once you're out there, stand back and observe."

Like most of the voyagers, Ridley and Carl wore high-end earbuds with the mike imbedded in the cord. A few wore over-ear headsets, Reese assumed because they wanted to be as cut off from the others as possible, even while still anchored.

Ridley said, "We got this."

"I know you do." Reese switched to com link one and went on, "Your objective is the same as last time. The target is Kray Armor, its owners and board of directors and senior executives. You are to make a general sweep of the terrain. You have ten minutes. You will stay safe at all times."

From the monitoring station's back wall, the small woman said, "Staying safe out there isn't the issue."

Karla started to turn around and snap at her, but Reese cut the com link and whispered, "Stay cool." When she was certain Karla was under control, Reese tabbed back to com link one and said, "I'm starting the count now."

The very instant Reese completed her return count, she was up and moving. She did not wait to hear from Karla that the voyagers were all safely back. Just then she had more important things on her mind.

As she passed the voyagers clustered along the back wall, Reese gripped the two closest by their shirts and swung them about. "Everybody come with me. Quick march."

She entered the departures lounge just as the first voyagers were opening their eyes. Reese positioned herself by the front wall, directly before Esteban's station. She lifted her sweatshirt and pulled the baton from where it had been digging into her back. She palmed the weapon, keeping it out of sight. And she waited.

Esteban's eyes shot open.

This was a very different beast from the one that had returned with Heather. Reese was confronted by two distinct images. One was of a body that unwound from the seat like a feral cat coming out of slumber. She watched the snarl, the delicious breath, the raised nostrils drawing in the scent of fresh prey. And still she waited.

The voyagers' collective fear was palpable. The beast emanated a putrid menace, strong as the stench of a fresh kill. Reese watched Esteban crouch and study her, the head swiveling slightly, side to side, taking her in with each eye. The sense of facing a reptile was even stronger than with Heather, as if the creature was unaccustomed to a head where both eyes faced directly forward.

The second image was unseen but just as clear as the physical. Reese was so amped she had time to examine herself as well as the fiend. She felt no fear this time. She was the hunter. The unexpected foe. And she was going to take this brute down.

The unseen beast was huge. She could sense the air shift as it hunched one shoulder and then the other, a carnivore limbering up before the strike. Esteban's body mimicked the greater force, a caricature of what Reese witnessed. The beast was so large it touched the ceiling.

Reese stepped forward and snapped the baton out to full length.

Esteban snarled a feral welcome.

Reese jammed the baton's tip into his chest and hit the button.

The zap was wicked, loud as a silenced pistol. The air was filled with the stench of burned clothes and skin.

Esteban spasmed so hard he flung himself into a backflip. Still the spasm clutched him, a puppet jerked by uneven strings. His head did a snare-drum rattle against the tiled floor.

Reese stepped up close and leaned over, getting down so close she was the only thing Esteban could see when his vision cleared. He blinked once, twice, and groaned. Esteban was fully back now, and seriously rocked by the electrocution.

Reese stabbed him again and hit the button. Right in the solar plexus. Hard enough to punch the wind from his body.

Esteban came back much more slowly. She was closer now, so tight she could dine upon the terror in his gaze. Reese settled the baton on his left cheek. Rubbed it up and down slowly. "You want more?"

Esteban whimpered and tried to push her hand away.

Reese used her free hand to slap his away. Then she positioned the baton's tip directly between his eyes. "I asked you a question."

"No, no, don't, I'm begging . . ." Esteban choked on fear and went still.

Reese used her free hand to slip the pistol from beneath her sweat-shirt. The guard had given her a Steyr, a sweet little 90 mil. The grip was small enough to fit her hand like it was made for her. The gun was not cocked, but Reese doubted Esteban was in any position to notice such minor details. She held the gun a few inches away from his face so he could inspect the gaping barrel. "Pay careful attention. I have a message I want you to pass on to all your little friends. Tell me you're listening."

"Yes, yes, don't—"

"If you or any of your buddies ever let one of those beasts into my departures lounge again, I will fry you until your heart stops. Then I'm going to hunt down the others. And I'm going to shoot them all dead. The same goes if any of my team don't make it back." Reese straightened slowly. She kept the gun aimed at Esteban, letting him drown in the black circle pointed at his face. "You breathe only so long as they stay safe. Tell me you understand."

The eyes were liquid with terror. Reese wondered if he had ever known fear before. It left him unable to rise an inch off the floor. "Sí . . . yes."

Gun in one hand, baton in the other, Reese walked over to where the others clustered by the exit. Then she turned back and said, "These are my voyagers. This is my team."

35

Reese left the departures lounge while Esteban was still prostrate and groaning on the floor. She assembled the team that had just gone out in the departures lounge. She took their report, thanked them, and said she had to deliver their findings. She left her weapons at the guards' station, then crossed the parking lot and entered the glass cube.

Kevin needed exactly two seconds to recognize the change. "What's wrong?"

Her response carried a confrontational edge, but she couldn't do anything about it. Reese expected Kevin to protest over how she had attacked one of the midnight crew. She hoped she could hold back and not blast him with the rage she struggled to keep suppressed. But within the space of five sentences, she realized that Kevin was neither sorry nor surprised.

When she was done, they sat there listening to the traffic rumble below his window. Finally Reese said, "You knew."

"Everybody knew. But we finally started getting the intel demanded by Vera. Plus there were no more coma victims among the voyagers.

And the ones who had been lost were all brought back. So the answer is, sure we knew, and we made do because we didn't have any choice." The old worry crimped the edges of his mouth and eyes. "I debated telling you. But I didn't want you to be confined by my own sense of helplessness."

Reese felt her emotions slowly drain down to a smoldering residue. "Nothing could have prepared me for what just happened."

His chair squeaked as he rocked back and forth, like he was sharing her own aftershocks. "We have to report in."

"You do it."

"No problem. Just tell me what you've uncovered."

She passed over the file with her handwritten notes, then gave him a summary. Kevin's chair continued to squeak as he listened and read. The conference table between them was dominated by a bulky speakerphone. The phone had a central mound the size and shape of an inverted snow cone. Seven lights blinked in frantic disarray. The device scrambled the outgoing signal and scanned constantly for listening devices. Their signal could only be interpreted by a matching phone on the other side. According to Kevin, a set of two calibrated phones retailed for eleven thousand dollars. The phone bore a corporate logo from the company they had been ordered to investigate.

When she completed her report, Kevin reached across the table, then hesitated, his hand upon the phone. "You did good, Reese."

"We're still faced with how to shield our voyagers."

He hit speed dial and replied, "You'll find a way. I'm certain of that now."

Kevin said to the speakerphone situated between them, "The board of Kray Armor, your target company, is squeaky clean. The same goes for their senior executives."

Vera's voice was crystal clear. There was none of the electronic distortion caused by most scrambling devices. "I'm waiting to hear what we use for an in. That is the only satisfactory answer here."

Kray Armor had been supplying Kevlar-style vests to police forces for two decades. Then four years back, they had designed a new product that was woven, reducing weight by ninety percent. Equally important, the vests became flexible. It could be shaped into true body armor, covering the upper arms, lower torso, and thighs, with an optional helmet shaped like a hoodie. Kray's turnover increased by eleven hundred percent. They were cash-rich and cautious. Four months back, they had acquired the nation's leading manufacturer of night scopes and laser sights.

Kevin said, "I have reviewed the intel gathered by Reese's team. She has made astonishing progress. I can find no—"

Vera cut in, "Reese using you as a cheerleader does not make this report acceptable."

Reese and Kevin exchanged a look across the conference table. Kevin sat with his back to the sunlit highway. "Give us a minute." He reached out and hit the mute button. "You notice anything different?"

Reese said, "She's not gloating over our apparent failure."

Kevin nodded. "I actually think she's nervous."

"Someone is monitoring her."

"That someone may actually be there in the room." He reached forward, hit the button, and said, "We did discover one thing. It's not an actual opening so much as an alternative take on the company's overall status."

"We're listening."

She and Kevin flashed another look across the table. *We.* Kevin said, "There's an issue regarding the ownership of their latest acquisition."

There was the sound of pages being turned. "Beadle Scopes."

"Reese has reformed the team. They have taken our work here to a completely different level, and done so in a matter of—"

"Skip the compliments," Vera said. "Get to the meat."

"John Beadle sold out because he doesn't trust his son," Kevin said.

"Which is wise, because according to what Reese's team has uncovered, Roger Beadle couldn't run a taco stand. He remains a member of society only because his juvie records have been sealed. For the past eight years, ever since he turned eighteen, he has lived in Australia, from where he supposedly runs Beadle's Far East office."

"Supposedly," Vera repeated.

"Correct. More capable people do all the heavy lifting. Roger's job is basically to stay out of trouble."

There was the sound of more pages turning. "Our records show Beadle Jr. is clean."

"Roger is anything but clean. He's just learned to hide his dark side. He's joined up with a local syndicate. They serve as a conduit for the Beadle products, reselling them for huge profits to paramilitary organizations and blacklisted governments. And now they're doing the same for Kray. Roger Beadle is his father's only living heir, who now owns a twenty-two percent share in Kray. Beadle Sr. is the second largest shareholder after the Kray family trust."

Vera went quiet.

Kevin's cadence slowed. Each thought carrying surgical precision. "The problem is, we're not sure how much of a lever this gives us. If Reese goes in and divulges this information, they all risk being brought up on federal charges. Every member of the board and every employee with prior knowledge would be facing serious jail time."

Vera did not respond.

"Say you send Reese in to address the Kray board. They might give us a onetime payment just to shut us up. But Roger Beadle is a rogue element. Kray bought into this company. It's not like we've discovered an inside problem."

Vera said, "Stay on the line." There was a sharp click, then nothing but the scrambler's muted whisper.

Kevin said, "She's discussing this with somebody else."

Reese kept her fists jammed to her gut, trying to still the creepy-crawlies. "Yes."

"So what—"

The line clicked again, and Vera said, "We'll take it from here." There was a single pop, sharp as a silenced gunshot. All the lights along the central cone went red.

Kevin said, "I think we just hit their button."

Reese returned from Kevin's office to her apartment and put on her training gear. She took the stairs to the basement gym, where she found Ridley working out while Carl sat on a weight bench. Reese liked how Carl met her eye, liked even better how he nodded a greeting.

Reese started her routine. It had been developed to fit a nine-by-eleven cage. She knew she could take up more space. But just then the important thing was to burn off the aftereffects. She felt tired and jittery, her muscles firing to a random pattern. She ignored the two other people. The room did not exist. There was nothing here but the invisible bars, the confines that still held her. She was going to break free. That or die trying. It was only a matter of time.

When she finished, Reese settled onto the mat, breathing hard. Ridley reached into the basket by the water fountain and tossed Reese a towel. Then she stationed herself by the wall, over next to where Carl still sat. "You did solid up there."

Carl said, "The voyagers are going to put your name in lights."

Reese used the towel to wipe her face. "You know I'm not after that."

Ridley felt comfortable enough to sit cross-legged on the mat by Carl's bench. "So what is it you want from us?"

"Three things now, one later. First, we need to find a way to anchor the voyagers without risking those beasts taking over."

Ridley did not so much nod as rock her upper body. "That's one."

"We are paid to find vulnerabilities in certain corporations. We keep doing our job, else the money faucet gets cut off and we're shut down."

"That's two."

Reese leaned forward. "Number three has to stay just between us."

Ridley responded by walking over and locking the door. Then she returned to the mat beside Carl's bench. "We're listening."

Reese told them, "We need to discover who is running this gig."

"You don't know?"

"I have a cutout named Vera. She's put me and Kevin in place. As far as the outside world is concerned, we're in complete control. But Vera fronts a group intent on remaining totally hidden. They are pulling our strings from the shadows."

Carl said, "They'll be watching and waiting to see if we go after them."

"That's right. They will."

"So we need to develop some stealth tactics." Ridley glanced at the big man. "Long as you got my back."

Carl shrugged. "That's my job."

Ridley offered him a fist. "Way to rock and roll, partner."

Carl studied the fist like he had never seen one before. Or at least never been offered one like this. Finally he lifted his own fist, held it an inch or so away from Ridley's. Ridley knocked him from the top, bottom, then straight on. When she turned back, Carl might have smiled.

Ridley asked, "So what's number four?"

"I told you. That's for later."

"When you trust us, right?"

"No, Ridley. I trust you now. With my life. But the last thing has to wait until we start extending ourselves further."

"I can dig that. Taking things to the limit."

"I'm not so sure there are any. Limits, I mean." Reese scrubbed her face again with the towel, anything to release some of the electric frisson. "But first we need to work out some form of a shield that doesn't rely on the midnight crew."

Ridley started rocking again. "You're thinking those four, sooner or later they're going off the reservation again."

"I know they will. It's only a matter of time."

"And when they do, you're going to take them down."

Reese did not reply.

"Well, you can count me in." Ridley glanced up. "Right, partner?"

"I'm only on day two and I'm already done with that group," Carl said.

Reese slid across the mat, moving closer. "Now start at the beginning and tell me everything that's happened since your first voyage."

36

"Outlier data is inevitable," Brett told the surgeon. "Run any experiment long enough, and there will always be measurements that don't fit logically within the research parameters. Scientists are human and their experiments are not perfect. So once in a while we are forced to deal with data that makes no sense. Either they file this away in a footnote, or they risk demolishing their experiment."

Bishop touched the open collar of his frayed shirt, the place where the knot of his tie would have been. Lena assumed it was a habit he had gained during his days and weeks and months in court. The surgeon opened his mouth as though he wanted to object, but no sound emerged.

Brett continued, "There was something special about your outlier data. It probably happened just once at first. If there had been several identical results, you would have been forced to include it. No matter how ridiculous, how bizarre, how insane. Then later it happened again. And a third time."

Lena enjoyed watching Brett. In moments like this, his intelligent magnetism was so powerful she could ignore the warning tingles in her gut. The ones that whispered about heartache to come. The guy, she realized, was born to challenge and inspire others.

Bishop said hoarsely, "And a fourth. And a fifth."

Brett nodded slowly, on the doctor's wavelength. "But you were already into human trials, weren't you. So the question was, what should you do? And the facts were crystal clear. These outlier events did not impact the data you were collecting. The subjects who had these experiences, they still recorded the same improvements to the problems that had brought them into your trial."

The doctor's right hand scrambled across the cardboard box next to him. The tremors were more pronounced as he asked a second time, "Did I kill them?"

"If what I suspect happens, your outlier events had nothing whatsoever to do with their deaths," Brett replied.

"How can you be so certain?"

"Because I have initiated these same events hundreds of times."

They took the three taxis back to the doctor's modest apartment and waited while he packed his things. Bishop had gradually been closing down on himself since they left the clinic. Lena understood. Relearning the challenge of hope was tough. It opened old wounds. She could see the cost there on his face. But Bishop plugged along, allowing them to help carry his four cases and one cardboard box.

The drivers let them stow the final bits in their front passenger seats. They drove to the inn and bribed the concierge to use his luggage room for the night. When they had unloaded all the cartons, Lena paid off two of the taxis and asked the third to wait. She made final plans with Robin as Chester checked them in. All the while, Brett stood on the inn's front veranda and talked softly into his phone.

When Lena said her farewells and stepped outside, Brett raised his hand, indicating he knew she was waiting. Lena did not mind the delay. The private jet was long gone, and the flight Robin had booked them on left in three hours. There was no rush, and the night was intensely beautiful.

The inn fronted a square filled with ancient oaks and the rush of an ocean breeze. Spanish moss drifted and swayed and whispered to her, inviting her to set down her burdens and rest a spell. The surrounding houses glowed softly, many of them burning gas lights by their entries. Lena stood by the porch railing and promised herself a few days here when things settled down.

Brett pocketed his phone and walked over. "Sorry to make you wait."

Lena remained where she was. "You reported to the people in Italy?"

"They're in Switzerland. Yes."

"You think all this is tied together?"

"I am certain of it." Brett leaned against the neighboring pillar. "The lines of convergence are not visible. But they exist. The leader of our group, Dr. Gabriella Speciale, agrees. She would like to speak with you."

"Now? It must be very late over there."

"Well after midnight. It doesn't matter. Gabriella has a scientist's ability to ignore the clock."

"What's she like?"

"Beautiful. Extremely intense. Highly intelligent. She has the ability to help draw elements together. Clarify directions."

"I've been thinking the same thing about you," Lena replied. She reached out. "Can I use your phone?"

Brett handed it over. It felt warm from his touch. "Hit redial."

Instead, she slipped it into her pocket. "While we were with Bishop, you mentioned two issues that we have to discuss."

Brett remained silent.

"First, you told him that he could be in danger. I need to know why. It so happens I think you're probably right. But I want to know why you thought you needed to say it."

Brett nodded slowly. "That's one."

"Number two is the outlier data. It's tied to the secret you're carrying, isn't it."

"Several secrets," Brett agreed. "Make the call. Then I'll tell you everything."

BOOK 3

37

As soon as Lena settled into the taxi, she placed the call. Dr. Gabriella Speciale said in greeting, "You must have many questions."

"So many," Lena replied, "I don't know where to start."

"So let me offer a few observations about what is happening. All this began as a small research project aimed at creating a measure of harmonious brain-wave patterns. It has evolved into something greater than any of us. Now there are a cluster of projects. A Tibetan doctor leads a team outside Rome. Brett travels the United States, revealing our preliminary ascent state to dying patients, working alone until he met you. A theoretical physicist and his business partner operate out of Santa Barbara. Associates continue our base trials at universities in Milan and Vienna and Rome. If I were forced to label our entire group, I would have to say we have not yet arrived at a point where we can even name what is happening. But if you like, I will tell you what I think."

Lena had heard enough to love the way Gabriella spoke. Her accent created a musical lilt, and her voice was honeyed in the manner of someone who was accustomed to being both beautiful and in charge. "Please do."

"I think we are evolving. We have received an invitation to move beyond our comfort zones. We are not in lockstep. Instead, we are each developing a crucial component of something far greater. So great, in fact, we have difficulty even seeing our own tiny fragments. You have made money from a rather incredible business project. Now you are being asked by your temporal self to step into something far more challenging. To you, all this seems both illogical and threatening. To me, it says that you are one of us."

To have a highly intelligent woman speak to her in such a manner, calmly declaring that everything she had endured actually made sense, left Lena's eyes burning. She swallowed against the emotions and asked, "Are we in danger?"

"Most definitely. Every step we have taken thus far has been met with severe opposition. That is why I wanted to speak with you to-night. I would like to have my beloved join you. His name is Charlie Hazard. You can ask Brett about him. Charlie is an expert at keeping people safe."

Lena supposed she should have been made more nervous by yet another person declaring that danger surrounded them. But the sense of being in the company of people she could trust grew stronger still. People who understood. She wiped her eyes. "All right. Yes."

"Good. Thank you." Gabriella sighed into the phone. "Now I will sleep easily. I loathe the prospect of this evolving project bringing anyone into danger."

"I know exactly what you mean," Lena said.

"Excellent. That is settled. Charlie has already left for the Zurich airport. He departed while I was still speaking to Brett. With your permission, Charlie will fly tomorrow morning to New York. Now tell me something about yourself. Please. I want to know who it is that is about to become one of my closest friends. It is a very Italian thing to say, yes? Completely illogical. We have never met, but our few words are enough to make me certain of this."

"I left logic behind a long time back," Lena replied. "And I feel the same way."

"That is so nice to hear. Do you have something you wish to share with me?"

Lena rolled down the taxi's window and spoke into the wash of warm Georgia breeze. "Things are moving so fast I haven't had time to digest anything. Or come to terms with what it might all mean. Not for your project. For me personally."

"You must still take time for yourself," Gabriella said. "Have a nice meal, savor the wonder of life. What is the one thing you most wish you had time to do?"

"I'm embarrassed to say it."

"Do so anyway. Please."

"Speak with my boss. Tell him everything."

Gabriella was silent for a long moment. "Do you trust him?"

"Yes."

"So much you are willing to place the lives of your entire team in his hands?"

It was Lena's turn to go quiet.

"This you must decide before you make any such declarations. I would suggest you enter into this slowly. Develop the groundwork that will lead him to accept the impossible before you actually declare it."

Lena nodded to the soft wind. "That makes perfect sense."

"See this as an expedition into life's wonders and mysteries. Taking such care frames a safe passage." If anything, Gabriella's accent had deepened, become even more lyrical. "What else excites you in this moment?"

Lena was silent. There was no way she would say what came to mind, which was, sitting and talking to Brett.

Somehow Gabriella caught a whiff of her repressed excitement, for she laughed softly, then said, "As one friend to another, I advise you to go and savor the exquisite joy of redefining your boundaries."

Brett stood behind Lena at the Delta check-in counter and had his ID ready when she asked. He could see she was surprised to discover that Robin had booked them into first-class seats.

He liked standing back and observing Lena. Her features were stained by a fatigue far deeper than this one day. He wished there was something he could do that would light up her face like Gabriella had in their conversation. Instead, he was going to offer her a perfectly valid reason to walk away.

He waited until they were seated in the same Starbucks where they had been earlier in the day. He felt extremely tense over what he was about to say. He liked her a great deal. The more he got to know Lena, the more he felt drawn to her on a variety of levels.

"All right," Lena said once they were seated. "Tell me."

So he did. Brett started at the beginning, described meeting Gabriella at a professional conference and falling head over heels in love with a married woman. He described her ex, the wealthy socialite who had financed Gabriella like he would a trophy racehorse, and how Gabriella's passionate drive conflicted with her ex's careless lifestyle. He related how an amorphous group called the Combine had begun tracking them through this same ex-husband. Which led Brett to Reese Clawson, and the villa above Como, and Charlie Hazard.

There he stopped and sipped from his tea. Taking a break. Drawing in the grim determination required to launch into the next phase of his secret. The dark tunnel he had walked after Gabriella chose Charlie over him.

Brett faced the rear wall. He stared at the grey paint like he was reading from a scientific journal about the measure of one man's guilt. He described his hunger to grow beyond Gabriella's staid and conservative set of experiments. Another sip, and he related his contact with Reese

Clawson's group and their offer of a lab and the freedom to go public. All because he had lost a woman who had never returned his love. Which led Brett to investigate the question of temporal boundaries, and how this had drawn him to the maw of the vortex. How even now he could hear the silent roar, the hungry viciousness.

Lena's response was the last Brett would ever have imagined. He did not actually believe it happened, not even after he felt the warm hand settle upon his own.

The expression she revealed was full of soft compassion. But all she said was, "It's time."

Brett had no idea what she was talking about. Lena rose from the table and lifted her carry-on with the hand not holding his. She led him from the café and down the central aisle and up to where the attendant was greeting the first-class passengers. They walked down the connecting tunnel and into the plane, where an attendant pointed them into the first row. Brett settled by the window because Lena directed him there, placing herself between him and the rest of the plane.

All without letting go of his hand.

38

Lena had always been a sucker for honest men.

Which made her previous romances absolutely laughable. Her love life was a comic opera of ridiculous moves. If she had taken a gun and shot herself in the heart, the result would not have been much worse. Certainly the pain would not have lasted as long.

But she refused to let herself dwell on past errors. This trip back to New York was not about her. Relating her own chorus of mistakes would come later. Lena had walked over an invisible boundary by listening to Brett's admission. She had not known it at the time, of course. But now that it was done, she knew that even if the warning lights had flashed across the airport tarmac, she still would have asked. She still would have listened. And she would still be sitting here, in the plane's first row, holding his hand.

She asked, "What about the women before Gabriella?"

Brett kept his gaze on the hand holding his own, as he had since taking the window seat. As though her grip was the one thing that kept him from falling back to earth. The texture of his sadness had shifted somewhat, still there, but calmer now. Resigned, quiet, steady. The sorrow of a man who had carried this burden for a long, long time.

He said, "There was only one who mattered. I met her the year I accepted my lectureship. Her name was Steffi. She was a senior at UCSB, film major, daughter of a Hollywood producer. Steffi had heard people say she was beautiful every single day of her life. She was so accustomed to having men try to reshape the world to suit her, she never actually thought about it. Getting everything she wanted came as naturally as sunshine. Until we met. Most of our fights were over how I did not drop everything and run to do her bidding."

"She sounds too shallow for you."

"That is too simplistic. She was a very good person in many ways. I never did feel comfortable with her beauty. Mostly because I never understood what she saw in me. So many other men chased after her. Richer men more connected to her LA life, more comfortable with small talk and high society."

Lena felt hollowed by his calm openness. Her heart was rendered and bruised by the act of listening. She opened her mouth, wanted to offer some form of comfort. But the words did not come.

"She liked to show up in the middle of the night," Brett went on. "Laughing and breathless and eager. But there was often the hint of other fragrances. She shrugged off my questions as unimportant. She always said I was a brilliant man doing important things. I needed to accept that sometimes she needed the party, the crowd, the action. What did it matter where she went, so long as she came back to me?"

Lena whispered, "The problem was, you loved her."

"It was a fatal error, falling for her like I did. Finally I broke it off. She was not hurt so much as astonished. And angry. No man had ever done that to her before. That was the line she repeated. Day after day. No man had ever left her." His smile was tragic. "So what do I do, after two years of solitude, but fall for Gabriella. Who was everything Steffi was not. A fellow scientist. Brilliant. Stable. Deep. Perceptive. Wise. Caring."

"And married," Lena murmured. "And in love with another man."

"I knew Charlie Hazard was a threat from the first time I laid eyes on him. Even before, actually. When Gabriella returned from an ascent where she had been shown where to meet him, she glowed. I was jealous of him a week before we even met."

Lena asked, "What about now?"

"You mean Charlie?" His smile was a Kabuki mask. "He is the best friend I've ever known."

Forty-two minutes later they landed at LaGuardia. As the plane taxied, Lena said, "I don't think you should be alone tonight."

A tension gripped his features, turning the skin around his mouth and nostrils parchment-white. He breathed in, not so much shaky as broken.

Lena felt awkward now that the thought was spoken aloud. "I mean, you know, as friends."

"I understand, Lena." He spoke to the same point on the wall before his face. "It's the nicest thing anyone has said to me in a very long while."

39

The instant Reese woke up, she realized she was back inside the cage.

The sounds came to her first, which was typical. The prison's noise always filtered through whatever dream ended the night. The shouts were predator calls, the shrieks and screams of marauding beasts hunting their next prey. Then she opened her eyes, and instantly she knew where she was. Somehow they had transported her back to Raiford, the first prison where she'd been held.

Her gut tensed with the rigid fear she had never allowed herself to reveal. The Raiford women's section had been dominated by two gangs, one Latino and the other African American. The Anglos had mostly been from Ukraine and Belarus, three drug-running crews who had been taken down in a series of stings. The Eastern European women hated each other with a stubborn viciousness that Reese considered idiotic. It was like watching the Soviet version of the Hatfields and McCoys. The other two prison gangs took advantage of their hatred and controlled the pen. Life for solitary beings like Reese was terrible. She had only stayed in Raiford for seven weeks.

She left convinced that one more week would have seen her laid out on the coroner's slab.

And now she was back. She recognized the Cyrillic script scrawled across the ceiling above her bunk. Her first cellmate had been from Minsk, a ruthless madam who used smuggled cell phones to run her string of girls from inside the pen. Two weeks after Reese arrived, the woman had been knifed in the yard. Now Reese lay with her eyes clenched shut, trying to remember who had taken the woman's place. But her mind was blank. It probably meant she had been drugged and transported while zonked out. According to prison lore the feds used that sometimes as a means to extract confessions.

Reese tensed and sprang from the top bunk, from prone to crouched in the middle of the cell, empty hands extended like claws.

The lower bunk was empty. The mattress was rolled up in a tight ball. Reese looked around. The shelf for a second inmate's personal belongings was bare. She had the cell to herself.

Which made no sense at all.

The morning claxon sounded and the cell door opened. Reese stepped carefully into the passageway. She expected to confront jailhouse snarls and women wearing gang paint. Reese was the new meat. They would measure, they would challenge. A fight was inevitable.

The passage was empty.

Reese's cell was on the third floor. The left-hand wall was a wire cage that overlooked the rectangular pen, with the rec benches and the concrete floor far below. The smell was overpowering, a wretched mix of disinfectant and human misery and blood not yet spilled. Reese took a slow look around, confused and uncertain. The noise was precisely as she remembered, the shouts and screams so loud she could not make out any actual words. But there was no one. Not a guard, not an inmate, nothing.

She started toward the door at the end of the aisle because she had no idea what else to do. She feared she might be marked down as late, which meant ten days in solitary. But she had moved as soon as the claxon blared and the door opened.

Reese walked the stairs alone, every nerve in her body on full alert. Being alone was a high-risk event, to be avoided at all times. Such isolation was usually arranged in advance, and always resulted in a severe beating or death. Reese heard her own breathing—tight, keening pants, an animal knowing she is being hunted, searching for safety, finding none.

She reached the ground floor, crossed the central pen, and walked the corridor leading to the cafeteria. The noise grew to where it pounded on her from all sides, battering her as strong as fists. Then she entered the cafeteria, and she froze.

The chamber was ten times larger than the prison's cafeteria. It was jammed full of beasts.

The creatures that had partly emerged with Heather's and Esteban's return. They were here. Hundreds of them. Every manner of horrible shape, heaving, surging, roaring.

Then they saw her. They wheeled about and crouched and bared their fangs. And roared at her with one voice. Delighted. Hungry. Vengeful.

They pounced.

Reese screamed. She tore from the bed, fighting the sweaty tangle of sheets like chains. She raced blindly across the unfamiliar apartment. She slammed into a chair, came up fighting. She flung it at the wall, still screaming.

Then she realized where she was.

When her heart finally calmed and her gasping whimpers ceased, Reese realized not a single member of her team had come by to check on her. Those screams should have brought the house down.

Reese crossed the room. She picked up the chair and set it down on its remaining three legs. She unlatched her door and stepped into the hall.

A dozen or so faces were there. All of them held to the exact same watchful caution. The voyagers crouched just inside their apartments, only part of each face visible. Showing just enough to observe. Ready to slam the door and retreat.

Reese asked, "This happens a lot?"

A voice from midway down the hall said, "Not every night."

"Often enough," another said.

Reese looked at them. Her rage was a bomb just begging to go off. But not at them. She said, "I'm okay. Go back to bed."

She shut her door. Crossed to the sliding doors and opened them and stepped onto the balcony. The night breeze felt good against her clammy skin. She stared up at clouds turned into silver ships by the moon and whispered, "This stops now."

Only when she had worked out her plan of attack did she return inside.

40

At dawn Reese phoned Kevin, surprised to learn he was already in his office. She showered and dressed and returned to the glass cube. Kevin made coffee, then took his mug over to the front window. Beyond the glass wall traffic already hummed, mostly pickups and the hard-used vehicles of hourly workers. Reese had come over hoping to do some forward thinking. But Kevin seemed distracted, so she began by reviewing the previous day's events. As she spoke she studied the man who was as close to a friend as she could probably come these days. Kevin did not look like he had slept at all. The hand holding his mug shook slightly. When she stopped talking, he remained as he had been throughout, watching the traffic and drinking from his mug.

Finally Reese said, "I want to walk back through what we discussed yesterday. From the very beginning."

He did not turn from the window. "This is about handling the midnight crew?"

"Yes."

"Good name, by the way." He waved his mug at her reflection. "Shoot."

"The mystery people hiding behind Vera found you and brought you in. You developed a basic method using this new technology. You signed up your first team. But your initial outings kept losing voyagers to comas. Just like we faced the last time we worked together. Then one of the four midnight crew hooked up with the beasts."

His words fogged the window in front of his face. "It was the guy with all the metal. Soon as I saw that first transformation, I knew I couldn't handle them. But we'd lost nine voyagers up to that point. Then the four made that connection to the monsters, and within a week all the coma victims had woken up. None of them fully recovered. We use them on the front desk now, and in the café. The important thing is, we haven't lost another since then."

Reese didn't like how Kevin was taking this. He seemed to find the traffic below his window more interesting than Reese's team. The man looked exhausted. And stressed. "Did you know the midnight crew has been extorting payment from the other voyagers?"

"Yes. That started the day before Vera finally agreed to bring you in. I had sent Vera a video of that moment when the beast appeared after a voyage." He set his mug on the desk, then went back to watching the traffic. "What makes somebody willing to get swallowed like that?"

"I think our four like that taste of danger. They like the power. The dark doesn't scare them like it does most people." When he did not respond, she pressed, "Tell me what's wrong, Kevin."

He tapped the glass with one hand. "They've murdered the old man."

"What?"

"John Beadle. Head of the scopes division. The official line is, he's suffered a stroke."

"How do you know?"

"I flag all the groups we're tasked to investigate. A news agency sends me an alert anytime there's a development. I've been wracking

234

my brain, trying to figure out our next move. But I can't get beyond the fact that we're working for a bunch of cold-blooded killers."

"Come over here and sit down."

He stayed where he was, tapping the glass. "Before, I thought, you know . . . all three targets so far have been military suppliers. Maybe Defense Intel decided to establish an outside group they could monitor and control."

Reese had thought the same thing. "Kevin. Please."

He slouched across the carpet and sighed into the chair opposite her. "DOD wouldn't murder a company exec to gain control. Not and put a criminal in his place."

"That's not the question we need to focus on here." She rapped the table with her knuckles and waited until Kevin lifted his gaze. "Vera and her group will assume we know."

Kevin stared at her.

"They'll gauge our response very carefully. If we don't react the way they want, they'll take us out."

"We're expendable."

"Of course we are. That's why we've been thinking about hunting them down. So we can know when to run." She leaned across the table. "I need you to focus."

He straightened in his seat. Or tried to. "I'm listening."

Reese worked out her strategy as she spoke. By the time she finished, Kevin's gaze had cleared. He still looked exhausted. But he was with her. "That could work."

She leaned back, satisfied and troubled at the same time. "Get Vera on the phone."

"We want a million dollars," Reese said. "Cash. Now."

Kevin's shoulders were bunched beneath the starched shirt. His gaze shifted between the speakerphone and Reese. Back and forth. Nervous as a cat.

Vera said, "Your Bridgeport contracts only netted three mil."

The tension was electric, but now it was all good. Reese had no problem with pressure. Stressing a situation had always brought her pleasure, so long as she was in control. Vera's response was all she needed to hear. She gave Kevin a tight smile. They were running in the green.

Reese said, "Our project is a whole lot bigger than a couple of jobs. Isn't it."

Vera did not reply.

"The contract payments we negotiated with that company were icing on the cake. It covers our costs. That's all—"

Vera interrupted with, "Break down this number of yours."

"For starters, two hundred and fifty each for Kevin and me."

"Your annual salary as bonus? You're out of line even suggesting such a thing."

"Two fifty each," Reese repeated. "For every successful project."

Vera went silent.

"Another two fifty to be split evenly among all the voyagers. Everyone gets something."

Vera did not respond.

"The final two fifty is for contingencies."

"Explain."

Reese pointed across the table. Kevin said, "You recall the video I sent."

Vera did not reply.

"The threat this represented has increased. Reese has worked out a possible means to overcome this. We want to reward—"

"All right. Hold on."

Kevin asked softly, "Think it worked?"

What she thought was, asking the question showed just how exhausted the man was. Reese replied, "You really need to get some sleep."

Vera came back on. "You get half a million."

"That's not enough."

"This sum is not negotiable. Split it however you like."

"Look, I'm trying—"

"And I'm looking for a reason to give out an all-points," Vera snapped. "'Escaped federal convict, multiple felonies, considered extremely dangerous, shoot to kill.'"

Reese smiled at the conference phone. Vera probably thought the silence was her way of tamping down on justifiable terror. But Vera was wrong. This was Reese taking aim. "Agreed."

"We have two more companies you need to investigate. High-priority targets. One British, the other Japanese. Is language a problem?"

"I have no idea," Reese said. "But first we need the funds to reward our team—"

"Payment will be effected immediately. Get to work."

41

Reese left Kevin's office and crossed the parking lot. It was almost nine o'clock, and traffic along the highway was heavy. As she entered their cafeteria and ordered a latte and a toasted bagel, Reese felt eyes follow her everywhere. The café was about half full, but no one was eating. Reese had developed the safety sense every inmate used to survive, the ability to see without actually looking, the skill of finding danger before it materialized.

She felt nothing bad. Just the eyes.

She walked over to a table occupied by three voyagers she had never spoken to directly and indicated the empty chair. "This taken?"

"It is now."

She slipped into the seat and asked their names. They responded without an instant's hesitation. She asked when was the last time they had been on a voyage. They told her. She asked if they ever visited the outside world. They talked about a trip to Disney. A couple of local restaurants. Cinema. Reese listened and ate her breakfast and hunted for the unspoken. Finally she acknowledged the change as real. These voyagers had accepted her. She was one of them. And it wasn't simply because she had confronted Heather and Esteban, or delivered an ultimatum to the midnight crew.

They bonded because she had known the nightmare.

Ridley entered the restaurant and came over, Carl one step behind. They pulled up two chairs and settled down a fraction removed from the others. Reese liked how they remained a team, even here in the café where everyone could see. She also liked how others drifted over, not asking permission to join them. She felt it as much as anything she was actually able to see, the sense that she was gathering them into a unit. They were willing to give her a chance to prove herself. Willing to expect a better outcome than they had known so far. Reese liked that a lot.

She said, "We've been given a new target. Two of them."

Carl said, "I've found a couple of others who want to try to link like me and Ridley."

"Excellent." Reese explained to all the others, "We want to develop an alternative midnight crew."

The same woman who had spoken in the hallway the night before said, "Those hungry ghosts, they scare me."

"Too right," another said. "Scare me white, almost."

"You wish," the woman said.

"Girl, I'm happy enough with my skin just how it is, thank you very much. I just don't like sharing it with no monster from dreamland."

"That time is over," Reese said.

"You're sure about that, are you," Ridley said.

Reese rose high enough to look over the group. Three more voyagers were clustered by the doorway. Another four were at the window table. "Can all of you join us, please?" When they were together and seated, Reese said, "Awhile back I was put in charge of the first-ever experimental team doing what we're doing now."

"What happened to them?"

"We were forcibly dispersed." She held up her hand. "I'll answer your questions. Only not now. We are on the clock, and we need to prep. Something we did back then might help us now."

Reese described how two of her team had gone hunting as a sniper-spotter team. She related how the pair had developed a weapon of sorts, drawn from negative energies and emotions they'd found waiting for them. Or perhaps had brought with them. Reese kept it vague, giving them only what was required, the bare bones. Then she waited.

To her surprise, it was Carl who got it. "We can make shields."

Ridley watched him. "You think?"

He shrugged. "Worth a try. Energy is energy."

The waifish young woman from the hallway said, "Or maybe even fashion a weapon."

A dark-skinned guy asked, "You'd take on a hungry ghost?"

"Hey. I am about done with running from them all night."

"Least you can run, girl. I wake up in my dreamtime, they're already wearing me like a human Gucci."

Reese showed her palm a second time. "Let's hear what she's thinking."

"If anger works as a weapon, I'm locked and loaded," the woman said. "And if fear works too, we're talking a nuclear bomb."

Reese had heard enough. "Okay. We're going out. With two changes. First off, we're blocking the midnight crew for today. If they ever work with us again, it's with a complete and total understanding that this is a whole new ball game."

Several of the faces blanched tight. The young woman asked, "Is it safe?"

"What's your name?"

"Erin."

"I need to learn all your names. And I will. For now, everybody, meet Carl. Carl is part of our first new protective team, a group I'm calling Lifeguards. That sound okay, Carl?"

"Works for me." He smiled for the first time Reese had ever seen. "Works just fine."

"And here's how confident I am that Carl can keep you safe." Reese did her best to hide the terror rush. "I'm going in with you."

·⫴·

This time, the security station's door clicked open before Reese lifted her hand to knock. She stepped inside and shut the door behind her. The guard who had loaned her the weapons lifted his baton and said, "You up for another barbecue?"

Reese smiled to acknowledge the jest, then asked, "Why don't you wear name badges?"

The guy shrugged. "Kevin said they weren't required."

The female guard was taut and solid and wore her T-shirt and jeans like a rumpled uniform. "We're only eight, two shifts doing twelve each. Which explains the dayroom. And Kevin's ordered us to stay unseen."

Reese asked, "What are your names again?"

"Val."

"Stu."

"Okay, Valerie and Stuart," she said, committing them to memory. "Can you work me up sheets with photographs and basic details of everyone here, including the staff? I need to fit names to faces."

"Sure thing."

"Great. But that's not why I stopped by." At this point the two other guards were standing in the doorway. "I want you to bar entry to the midnight crew."

Stu asked, "Who?"

"The four weirdos," Valerie said.

"Oh. Right. Sure." He grinned. "A pleasure. Really."

"One or more of them should be coming downstairs any moment now. I'd like one of you on station in the hall leading back to departures. Tell them the whole area is off-limits."

"I'm volunteering," Stu said. "What should I say when they ask why?"

"Tell them they're on probation. And that I want to see them all after the next voyage. And they better be on time."

"What if they object?" Stu was just loving this. "Or like, you know, try to get past me."

But Reese was already turning away, focused on the unseen next step, fighting down her fear. "Use your imagination."

42

Kevin's chief technician responsible for calibrating each individual neural net was a dull-faced Salvadoran with a heavy accent and heavier build. She fitted Reese with nicotine-stained fingers. Even when she was back behind the monitor, Reese could smell the ashes on her clothes. The woman asked her questions for over two hours, continually making adjustments on her computer as Reese responded. The questions were endless and extremely personal and intended to elicit emotional reactions. Reese endured it because she had to. The woman's flat, uncaring tone made it easier.

When it was over, Reese returned to the monitoring station. Karla disliked the idea of Reese heading into Indian country, but she kept her objections to herself. Reese counted the main team in and gave them the targets. Then she gave Karla a set of handwritten instructions and said, "Read this when you count down me, Ridley, and Carl."

Karla frowned at the page. "The standard first voyage is simple in the extreme. You're counted down and given very basic instructions. Come up from your body. Take a careful look around. Return. That's it."

"I want you to give me a little more than that."

"More . . ."

Reese started to say the word *freedom*. But decided it didn't fit. "Mobility. Our aim is to find a way to operate without the midnight crew, and stop the voyagers from suffering through any more nightmares."

Karla nodded slowly. "It is all becoming clear."

Reese left the monitoring station and entered the second departures lounge. She settled into the seat on Carl's opposite side from Ridley. Reese hated how the helmet fit on her, clamping down over her hair with probes like blunt needles pressing into her temples and forehead and rimming her skull. The chin strap was tight enough to make the helmet wiggle every time she opened her mouth. The cables dangled down behind her like metallic braids.

She did her best to ignore the discomfort and said, "Karla, can you hear me?"

"Loud and clear."

Reese shut her eyes and did her best to push away her dread. "Let's get this show on the road."

Reese had little experience with the immediacy of terror. She had been afraid many times, but it usually hit her long after the event. When she reviewed the closeness of peril, when she recalled the way she had survived and saw how near she had been to her final breath, she knew fear then.

Not like this.

Reese decorated the space behind her closed eyelids with the beasts from her nightmare. Always before, she had survived by going in prepped and ready for battle. But this time she had no idea how to prepare, or what to do, or how to come back.

A faint hiss sounded in her ears. Reese recognized it as the starting murmur that would rise into the auditory signal patterned after the optimal brain waves. In the chairs to her left, Reese heard Carl and Ridley exhale long and slow.

Karla's voice came through the headphones. But as she started her instructions, Reese opened her eyes and said, "Hang on a second."

Karla asked, "Something is wrong?"

"No." Reese turned to Ridley and said, "I want to try something. You remember what I told you earlier?"

"About the energy weapon."

"The energy. That's the key. So what if we use the energy to fashion an anchor as well as a shield?"

Carl asked, "Can we do that?"

"We can try," Ridley replied. "I like it."

Reese was thinking out loud. "Carl, you bind yourself to me and Ridley. That's your number one job. You station yourself in safety and you anchor us. Ridley, you—"

"Fashion a shield against the hungry ghosts and move forward," Ridley finished.

"Right. And I play the observer."

"Hungry ghosts," Carl said. "That's good."

Reese lay back and released the tension. The fear she could handle now. "Karla, you there?"

"Of course."

She shut her eyes. "Start the count."

Reese had secretly been hoping that it wouldn't take. She knew how few trial subjects were able to extract themselves. Or willing to take that step toward what her earlier team had called a small death. Releasing their consciousness voluntarily from their physical bodies. Looking beyond the confines of what was called normal life.

As if anything in her recent existence had been normal.

Reese half expected that she would be one of the majority. Unable to enter the state of voyaging, blocked by some internal resistance over which she had no control. But as soon as the auditory patterns increased in volume and Karla began her count, Reese felt the release.

She sensed its arrival before it actually happened. As though all the close calls she had known, the fractional distance she had maintained from death, had readied her for this moment. When she did what Karla told her to do. Almost before Karla shaped the words.

"Now open your other eyes."

Reese did just that. She felt her consciousness lift away from the physical form that she knew—she knew—was still prone in the chair. She did not need to turn around and look down at herself. But she did so anyway. She saw the slightly canted features, the indentation in her skull. But this time she felt none of the customary rage that struck her whenever she studied her reflection. Reese inspected herself with the mild curiosity she would have shown a stranger.

Reese was ready to move when Karla said, "You are to inspect your environment. See whatever it is that you need to observe in order to build a greater sense of safety for you and your team."

At one level, the instructions seemed unnecessary, because long before the words took shape, Reese was already in motion.

What Reese had not expected, what she was not prepared for, was the sense of exultation.

The weight and shadows of the past fourteen months, all the failures and rages that preceded her incarceration—they were just gone. Not merely erased. They had never happened. She recalled the events only with effort, like dredging up some long-ago conversation. But the exhilaration was far more than a simple freedom from the past. She was filled with a sense of potential. She could do anything. She could go anywhere.

Power. Just thinking the word filled her to the point that she would have wept, if such an act were possible. Instead, she felt tremors course through her, tight as repressed sobs. She vibrated to the latent force that was hers to call upon.

She felt a tug at the small of her back and turned around. The ephemeral Carl stood by his chair. His disembodied form was large and solid as a concrete block. Which was what he was focusing upon.

She understood his intent. He was linking to her by an imagined chain, light as air, strong as titanium. He held a second link that bonded him to Ridley. Reese did not see the woman until she focused in that direction. Here was a limitation, she realized. She could only see the one thing upon which she focused.

Ridley had fashioned a shield as tall as she was, an oval with a peaked top and bottom, like those carried by Zulu warriors. She pushed forward, and as she did streamers of incoming force flowed to all sides of her. Ridley was under attack. Yet she moved in safety and remained linked to her lifeguard.

It was working.

Reese focused outward and saw the assailants. The beasts formed an encircling mob, raging and toxic. But they could not touch them. Ridley's shield deflected the incoming barrage from reaching any of them.

Ridley moved forward, out to where the other voyagers searched for answers to their new quest.

Reese could see how they clutched one another, her shadow company. Using this unity as a means of safety. Bound together by . . . what? Their experience, or newfound trust? Reese had no idea. So many questions she had to work through. The prospect of hunting down answers was positively thrilling.

"Your ten minutes are ended," Karla said. "You are returning now. You remain in absolute safety, in total control. I am beginning the count now."

Reese slipped back into the confines of her physical existence, breathed, sighed, breathed again. She opened her eyes because she had to. There were things to do.

But all she could think was, *Too soon, too soon.*

43

When Lena woke up, she knew a quick wash of fear before she remembered where she was, and why. The previous evening Brett had wanted her to take the apartment bedroom, but she had refused. Lena had not needed to insist or argue—the man had no strength for either. Brett had brought out sheets and a blanket and pillow and a clean T-shirt, then entered the kitchen and prepared a morning coffee service. At the bedroom doorway he had paused and thanked her, his voice so soft it might have gone unheard had she not been listening carefully. He was a strong and intelligent man brought very low indeed.

Now she lay on her side, staring out the sun-splashed glass wall at an emerald garden. She heard only birdsong. She rose from the sofa, entered the kitchen, and switched on the coffeemaker. She then took her carry-on bag into the guest washroom. When she emerged she was dressed for the day ahead, though her feet were still bare. The floor was an inlaid pattern of marble and granite and coquina. Her heels would have made a racket, and she wanted to be alone.

She sipped her coffee and studied the apartment. There were subtle hints everywhere suggesting that it had never been lived in. Brett's presence was overlaid upon the formal setting like someone who had entered a hotel room and not yet had time to settle. Lena was fairly certain the apartment had been designed with a woman in mind. She walked slowly around and imagined what it would be like to live in such a luxurious place, a block off Park Avenue.

She took her second cup and her briefcase out the glass doors and seated herself on a metal bench beneath a trio of blooming cherry trees. The rear garden was laid out with Oriental precision, the springtime flowers as fastidious as a wedding bouquet. She had come here for Brett. But the quiet hour felt like a gift intended for her alone. Since arriving in New York, Lena had known so few opportunities to sit and reflect.

She was fully aware that her world was undergoing significant changes. The new job, the private jet, the meeting with Roger, the trip to Savannah, the formation of her own team, the bank account . . . All these were fragments that could easily remain disconnected through the speed of life. But the memory of Gabriella's voice rustled with the morning breeze, and Lena nodded to the sunlight. She was part of something far greater. She needed to prepare. She needed to be ready for the unseen.

She took her phone from her briefcase.

Roger Foretrain answered her call with, "This has to wait."

"It can't," Lena replied. "I really need—" She was halted by the click of the line going dead.

Lena compressed the phone between her hands. The audacity of what she was considering shocked her. But the longer she sat there, the more certain she became. She pulled the card from her wallet and dialed.

When Roger's wife answered, Lena said, "I need something. And even asking is so far out of line—"

"Skip the windup and tell me what it is," Marjorie said.

Lena stumbled through a basic description of what had been going on. Marjorie cut her off in mid-flow. "You and Roger need to meet."

"Outside the office if at all possible." Lena breathed fractionally easier, having someone else catch the jagged urgency. "I can lay it out in twenty minutes. Half hour tops."

"You just stay right there." The phone clicked.

The silence held an electric tension, as though the argument she could not hear infected the sunlit garden. Lena rose from the bench and paced the narrow path.

When Marjorie returned to the line, her words carried the crisp hint of smoke and cinders. "MOMA, the café, quarter to one." Then she was gone.

There was no reason why the brief back-and-forth should have left Lena slightly breathless. She stood and cradled her phone with both hands, waiting for the world to rebalance. Then she noticed Brett standing by the glass alcove's open doorway, waiting.

He was dressed in another outfit, smoky blue trousers and a navy jacket with a subtle stripe matching shirt and tie. Only his eyes carried the shadows of the previous evening. "Someday I hope to be able to tell you what it meant, having you stay here last night."

She pocketed the phone, and only then did she realize she was blanketed by the aroma of cherry blossoms, gentle as a lover's midnight whisper. "I'm glad I could help."

He gave that a moment's silence, then said, "Charlie's plane lands at Kennedy in just over an hour. He has a two-hour layover before flying on to Savannah. I think we should go out together so you can meet him."

"That makes sense."

"Then I have to teach my class." Brett pointed at the house rising behind him. "After that I've just arranged with Agnes for her to have another session. She wants to meet you this afternoon. I explained you're a friend. She . . ." Brett studied the sunlit garden. "She is a wonderful person."

On the ride into New York the previous evening, Brett had told her about the wealthy woman and her meeting with Brett's own temporal self. The first time such a transference had happened, as far as their team was aware.

Lena said, "She is concerned about you."

"She wants to be involved," Brett replied. "Her body is failing, but her curiosity is a living flame."

"After we meet Charlie at the airport I need to speak with my boss. But later, of course, I'd like that."

Brett remained where he was. "Agnes has two people who care for her. They want to ascend. Today. With Agnes."

Lena took that as an invitation and replied, "Count me in."

The MOMA coffee shop was no great shakes. For such an astonishing museum, it was almost a disappointment. The cavernous room held long rows of identical tables and chairs. The clinical sameness stripped away any sense of artistry or uniqueness. It was a factory designed to swallow the hordes and send them on their way again. But it suited Lena just fine.

The café was less than half full. Even so, the noise was a quiet and steady wash, like a sound machine designed to render every conversation completely private. Lena had a tray in front of her, holding a steaming mug of green tea and a poppy-seed bun. She picked tiny fragments off the rim of the roll, something she used to do as a child, creating little white crevices around the rim.

Roger approached the table bearing a full head of steam. Marjorie followed, her face set in determined lines. She said, "I invited myself."

Roger dragged out a chair. "I don't have time for this."

Marjorie seated herself and pulled Roger down so he took the place between them. She said, "He left for the office at five thirty this morning. Skipped breakfast. Ditto for lunch. I brought him uptown so he'd be forced to take time for a hot meal. It's called dining by limo."

"I would have eaten," Roger groused.

"Of course you would," Marjorie said. "And on the way back you can write the speech you're delivering tonight."

He froze. "I forgot the speech."

Marjorie shot Lena a smug glance. "I know you did."

Roger said to Lena, "We're preparing a package for a major new investor."

"They just showed up last night," Marjorie offered. "Russian oil money."

"I doubt the board would be happy to learn my youngest associate is party to that knowledge," Roger said.

Marjorie sniffed. "The board."

Roger turned to Lena and asked, "Why am I here?"

"Because my project's potential is real," Lena replied. "What we're coming to realize is the project's risk is also real. As is the need for you to know what is going on."

As Lena began describing what had happened in Savannah, Roger gazed through the café's rear windows to the trees rising in the central garden. He looked as rumpled and intense as usual. From the side, his grey-green eyes held a crystal quality, like a prism through which the café's light was distilled. He only granted Lena space for a few sentences before he softly declared, "What you're telling me is only more ammunition for my opponents."

Marjorie protested, "Roger, please."

"I'm getting serious blowback from Wesley's uncle. The Baker Meredith partners went over my head. They want you gone."

"Major mistake," Marjorie said.

Roger turned to his wife. "You know this how?"

"Lena costs the bank nothing. Isn't that the first thing you told me? But that isn't the issue. Lena works outside the lines. She scares the lesser minds on your board."

"Those lesser minds," Roger pointed out, "are responsible for my job."

Marjorie pressed on, "They can't control Lena. It terrifies them."

Roger tapped the table, softly drumming along with his thoughts. "I am going to try and arrange for you to present your findings to my allies."

Lena swallowed. "All right."

"You need to bring some undeniable evidence to the table," Roger went on. "That's your job now. Find me something so compelling not even the Weasel's uncle can shoot it down."

Lena thought of what the afternoon might hold and said, "I can do that. I think."

Roger rose from the table. "Be ready for my call."

Lena followed Roger and Marjorie from the museum and stood somewhat removed as her boss spoke intently with his wife. Lena most certainly did not mind waiting. This was the best time of year to be in New York. The air carried a sweet flavor of spring that not even a passing truck's exhaust could erase.

Roger slipped back into the limo and left without glancing Lena's way. Marjorie stepped over to her and said, "Roger is glad he came."

The day's burdens lifted somewhat. "Is that your way of trying to make me feel better?"

"I am a born-and-bred New Yorker. I'm not capable of sugarcoating." She smiled. "Tell me what you need."

"My team is driving up from Savannah. I'm supposed to find us a place to work."

The older woman opened her purse and brought out her phone. "How big?"

Lena gave her what Charlie had said at the airport. "We need a place that is off the map. One access portal would be preferable. In an area where there isn't too much foot traffic. A clean line of—" She noticed Marjorie's expression. "What?"

"You sound like one of the bank's security team."

Lena hesitated, then decided there was no need to try to describe Charlie Hazard just yet. She finished with, "Size and comfort take second place to safety."

While Brett was in the taxi returning from Columbia, Lena called to report that she and Marjorie were working on the secure location Charlie had requested. As soon as the butler opened the door and ushered him inside the Park Avenue house, Brett knew something was wrong. All Frederick said was, Agnes had had a difficult morning. But one look at the lady in the bed was enough for Brett to know that Agnes Lockwood was not ascending today. At least, not with his apparatus.

Her eyes drifted slightly, then focused on him. She said weakly, "There's never enough time."

He seated himself by the bed and took her hand. Like he had been doing it for years. Like they were the best of friends.

Agnes asked, "Where is your young lady?"

"Lena's been held up. But she's coming." Brett glanced over to where Frederick and Doris hovered on the bed's other side. "Lena wants to ascend with you."

Agnes asked, "Can you do it in here? I'd like to observe."

"Of course." Brett said to the pair, "There is no assurance either of you will manage an ascent. The success rate with nonterminal subjects on their first try is very low."

Frederick replied for them both, "We want to understand what the missus has seen."

"Frederick positively thrives on meddling," Agnes said weakly.

Brett indicated the box in the corridor and said to the old woman, "I have a new system I was hoping to try out. It requires some calibration. But if it works as I expect, it could alleviate some of your pain without drugs."

She could still command with a murmur. "What a delightful thought. Sit down and get to work."

"There could be side effects," Brett said. "I don't think they are a real threat. But you need to be aware just the same."

"Now you sound like my doctors. Side effects. Those words have lost all possible significance." She rested with eyes closed for a long moment, then went on, "Young man, you may begin."

The calibration process was finicky. Bishop's system utilized software whose user interface was ten years out of date. But Brett had worked with far worse. What required more time was Agnes, who floated in and out of a drug-induced doze. Brett was certain he would eventually find ways to work around the subject's sleep-wave patterns. But Bishop's current protocol was based upon patients replying directly to questions. Brett suspected much of the resulting data was unnecessary. It was a structure set in place by a doctor who had spent a lifetime interpreting patients' verbal responses.

Bernard's questions were designed to illicit emotions: Recall a situation where you were hurt, where you were angry, where you were disappointed. Focus upon your pain, describe your current emotional state, identify what in particular causes you to feel as you do. Many of them were clearly uncomfortable for a woman as reserved as Agnes. But she did not protest. Her features contorted from time to time, but she did as Brett requested. Her only refuge was the occasional nap.

Brett used the downtime to transfer a copy of the software to the nurse's laptop. She and Frederick drew up chairs to either side of Brett's station and listened as he described the process of linking the neural net to the patient's individual brain-wave patterns. Minute electromagnetic impulses could then be sent into the brain via the microchips positioned within the neural net, damping down both the pain itself and the related emotional responses.

By the time Brett completed the explanation, he had also finished the questions. He powered down the second laptop, handed it to Doris, and said, "What we're doing here is totally off the books. I'm probably breaking a dozen laws. But if it helps Agnes deal with her pain . . ."

"And offer her clarity in the days between now and her departure," Doris added. "I understand."

"Just don't share this with anyone else," Brett said.

"You have my word."

Agnes opened her eyes. "Are we done?"

"We are." He glanced at his watch. The questioning had required two hours and forty-seven minutes. "You did great."

"That was a trial. Quite horrid, actually."

"How long before your next dose?"

Doris replied, "Anytime she wants."

"Get her meds ready," Brett suggested, watching Agnes. "But hold off and let's see if this has any impact. That is, if you're game."

"Why do you think I put up with those wretched questions of yours?"

"Those questions are specifically designed to assist in the calibration—" Brett noticed she was smiling. "What is it?"

"Do all your female students fall head over heels in love with the dashing professor?"

"Not nearly enough of them," Brett replied.

Agnes shut her eyes. "Crank up your gizmo."

Brett hesitated. "As I mentioned, there have possibly been severe side effects."

"Five deaths. I know. Do it."

Brett should have been used to the silent and unseen process by now. But the seconds clicked by with maddening slowness.

He decided to give it two full minutes. But ninety-two seconds in, Doris asked, "Are you showing any response?"

"Her alpha patterns indicate a strong harmonization . . ." Brett stopped as Agnes opened her eyes and looked at him, alert and focused for the first time that day. "Something wrong?"

"On the contrary," Agnes replied. "The pain. It is gone."

44

alf an hour after Reese returned from her first voyage, Kevin found her in the lounge, wrapped in a pashmina blanket and sipping on a coffee. He waved the other voyagers away, then announced, "The money's in our account. Sun Trust, south two blocks. I've already made you coexecutor. You just need to sign the forms."

Reese knew at some level the money was important. But just then she could not say why, or even feel a need to understand. The disconnect from reality remained that strong. "I'll stop by after the next voyage."

Kevin looked tired, stressed, and confused. A dangerous combination. "Security wants to speak with you. They say it can't wait."

Reese asked, "How much sleep did you get last night?"

Kevin ran a hand through his remaining hair. "Hard to say."

"Go sack out. For both our sakes."

When he had left, Reese dropped the blanket and walked slowly down the hall to the front lobby. She wished she could just get back to flying. The buzzer opening the security door had never sounded more irritating.

She entered, waited until the door clicked shut, and asked, "You wanted to see me?"

Val, the female guard, said, "There's something going on with the four weirdos."

Stu explained, "Kevin ordered us to wire their rooms. We've got audio and visual feeds, phones, computers, the works."

Reese forced herself to concentrate. "Can you observe any other apartments?"

"Just theirs. As per orders."

"Show me."

He tapped the keyboard, and the central monitor displayed three of the four together. Esteban was sprawled on the sofa, his right hand massaging a bandage at the base of his bare rib cage. Reese heard him say, "This still hurts really bad."

Val said, "This is Esteban's apartment. He howled like a little girl when they treated his wound."

Reese heard Heather say through the wall speaker, "We'll get Reese. It's only a matter of time. Now shut up."

Stu said, "That Heather is the walking dead."

The monitor showed a view about three feet off the floor. Reese assumed the feeds were imbedded in the television. She made a mental note to use Kevin's tools and check her own place for bugs.

The sound of furious typing came over the speakers, then Lilly pushed back from the desk that ran between the television and the sliding glass doors. Reese heard her say, "Okay, the bossman has come back. He says they'll have a response to our request ASAP."

Reese asked, "Any idea what they're talking about?"

"Not a clue," Val replied. "They go out for breakfast most mornings. My guess is they worked out some kind of plan while they were away. Been camped in Esteban's room ever since they got back."

Reese shook her head. Clearly the midnight crew had connected to some outside force and were seeking to circumvent her new order. Which could only mean one thing.

She heard Esteban say, "We go downstairs, I'm carrying my pal Smith & Wesson."

Stu asked Reese, "Want me to check them for weapons?"

"Thanks, but no." Reese headed for the door. "I've had a year to learn how to take care of myself."

As soon as Reese reentered the lounge, the voyagers began drifting over. She saw the same expression on most of the faces, the unspoken question, the wondering if things were really moving in the right direction.

She asked, "Any trouble with the hungry ghosts while you were out?"

"They watched, but they didn't attack," one said.

"We sort of clutched each other," another said. "That might've helped."

Reese described what she'd worked out with Ridley and Carl. The assembled voyagers joined into the discussion, nineteen of them now—Reese knew because she counted. She broke in with, "What if we stopped splitting you up and instead everybody goes out together? We're coming together solid, why not try to keep this bond on the other side?" When she received a general agreement in reply, she turned to where Ridley and Carl stood by the side wall. "The increased numbers will mean your scouting techniques go from important to critical."

Ridley creased Carl's ribs with an inked fist. "You hear that? They're singing our tune."

Carl rubbed the point on his chest, but he did not look like he minded the contact. "I heard."

Reese said to the group at large, "I'm thinking you should all pair up. One serves as anchor, the other hunts. Choose your partner and decide who holds back this first round." She gave that a beat, then concluded, "I'll be on duty in the monitoring station. Your objective is to stay safe while we go after the required intel. We clear?"

"Protect and serve," Ridley said.

"We roll in ten," Reese said. "But first I need to have a word with the midnight crew."

Most of the voyagers decided to walk with her. Reese listened to the easy chatter that trailed in her wake. She did not hear the words so much as the tone. They talked like kids let out early from school. Released from some restrictive and uncomfortable hour. Free to do whatever. Because of her.

Her posse. Ready to go wherever she asked. Do whatever she said.

The midnight crew was clumped together on a sofa and uncomfortable chair positioned between the reception desk and the front window. They were being watched by Stu, who greeted Reese with, "One big happy family."

Reese wondered if there would ever come a time when she would feel relaxed around armed guards. "Thanks. A lot."

"De nada."

"I got this."

Stu took that as his dismissal and slipped back into the security suite. Reese surveyed the four in silence until the door clicked shut, then told the midnight crew, "Everything's changed."

Heather must have been their appointed spokesman. "They're going to get you. Sooner or later. It's inevitable."

Reese saw no need to ask who Heather meant. "We'll see."

Carl told the midnight crew, "Haven't you heard? We ate your pets for lunch."

Heather looked over, the cold gaze meant to terrify. Then back to Reese. "They can't watch you forever."

The young woman, Erin, spoke from the group behind them. "Actually, we can."

Carl said, "We got her back, 24-7."

Erin added, "New game, new rules."

Carl said, "We're posting our own guards. Night and day."

Ridley stepped in tight, right in the midnight crew's personal space, and crouched down. Her voice barely above a whisper. Like it was an intimate moment just between them. "Here's the thing. You come for any of us, or you let your little friends try anything, we're coming for you."

A dark, rich female voice said, "Tell them, girl."

"It doesn't matter what you do. It doesn't matter how you plan."

Carl said, "You got to sleep sometime, right?"

"The deal is simple," Ridley said. "Forget what your little friends want. You keep them caged, or we take you out."

The united response caused all four to waver. Reese saw it happen because she was watching for it. She knew it had little to do with Ridley's threat. These four were true psychopaths. They did not respond to fear like others did. Their world was not defined the same way. What troubled them now was the prospect Reese saw in all their eyes. They were no longer needed. She could shut them out. One word from Reese and their days of moving beyond the physical realm were finished. Over.

They knew this. And it terrified them.

Reese said, "You're welcome to stay."

They clearly did not believe her. It was Carl who said, "And do what? Didn't you get the memo? We got your back."

Reese nodded and continued to address the crew. "All you need to do is obey the new rules."

But she did not really want them to stay. Reese had spoken because she wanted to gauge their reaction. And there beneath the flat gazes and silent rage, she saw the same response. They had no intention of doing what she wanted. Which could only mean one thing.

There on the sofa were Vera's watchdogs.

Reese dismissed them and headed back down the hall, followed by her crew. If anything, the voyagers were even more amped. They thought the threat was vanquished. They were safe. Because of Reese.

She decided to let them live that myth a little bit longer.

45

ena climbed the stairs to the townhouse off Park Avenue and rang the bell. A woman in a nurse's uniform opened the door and asked, "Yes?"

"I'm Lena Fennan—"

"Of course, Ms. Fennan. Dr. Riffkind is expecting you." The nurse had greying hair and the over-bright eyes of recent tears. "Do come in."

"This is Marjorie Foretrain—"

"Yes, yes, Dr. Riffkind said you'd be coming with a guest. I'm Doris, Mrs. Lockwood's nurse." She locked the front door, then hurried across the foyer, almost running by the time she entered the hall. "This way."

The corridor opened into a very grand sitting room, totally at odds with the hospital bed and the clinical smells. One look at the old woman left Lena certain she stared into the face of death. Agnes Lockwood wore a neural net, which compressed her slack features. Wisps of translucent hair stuck out in various places. A hand that appeared little more than bones and parchment lifted from the covers and waved them forward. "Do come in, my dears. Forgive me for receiving you in this manner. I realize I might appear rather, well, horrid."

"You are nothing of the sort," chided a man seated in the chair by her bed. He wore the vest and trousers of a black suit, a starched white shirt, and another neural net.

The cables draped over his chair back and wound into the laptop monitored by Brett, who turned and smiled and said, "Almost done."

"Thank goodness." The man shook his head. "I find these questions most unsettling."

"That's pretty much their intention," Brett replied.

A second laptop was placed on the table beside his own, this one containing four graphs with a myriad of wave patterns. Most were jagged and uneven, and these were colored either red or green. Overlaid upon them was another wave, this one golden, steady and flowing like an ocean current. Every few seconds all the graphs but one were replaced by others.

Lena asked, "They're showing the different segments of Mrs. Lockwood's brain?"

"Please, dear," the old woman said. "I insist you call me Agnes."

"Exactly," Brett said. He stopped long enough to tap the central graph. "This is the mother lode. What you might refer to as pain central." He tapped the screen. "See that clear rhythm? Not even a shadow of disturbance."

Lena looked at the woman on the bed. "You don't feel anything?"

"Not a tickle," she replied. "Isn't it marvelous?"

Lena was by nature an extremely private person. And yet, as Brett asked her the probing questions, Lena did not feel the least bit disconcerted. What was more, the presence of others made the calibration process feel almost comfortable. They were bound together by something they did not fully understand. There on the bed lay the living testimony of just how important this entire episode truly was. Agnes Lockwood now approached death free of pain, free of drugs, alert, at peace. And something more.

Agnes Lockwood was happy.

She radiated a joy that embraced them all. She had been unable to describe what was happening, but it did not really matter. They could all see the impact the neural net was having. The electromagnetic process was not a dominating force. It did not control her mind.

It freed her.

Agnes was able to die on her own terms. Alert and engaged.

When Brett asked her to recall a scene when she had been emotionally hurt by another person, Lena relived the episode. On and on it went, eighty-nine minutes of difficult recollections and emotions. She knew the neural net made her look ridiculous. It mashed her hair and compressed her face. Lena accepted it all as the price of admission.

Marjorie's calibration followed. Lena accompanied the nurse into the kitchen, where Doris made her a cup of tea. When they returned to the sickroom, Agnes gestured to Lena, who understood the invitation and shifted a chair over to the bed's other side.

Agnes said, "Brett tells me you've had some experiences of your own."

"Not the same," Lena replied. "But Brett thinks they're related."

"Not think, know," Brett said. "Okay, Marjorie, we're done."

Marjorie slipped off the net, gave her scalp a good scratching, and asked Lena, "What haven't you told me?"

"There's no way to describe what I've been through in a few minutes," Lena replied. "I'll tell you, just not now."

Marjorie sniffed. "You sound just like my husband."

Brett stood, stretched his back, said, "Where do we want to do this?"

"Here, of course," Agnes said. "What an absurd question."

He looked down at the lady in the bed and said gently, "This technology is new to me. I'm concerned that if I insert the ascendant commands into your system, the pain control might be diminished."

Lena shivered slightly and wondered if the words impacted anyone else. Ascendant commands. Pain control. Gentle verbal bombs lobbed into the realm they called reality.

Agnes replied, "I have no intention of ascending again. I shall be making that final flight soon enough. I am quite content to play the observer."

Brett turned to Doris. "We need to make up four pallets."

Lena asked, "What about you?"

"My thoughts exactly," Agnes said.

Brett froze in the process of uncoiling cables. "You received a message about this?"

"I did not require one." Agnes pointed the translucent hand at Lena. "She knows it is time. As do I."

Brett resumed keying in the four neural nets. But his motions were slower, his hands somewhat unsteady. "I'll think about it."

The transition was very frightening, such that Lena instinctively drew back. The terror formed a repulsive barrier. She jerked in a panic, as though she fled a premature death.

At that exact moment, Brett's calm voice repeated the words for the third time, "You are in complete control."

Control was the issue. Control was the anchor. Lena grasped this with a swiftness that defied the speed of thought.

One instant she was retreating in dread. The next and she . . .

Just.

Went.

The fear vanished so completely it might as well have never existed. In its place Lena knew a sense of exhilarated release. The world of the physical still surrounded her. But it no longer held her.

She saw a vivid portion of the world wherever she looked, on whatever she focused. Yet overlaid upon the physical reality was something new. Lena's perspective felt scrubbed clean. Not in terms of image. Rather, in terms of the viewer.

Lena could have remained there forever, hovering above her body. She turned and looked at the form upon the bed, and saw the beauty of a woman who was a few breaths from her next transition. She felt the woman's peace. She knew the strength this represented. Then she turned away and looked at Brett.

All the barriers she had known were no more. The fact that her temporal self had promised coming heartache no longer existed. Brett was a wounded soul who was doing his best to make amends. He was . . .

Beautiful.

46

When Brett finished bringing everyone back, Doris rose from her pallet and served them all tea. The nurse raised Agnes's bed and held a mug with a straw so the old lady could sip. Brett asked the others if they had ascended. Doris and Frederick said they had not, and yet there was a calm satisfaction to both their expressions and their voices. Lena had the distinct impression something concrete had been experienced, but she felt no need to press. Marjorie did not respond at all. She sat cross-legged upon her pallet and stared at the steam rising from her tea. Brett observed her thoughtfully and did not press.

Doris said, "I don't know if I dreamed or if it was real. But I had a conversation with my late mother. It was . . ."

"Remarkable," Frederick murmured. The butler's vest and trousers and tie and starched white shirt formed a sharp contrast to his position on the pallet, legs outstretched, his back against the side wall. His shoes were lined up like two soldiers next to his mug.

Doris gave him time to say more, but when he remained silent, she turned to Agnes and said, "You never told me how wonderful it was."

"I thought perhaps it was only because of my state."

Brett quietly asked, "Marjorie, did you—"

"No."

The sharpness of her response drew them all around. Brett asked, "Is there anything I need to know?" When Marjorie continued to stare at the mug in her hands, he asked, "Are you all right?"

"Fine." She rose in the jerky swiftness of an angry teen. "Just drop it."

"Don't go." Agnes spoke hardly above a whisper, but it carried enough force to halt Marjorie in the doorway. "My dear, we can't drop it. Brett needs to know—"

"There was a message waiting for me. It said I'm pregnant." Marjorie leaned her head against the door frame. "We've tried for eleven years. And now . . . What if it's a lie?"

Lena rose and walked over. She said to Marjorie, "I need to tell you what has been going on."

They stood like that while Lena related the events and the messages and her actions and everything that had happened as a result. She finished with, "I'm not sure it would be a good idea for me to tell Roger—"

"Don't," Marjorie said. "Not yet. First Roger needs to do this for himself. Or at least try. Then you tell him. Until then it won't make sense."

"I agree."

Marjorie's eyes were coal-black diamonds, washed by a river of hope. "There was a second message. It said that I am to help you any way I can. I think that's why I was told about my child. So I would understand how important this is."

Agnes grew very tired after that, so they moved into the living room. Frederick left and returned with takeout from a Park Avenue deli. The elegant onyx coffee table was soon littered with cardboard cartons and sterling silver cutlery and linen napkins and Limoges china plates.

No one said much. Marjorie called her husband, left a message, and spent the meal watching her phone.

When Roger called back, Marjorie left the room, only to return and announce that her husband was rushing to complete the same urgent matter that had compressed so many of his recent hours. He had agreed to meet with her, but only if she could come join him at the bank. Marjorie gathered up her things, hugged Lena and Brett once more, promised to return the next day, and was gone.

When Brett left to teach an afternoon class, Lena carried a sense of pleasant exhaustion downstairs. She lay down on the sofa, expecting to rest for a few moments, and the next thing she knew it was two in the morning. Brett had obviously come in, for she was covered with a quilt. Lena was amazed he had not woken her. Normally she remained completely aware of her surroundings at all times and could be woken by the tiniest of changes to her room's atmosphere. Yet Brett had come in, obviously seen her asleep, moved about the apartment, spread a covering over her, and then gone to bed. The longer she thought on this, the more convinced she became that it represented far more than a simple case of needing sleep.

The next morning she was making coffee when Marjorie texted that she had finished with the arrangements for the place where Charlie and the team could locate. She and Roger were having coffee, and then she would come by and pick up Lena. Twenty minutes later, Robin called Lena to say they were making good time, and finished with the news, "Bernie is one amazing mind."

"So it's Bernie now."

"The guy has a photographic recollection of every step of his research, every circuit of the neural net, every patient right back to med school. He'd be scary if he wasn't so nice."

"I kind of figured Charlie Hazard would give you all the scary you need."

"No, Charlie's just a big puppy at heart."

Lena listened to laughter rock the truck. "You've been making friends."

"Thirteen hours in a truck with this crew, it's either become pals or borrow Charlie's gun."

Lena gave her the address Marjorie had located, then asked to speak with Bishop. When the surgeon came on the line, she said, "Brett calibrated five neural nets, and with four of them he added the brain-wave pattern that stimulates ascending. The fifth neural net is being used by our host, Agnes Lockwood. She's dying. What I wanted you to know is, yesterday Agnes remained without pain all afternoon."

"Wait, he's . . . You've . . ."

"Brett then counted the four of us up. I ascended. The other three all reported having experiences. Not actual ascents, but very important just the same. All because of your wonderful, amazing, incredible invention."

There was a long silence, a fumbling noise, then Robin came back on the line and asked, "What did you say to make Bernie cry?"

Brett entered the kitchen as Lena cut the connection. His hair was still wet from the shower, and his eyes were clouded. Lena wanted to tell him about yesterday's ascent. She wanted to thank him for the quilt. She wanted him to help her adjust to this strange mix of emotions that filled her heart and mind. But as she watched him move with careful deliberation around the kitchen, then frown out the rear window as he sipped his coffee, she knew now was not the time.

Finally he said, "I woke up to a very strong impression that you need to ascend again."

"All right."

"This raises a number of issues." He did not seem to have heard her. He stared at the garden as he continued, "I have not had any direct contact with . . ."

"Whatever this is," Lena offered.

"With anything related to ascents for over a year. And yet, that was how it felt. As though I walked into some message that was . . ." He grasped the air in front of his face. "I can't describe what just happened. Much less explain it."

"Brett." She waited until he turned around. "It's okay. I understand. These sorts of events are why I'm here. Remember?"

His gaze was hollow. "But you're not carrying my baggage."

She clamped down on the urge to tell him what she'd seen of him the previous day. "Maybe we better get started."

Brett brought the gear downstairs and set it up on the coffee table. He drew a chair over from the dining table, helped Lena fit on the neural net, then waited while she settled back down on the sofa. When she was comfortable, he ran through the same initial phrases, then counted her up.

This time she knew an instant's hesitation, a mere flash of fear, and then she was up. Ascending.

Free.

Then he spoke. "If there is anything you need to see, you will do this now. You remain in complete control. You will only experience what keeps you in complete safety. You are going now."

Even before she heard the words, she was moving. She rose from the room, from the house, from the city. She saw none of this, and yet she knew this had occurred. Lena's focus was gradually drawn south, farther and farther, to where she could see a GMC truck traveling north on I-95. The rear hold was jammed with gear. The truck's two rows held four people. Charlie Hazard drove and listened as Robin and Chester peppered Bernard Bishop with questions.

She remained there a single breath, then she was drawn even higher. Lena observed the highway and the traffic and the people and the dreams and the frustrations and the needs, a flowing river of human life. The act of being directed was so gentle, Lena could easily have broken free.

Then in the distance a cloud formed. Far to the south, the asphalt ribbon became swallowed by a dark menace. Every kind of malevolent spirit, every form of dark and tainted soul. They knew who she was, they knew about Charlie Hazard, they knew about Bishop, and they were bound together by the aim to destroy them all.

Lena's form was wracked by a somber tolling, a thunderous message so potent it flung her back and into her physical form.

"You are returning now," Brett said. His eyes went round as she jerked from the sofa and flung the neural net to the floor.

Lena waited until her breathing had eased, until she could form the words without shrieking them out loud. "They're coming."

47

arjorie's limo pulled up fifteen minutes later. Lena and Brett went upstairs for a brief moment with Agnes. The old lady was calm and accepting and brilliantly alive. She had remained pain free, without drugs, all night. Lena felt pierced by the uncertainty of whether they might meet again as Frederick helped them load the gear into Marjorie's waiting limo. The butler's farewell carried a solemn formality, and he remained standing at the curb until they turned south on Madison and vanished.

On the journey through the Theater District, Brett quietly described the project's early days. Marjorie sat between them, her gaze aimed straight forward, not moving, not even blinking. Absorbing every word.

Their destination was a rundown warehouse three blocks off the Hudson River. According to Marjorie, the entire block was now owned by one of the bank's subsidiaries, kept empty while the developers ran the city's permitting maze.

"Roger has officially leased this to me," Marjorie told Lena as they rose from the limo. "I quite like playing landlord to a world-changing event."

Lena asked, "Did you tell Roger about your . . . ?"

"Message," Marjorie finished. "Not yet. That sort of news requires . . ."

"Delicacy," Lena offered. "Proper timing."

"Roger has wanted this far more than me," Marjorie said. "He has forced himself to move on. This is going to be . . ."

"Special."

"And intensely difficult for him to accept." Marjorie hugged herself.

They crossed Tenth Avenue and entered a diner. The linoleum table was sticky and Lena's coffee mug had crevices around the rim, like someone had tried to eat the ceramic. A secretary from the developer's office arrived with a set of keys and the rental contract. Fifteen minutes later, Lena's phone rang. She spoke briefly, then announced, "They're here."

As Lena left the diner and crossed the street, she watched the four emerge slowly from the truck. Their motions were stiff in the manner of people who had been driving for a very long while. But they were easy with one another, that much was very clear. They spoke and they smiled, and Robin even gave Charlie a mock blow to the shoulder. Charlie saw them first and spoke a few words that drew the others around.

Robin said in greeting, "Next time you can drive fourteen hours and I'll go to the spa."

Charlie and the others stepped up beside Robin. He moved with quiet grace, a hunting cat in chinos and a denim work shirt. The open collar revealed ragged scars to his collarbone and chest. He waited through the introductions, then said, "You need to lose the limo."

Marjorie appeared fascinated by the man. "Of course."

Brett told Charlie, "Lena has received a warning that we are already being tracked."

Charlie's gaze held the calm finality of prehistoric diamonds, compressed by eons into something hard enough to fracture light. "You ascended?"

"Twice," Brett replied for her. "The second time was because I received . . . I'm not sure what to call it."

Charlie nodded, clearly comfortable with the lack of proper words. He said to Lena, "Describe what happened."

They all gathered there on the broken sidewalk in a condemned neighborhood, chilled by far more than the wind. Robin and Chester listened agog as Lena related her experience.

When she finished, Charlie said, "For the moment, we'll assume it's correct. I'll ask others to confirm your findings."

"Can I try this thing?" Robin said.

Brett replied, "The stats on first timers are not great. Less than ten percent who try can ascend."

"Still, I want to give it a go."

He nodded. "Then we'll make it happen."

Robin actually bounced on her toes. She asked Lena, "Is it as cool as it sounds?"

"Better," Lena replied. "By about ten thousand percent."

Brett told Charlie, "The neural nets seem to increase the success rate. We tried with four. Only one ascended. But what was most interesting is that the other three had what can only be described as unique experiences."

Bishop asked softly, "And the patient?"

"As of an hour ago, Mrs. Lockwood remained off her meds and pain free."

Bishop wiped his mouth slowly, back and forth, compressing the emotions that creased his face.

Charlie patted the doctor's shoulder and said, "Let's get out of this wind."

⁂

The nicest part of the warehouse was the upstairs, reached by a metal stairwell that climbed the right-hand wall. There was nothing to suggest it would be anything more than a suite of threadbare offices. Marjorie unlocked a solid wood door and they entered a three-bedroom apartment. The setting held a certain Zen-like quality, with muted lighting and woven tatami carpets and lotus blossoms imprinted into the off-white wallpaper. The front room had done service as an office, evident from the multiple cables still sprouting from every wall. Two skylights adorned with stained glass painted the room in hues of rose and umber.

Robin took one look and declared, "I'm moving in."

"Actually," Charlie replied, "we all are."

Marjorie cleared her throat. "Now may be a good time to offer my husband's objections to that idea."

"You don't need to stay," Charlie replied. "No one is required to take it to the next level. But if you're in, this is home for the duration."

Marjorie waited until Charlie led Bishop into the rear bedrooms to say, "That man scares me a little."

Brett replied, "Probably a good thing."

Lena asked, "Does he frighten you too?"

"Not the man," Brett replied. "But the reason why he's here. What he represents."

"The cloud beyond the horizon," Lena said. "The boogeymen who are hunting us."

Marjorie shivered.

Brett faced the four of them, Lena and Marjorie and Robin and Chester. "Here's what you need to remember. Charlie Hazard will die before he lets anyone in his team get hurt."

Chester said, "Is it true what he said, we can leave?"

Lena replied, "Absolutely."

"You're kidding, right?" Robin protested.

"Hey, this has been fun and all, but I'm a banker," Chester said.

"What am I, the nanny?" Robin shot back. "Did you even hear what Bernie was saying?"

"I was sitting right there beside you. I heard every word."

"All this represents a major breakthrough," Robin said. "Besides which, it could be fun."

"This guy talked about dying and you call it fun?" Chester looked from one to the other. "You're all nuts."

Lena settled a hand on Robin's arm, cutting off her next comment. "Go back to the office. Play damage control. We need somebody protecting our backs, right, Robin?"

She muttered something that Lena was fairly certain had nothing to do with agreement. Chester looked from one to the other, then turned and left without a backward glance.

Robin took a hard breath. "I actually liked the guy."

"There's nothing wrong with knowing your limits," Marjorie said.

Lena took that as her cue. "Maybe you should go."

Marjorie was clearly tempted, but in the end she shook her head and said, "So what happens now?"

Brett's voice had gone quiet, somber as a messenger of death. "In a few minutes Charlie will come back and say that our first objective is to define the danger. And the second is to define our defense."

Lena read the unspoken in Brett's gaze. "I'll need to go back up again?"

"Ascend," Brett corrected. "Since you found the threat, he'll probably think it's a good idea."

"Will you come with me?"

She could see the objections in his gaze. And was ready to accept them all. Now was definitely not a time for arguments. The threat was too real, their numbers too paltry. But when he spoke, it was to say, "Yes, Lena. If I can."

48

Reese awoke to the sound of a prison claxon. She jerked awake, gasping with fear of the nightmare's return. But her eyes focused upon a beautiful little apartment, with sliding glass doors that reflected nothing more dangerous than a dark night. She rose from the bed and opened the doors and stepped outside. Her apartment was on the third floor and faced east, over the pool enclosure and the residential community beyond. Dawn was a pale hue of promise and calm. The houses beyond the motel's enclosure were silent, the wind still. The air was perfumed by late spring jasmine and a distant orange grove.

The balcony chairs were old and worn, remnants from the motel's previous incarnation. She sat until the sun's rim emerged from the trees and the rooftops, and the birds rose in chattering clouds, and the neighborhood streets came to life. She returned inside, showered, and dressed. The tension remained with her, a tight ball that she doubted would ever fully unravel. But she had slept well, and there had been no repeat of the monster dreams. For today, it was enough.

The café operated on a twenty-four-hour clock. A couple of voyagers offered her a sleepy hello, then went back to their eggs and soft conversation. Through the rear doors she saw that another few surrounded one of the tables by the pool.

While she was waiting for her breakfast, Kevin appeared in the doorway. He looked as rumpled and exhausted as the previous day. He hurried over and said, "You need to come."

"Can I get my coffee?"

Kevin barked across the counter, "Coffee. Large. Two. Now."

"Did you get any sleep?"

"Not enough." He accepted the two paper cups and handed one to her. "Let's go."

Every eye in the room and beyond watched them hurry back down the hall and through the lobby and out into the early morning heat. "What's the matter?"

Kevin crossed the parking lot. When the office building's glass doors did not slide back fast enough, he kicked them impatiently. "I have no idea."

"We have a very serious problem," Vera announced.

Kevin's chair could not contain him. He stood by the window, shifting from heel to toe and back again. His nervousness was contagious. Reese could feel the ropy tendrils swirl across the table's polished surface and ensnare her.

Vera went on, "There is a man we must find. His name is Dr. Bernard Bishop."

Reese waited for Kevin to ask the necessary questions. But his only response to the news was to start pacing. Back and forth, the length of his office, moving from shadow to the window's light to shadow again.

Reese reached across the table for his yellow pad and pen. She asked, "Doctor of what?"

"He was formerly a spinal surgeon. More recently he has been working as a GP in an urgent-care clinic."

"Where?"

"Savannah."

"Is that where he was a surgeon?"

"Yes. There and Jacksonville. Is this really necessary?"

"I have no idea."

"The man has gone missing. We want you to find him."

But Reese was no longer paying attention to the new task. Kevin's nervous motions were a distraction. She swiveled her chair so she was looking at the wall beyond his desk. Thinking.

Vera demanded, "Are you there?"

"Give me a minute." Reese heard something. A vague hint, nothing more. She felt like a feral cat that had caught the first scent upon the wind. She pulled the speaker closer to her. It was just her and Vera now. "This means a new duty. Something we've never tried before. It may help us to have details of this guy's life."

It was Vera's turn to go quiet. Then, "Hold on."

When the phone went quiet, Kevin asked, "What are you—"

"Not now." She kept her gaze upon the empty legal pad in her lap. Writing her thoughts in a secret script. When Vera came back on, Reese was ready.

"All right," Vera said. "Ask your questions."

"Why did this man stop being a surgeon?"

Again there was a long silent moment, then Vera said, "We might have had something to do with that."

"Understood." There it was again. The vague wisp telling her that the quarry she had been hunting was close. "You've had this Bishop under surveillance?"

"Off and on. Mostly via bugs and cameras."

"When did he go off grid?"

"The day before yesterday, Bishop left his place of employment in the late afternoon. We don't have the exact time yet. He went by a storage unit where he kept . . . certain elements from his . . . previous work. He stopped by a bank. Then he went to his apartment. Our knowledge becomes sketchy after that. He may have checked into a local hotel, but if so the room was under a different name."

"Was he alone?"

"No. Four people we have not yet identified came and took him. Or he went voluntarily. We don't know."

"Were they police?"

"We don't think so. They showed the clinic receptionist no badges."

Reese stared at the pad and sorted through all her unwritten thoughts. "So what you're saying is, it took a day and a half to sound the alarm."

"The doctor has made no change to his routine in almost a year. The surveillance understandably grew lax." Vera hesitated, then added, "We also want you to tell us who took him."

"Give me those addresses for where you know and where you suspect he went after going off grid." But when Vera rattled them off, Reese did not write them down. She was not after data. She wanted to keep the woman talking. Because the breeze had shifted in her direction now, carrying the first clear confirmation that the prey was close. And vulnerable. "What would be your ideal outcome here?"

"My ideal . . . We want you to find the man and these four others. Immediately!"

"Do you want where he is at the moment, or where he will be in the future?"

Vera's standard ire shattered like a crystal globe hitting granite. "You can do that?"

"We can try. Give me your optimal solution."

"Wait." The phone clicked off. Reese drew a circle in the middle of the yellow page. Then she drew a vertical line down the center of the circle, and another line at a ninety-degree angle. Creating a target with crosshairs. She ground the pen into the juncture of the two lines. A bullet hole right through Vera's heart.

Vera came back on and said, "We want the individual's position twelve hours out. At a point where he is isolated."

Reese kept enlarging the dark point at the target's center. "I have no idea how long we will require to obtain this information, or even if it's possible."

"We need this immediately. Now get to work."

But when the call ended, Reese remained there in the chair, staring down at the pad in her lap. She knew Kevin kept pacing because his shadow passed back and forth over the target Reese had drawn. She also knew what it was that had robbed him of sleep and kept him moving. The tension had a name now.

"The key is the missing neural nets," Reese said.

"They're not missing," Kevin replied. "A van comes and picks them up."

"But we don't know where they're going."

"They're developing their own team. A second set of voyagers." Kevin's fear was palpable. "Soon as they're operational, we're surplus material. They'll take us out."

Reese responded because she wanted him to understand his fear. Though she did not share it. Not at all. "You've always operated by the book," Reese said. "You were a good physicist, and then a better administrator. You handled a nation's darkest secrets. You got burned, you came back. You are giving this your very best. And for what. So you can wake up and wonder if today's the day they deliver a bullet with your name etched on it."

Kevin stopped, halted by the truth. He waited.

Reese swiveled around. Met his gaze. "What they don't realize is, they've just given us our way out."

Kevin's anguish creased both his features and his voice. "Where are we going to run?"

"It's not about hiding," she replied. "It's about making them stay away."

Kevin squinted, like he was straining to hear her words.

Reese went on, "Why are they so worried about a guy who's vanished?"

He did not reply.

"What happened that reduced a surgeon to a GP in some late-night clinic?"

Kevin opened his mouth, but no sound emerged.

"There's only one answer that works. This Bishop guy developed the technology we're using. Vera's secret bosses stole it. And they made certain nobody ever came looking to use his discovery. Murdering him would leave a trail. So they disgraced him. And blinded the world in the process."

Kevin's hand shook slightly as he searched for the chair. He dropped into the seat. All without taking his gaze off Reese.

"We follow the trail," Reese said. "Backward and forward. We give them what they want. The target's location twelve hours from when we report in. But we hunt back at the same time."

"We use the information as blackmail," Kevin said.

She wanted to reach across the table and slap him, jolt him to full alert. But she stayed where she was and kept her voice calm. "No, Kevin. That's not it at all."

"Then why . . ."

"We track down the people who were behind this. We follow them to their lair. We make a firm ID. We give the puppet masters a name." Reese felt the tense pleasure only a predator ever knew. "And just when they think it's time to take us out, they'll discover . . ."

When she did not continue, Kevin pressed, "Discover what?"

Reese knew he was not ready to hear what she had in mind. "Whatever we want them to see."

But the truth was, by this time tomorrow the group hiding behind Vera would no longer be the people in control.

49

On her way back across the parking lot, it struck Reese that Kevin had relinquished his position as team leader. He shuffled a half step behind her, there to support and there to follow. Reese slowed a fraction, just to see his response.

Kevin slowed with her. He asked, "Something wrong?"

"Just working things through."

"Are you sure it's wise, you taking another voyage with them?"

"Yes, Kevin. I need to help with the hunt." Though in truth his concerns were valid. But Reese had no interest in leading from the rear.

A male security guard Reese had not seen before rushed through the motel's doors and started toward them. He announced, "There's something you need to see."

⫙

The guard's name was Colin, and Reese was fairly certain he was a retired cop. There was a vibration or a scent or some edge to his voice that set her off, like a dog yammering over a coming storm. Reese stood behind Kevin, to the right of the female guard named Loren.

Reese did not want to be here. The ticking clock was a drum rattling inside her brain.

"Loren was the one who spotted the action." For such a big man, Colin had a very light touch on the computer console. He stopped typing and manipulated the joystick. "Watch the central monitor."

Kevin asked, "What are we supposed to be seeing?"

"You tell me. Here we go."

Two voyagers crossed the lobby. One was male, the other female. Reese knew them both by sight. The pair wore backpacks and dragged wheelie cases across the carpet.

Kevin said, "I suspected these two of being Vera's spies."

"Your alert was why I've been keeping an eye on them," Loren said.

Reese nodded but did not speak. It was smart of Kevin to have the guards track anyone possibly spying for the opposition. That was increasingly how Reese thought of the unseen puppet masters. They weren't enemies yet. But they were moving in that direction. It was only a matter of time.

Kevin said, "You didn't ask where they were headed?"

"Your instructions were, long as they sign out, they're free to come and go at will." Colin pointed at the monitor showing the motel's forecourt. "They've moved over into the shaded area to the right of the entry. Probably for the breeze. The cameras miss that spot. There's nine and a half minutes of nothing, so I'm going to speed things up."

Several people zipped in and out of the doors. Twice, shadowy bits of someone's body popped into the screen's right-hand edge, then disappeared.

Colin watched the clock above the monitors. "Okay, now we're back on real time."

A minivan pulled up. Kevin squinted and demanded, "Who's that driving?"

"Esteban," Reese said. Insects started moving around in her gut, even before she had worked out the reason. She watched as the side door opened and Heather stepped out. She gave the pair that same hateful-bright smile. They stowed the pair's cases and backpacks in the rear hold. All three clambered into the van. The door slid shut. The van started forward.

"Keep watching," Colin said.

The van departed, and a Nissan Altima passed in front of the camera. It followed the van across the screen. The light glinted off the windows, but Reese recognized both the driver and her passenger.

"Play that back," Kevin said.

"There's no need," Reese replied. And no time. "It's them. The whole midnight crew and Vera's two spies. They're gone."

Kevin kept watching the image now frozen on the monitor. "Gone where?"

Reese thanked the guards, then waited until they were back in the lobby to reply, "There's only one answer. They're going to be part of Vera's new team."

Kevin mulled that over. "I'll have security run a search of all private jets taking off from the regional airports."

Reese thought that was a total waste of time, but all she said was, "The doctor's disappearance obviously hit their panic button. My guess is, they'll be up and running in a matter of days. Which means we need to accelerate."

Kevin responded like a willing subordinate. "How will you handle this?"

"As far as Vera and her associates are concerned, we will perform as ordered. Track their man. Everything else stays off the grid." Reese could see Kevin was not moving fast enough. She wanted to grip him and shake him so hard his teeth rattled. Instead, she said, "You need to start prepping for an emergency evac. Shift the money into cash and gold. Get transport for us all."

"Wait . . . We're leaving?"

"Wake up, Kevin. They're going to equip their own team with the midnight crew, probably offering the protection they've lacked until now. Soon as they're up operational, they don't need us anymore. Would you leave us out here, knowing what we know?"

The same haunted look returned to his weary features. "All right. Yes."

"One more thing. Kevin, this is the most important of all. Stop shipping out your products. Duplicate all the monitoring equipment. Stow away as many neural nets as you can. Be ready to move."

"When do we . . ."

But Reese had already started for the doors. "I'm about to find that out."

Reese split most of the voyagers into two groups and prepped them together. As soon as one returned and reported in, the second would go out. Obtaining all the data required by Vera and the unseen people pulling their strings.

And while this happened, Reese's secret crew would target the real issue.

Reese sent them out, giving the voyagers thirty minutes. Then she asked Karla, "We clear on the instructions?"

"Yes, but who will shield you?"

"Carl will handle me and Ridley both." Reese left the monitoring station and entered the second departures lounge, the one reserved for her core team, and said, "New day, new target. We're going to have to assume the midnight crew has shifted over to the opposition."

They exchanged a worried look. Ridley asked, "What does that mean?"

"I have no idea. We need to be ready for incoming fire, but not today. We've got at least twenty-four hours before they're operational. So we're splitting up. Ridley, you're going after the missing crew. Karla will count you down and tell you to find out where they're heading. This is important. We don't need to know where they are now. We need to know where their point of operation is located. Clear?"

"Yes."

Carl asked, "What about you?"

"Karla is going to give me different instructions. We need to know if and when the opposition is going to come for us. Karla will tell me to stay here and move forward."

Ridley asked, "We're in danger?"

"Not if we're already gone. You see?"

Carl revealed a remarkably sweet smile. "You're our early warning system."

"If it works," Reese said, glad she had decided to tell them. "Can you stay linked with both of us if we move in totally different directions?"

Carl shrugged. "I've got two hands. Sort of."

Reese settled into her chair. "We probably don't need to share this item with the others just yet."

"No need to spook them," Ridley agreed.

"Terrible pun," Carl said. "Awful."

"Then why are you smiling?"

Reese fitted on her net. "Let's get to work."

50

wo hours later, Reese and Kevin were back in his office, talking on the scrambler phone. Reese did not want to be there. But Vera had demanded an update.

"My people have made a number of searches, but so far we're coming up blank," Reese reported.

"Send them out again."

She resisted the urge to snap at the woman. She was tired and stressed and worried about her team. They were doing everything right. But learning how to anchor and protect themselves was proving both difficult and time consuming. So far, their voyages had done little except keep them safe. Which was in itself a huge success. But not to Vera.

Reese said, "I am. Repeatedly. We will get this done."

Vera demanded, "Do I need to remind you how urgent this is?"

Kevin replied for her, "We are all aware of the ticking clock."

"Time bomb is more like it." Vera went silent, then said, "Stay where you are."

When the phone clicked off, Kevin muttered, "This is the first time we've not had anything positive to report."

Reese did not reply.

The phone clicked back. Vera said, "This issue could not be more crucial."

When Reese remained silent, Kevin answered, "We will get this done."

⸎

Reese sent the crew out once more. They returned exhausted. Despite the lack of progress on the intel front, Reese found a deep sense of satisfaction in how they all rose from their stations, alert and present and on her side. When she returned to the glass cube to report, Kevin met her upstairs in the production room. Around two dozen dark-skinned men and women worked at long benches, soldering wires and shaping flexible helmets and snipping cables and checking leads with various calibration equipment. Even the production manager, a tall Anglo with snow-white hair, occupied one of the benches. Reese thought their motions looked borderline frantic, but she had no frame of reference, as she'd never been up here before.

Kevin greeted her with, "Anything?"

"Not yet, but I think we're getting close."

His features were crimped tight by the strain. "Still think it was a good idea to get rid of the midnight crew?"

Reese thought nothing good could come from reworking past events. She remained silent.

Kevin turned back to the factory floor. "I promised them triple overtime if they can complete new helmets for all of us by midnight."

"And the monitoring station?"

"That comes after. The technicians are all on this now. I'll give them a couple of hours off, then another triple pay to complete five sets of portable monitors before dawn. We'll check their work by using the new monitors to fix the new nets to each voyager."

"How long will that take?"

He shrugged. "Should be relatively fast. We have each voyager's mind print on record now. They'll duplicate the frequency settings, then bring the voyagers in and check."

"How long?"

"Three days, maybe four."

"We don't have that long," Reese replied.

He pulled his gaze away from the workers. "You're sure about that?"

"Yes, Kevin. I am."

"Why is that?"

"Because the reason why I think we're close to identifying Bishop's location is, I had a second team trying to track the midnight crew. This team was successful. Finally."

He saw it in her face. "It's bad, isn't it."

"You tell me. They're outside Havana."

Kevin jerked a half step away.

"Vera's group has taken a waterfront estate south of the city that looks like a palace. It's leased to the Russian government."

Kevin did not respond.

"It makes sense, though," Reese went on. "I mean, let's back up. Somebody who can arrange murders on the other side of the globe at an instant's notice could also be powerful enough to spring me from federal prison, right? So that same group steals a doctor's new technology. They don't kill this guy, because it might raise red flags. Instead, they disgrace him. How really doesn't matter at this point, does it, Kevin."

He watched her, his gaze unblinking, the production room forgotten.

"Once they obtained the doctor's technology and quashed any potential interest by outsiders, they went on the hunt," Reese said. "Gathering up a collection of military suppliers. Their aim was to build their own intelligence cabal. Not just here in the United States. Around the globe. And it's not just so they can access the latest technology as soon as it's developed. They want to know what their enemies are spending money on. Using us to do it. And at the same time, the Russians began working up a voyager team of their own."

"Havana is . . ."

"A perfect cutout," she finished for him. "Even if they're detected, they can deny any involvement. And now they have our midnight crew to prevent their own voyagers from sinking into comas. They probably don't like the idea of unleashing shadow monsters any more than we did. But Russia will take that risk. Soon as they confirm that their own crews are stabilized and bringing in the required intel, we're history. Because we know too much. We've become a liability."

Reese let that sink in, then added, "We don't have four more days, Kevin. In thirty-six hours, we are either gone or dead."

51

Brett's first real interaction with Bernard Bishop came when he described inserting the brain-wave patterns to stimulate an ascent. Bishop looked very tired. Brett assumed it was not so much from the journey as from the year of futile days and all the crushing blows that had come before.

Bishop ignored his fatigue as only a professional surgeon could. He stood at the kitchen counter beside Brett and said, "I'm still struggling with the idea that these supposedly random experiences of my trial subjects are your mainline event."

"They weren't random," Brett replied. "Gabriella thinks they are a component of every human's core brain-wave structure. What happens here is they become a dominant force."

"And allow the subject's consciousness to separate from their physical form."

"In a controlled pattern," Brett said. "Which is both the beauty and the danger of this entire process."

Bishop was moving with him now. "Control means direction."

"Access," Brett confirmed. "No secret is safe from a spy who uses this technology to observe and remain undetected."

Bishop's gaze burned within the hollow cave of the events now behind him. "What is your ultimate aim, Dr. Riffkind?"

"Call me Brett. I don't know how to answer that. I thought I did, before . . ."

Bishop gave him a minute, then said softly, "I have the impression you carry your own shadows because of all this."

Charlie surprised them both by responding, "Brett's not alone there."

Bishop jerked around. "You would make a cat jealous."

Brett knew the reason Charlie had spoken was to save him from needing to respond. But he did so anyway. "My original ambition was to prove that human thought and perception were not tied to the Newtonian concept of time. That Einstein's barrier did not exist at this level. That here was the juncture at which human existence and the quantum world combined."

"They would all seem to be worthy of a life's work," Bishop said. "Why did you drop them?"

"He didn't," Charlie replied, settling a hand on Brett's shoulder. "But this isn't the time for Brett to go deeper into his recent activities."

Bishop still possessed a surgeon's ego and a scientist's inquisitive nature. He looked ready to argue. Brett understood the urge. They were here because of what Bishop had discovered, so he had a right to know why things had been brought to this juncture. But the past eighteen months of living down and out had taught Bishop patience as well. He asked, "So what happens now?"

"The ladies should be back soon. We'll have a meal and go on the hunt."

"Through an ascent," Bishop said.

"Right."

"I want to do this also," Bishop told him.

"Not just yet," Charlie replied. "We're headed into Indian country. You understand the term? It's military-speak for a free-fire zone.

293

There is no telling what we are going to find. I'm already concerned about sending Lena, but since she was our first spotter, I think it's a necessary risk."

Brett understood the unspoken. How Charlie was concerned about Brett taking such a high-risk ascent. But all he felt was calm certainty. He said, "I need to go with her."

Charlie nodded acceptance. "Soon as the ladies return, I'll count you both up."

Lena and Robin and Marjorie went off shopping. Three minivan taxis, three different lists. Lena found an outdoor sports-supply house that was open late and bought nine sleeping bags and blow-up mattresses and two portable camp tables and chairs. She deposited her wares in the taxi and went next door for shampoo and conditioner and makeup remover and other such vital items as Oreos and, for those who were not dedicated chocoholics, Fig Newtons.

When Lena returned to the warehouse, she helped Brett and Bishop set up pallets in a rear bedroom that would serve as their ascending station. She then sat in a camp chair and watched as Bishop took Brett through the questioning process, then did the same for Charlie, who interrupted his own calibration to take three phone calls.

Lena found a soft pleasure in the inactivity. She heard the others return but did not feel any need to go join them. Lena smelled the odors of takeout being unpacked and knew a keen sense of hunger. Still she did not move. There was a need to assimilate the day and see it from the perspective of what would probably happen tomorrow. As far as she was concerned, it all came down to this. From the very first contact with her temporal self, Lena had been moving toward this point in time and space. Seated in a canvas camp chair, watching a professional warrior and a California scientist and a Savannah surgeon prepare for an incoming assault.

While they shared a subdued meal, Charlie related how he had reached out to a few friends and they would be arriving soon. Marjorie took another phone call and stepped from the room. When she returned, she slipped into the chair beside Lena and said, "Roger had to attend a dinner with the board. He's on his way over. He wants me to come home with him."

"Maybe he's right." Charlie said, then told Lena, "It's almost eleven. I know you're tired. But we need to do a recce."

"I'm ready," Lena said. Her calm felt generated by something outside herself. A by-product of all the events swirling and tightening and focusing. On her. Here and now.

"Brett?"

"I'm good to go."

"I'll count you up," Charlie said. "Bernie, I need you to ready Brett for an ascent using one of your neural nets. When they ascend, I need you beside me to ensure I get the technical sequencing correct."

"Of course."

Charlie focused on Lena. "Your aim is simple. Your ascent needs to stay tight and on target. You are to determine three things: What form the first assault will take. Will there be a psychic element to this first attack. And when will they strike. Is that clear?"

Lena had the impression he was not speaking just to her and Brett. He spoke so that everyone could hear and understand. Building them into a squad. Readying them all.

She said, "Perfectly clear."

"The risk is that they are already here. So before you ascend, I'm going to instruct you to form a shield. We haven't done this before. But I want to try it."

Brett sounded as calm as she felt. "Understood."

Charlie finished his mug, set it on the counter, and said, "We ascend in five."

52

J ust after sunset, Reese's voyagers came back with solid gold.

As far as her team was concerned, locating Bernard Bishop was less important than the sheer pleasure of being freed from the midnight crew and staying protected. They constantly interrupted Reese's debriefing with laughter, tag teams, impromptu dances, basically letting off steam. Time and again Reese needed to check her desire to scream at them to focus.

When she finally had all she needed, Reese dismissed them and walked as calmly as she could down the corridor and through the reception area. Then she sprinted across the parking lot and punched the glass entry and bolted up the stairs. But Kevin was not in his office or in the assembly area, and the foreman had no idea where he was. His cell phone went straight to voice mail. She thought maybe he was sacked out, so she raced back, flying through the clutch of voyagers and up yet more stairs. She pounded on his door until one of the guards came up behind her and said, "What's going on?"

Only then did Reese hear her own breathing, a teakettle hiss one degree off a soft scream. "What a time for him to go off grid."

"He left while you were getting ready for that last voyage."

Reese punctuated each word with a fist to his door. "I need him now."

"Can't help you." The guard pulled the chain that connected the passkey to her belt, pushed it into the slot, and opened the door. "See for yourself."

Reese glanced inside but did not enter. "Gone where?"

"He didn't say. Which for Kevin is kinda strange." She watched as Reese leaned her forehead on the doorjamb. "What's going on?"

"The team did their job." There was a somber quality to accepting the fact that she had to handle this on her own. Because she was certain there was no way this could wait. The guard followed her back down the stairs. A lot of worried faces watched her come into view. Reese told them to eat and get some rest while they could, because they would be going out again before dawn.

Reese tried to hold it together as she recrossed the parking lot. A faint evening breeze whispered threats of what would happen if she got this wrong. She entered the glass cube and climbed the stairs and walked into Kevin's office. She seated herself in Kevin's chair so her back was to the window and the dusk. She was terrified of losing what was probably the only chance they had left. But the clock kept banging in her head, counting down the seconds. So she coded in the scrambler and dialed the number. Each ring was a drill puncturing her future.

When Vera finally answered, Reese said, "I want five million dollars."

Vera's voice caught momentarily. "You . . ."

"You heard me."

"It's no more about what you want than the last time."

Reese hoped the jerky quality to Vera's response was not just her imagination. She hoped the uncertainty was real. She hoped . . .

Vera demanded, "Did you hear me?"

Reese took a long breath. "Actually, I want two million. But this way you can say you beat me down."

Vera was silent.

"I have it all," Reese said. "Bishop's location now. Where he will be tomorrow. And the danger you're going to face when you go after him."

"Tell me."

"No problem. Soon as the money is in Kevin's account."

"You will tell me this instant."

"The clock is ticking," Reese replied.

"You took the words out of my mouth," Vera said. "You have no idea how close you are —"

"No threats!" Reese shouted with fourteen months of pent-up rage. She panted through the comedown, then went on, "You will reward my team. On my terms."

Reese cut the connection. She sat there, her hands compressed between her thighs, her entire body curled with the effort of holding it together. Then her cell phone jangled in her pocket.

When she answered, the guard said, "We've located Kevin."

Reese found Kevin exactly where he said he'd be. The café was across a six-lane intersection from the world's largest waterslide, a behemoth that took up a full city block. The café had a long canvas overhang girded by steel supports. The metal pillars glinted in the streetlights. The canvas was tight as a beige sail and fluttered in the night breeze.

Kevin was at a table toward the back, the only man seated there alone, the only guy in a tie. He was studiously ignored by the teens and families laughing over the safe adventures they'd enjoyed across the street. He had a draft beer in front of him. It had been sitting there long enough for the foam to settle and the bubbles to fade. He had torn strips from the coaster and formed tiny sodden balls that littered the table.

He watched Reese approach and asked, "You want anything?"

Reese felt utterly drained from handling Vera on her own. The drive here had taken over an hour. The traffic had been awful. But the distance and the time alone had helped. She was no longer angry with Kevin. There was no time for recriminations. Things were going to enter a critical phase. All nonessentials had to wait.

Reese was not hungry, but she had skipped lunch and knew she had to eat. She ordered a burger and Coke from a passing waitress, then asked Kevin, "Why did you go off grid?"

"I needed some space, is all."

Across the street, a trio of teen girls reached the top of the waterslide's highest ladder. They stared down the glistening plastic tube and played at screams. A boy and girl with toffee curls pointed from the next table and laughed at their antics. She saw it and yet none of it touched her. On the drive over she had feared Kevin was going to walk away. But now she knew the man had nowhere to go.

Kevin watched the shrieking girls take the slide hand in hand. "Do you remember the last time you were happy?"

Reese waited while the young woman in the candy-stripe uniform deposited her Coke on the table. She kept her voice calm as she replied, "That's not the question we need to be dealing with."

He tore off another strip and rolled it between thumb and forefinger.

"The question is, what do we need to do in order to have a chance at happiness tomorrow."

He stared across the traffic at the slide, seeing nothing. "Always before I could excuse the limits I'd set on my world. No home life to speak of. Wife and kids were strangers long before they left me. It was all for the agency. Or the country. Something worth the sacrifice."

Reese studied him with the objectivity of a scientist inspecting an amoeba. This was her friend coming undone. Explaining why he was relinquishing the lead. Handing control over to his number two.

Kevin went on, "Now I'm working for the enemy. There aren't any excuses I can hide behind. Now it's just . . ."

Reese waited to make sure he was done, then finished for him, "Now it's about survival."

The waitress returned with her burger. Reese ate without tasting. Holding back, wanting to see if Kevin could draw the world into focus. Because the truth was, she needed him desperately. She wasn't sure she could do everything that was required without him.

Kevin neither spoke nor looked her way. When she finished her meal, she asked, "What are we doing here?"

"The biggest dealership in Florida for campers and stuff is just down the road. I got a bus, one big enough to handle all of us. I assume you didn't want to separate us."

Reese heard the resumed clarity to his voice and sighed away a great lump of tension. "You got that right."

He lifted his glass, stared into the contents, and set it down again. "So what now?"

Reese laid out what the voyagers had discovered, and how she had confronted Vera. Her words were punctuated by more screams from across the street.

Kevin nodded slowly as she laid out what she had in mind, then asked, "Is the money in place?"

"Two million dollars. I checked before I came out here."

"Your plan succeeded."

"So far."

"You worked out this idea before you called Vera?"

"Most of the framework," she replied. "The details I put together on the drive here."

"Good strategy often comes down to the details," Kevin said.

"Is this good?"

He shrugged. "We'll know when the bullets start flying."

53

When Lena and Brett settled onto the pallets and fitted on their neural nets, the others did not ask if they could observe and Charlie did not caution them that there was nothing to see. Lena could sense them coalescing into a functioning unit.

Robin settled down by the wall next to Lena's pallet and watched her fit on the neural net. "You'll help me ascend?"

"As soon as we return," Lena said.

"Tomorrow is better," Brett said, laying back. "When you're fresh. It will heighten your chances of success."

"Leaving my body," Robin said. "Success."

"We'll do it whenever you want," Lena said.

Charlie interrupted with, "Time to take aim."

The net's earphones flapped down like a hunter's hood. Lena fitted them in place, found a comfortable position, and closed her eyes. The rushing sound was oddly familiar. Her heart rate rose to meet the anticipated thrill.

Charlie said, "Brett, you've done this a hundred times before. The past few months are an interruption, nothing more. Lena, Brett is here to help secure you throughout the ascent. I will count you up, and you will remain in ascent only so long as you are in complete control and absolute safety. Before the first risk arrives, you will have returned. Given those parameters, you have three targets: What form the first assault will take. Will there be a psychic element to this first attack. And when will they strike." He gave that a brief moment, then said, "I am beginning the count now."

The simple rush of sound was followed by a distinct sense of invitation. The urge to rise beyond the familiar was not a demand, not a command.

Charlie repeated, "You are in complete control."

Lena already knew this, just as she knew she could use the lancing fear as a means of withdrawing from the experience. She wanted to do just that—retreat from the sense of final disconnect. And yet her desire to move forward was stronger.

". . . Nine. Ten. Now open your other eyes."

She floated just above her body. She made a slow circuit. It probably lasted only a few moments, but the time was less important here. As though the restraint of counting seconds no longer held her. She saw Robin, sensed her trusting nature, her desire to accept Lena's quest. Then she looked at Marjorie and noticed for the first time how she held one hand upon her stomach, sheltering the new life within. Then Bishop, the spark of hope rising now, a piercing note she could almost hear. Then Charlie Hazard, the denseness of his being, the ready ability to do whatever it took.

Then she saw Brett.

Lena actually seemed to inspect herself first. As though clarity about the observer was vital to understanding the event. And that was how it seemed. A moment with the magnified intensity of an event that would change her world. Permanently.

She saw how her passion for risk analysis reflected her deepest nature. She held all life, all people, at arm's length. Especially men. She wanted to calculate the risk of every relationship, compute the hazards to every new beginning. And since she couldn't, she failed every relationship before it started.

Until now. When the outcome was foreordained. This man would break her heart and leave her destitute. But it did not matter. Not now that she had seen him.

Brett was as captivated as her. Lena understood that partly it was due to his joy over ascending again. His body breathed a long, pure breath, the lone physical expression of having realized a yearning he thought would never be his again. She did not merely understand. She experienced.

But that was not what held her.

She moved forward slowly. Or so it seemed. There was no reluctance, but rather a need to gradually give in to what they were doing. Moving together and experiencing the melding of two spirits.

Her every jagged edge, her every perceived flaw, her yearnings and her hopes, they all merged smoothly into his own. They were intended to do this. Join with such force that time literally stopped. Lena had no ability to turn her focus anywhere else, and yet she sensed that Charlie's lips moved, a fraction at a time, forming the words that would pry them apart. But not even the demands of coming peril could faze this event, drawn as it was from a universe never touched by the chains of time or risk.

She flowed to him. The unanswered need to love and be loved, the hunger she quashed because it hurt too much to inspect—all of this empowered her. And even this was shared. He flowed to her, and into her.

They breathed as one.

She knew the words were arriving, vibratory patterns in the air between them and Charlie. Lena did not want anyone else to sever this bond. And Brett was literally blinded by the act of joining. So she did it for them. Gently, firmly, lovingly, she pried herself loose, until one tendril of connection remained. The hand that had no physical presence reached out. And touched his formless face.

Then time retook hold upon them both, and Charlie said, "You will begin scouting now."

54

Reese directed her words to the encryption phone at the center of Kevin's conference table. "The target is no longer your primary problem."

"Is Kevin there?"

His chair was turned so that Reese saw his right side in silhouette. Like he wanted to remain disassociated. "Right here."

Vera demanded, "Why am I listening to your associate and not you?"

He swiveled around, the movement reluctant. "Reese and her team made the discovery. They are responsible for the intel. It is her report."

Reese waited through a pair of tight breaths, then Vera said, "So report."

"Dr. Bernard Bishop has sold a majority interest of his company. He is—"

"Hold it right there. Bishop's company is defunct."

"Not anymore."

"His reputation was destroyed. He has nothing left."

"If that is the case," Reese countered, "why did you order us to drop everything and hunt him down?"

Vera's breathing was audible over the scrambled line. "You stay right there. The both of you. Don't move."

When the line clicked, Kevin asked, "What just happened?"

The answer seemed obvious to Reese. "Vera was tasked with obliterating this guy. Having Bishop rise from the ashes threatens her position."

The streetlights painted his face in shadows. "So you think Vera was involved in murdering five innocent patients."

"Come on, Kevin. Snap out of it."

"Snap out . . . We're employed by animals."

Reese was a thousand miles removed from his distress. She was too intent on taking control of the last operation either of them would ever run for these puppet masters. Because Reese's new intel held the opportunity to pave the way to a very comfortable future. Or render them stone-dead. She was certain there was no third option.

But she did not tell Kevin any of this. Right now, there was room for one thing only. Making the next step. And surviving. So she said, "That's right. Animals who will kill us too. Unless every move we make is totally correct." Reese leaned forward and gripped his arm. "I will handle the opposition. But I need you to stay tight. Okay?"

She was close enough to see the loose skin of Kevin's neck tremble as he replied, "I won't let you down."

Vera kept them hanging for almost an hour. When she returned, her voice held a flat edge, almost resigned. She reported, "We can confirm that a personal check was written by Lena Fennan for five hundred thousand dollars and deposited in Bishop's account. Lena Fennan was until this week an analyst at First American Bank's Wall Street headquarters. She is now a fund manager with Baker Meredith. The branch manager of Bishop's bank notarized what she thinks were three copies of a contract."

Reese replied, "Lena Fennan is not your problem."

There was another extended silence. The tension grew until Kevin was no longer able to be held by his chair. He rose and started toward the window, when a new voice came over the speakerphone. "Ms. Clawson, am I correct in assuming you have had training as an operative?"

Reese shifted forward, drawing her face close to the phone. "Affirmative."

"Excellent. As one operative to another, may I suggest that we cut to the chase."

The man's English was both precise and very polished. But Reese heard the hint of an accent, almost impossible for an adult to totally lose. Kevin heard it as well, for he came back to the table and wrote a single word on his legal pad: *Russian.*

Reese said, "Can I ask your name?"

"Most certainly." The man seemed to find something humorous in her question. "As far as you and your associate are concerned, I am Jones."

"Bishop is now under the protection of a security specialist named Charlie Hazard."

"Am I correct in assuming that you and this specialist have a personal history?"

"I've come up against him twice. Both times he and his team took us out."

"This Hazard is behind your recent incarceration?"

"Directly responsible."

"Is his team already in place?"

"They don't need to be."

"Ah. So this Hazard and his team are in possession of our technology."

"They developed it. We stole it."

"Hazard is in the employ of . . ." There was a rustle of pages. "Dr. Gabriella Speciale?"

"Correct."

There was a brief pause. Kevin took the pad back and started writing. When he swiveled it around, Reese ignored it entirely. She remained intent upon Jones. Their survival depended upon her getting this right.

Jones said, "Be so good as to describe your previous encounters with this specialist."

Reese gave him the sort of abbreviated account she would have used with a visiting general or head of state. In her previous existence, back before she was locked in the federal cage, this had formed a regular part of her world. She assumed Jones already knew everything. He did not come on the phone to discuss the past. He was here to take her measure. Decide whether she was part of the solution or just another loose end to be obliterated.

When she was done, Jones gave her a few moments' silence, then said, "Very good. I assume you have worked out a means by which we can eliminate this Hazard."

"Him and everybody else working with Bishop."

"Because I would be quite displeased to think we have wired you two million dollars merely to obtain the doctor's whereabouts."

Reese laid out her idea. Six sentences. A pause. Three more. Then she stopped. She did not simply stop talking. Time itself seemed to freeze.

Finally Jones said, "This is most impressive."

Reese opened her mouth wide, forcing her chest to unlock, drawing a silent breath.

"So where did you locate Dr. Bishop?"

"Hazard and two of Lena Fennan's associates have driven him to Manhattan."

"You have their specific location?"

"Yes." Reese spelled out the address and described the building.

"Did their transport contain all of Bishop's remaining items?"

"No. A box of the neural nets was already in Manhattan."

"Ah. Which means they have already started monitoring your, shall we say, frequency?"

"There is no question. They know we're coming."

Jones's sigh was almost theatrical. "Well, in that case I suppose a little noise is inevitable."

55

Twenty minutes after Lena and Brett finished briefing the others about their ascent, Charlie's three associates arrived. Charlie greeted them with what Lena had always thought of as a warrior's embrace—thumbs-up handshake and free arm gripping the other's back for barely a second. An easy dance of muscle and steel, an affirmation they were joined against whatever threat was beyond the horizon.

The trio was shaped by the same ferocious mold, tight and tattooed and shave-headed and deadly. The Anglo wore an ammo vest over massive shoulders, black drawstring trousers, and canvas paratrooper boots. The African American and the Latino matched him for build and tats and manners, but they both wore jeans and sleeveless hooded sweatshirts and leather lace-ups. The African American bore two scars that ran forehead to neck, like he had been raked by a dragon's claw.

Charlie's team was still unloading their gear when Roger Foretrain stepped through the door. He did not return his wife's embrace because he was too busy dealing with the sight of the weapons. "Tell me this isn't happening."

Marjorie repeated what Charlie had told them. "These are our security. They're here to make sure we stay safe."

"They're mercenaries." Roger gave an angry swipe, as though he wanted to erase the whole thing. "This is Manhattan."

"I told you the situation was serious," Marjorie persisted.

"This isn't serious." His face was drained of blood. "This is war."

Charlie stepped up beside her. "There are just these three. All the armament is designed for two purposes."

"No. I do not want to hear—"

"Let him finish," Marjorie said softly.

"Their primary job is to make noise," Charlie went on. "The opposition will be after stealth. They want to sneak in, do their job, and leave unnoticed. This team is tasked with the job of waking up Manhattan."

The Latino was handsome in the manner of a weaving cobra. What was more, he knew it. He flashed a smile at Robin and said, "We are very good at our job. Charlie, tell the lady how good I can be."

Charlie went on, "I will be stationed across the street. The instant the opposition reveals their hand, I will phone the police, then take them from behind."

Roger's words rang through the cement chamber. "You are not putting my wife in danger."

Marjorie snapped, "Roger. Upstairs. Now." She wheeled about and drummed her heels up the metal stairs. When Roger did not follow, she shouted down, "Now!"

The handsome Latino murmured, "Adios, Roger."

"Hector," Charlie said. "Shut it."

"Hey, I'm just—"

"That's your quota all used up," Charlie said. "We clear?"

Hector made a big thing of the shrug. "Sí, jefe. Claro."

Lena remained downstairs both because she wanted to give Marjorie space and because Brett was there. She stood a few feet from where he and Bishop continued their ongoing dialogue. The pair remained intent upon their quiet discussion. Brett sketched graphs and calculations in the air. Bishop tracked Brett's finger like he could read the unwritten script.

Lena felt a faint electric charge compressing the air between Brett and herself. It was not desire and it was not impatience and it was not love. It was all of that and more. Brett shot her a look, freezing her solid and him as well, the finger poised in mid-stroke. The look was enough. For now.

Robin stepped to her other side and murmured, "I can't even name half the gear they're laying out."

Lena's attention drifted back over to where the Anglo broke down an assault rifle and cleaned each component carefully. The clink of metal on metal rang through the concrete chamber. She replied, "It's not just the gear that fascinates you."

Hector could not possibly have heard their conversation, perfected over months of hovering at the back of rooms, the gophers paid to disappear in plain view. Even so, Hector lifted his head and gave Robin a visual scalding.

"Like you're one to talk," Robin countered. "You and the scientist over there melting the walls."

Lena glanced back to Brett and the surgeon. "We are, aren't we."

"So when did that start?"

Lena was saved from needing to respond by Marjorie appearing at the top of the stairs and calling her name. Hector polished the barrel of his rifle and sang a soft, "Leeeena."

Charlie hissed. A cobra's warning. Hector ducked his head and resumed his work.

Marjorie halted Lena on the top step, holding the apartment door shut with the hand not gripping the rail. Needing both grips to maintain her balance. "Roger is extremely upset."

"I already got that memo."

Marjorie indicated the action downstairs. "This couldn't have come at a worse time. The board is gunning for him."

Lena knew why Marjorie was saying this. "He's taking you away."

"He needs me to be with him."

"Marjorie, I totally get it. Roger is worried about you. Did you tell him about the other thing?"

"Not yet."

"That's going to take his arguments to a totally new level."

Marjorie might have nodded. "He won't want to accept it now. He won't hear me. So I wrote him a note. I asked him to wait and read it in a few days. After . . ."

"When it's safe," Lena finished. "When you can see a doctor and have it medically confirmed, and then you can tell him. And he reads the note, and he remembers how all this happened. Bring it home to him. Smart." Then Lena realized what was behind the bleak expression. It had nothing to do with Roger making her leave. She asked, "Roger is going to fire me?"

Marjorie's eyes glittered in a very New York fashion, the misery of city life barely held in check. "Be nice. Please. Accept this with grace. It's coming from the board, not him. He fought for you. That's why it took him so long to arrive. Maybe later he can rally enough support to reinstate you."

Lena turned from the woman, the reality and the pain too great to watch her a single second longer. And the act saved Lena, for when she looked down into the main warehouse, Brett chose that moment to glance up. He had no idea what was happening, but the electric frisson sparked the air. The communication did not come from him directly, but rather through the act of bonding. Lena realized she was already moving into a new future. This was merely another step along the way.

She found the strength to turn and say calmly, "Let's get this over with."

⫘

"The granddaddy of brain stimulus methods is electroconvulsive therapy," Brett said. "Its name pretty much describes what it does."

They had returned upstairs. Lena was seated next to Brett on the sofa closest to the apartment's open door. She could hear the mercs downstairs talking softly and laughing. Occasionally there was the clink of metal on stone.

"Over the past few years, the entire direct-stimulation concept has been transformed," Brett went on. "There are now four entirely new methods being studied."

Bernard Bishop was seated in a camp chair he had pulled over from the dining table. Robin sat on a throw cushion supported by the side wall. The central table was littered with remnants of midnight takeout. Charlie wandered around the apartment, checking the windows, padding downstairs to speak with his team, then returning to plant himself by the open door. Lena found his actions as comforting as the sounds drifting up from below.

"My least favorite method is vagus nerve stimulation," Brett said. "A device is implanted under the skull, sending electrical impulses through the brain stem. Recently the FDA approved this as treatment for epilepsy, MS, and Alzheimer's."

What Lena most wanted from this moment was privacy, so she could wrap her arms around Brett and squeeze the man tightly enough that she could breathe with him. Have his presence fill the void where her job on Wall Street had resided. Her logical brain kept offering the reassurance of a job in Denver, the money in her account, all the reasons not to let this impact her. But Lena had never been fired before. Logic played no role in how she felt.

"Transcranial stimulation comes in two forms, electrical and magnetic," Brett continued. Bernard Bishop listened with the first easy smile Lena had ever seen him offer, the experienced surgeon pleased with his new student. "Electrical is being considered as having the best possibilities for cognitive enhancement. Magnetic impulses take longer to have an impact, up to an hour, but human studies are currently under way for the treatment of migraines, severe depression, and psychosis." Brett met Bishop's gaze and added, "And then there is deep-brain stimulation."

Lena was both involved and able to analyze her torrent of conflicting emotions. She remained hollowed by Roger's official farewell. And yet Brett's closeness only heightened the sense that she was accelerating into a totally new future. The danger she had twice witnessed when ascending, the smell of gun oil drifting through the open doorway, Charlie's silent presence—none of this could stifle her sense of purpose. She reached over and pulled Brett's hand into her lap so she could cradle it with both her own.

Brett broke off and gave her a look that brought to mind the word *smoking*. Then he glanced back at Bishop and said, "Where was I?"

"Stimulation," Robin said. When Brett's gaze tracked back to Bishop, Robin smirked at Lena and fanned her face with the takeout menu.

"Right. The current research on cranial mapping is in its infancy. We have the tools, the National Institutes of Health has licensed several new projects, but the spotlight is on the academics. As a result, they move forward carefully—"

Bishop spoke for the first time. "And all the while, patients are suffering from pain. They're given the choice of agony or drugs that blanket all senses and carry severe side effects. Which isn't much of a choice at all."

Brett went on, "Bernard took a surgeon's approach. He applied the scalpel to the entire academic world. He carved away all those artificial boundaries. He showed that if you combine the magnetic and the electric, and if you add the individual brain-wave patterns, you can create deep-brain stimulation without all the risks involved in drilling holes into patients' skulls and implanting electrodes."

Robin asked the surgeon, "What was the trigger? For you, I mean."

"Five years ago, there was an article in *Science*." Bishop sat like a man who had lost the ability to relax. "It proved that the same transcranial electrical and magnetic impulses caused completely opposite responses in patients, based upon age or sex or other causal factors. The researchers concluded they would need years to unravel the linkages."

"Ridiculous," Brett said.

"My word exactly," Bishop said.

"So you ignored the question," Robin said. "You decided to unravel the brain-wave patterns on an individual basis. That was . . ."

"Brilliant," Brett said.

Charlie stepped forward and inserted himself into the group. "Time to take another ascent."

"I'll go," Lena said.

"Me too," Brett said.

Robin asked, "What are you two smiling about?"

Charlie said, "From now on, we'll need to make a recce every couple of hours. Toward dawn, I want this to become watch-on-watch."

Lena caught the edge to his voice, and knew Charlie would soon split up her and Brett. Her last thought, as she fitted on the neural net and lay down on the pallet, was that she and Brett had not yet found a private space to talk about what was happening.

She was still reflecting on this when Charlie counted her up. The union was as blissful as before, perhaps even more so. This time Lena knew what was coming. She hungered for it. When Brett appeared, she flew at him.

And he at her.

There was no body, no vision, no touch. And yet the intensity of their moment-beyond-moments made all of this relatively unimportant. The harmony she felt was a vibration that caused her physical form to give off a tuning-fork hum, one she could sense from her position across the room.

This time it was Brett who pried them apart. The act of separation carried an exquisite distress for Lena. She wished she had the capacity to weep. And that Brett had hands with which he might dry her eyes.

Lena shifted away and refocused upon Charlie's voice. The words flowed into a coherent pattern, and she followed them out, hunting.

The search took only as long as Charlie required to speak the words,

"You will now determine who the opposition is, and when precisely they will arrive. You will remain in complete safety and control . . ."

Lena opened her physical eyes with the gasp of being drawn from a living nightmare. The room watched as she ripped off the neural net and flung it as far as the cables allowed.

Charlie demanded, "What did you see?"

Lena's limbs did not feel capable of holding her full weight. She crawled over to Brett. Only from the safety of his arms could she look at Charlie and reply, "Monsters."

56

Brett came back from the second ascent feeling disconnected from reality. The intensity of bonding with Lena had overwhelmed his senses. He walked the empty street in front of the warehouse behind Charlie and Lena, struggling to draw the danger into focus.

He heard Charlie say, "Tell me about the monsters."

"Again," Lena replied. "Tell you again."

"Sometimes it helps to remember if you repeat the story," Charlie said.

"There were a lot of the beasts," Lena said. She hugged her arms tightly around her middle. The night was cold, but Brett did not think that was why she shivered. "Too many to count. A couple dozen, maybe more."

"You said they filled the street," Charlie said.

"Because they were big."

"And you said they kept shifting shape. Can you describe that for me?"

Lena hesitated. Charlie walked on beside her, matching her choppy stride, not pressing.

Brett liked being able to hang back. The slow pace down the center of the street suited him. Behind them, one of Charlie's team lounged in the warehouse doorway, smoking and keeping watch.

Lena said, "It's really hard to describe."

Charlie nodded with his entire upper body. "I can imagine."

"They were huge, and then they shifted into human shape. Then huge again. Like I was seeing two different groups, only they weren't." Lena shook her head. "I can't describe it better than that."

"You didn't mention this before, about them shape-shifting."

"Because it sounds crazy."

Charlie touched her arm. "You're with friends. We trust you and we believe you. There's no telling what will prove important. Now, was there anything else?"

Lena pointed toward the east. "They came from out of the sun."

Brett held back a couple of steps so he could watch Lena. Five minutes to two in the morning, they owned the night. The first ascent in over a year had rocked Brett in so many different ways he could not catalog the sensations. The shock of meeting Lena in the bodiless realm was . . . exquisite.

Charlie said, "You're sure they came at dawn?"

"This is the third time you've asked that," Lena replied.

"Waning light could also have meant sunset," Charlie said.

"It was dawn." Again Lena pointed to the east. "The sun was fully over the horizon, but still touching the earth."

They walked on in silence. Three blocks to the south, a bevy of flags snapped in the night wind, surrounding the USS *Intrepid*'s spotlighted superstructure. The mothballed aircraft carrier was permanently moored at the pier by West 46th Street.

Finally Charlie asked, "You were seeing this from a height above the rooftops. Sunrise today is six thirteen. This is officially defined by the first sighting of the sun's edge from sea level. So we'll call it from six to six thirty."

"Why is the precise time so important?"

"They'll have watchers in place."

"You mean—"

"Just like us. Looking forward. Our best hope is to be one step ahead of them. Which is why you need to keep ascending."

"I can do that."

"I'll need to separate you and Brett. Watch-on-watch. From now until dawn. Bernie or Robin will serve as backup."

Lena's flat tone reflected Brett's own disappointment, but all she said was, "What about you?"

"I'll stay on constant watch here in the physical realm. That's my duty station throughout." He gestured toward the buildings and the shadows that swallowed their every sound. "I'll be switching positions every few minutes. Making my pattern as random and unpredictable as possible."

"So what you told Roger—"

Charlie pointed across the street at a blank window. "I've rented that room. But I won't be there. Are you okay going without sleep?"

"Yes."

"Brett?"

"Fine."

Lena stopped. "What are we doing out here?"

"I need to establish optimal shooting sites. A kill zone is all about angles and distance." Charlie might as well have been discussing a shopping list. "Knowing where I can be positioned and still—"

"No," Lena said. "What are we doing here?"

Brett had difficulty hearing Charlie's reply. The words crystallized in the darkness before his face. *Kill zone*. Brett sensed at a level beyond the physical that Charlie was both telling the truth and leaving a great deal out.

He heard Charlie say, "I'm not tracking."

"Yes you are. You know exactly what I mean. Why are we standing here waiting for the bad guys to show up?"

"Where would you want us to be, Lena? In some crowded hotel where we put civilians at risk? Could you live with yourself?"

"How about a police station?"

"And tell them what? Sooner or later, we would be back on the street, only without the ability that we have now to control the terrain."

"So we're basically just waiting for them to attack."

"No, Lena. That's why you have me. That's why I'm out here. That's why in about ten minutes you and Brett are going back inside . . ."

Brett stopped following them. He turned and looked back the way they had come. The sunrise was out there somewhere, four hours and counting. But Charlie was not concerned about the exact timing so he could switch positions, and his actions would not be random.

Brett took a long breath. He knew what was happening. The logical linkage that dominated his life no longer held him. This night he had been taken beyond logic, beyond the physical reality, and shown a different perspective. And this outlook held him still. He knew why they were out here.

Charlie intended to sacrifice himself.

Charlie was going to plant himself as a target. Let the bad guys zero in on him. Give New York's finest a reason to roll.

Lena called, "Brett?"

"Coming." Brett smiled to the darkness. It all made sense now. This opportunity he had been given to ascend. The chance to witness the true power of selfless love. Despite everything he had done, all the shadows he had introduced into the world. Every possible reason to be denied these gifts. All this was life's way of saying farewell.

Because Charlie Hazard was not going to sacrifice himself. Gabriella was not going to lose her life's love. They deserved happiness. They deserved a future. They had a role to play in tomorrow's world.

Charlie called, "It's time."

"Yes," Brett agreed. It certainly was.

57

When Reese entered the lobby area outside the departures lounge, Ridley was talking as though it was only her and Carl. But the place was jammed with bodies, the entire voyager team swamping the sofas, the chairs, lining the carpet by the refreshment stand. Ridley was saying, "We got to come up with some tag that fits us. I mean, what we're doing is totally world-class. We've got to have a handle."

If Carl was even aware of all the others listening in, he gave no sign. For him, it was just his partner talking. "They talk about surfing the web. They don't know what they're missing."

"There you go." Ridley started to punch his shoulder.

"No hitting."

"I stopped, see?" She held her hand out for Carl to do the fist-on-fist thing. "We're out there surfing the unseen winds."

The waifish young woman was closest to the pair. Erin looked about fifteen, but Reese had heard from one of the other voyagers that she was twenty-eight. Erin said, "We need superhero uniforms. You know, over there."

The man seated on the carpet next to her was named, of all things, Rupert. The others called him Rube. He said, "Something with a space-suit feel. All shiny with a flip-down visor for the stellar voyages."

Ridley pretended to notice Reese for the first time. "Here she is, ladies and gentlemen. Our very own launch director."

Reese knew her team was frightened. Which was probably a good thing. It meant they had less distance to travel before they arrived at true terror. Which was bound to come as soon as she told them what was happening.

Ridley asked, "Is the boss okay?"

"Kevin is fine. Everything is . . ." Reese stopped. No false assurances. She finished, "Kevin is not the issue."

Reese had phoned the security station before she left the café and asked the duty officers to round up the voyagers. They had been stewing here for over half an hour. They had heard about her little tirade when she couldn't find Kevin. They knew something was up.

She began, "There is a second set of voyagers. Like us, but not at all the same. For one thing, they're a couple of steps behind us."

Erin asked, "Who are they?"

Reese liked how Ridley and Carl turned to her, asking permission. She liked that a lot. The impossible duo was hers. Which meant they might just survive.

Reese said, "Go ahead. Tell them."

Ridley said, "The lady had us track them. They went to a place outside Havana."

"So . . . they're working for . . ." Erin's eyes widened. "Oh wow."

A guy on the sofa to Reese's left said, "They're working for the Cubans? Really?"

"Dude, wake up." Ridley looked at Carl. "You believe this guy?"

Carl said, "We saw Russians all over the place."

"No way," Erin said.

Reese needed to be certain they all understood, so she said, "Ridley and Carl are our first team of perimeter scouts. Their objective was to track the midnight crew. The Russians are our backers. And they are developing a second team. We have to assume the group's progress will accelerate now that they have the midnight crew as backup."

The waif asked, "So where does that leave us?"

Reese nodded. "That is the question. And the answer is, it's up to you. Anybody who wants out, you need to leave now. This is probably your last chance to walk away. Because if you stay, things are going to get hot."

Rube asked, "What, they're coming for us?"

"What do they need us for once they're up and running?" Ridley said. "We're as good as toast."

"Ridley's correct. Not this very instant. Maybe not today. But soon." Reese pointed at the hallway leading to the front lobby. "The exit is that way. If you're going, leave now."

Ridley looked at her partner. "What do you say, big guy? We staying?"

Carl shrugged one massive shoulder. "What do I have out there that's half as good as this?"

This time Ridley's fist made soft contact. "My man."

"Ow again."

Reese laid it out. She figured some would take off as soon as they learned what was happening. But they had to know. Even when almost everyone showed fear long before Reese was done.

All but Ridley, who was grinning, and Carl, who showed no reaction at all.

Erin said, "This could be a total suicide mission."

"Lighten up," Carl said.

Ridley said, "My money is on the lady getting us out intact."

Reese walked over and squatted down between the duo. She wrapped one arm around each of them. It wasn't much of a thanks for having said the exact right thing at the ideal moment. Her two voyagers exploring the outermost edge, the pair who would face the greatest danger, were cool with it. They trusted her. Their example swayed the group. Reese could feel it happen.

Reese hoped she would find a way to tell the pair what that gift of trust meant. But for the moment, a one-armed hug would do.

She straightened and addressed the group. "From this point on, you do exactly what I say. No questions. No argument. We move in sync. And we get out of this. Alive."

"Call it out," Reese said. She stood in the lobby area, far enough from the two entries so most of the voyagers could see her. Sixteen were linked and ready. Even so, she did not need to raise her voice. The two departures lounges were that silent, the voyagers totally intent upon her. "Who's on lead?"

Four hands went up. All were volunteers. Ridley, who was lead on the fifth and most important team, pretended to inspect the tats on her left wrist. Reese said, "Good. Now a show of hands from the first backup. Excellent."

Reese ran them through the sequencing once more. She knew her voice was tight and that the words held a drumbeat cadence. She felt the old familiar adrenaline surge that had always sparked the moments before action. The rush was indescribable to anyone who had never known the kick of high-risk engagements. The strategy she had worked out was probably overkill. But the voyagers were scared, and they needed the assurance of knowing she was on their case. Taking them out, doing the job, bringing them home.

The four voyagers serving on the front line each had backup that alternated between shield and anchor. Erin and Rube were joined with Carl and Ridley, her forward scouts. Their task was to move unseen through the high grass, stalking the predators.

Reese entered the monitoring station. The ranks of empty chairs to either side of the entrance were occupied by all the fears and doubts she could not share with anyone. Now there was space for only one thing. Bringing her team home.

She slipped into the chair next to Karla and said, "They're all in the green?"

"Barely." Karla's hands shook as she worked the controls. There were seven monitors on the wall above the long desk. Karla had split the screens so they showed a face and the rapid-fire heart rates and breathing rhythms. She switched back and forth, blipping through all twenty. Ridley and Carl were the only voyagers who appeared calm.

Kevin entered the room and declared, "The guy Jones just called it in. They're going on the attack. Ten minutes."

"From when you spoke to them, or now?"

Kevin slipped into the chair next to hers and pointed at the digital clock above the top line of monitors. "Nine minutes and thirty-eight seconds."

"Okay." She turned to Karla. "I get the four teams started, then we release the scouts. Just like we prepped. Ready?"

"Yes."

"Now listen carefully. You heard what I said to the team. No questions, no arguments. The same applies to you." When Karla looked ready to complain, Reese stabbed her ribs with one finger, hard as a gun barrel. "Pay attention. I am going to count them up. Then I am handing the controls over to Kevin. You've worked with him before."

Reese did not give the technician time to whine. She swiveled her chair around and said, "Give the four main teams thirty minutes. Either that's enough or . . ."

Kevin watched her with a gaze hardened by years of smoke and cordite. "You're going after him, aren't you. Hazard."

Reese slipped an envelope from her pocket and replied, "I don't want you to open this until I'm hooked up with Ridley and Carl."

"What's in here?"

"Instructions for my crew," Reese replied. "You give us twenty-five minutes and the directive you've been waiting a year to say."

Kevin nodded slowly. "I can do that."

Reese turned back to the controls, ignored Karla's tremors, and said, "Here we go."

She gave her four main teams their instructions, she watched the clock, and when it was time she sent them out. All but the four voyagers waiting in the other chamber.

She knew she left the monitoring station at a calm walk. She felt her feet tread across the carpet. But inside, where it counted, she felt as though she flew in a low-altitude orbit.

Ridley greeted her with, "I knew you wouldn't miss the fun."

58

Lena stood on the rooftop waiting for Brett and watched the fog silently unfurl. The river vanished, then the aircraft carrier. But the mist that drifted down the roads toward them was not so heavy as to blanket her vision. It was more of a gentle veil, an Impressionist rendering of a poor New York neighborhood.

The door opened behind her. Lena heard Brett say, "Aren't you cold?"

"Basically all I feel is numb," Lena said. "Too many late nights. Too many intense events."

When Brett settled his sweatshirt over her shoulders, Lena snagged his right hand. She wrapped his other arm around her middle, like she'd been doing it for years. Like they were a couple. Brett moved in close enough that she could feel his warmth, feed off the masculine strength.

Lena said, "We need to talk about what happened."

Brett freed his left arm so he could trace the line of hair framing her forehead and ear and neck. "I've wanted to do that for days."

"Did you hear what I said?"

"Yes, Lena. And I'll talk about it whenever you want. But we're watch-on-watch until dawn, remember?"

"How much time do we have?"

He moved in closer still. "Not enough."

Lena resisted the urge to turn around and kiss him. It was silly in this day and age to give so much importance to such a simple act. But she did not want that moment to arrive on the rooftop of a warehouse before the monsters attacked.

So she asked, "Did you ascend again?"

"I did. Yes."

"Are they still coming?"

"Let Charlie fill you in, all right?" He buried his face in her hair. "Please."

She rewarded that request by closing her eyes and leaning back, nestling against him from heel to hairline. They were still like that, immersed in each other, when Robin came to bring her down.

☁

Robin replaced Bishop at the camp table holding the laptop monitor as Lena entered the room. Brett stood in the doorway, observing her with a gaze that could only be described as electric. Robin waited until Lena fitted on her neural net, then asked, "Can you hear me?"

"Five by five."

"Charlie says we're supposed to fill you in. Nothing's changed. They strike in about . . ." Robin checked the computer's clock. "Forty-seven minutes."

"Okay."

"He says to tell you the guys downstairs are on high alert. You're to focus on . . . you know."

"The monsters," Lena confirmed. She settled down on the pallet and offered Brett as potent a smile as the people and place allowed.

Robin said, "Nobody else has seen them. Your monsters, I mean."

327

"Just the same," Lena said. "They're coming."

"I believe you." Robin watched Lena settle onto the pallet. "In case I get too busy later, I just want to say, you know, thanks."

"De nada."

Bishop added, "That goes double for me, young lady."

Lena opened her eyes. Bernard stood between the monitor station and Brett. He was a stubby man in need of a shave and a week's rest. His beard grew in unattractive patches. His shirt was wrinkled and there was a hole in his left sock. But his eyes burned with the fire of bygone days, intelligent and ambitious and something more. His gaze carried a new focus. His features were carved with a future he thought had been ripped away. "It's really good to have you all here."

Robin said, "I'm starting the count now."

The ascent started and Lena entered a white room. Even before Robin said, "Go and check for any incoming threat and remain safe," Lena knew she wasn't going anywhere at all.

The room was boundless, yet tightly confined at the same time. Lena touched the wall and felt an unwelcome friction, like she had been repelled at the very core of her being. She backed away. And stood in the center of white nothingness. Everywhere she looked, she saw the same smooth curvature. Not exactly an oval or a globe. The only way to describe the setting was, Lena rested in the middle of a white womb.

Her ascents had all felt smooth. This one was the same, only now it carried a special intensity. Not bad, not good. Just . . . Lena used her white cage as an opportunity to study what before had been too overwhelming. She realized that the event now carried a naturalness. Ascending was now part of her world. She had moved beyond the initial shock. The question was, once this threat was behind them, where would she go next?

A voice said, "That is an excellent question."

Lena stared at a version of herself. Only this woman was so alien it would have been easier to face a stranger. The woman who confronted her was utterly content, an emotion so foreign to Lena's existence that it took her a moment to even shape the word. She was also in love.

And she was pregnant.

The stranger wearing Lena's face cradled her distended belly and said, "This is our second. We are naming him Brett. And that's all the time we can spare for us."

But Lena had to ask, "Am I with him?"

"There are restrictions to what we can discuss, you and I. Many, in fact. But you need to remember, the promise you see in me is intended to help you get through what comes next."

A terror flooded her, so potent it almost wrenched Lena out of the ascent. She wanted to depart and find Brett and shield him from whatever might take him from her. And yet Lena was trapped by her need to hear what this woman had to say.

"We meet because the purpose justifies the deed," the woman said.

"I don't understand," Lena replied.

"You will," the woman assured her. "Now pay attention."

There were two flashes, similar to the events Lena had experienced with her temporal self, but far more intense. One lightning bolt of warning, another of response.

Clearly the woman knew Lena wanted to depart. But she held her in the white room long enough to say, "Here is the key to us having any future at all. When the monsters enter your lair, you strike. Do not think, do not hesitate. It all comes down to this."

And it was over.

Lena bounced up to a seated position, halting Robin in the middle of counting her back. She ripped off the neural net and felt her heart squeeze at the empty space by the doorway. "Where's Brett?"

"He went to help Charlie."

Lena staggered to her feet, her limbs caught in the quicksand of returning from another ascent. She reached out, and Bishop offered her a strong right hand. She gasped, "Outside. Hurry!"

"What's the matter?" Robin cried.

Lena hated how she could not support her own weight. Hated how she had to slow down even more to reply, "They're here."

59

Reese waited until she had fit the neural net into place, then told Carl and Ridley and their backups, "We're going after something entirely different from what we discussed."

Ridley asked, "Why are we only hearing about this now?"

"Just in case," Reese said. "They might be listening."

Carl nodded slowly. "You mean, the crew in Havana could be monitoring us."

"I had to plan for that. But my guess is they're too busy right now."

"Which gives us a window," Carl said. "Smart."

"I think they're planning to finish this business in New York, then come for us." Reese fingered the mike. "Kevin, you getting this?"

"Roger that. And I agree."

"Our task is to build us a window we can all climb through."

Ridley asked, "So what are we going to do?"

Reese told Kevin to break the seal and read the handwritten instructions out loud. When Kevin finished, Ridley said softly, "Oh man."

Carl shrugged his massive shoulders. "Works for me."

Ridley studied her partner. "What if, you know, they eat us?"

"You heard what the lady said," Carl replied, watching Reese. "You'll protect us, right?"

"With my dying breath," Reese said.

"Let's hope it doesn't come down to that," Ridley said. "For all our sakes."

"Roger that," Kevin said. "I'm starting the count now."

Identify the enemy's core element, their primary purpose, the real reason why they are on the field at all. Shift it slightly, and everything changes. Those were the words written across the top of the whiteboard in Reese Clawson's first class on tradecraft.

Reese had been approached late in her junior year at university. She was sulking in a Starbucks after another oh-so-boring job fair in the rec center. Just one of six hundred juniors desperate for an internship, a summer paycheck, a chance to carve a chink from the mountain of student debt.

Reese had said yes before the guy finished his windup. When he had asked what fueled her eagerness, she replied, "I've wanted this my whole life." Even then, Reese Clawson could lie with utmost sincerity.

What she had thought was, the man and his pitch both smelled of danger. And she wanted in. Desperately.

Tradecraft had been taught by a grandmotherly woman who had peppered her lectures on stealth and tracking and eliminating opposition with real-world tales from the field. The instructor had been a black-ops agent for twenty-one years, a specialist at blending into the scenery and attacking with a smile. She had a musical lilt to her voice and gave most of the class nightmares. Reese had gone up after the first class and said, "I want to be you."

Throughout that first summer of training, Reese had often thought of that first class and the words written on the whiteboard. The instructor had called it "stressing the situation." The aim was to keep the opposition off balance by never doing the expected. Finding their core

332

assumptions and breaking them in subtle and unseen ways. During the final assessments, the woman had described Reese as a natural, perhaps the best she had ever taught at stressing.

As Reese listened to Kevin count them down, she had the sensation that the instructor was there in the departures lounge with them. Watching and smiling in approval. She whispered the words, "Here we go."

60

Brett stepped through the doorway and entered the empty street. Dawn was less than fifteen minutes away, according to Charlie's timing. Which meant the apparitions that only Lena had seen were on the move. In Brett's own ascent, he had witnessed an assault by two Russians and four Cubans, all heavily armed. Each of his ascents ended the same way, with gunfire and police sirens.

As he started forward, Brett felt a single gnawing ache that he and Lena had never kissed.

Charlie moved like liquid through the floating mist. He told Brett, "Go back inside."

"Save your breath." Brett turned and faced the direction from which the enemy would arrive. And waited.

The fog seemed unsettled by the pre-dawn light. There was no wind. The air was utterly still. Even so, tendrils of vapor writhed and weaved, like an underground cauldron was being kept one degree off full boil.

Charlie's voice took on a military edge. "This is a direct order, mister."

Brett did not turn around. "You're not sacrificing yourself. I'm not letting you."

Charlie's only response was to grip Brett's arm and start pulling him toward the entrance.

"Go ahead, take me inside. I won't stay." Brett felt Charlie's pace falter. "If anyone takes a hit for the team today—"

"No."

"It will be me," Brett persisted.

"Not happening."

Brett lifted the phone in his hand, placed it directly before Charlie's eyes. "How about we call Gabriella, let her decide?"

Charlie froze.

"That's what I thought." Brett shook his arm free. "So you've got about three minutes to figure out a different way to save us both."

Whatever Charlie's response might have been, Brett never had a chance to hear it. Because that was when the attack began. Not with the bang he had always heard during his ascents. Rather, with a scrape of leather and one small, metallic laugh.

61

At first Brett thought the two couples walked hand in hand. Then he realized it wasn't like that at all.

They drifted into sight through the shifting fog. The light was vague enough to leave him feeling as though great fists unfurled, releasing the four.

One of the ladies had blonde hair that gleamed in the dim light like a brass helmet. She called down the half block that separated them, "Well, well. What do we have here?"

The other woman did not actually laugh. The sound she made was like a bird's call, high-pitched, staccato.

Charlie tried to step in front of him, but Brett moved forward, keeping himself between Charlie and the enemy. Because this was who they faced. Of that Brett had no question. The motions caused the woman to emit another of those sounds, ack-ack-ack-ack, up and down an inhuman scale.

Charlie said, "Tell my team to come out."

"You go ahead," Brett said. "I'm good right here."

The four held empty hands out from their sides. Which was why

Brett had thought they were holding on to each other. They were less than forty paces away now, and Brett could see how unsteadily they moved. Part shuffle, part stagger. They bounced off one another every now and then. Their heads shifted up, down, side to side. Brett had seen the motions before but could not place where.

Charlie said, "I need to clear the range of fire."

"Couldn't agree more," Brett said. "Go inside."

The four were within thirty paces now, moving so slowly they could not logically represent any threat. And yet the sight of them made Brett's skin crawl. Around them the fog boiled like a live thing. Figures seemed to appear in the mist, four nightmarish beasts that staggered and stretched and moved forward. The images mocked the dawn light, keeping ragged cadence with the approaching figures.

The warehouse door slammed against the concrete siding with a crack so loud one of the guys backed up and tripped over his own feet and almost went down. Lena rushed out, followed by Bishop and the Latino security guy. Bishop had one arm outstretched, like he was concerned Lena might fall without his support, which was not altogether a bad thing, because Lena staggered as she shrieked, "Get inside!"

Brett turned from the four and saw how Charlie scouted the surrounding rooftops. He was about to say something about snipers when Lena slammed into them both, a football tackle that caught them so completely off guard they fell in a heap on the pavement.

Two things happened instantaneously. The approaching woman gave off another of those impossible cackles, and the pavement beside Brett's head was scored by something, a dark gouge that gleamed in the growing light.

Charlie plucked them up, one fist gripping Lena's arm and the other holding Brett's collar. From prone to racing in half a second. "Ten o'clock and two, rooftops!"

Hector did not bother aiming. Raising his rifle to his shoulder would have cost precious moments. He lay down a covering fire, racing through a clip in three seconds and flaying the buildings across from them.

Brett tried to protest, tell Charlie he was not going anywhere, but the soldier's grip on his collar cut off his air. As they passed the doctor at a full-bore sprint, Bishop spun like a convulsive top and fell.

"Bernard!" Lena did not quite manage to break free of Charlie's hold.

Charlie responded by lifting her off her feet and flinging her through the warehouse door. "Gun! Gun!"

Brett knew Charlie was heading out, the officer who only knew one way to lead his troops, and that was from the front. Taking the worst of whatever was incoming. Brett gripped the doorjamb, refusing to allow Charlie to push him into safety. He blocked the door with his body.

The hit, when it came, was astonishing on many levels. He did not feel a bullet. Instead, it seemed as though an invisible flame shot through his side. The pain was so intense he could not even breathe.

"No!"

Brett slipped to the earth because he no longer had legs to support him. The sounds were a furious barrage now, gunfire and Lena screaming and the woman outside still giving off that strange reptilian cackle. Then he stopped hearing anything at all.

62

Lena gripped Brett's arm and struggled to shift his inert form out of the entryway. Charlie and his two remaining team members were firing and shouting for Hector to "Move, man, move!" Bullets whacked chips from the door frame and the cement wall, showering Lena with debris. She wanted to shriek for somebody to help her, but the dust and the cordite choked her. Then Robin shoved in beside her and grabbed Brett's other arm.

Brett's left foot snagged the Anglo security agent, spoiling his aim. He snarled something that Lena did not bother hearing. As she and Robin pulled Brett away from the gunfire and the danger, they left behind a trail that glistened blackish-red in the smoke. Lena forced down the gorge that rose in the back of her throat. She did not have time for nausea.

As she knelt beside Brett, Hector appeared in the doorway. He hauled Bishop with him. The doctor's head lolled at a sloppy angle. Both men were stained black with blood. Hector grimaced and gasped as the Anglo dropped his rifle and shouldered Bishop. Together they dragged the doctor back and settled him beside Brett. Hector waved away whatever his mate said and started toward the doorway. Charlie shouted and pointed back behind them. The rear access portals were locked down, but Charlie wanted them covered. The Anglo helped support Hector as they hurried back.

Lena laid her head on Brett's chest. The wet stain was warm as a departing life. "I can't hear anything!"

Robin's response was lost to a rain of bullets that hammered the metal shutter over the front window. She pointed at Brett and crawled toward the pile of gear that Charlie's crew had brought with them. Then Lena felt Brett's chest moving beneath her stained hands. A fractional gasp, up and down. He was breathing.

Robin dropped back down beside her, holding a black nylon kit the size of a large briefcase. A red cross was stitched into every side. She used a sudden gap in the noise to say, "Guys like this always come prepared."

Lena watched as Robin unzipped the case and started sorting through the contents. Lena stroked Brett's forehead and left a red streak from the blood staining her hands. She had no idea what to do except yell, "Please wake up!"

Charlie dropped down beside her. He dug two fingers into Brett's neck, then used the scissors Robin handed him to cut away the sodden shirt. He inspected the wound to Brett's lower left side, then pointed to the wound and said something lost to the shooting. But Lena found a hint of reassurance in the way he swiveled away and started working on Bishop.

A sudden silence filtered through Lena's frantic helplessness. Charlie shouted, "Cease-fire!"

The quiet was deafening. Charlie asked the man by the front door, "See anything?"

"The shooters have vanished." He risked another peek. "Looks like the four civvies are coming our way."

"They armed?"

From his prone position on the floor, he shot a glance around the door frame. "Their hands are empty and over their heads."

Charlie shouted, "Hector, you okay?"

"Just a scratch, jefe. Everything's cool back here."

The guy by the front door asked, "Do I let them in?"

"Tell them to wait." As the guy shouted orders, Charlie ripped open a pack and sprinkled a yellowish grit all over Brett's wound. Then he set a bulky bandage in place and said to Robin, "Apply steady pressure."

"Got it."

The guy by the front door called, "Charlie!"

"Hold them where they are." Charlie inspected Brett's wound, then said, "No bubbles."

Lena was almost afraid to let in hope. "W-what?"

"If the lung was punctured, the wound would bubble. It's not, see?"

"There's so much blood."

"Probably nicked an artery." He tore open another packet, motioned Robin to peel off the gauze, and sprinkled more granules liberally over the wound. "Okay, apply the pressure again. Good. Lena, help me roll him over. Gentle, now."

The guy by the front door flicked his head in and out of low-level view, then called, "Charlie, they're still coming."

"Watch their hands and don't let them enter. They show a weapon, take them out." Together they turned Brett far enough to inspect his back. "Okay. Clean exit. Same thing, no bubbles. Just below the lung is my guess. Maybe nicked a rib."

"H-he's okay?"

Charlie ripped open a third packet, covered the area, applied another bandage, then settled Brett back. "Too soon to say for certain. But he doesn't appear to be critical. I want you to lift his head just in case there's some leakage into his lung, help him breathe."

"Can't we do something?"

"Absolutely." Charlie raised his voice. "Hector, 911!"

"On it!"

The guy by the front door shouted, more frantic now, "Charlie!"

Charlie started to rise and was reaching out for his gun when it happened.

Lena was moving to cradle Brett's head in her lap as the first woman entered. Her hands were high overhead, which was possibly what caused her to wobble into the door frame. Lena thought she was drunk or drugged from the canted way she held her head. Her blonde hair was shellacked into place and mashed flat on one side. Bits of gravel flecked that side of her face. She leered at them, her grin as lopsided as her stance, and shrieked, "Hello, boys!"

The fog seemed to boil into the warehouse, surging around her like it was pushed in by an unseen wind. Only the fog did not dissipate. Instead, it fed upon the cordite fumes, sucking and heaving and growing into a form that Lena could actually see. The behemoth grew and mimicked the way the woman now stretched out her arms, the hands fashioned into the talons that tore through the air overhead.

Then the woman and the beast looked together, taking in the frozen soldiers and the guns that were held by numb fingers. And they saw the two bodies bleeding onto the concrete. The woman cackled and started forward. Bringing the beast of smoke with her.

Lena leapt up before the thought was fully formed. Her body responded to a primitive rage, the mother bear protecting her own. She tore the rifle from Charlie's limp fingers, gripped the barrel's hot metal, and raced forward. The smoking beast swooped down, the translucent talons aimed for her face. Lena swatted it aside and kept moving, until she was face-to-face with the leering blonde woman.

She rocked back, then forward, putting all her weight into the swing. The woman's vision seemed to clear enough for her to show momentary dismay and raise one arm. Lena's swing connected with her elbow, and the woman shrieked once more, only this time there was a human note to the distress. Lena took a two-fisted grip on the weapon and hammered the stock into the woman's forehead. Her eyelids flickered once, twice, and she went down hard.

Lena raced past the still-prone guard and flew out. The three remaining civilians were clustered in the doorway, oblivious to the cordite stench. Lena smashed her way forward, using the rifle as a battering ram.

The three somersaulted back, then rose to their feet, swaying like partygoers long after the music has stopped. The mist boiled and wrenched about them as a guy with multiple piercings called, "Did you come out to play?"

The woman cackled like a bird of prey. The three started toward Lena.

Lena swung the rifle like a misshapen baseball bat, scything through the mist between them and her. "Get out of here!"

The other young man, a Latino, sneered, "You're nothing but fresh kill."

Then Lena heard the sirens.

63

As Reese entered the voyage, Kevin's instructions were as precise as his voice. "Find the team and track them. Remain unseen at all times."

The other voyagers had been given the command that Reese had outlined for the Russian named Jones. They were tasked with protecting the unseen periphery as Jones and his team attacked Bishop and Hazard. Reese was to report through Kevin the instant an enemy was identified. In fact, report to Jones before the attack.

Ridley held the Zulu-shaped shield in front of her, but there was no sense of opposing forces. Instead, she voyaged and Reese followed. Simple as breath.

They hovered somewhere above a rooftop in a derelict section of New York. Reese knew it was the fringe area of Hell's Kitchen, because her team had identified the warehouse. The scene was exactly as the voyagers had described to her.

Jones's team had taken up positions on two rooftops. The warehouse holding Bishop and the others was to her left. And inside the warehouse was Charlie Hazard. Reese was certain he was there. She tracked him like a predator sensing the unseen enemy.

She watched with genuine pleasure as the six attackers fired on the warehouse's entry. She saw the wounded merc drag Bishop inside while Hazard and his team poured out withering cover fire. She knew in that first glimpse what she had suspected all along.

Jones's cover was blown. The attack was going to fail. His team was already losing. Charlie and his team would survive.

As far as Reese was concerned, it had never been about defeating Hazard. That would have been fine, of course. But Reese had known this was not the time. Her team was splintered by the tasks handed down by their Russian puppet masters. Taking down Charlie Hazard would require careful planning and total focus. Victory at this stage was a forlorn hope.

Reese was all about escape.

Her aim was simple in the extreme. Disrupt the situation so effectively that the Russians were blinded. Then make her getaway. And take her entire team with her. Vanish in a cloud of smoke.

The question was how to make that happen.

As though responding to her quandary, Kevin read the next line off her secret instructions, the ones she did not want revealed to any watcher until it was too late. "You will find a means to create havoc."

Even before Kevin finished shaping the words, Reese spotted the beast.

The monster was the one that had entered the departures lounge riding inside Esteban's skin. Reese instantly recognized the fiend. It loomed massive and fierce, taller than the warehouse.

Reese realized the beast was not alone. Her vision expanded to where she could see a crowd of the fiends, hovering like vultures around the periphery.

At that same moment, the fiend swept its talons downward toward a woman who appeared in the warehouse portal. She was smeared from face to knees with someone else's blood, and shrieked a warrior's cry as she met Esteban with the wrong end of a rifle.

All the surrounding beasts watched the assault. Which granted Reese the lone instant, tight as a racing heartbeat, to go on the attack herself.

Reese took the power of her rage and reshaped it. She fashioned a whip from her fury. Long and alive, a bullwhip with a serpent's fangs at its tip. The whip shot tiny sparks as she moved, the snake hissing fire. Then a monster crouched on the nearest rooftop spied her.

The beast was mountainous, a looming gargantuan that bore down upon so many legs she could not count them. They blurred together as the monster reached ramming speed.

Reese unleashed the whip and screamed her welcome. The rage erupted from her mouth and her whip both.

The whip came down and through the monster. One moment she faced a doom beyond her senses. The next and the behemoth was gone. Not even smoke remained.

Ridley appeared beside her, only it was a Ridley transformed. Her right hand carried a flaming spear, and she shrieked her battle cry with such force it caused Reese's vision to tremble.

Their communication, hers and Ridley's, was instantaneous and total. Reese took one line of rooftops, Ridley the other. They screamed in tandem, Ridley shooting flames from her spear point and Reese snapping her lightning whip.

The beasts of smoke and fury turned away from their approach. And they stampeded.

Reese and Ridley drove them in a solid pack that filled the concrete valley. The three remaining midnight crew and their attached beasts turned and gaped at what only they could see.

Then Reese noticed the shooters. They had gone silent when Heather and the other midnight crew members had stepped from the warehouse doorway and reentered their line of fire. The Russian and Cuban assailants were all directly in the path of the invisible horde. Reese watched the shooters key their throat mikes and call to one another. Confused. Frightened.

Reese used her whip to snag one of the rearmost fiends. She tugged hard on her razor leash, redirecting it so that the beast ran straight through the line of armed assailants.

Down below, the three remaining midnight crew writhed in a unified spasm as the monsters they had joined with were caught up by the horde. Up above, the shooters became snared by the same violent flow. Only they had no idea what was happening. Just that some force, a cyclone of dire fury, ripped right through them. They shrieked and flung their guns aside and ran. One was so blinded by the onslaught he slammed straight into a wall and slumped down, unconscious. Another took a severe tumble down metal stairs, broke his shoulder, and still came up at full speed.

Reese observed the pandemonium from a position that suited her perfectly. She rode on the back of the last beast, shouting a gleeful hello at the shooters who most likely would have been the ones sent to take out her and her team.

Stressing a situation had never been so much fun.

Reese unleashed the fiend and snapped her whip a final time, sending it flying off with all the others, including those from the midnight crew. Ridley stood at the end of the city canyon, hands on hips. Reese could not hear her, but she knew Ridley shrieked with the laughter of pure triumph.

The gunmen broke from cover, screaming and flailing at what was now passed. Charlie Hazard and one of his team came out, guns at the ready, and knocked the assailants to their knees. Reese watched as Charlie's teammate secured wrists and ankles with plastic strips while Charlie kept them all covered.

Reese studied her enemy with deadly intent, taking careful aim.

The sirens howled as multiple police cars roared up and sealed the almost-empty street.

Then Carl tugged on her safety leash. Drawing her and Ridley back to base.

Reese cast Charlie a final glance before turning away.

It was only a matter of time.

64

The police were moderately kind, or so it seemed to Lena. After all, she and her team had brought mayhem to Manhattan. When the ambulances carried off Brett and Bishop and Hector, Lena begged to go with them. The police refused, but even here they showed some consideration. The detective interviewing her was a woman with a Marine officer's voice, hard and cold and aware. But three times she had her partner radio the officer on duty at the ER. She relayed the information on Brett's surgery to Lena, then continued with the questions.

Police took Charlie and his team away. Lena asked where to, but the detective merely continued with the questions. Lena felt mildly abandoned and extremely vulnerable. The detective used Lena's isolation to pry out a great deal of information.

It was late afternoon when the detective finally released her. A squad car drove Lena to the hospital. Brett was out of surgery and his condition was classed as serious but stable. Bishop had been hit twice, in the leg and shoulder, and was expected to make a full recovery.

When she asked about Hector, Lena was told his condition was a matter for the courts.

They had put Brett and Bishop in the same room so that a single police officer could stand duty over both of them. The two patients were zonked out when Lena arrived. The nurse gave Lena a few minutes to sit by Brett's side, then guided her into the shower and kitted her out with a set of surgical blues. When Lena emerged, a meal was waiting for her on the bedside table. She ate everything, then was swamped by waves of fatigue. The room was overly cold, but she found a pair of blankets in the closet. The chair folded down flat, and the footstool could be positioned to make for a narrow bed. Lena stretched out, took hold of Brett's hand, and within a pair of breaths was asleep.

·ı||ı·

Lena awoke to daylight outside the room's narrow window. Her rest had been so profound she needed a moment to remember where she was. Then she turned her head and saw Brett watching her. And smiling.

She loved that she still held his hand.

Bishop's bed was down prone and his eyes were closed. Lena decided that was about as close to privacy as they were going to get. She raised her chair back and whispered, "How are you?"

"Awake. Alive. With you." He paused, then added, "Thirsty."

Lena lifted the cup and fitted the straw into his mouth. Brett watched her as he drank. When he finished she said, "There is something we need to get straight right now."

Brett nodded. "All right."

"You are part of two people now. Which means certain things you could get away with while single won't work anymore."

"Lena . . ."

"No. I'll tell you when it's your turn to speak. Right now your job is to pay attention. You can't risk your life like that ever again. If you feel like you don't have any choice, that it's absolutely the right thing

350

and you're on point, you can come and ask my opinion. And I'll tell you, 'Don't do it.' And what are you going to do?"

He nodded again. "Stay safe."

"I'm glad to hear you say that. Because if I'd heard any other answer, I'd have been tempted to go ask the cop outside our door if I could borrow his gun. Now tell me you'll remember this conversation."

"I will remember every moment."

"And even when your guy genes are electrified and your adrenaline is maxed out, you won't forget."

"I have an eidetic memory," Brett replied. "I don't forget anything."

Lena felt the hot pressure against the back of her eyes as she recalled, "When I knelt by you on the floor and watched you bleed . . ."

Brett reached over with his free hand, though the motion caused him to wince. He touched her face and asked, "Do you think it's time we kissed?"

Lena sat and held Brett's hand until he drifted off again. Then she retreated to the bathroom and took another long shower. She dressed in a fresh set of surgical blues because they were all she had. The bloodstained clothes she had arrived in had hopefully been taken away and burned.

When she emerged, Bishop's bed was angled so he could sit upright. The breakfast tray was drawn up in front of him, the meal untouched. He glanced at her, but his eyes remained blank. Almost as though he could look straight through her. Almost like all he had room for was the havoc his invention had caused.

Another breakfast tray was set on the table beside her chair. Brett remained deeply asleep. She seated herself and whispered across to Bishop, "The service in this place is wonderful."

Bishop gave no sign he heard her at all.

Lena whispered, "Any word about Charlie and the others?"

Again, no response.

As she was finishing her meal, the nurse came in, checked on the patients, then reached into her pocket for Lena's phone. "This thing kept buzzing, so the night nurse took it to the station."

Lena thanked her and took it outside. She found she had sixteen messages, nine of them from Robin, which she took as a very good sign. Lena decided to return two other calls first.

Gabriella Speciale answered on the first ring. There followed a warm conversation between two women who were glad for the chance to weep together over the safety of their men. When she cut the connection, Lena sat on the bench in the hallway and waited until she regained control. The nurse on duty at the central station glanced over and smiled, but did not bother to ask if Lena was all right. Clearly tears were an acceptable component of life in the wards.

Then Lena placed the second call, which was enough to leave her wanting to weep all over again, but for different reasons.

She recovered more swiftly this time, and when she was ready she returned Robin's call.

Robin came on the line with, "We're all over the news."

"Forget that. How are you?"

"Fine. Well, not fine. But I haven't been arrested and I'm home. Charlie just called from the lockup. When he couldn't reach you he phoned me. He's lawyered up and should be out this afternoon."

"I just got that news from Gabriella."

"Are you safe?"

"There are cops at our door."

"The attack is big news. So are you." Robin's voice carried strain. "They even mentioned you by name."

"So give me the flip side."

"Maybe it should wait."

"Tell me now, Robin."

She sighed. "Chester phoned. I've been sacked. Roger was on TV, saying you are no longer affiliated with his group."

"I know."

"You know? Since when?"

"Yesterday. About five minutes before things got very hot."

"So . . . we're out of a job."

"No, Robin. We're not. Nothing's changed. Well, it has, but it hasn't."

"You know that doesn't make any sense."

"We've been offered something a whole lot better," Lena said. "If you don't mind moving to Denver."

Robin breathed in, held it, then said, "Get out."

"I just spoke with Charles Farlow himself. He wants me to run part of his financial operations. I can bring the whole team. And he's agreed to take Bishop's project on as a major component of my new division."

Robin did not respond.

"Are you there?"

"Give me a minute."

"I don't have a minute. Are you in?"

"Am I . . . You're serious."

"I'll take that as a yes," Lena said. "Start packing."

Lena nodded to the police officer and reentered the patients' room. Brett was still sound asleep. Bishop was exactly as Lena had left him, seated upright in bed, the breakfast tray still untouched. His gaze shifted slightly, then he resumed his fixation upon the opposite wall. A flat-screen television was connected to a wall clamp about five feet up. Bishop stared at the blank screen with the intensity of a man who supplied his own visuals and running commentary.

Lena stepped up close to the bed and waited. Three minutes passed, four, then finally he turned her way. He still did not look directly at her, but rather focused upon a point just beyond her left shoulder.

"I was called last night by Frederick. You remember him. The butler. Frederick left us a message. Agnes passed away just after eleven." Perhaps the weepy spell Lena had endured out in the hallway now played a vital function, granting her the ability to meet Bishop's gaze

353

when he finally looked directly at her. And to continue with the message she knew was intended for him all along. "Frederick called to thank you. He wants you to know that Agnes died at peace. Without any pain. And without drugs. All because of you."

Bishop's mouth worked, but no words came out.

"Everything we've been through, none of it is your fault," Lena said. "The only thing of any importance today is Agnes. The freedom you gave her. And the hope your invention holds for tomorrow." She gave that a beat, then offered him the phone. "I think you should be the one to call him back."

65

The island of Yakushima was located about forty miles south of the southern tip of the Ōsumi peninsula, which extended like a finger pointing straight down from Kyushu province. Once she and Ridley had identified this as their destination, Reese had researched the island as thoroughly as time had allowed. The island had a population of thirty thousand, and all its citizens lived either in Yakushima town or five adjacent villages.

Since their arrival, Reese had heard multiple legends about mainlanders who ventured into the mountainous interior, determined to live a basic existence, cut off from all elements of civilization and people. There were supposed to be several hundred of these neo-primitives scattered through the island's two hundred square miles. The rain forest was a nationally protected preserve, mostly without trails, much less roads. Yakushima had any number of traditional inns, but only one five-star resort. Then again, one was all they needed.

The meeting took place on the veranda of Kevin's villa, the plushest that the spa hotel had on offer. The veranda faced south over a pearl-sand beach. The sea was dotted with over a dozen smaller islands, all jade green in the afternoon light. The villa was separated from the hotel's sculpted gardens by a stand of Japanese cedars, which grew wild all over the island.

The hotel manager personally supervised as three female attendants laid out a formal Japanese tea service. The hotel manager and Reese's seven guests—all male—wore dark suits. Reese and Kevin were intentionally dressed in pressed but casual shirts and slacks. Their main guest, as far as Reese was concerned, sat in the second row facing them. Everybody else was window dressing.

The front row was dominated by a prune-faced deputy minister of Japan's Department of the Interior. He was flanked by a male secretary and an official interpreter. The trio was here only because the man seated behind them had forced the government to act.

The focal point for Reese's attention had steel-grey hair and a hard onyx gaze. His official position was CEO of a family-owned company making machine parts. But the title on his business card held all the reality of a Kabuki mask. His real position was as head of Japan's third-largest keiretsu. The keiretsu was a collection of tightly linked companies whose intertwined ownership resulted in a collective force that could even bring a deputy minister to this veranda, a world removed from Tokyo and the halls of power. It was no wonder the government officials looked so irate.

This particular keiretsu was aggressive and ruthlessly ambitious. Reese had obtained this intel by hiring the attorney seated next to the CEO. The lawyer was one of the most powerful in Japan. Arranging this meeting had cost Reese one hundred and seven thousand dollars. She already considered the money well spent.

After the tea was served and the attendants were dismissed, the hotel manager bowed low and spoke solemnly to the deputy minister. Whatever the manager said did not improve the government official's disposition. Then the manager departed.

There followed over an hour of polite conversation. Kevin shifted impatiently from time to time, but he held to their agreed-upon strategy and did not speak. This lengthy discussion, required by Japanese protocol, was why Reese had ordered her team to stay away. She had no problem with the empty chatter. Arriving at this point was a triumph of global proportions. She was ready to sit here for days.

Reese also knew these formalities were intended as a means of testing. Foreigners were expected to demand swiftness, and thus cede the advantage in the negotiations that followed. But Reese had spent several pleasant years learning the gentle art of Oriental aggression. What was more, sitting here on the teak veranda of a world-class villa, facing these movers and shakers within Japanese business and government, filled Reese with a sense of well-earned triumph.

The shift, when it came, arrived from the bullish man in the second row. His voice matched his demeanor, an aggressive growl that deepened the deputy minister's frown.

The minister's official translator said, "Our associate representing Japanese industry says the information you supplied was possibly of some minor interest."

The veranda behind Kevin and Reese was empty, save for one lone chair situated far back from the group. It was the subservient position of a lowly attendant. The woman seated there had not been introduced. Her instructions were precise: remain invisible unless one thing happened.

The woman spoke now. "So sorry, Ms. Clawson. That was not an exact translation." Despite several practice attempts, Reese's interpreter found it difficult to pronounce her name. "The honored gentleman said, 'The information you supplied has proven to be of enormous importance.'"

The deputy minister lashed out at his interpreter, revealing his working knowledge of the English language. Reese was certain the condemnation was a futile attempt at saving face. The bullish man's tight smile was all the confirmation Reese needed that the deputy minister had been caught out.

Reese said, "Perhaps your translator is tired from the journey and the hour-long conversation. If you wish, my interpreter can—"

"That is not necessary," the deputy minister said, then barked a second time at his translator, who responded by bowing while still seated.

Reese focused upon the man in the second row. "You may come to us once each year. You can ask anything you like. If our information proves to be correct, we will receive one million dollars."

"Impossible." The deputy minister did not bother to wait for his translator. "Out of the question, so sorry."

"We will also require a well-protected villa with twenty-five bedrooms, or a luxury apartment block, whichever you prefer."

"These demands of yours are without merit."

"We will also be granted full immunity from prosecution, permanent residence visas, and full protection," Reese finished.

The bullish man interrupted the deputy minister. Reese's translator said, "The honored gentleman asks, 'Why is protection important?'"

"You've seen what we're offering," Reese said. "No secrets are beyond our reach. Ask the question, we will deliver. So long as you meet our terms and keep us safe."

The deputy minister's protest was halted this time by a short bark from the businessman, so swift Reese could not actually call it words. Even so, it was enough to freeze the official up solid. Then the industrialist addressed Reese directly. Her translator said, "The honored gentleman says, 'So sorry, Ms. Clawson, but one such request each year is not sufficient.' He says, 'One question each month would be much more acceptable. And payment should respectfully be limited to one hundred thousand dollars.'"

"One request every six months, seven hundred and fifty thousand dollars per question."

"Two requests every three months, one from government, one from industry. One hundred thousand dollars payment for each."

"Two requests are okay, but a quarter million per question."

The man barked, stood, and bowed. The translator said, "The honored gentleman agrees to your terms."

Reese felt flooded with a sense of victory so intense she could have wept. Instead, she rose and returned the bow, holding her position until she had brought her emotions under control. When she straightened, she saw the man was smiling.

She said, "Always a pleasure, doing business with a pro."

Thomas Locke is a pseudonym for Davis Bunn, an award-winning novelist whose work has been published in twenty languages. He has sales in excess of seven million copies and has appeared on numerous national bestseller lists. His titles have been main or featured selections for every major US book club.

Davis serves as Writer-in-Residence at Regent's Park College, Oxford University, and has served as lecturer in Oxford's new creative writing program. In 2011 his novel *Lion of Babylon* was named a Best Book of the Year by *Library Journal*. The sequel, *Rare Earth*, won Davis his fourth Christy Award for excellence in fiction in 2013. In 2014 he was granted the Lifetime Achievement Award by the Christy board of judges.

A film based upon *Emissary*, the first novel in the Legends of the Realm series, is now in development.

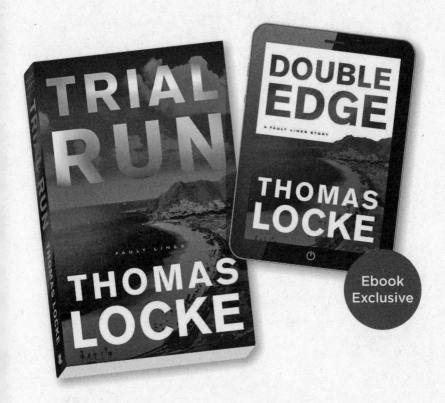